PRINCE OF SAVOY

Witnesses Of The Light

Prince
of
Savoy

a novel of the Waldensians

D. J. Speckhals

LOCUST LAMP PRESS

Copyright © 2025 by D. J. Speckhals
All rights reserved. Published in the United States by Locust Lamp Press, Pennsylvania,
United States of America
www.djspeckhals.com

Trade Paperback edition ISBN: 978-1-7375364-7-5
eBook ISBN: 978-1-7375364-6-8

Front cover illustration: *The Departure* by Thomas Cole
Back cover illustration: *The Return* by Thomas Cole
Maps by D. J. Speckhals
Author photograph: Following Splendor Images

3 5 7 9 10 8 6 4 2

First Edition

For Dave Wilbur

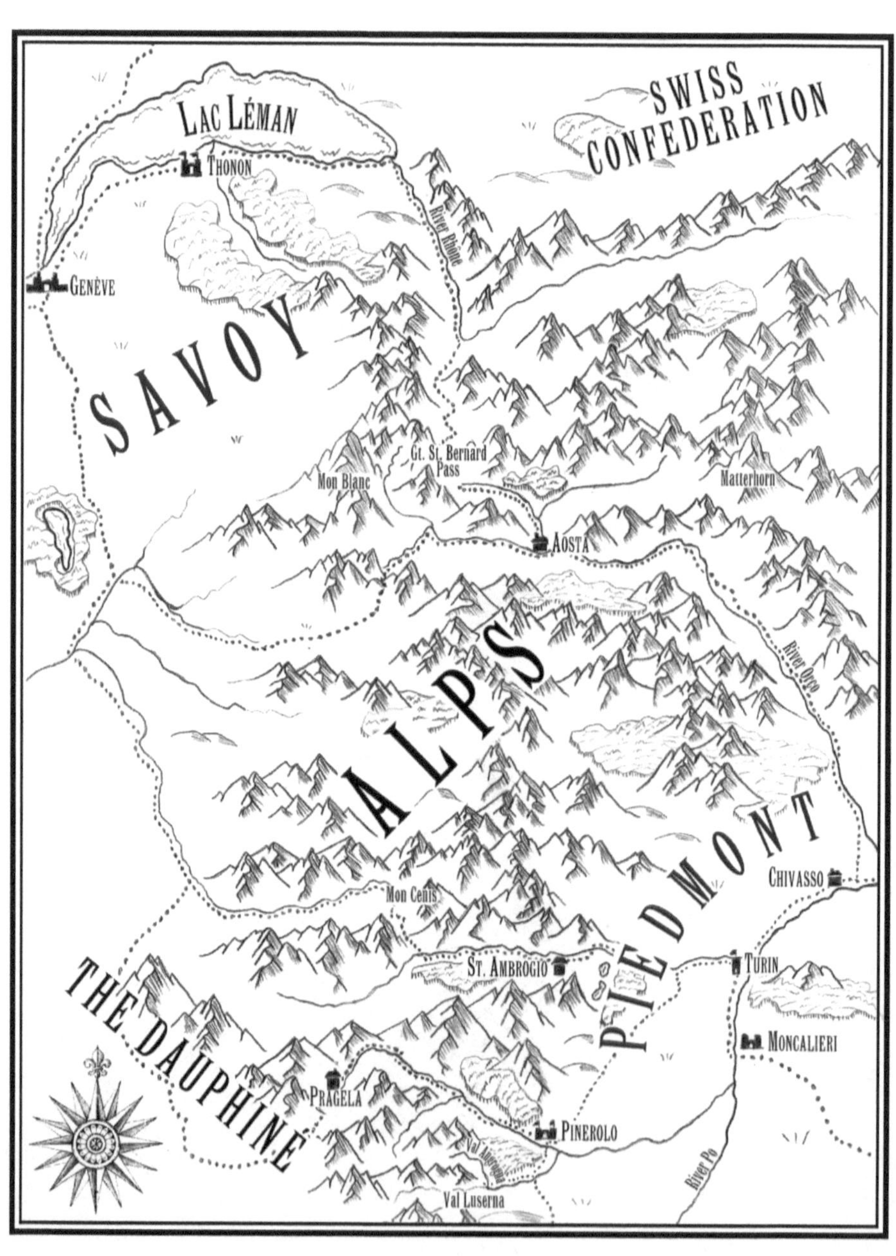

SWISS CONFEDERATION
Lac Léman
Thonon
Genève
River Rhone
SAVOY
Gt. St. Bernard Pass
Mon Blanc
Matterhorn
Aosta
ALPS
River Orco
PIEDMONT
Chivasso
Mon Cenis
St. Ambrogio
Turin
THE DAUPHINÉ
Moncalieri
Pragelà
Pinerolo
Val Luserna
River Po

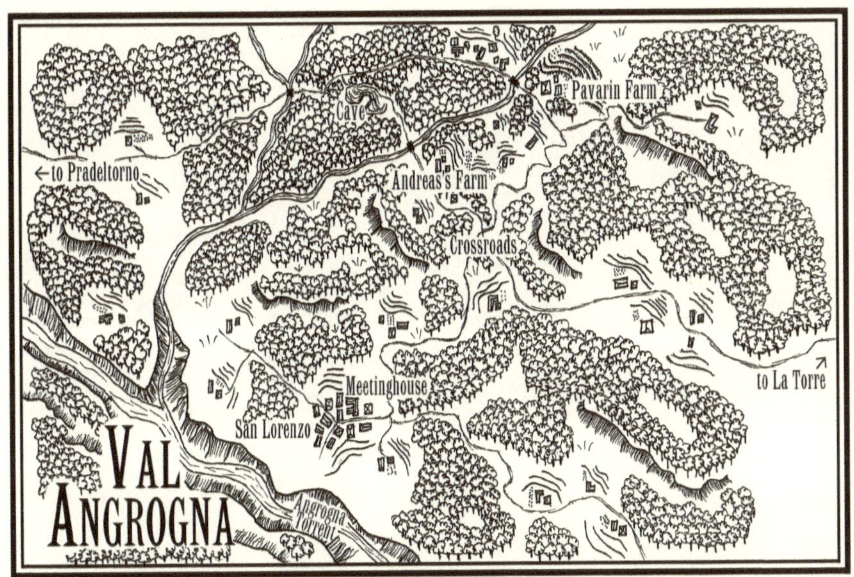
to Pradeltorno
Cave
Pavarin Farm
Andreas's Farm
Crossroads
to La Torre
Meetinghouse
San Lorenzo
Angrogna Torrent 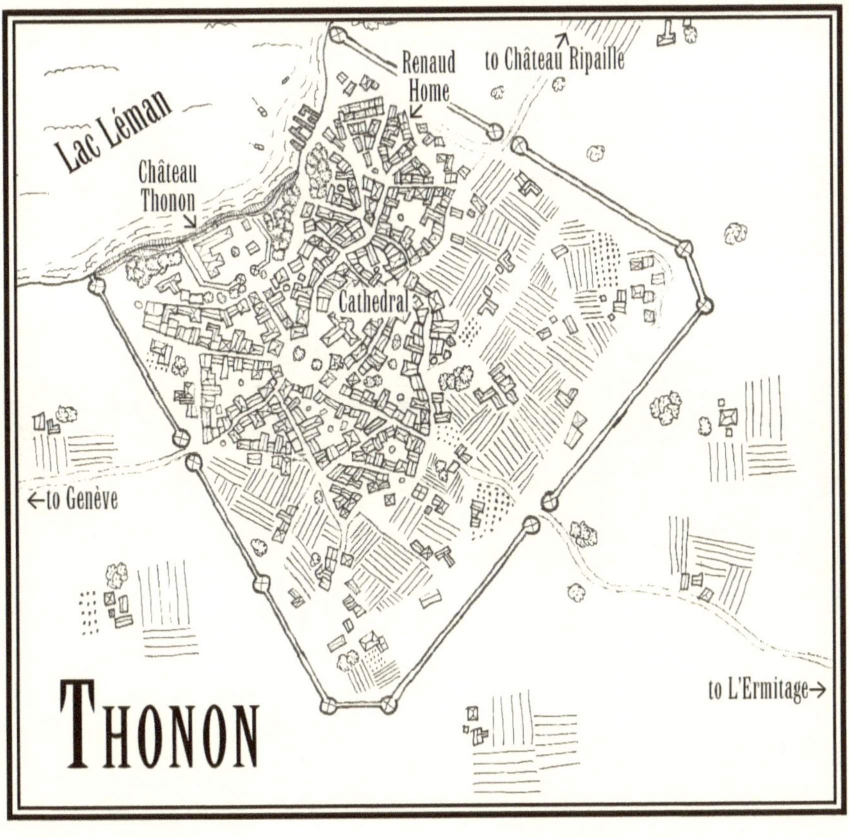
VAL ANGROGNA

Lac Léman
Renaud Home
to Château Ripaille
Château Thonon
Cathedral
to Genève
to L'Ermitage
THONON

1

There was a "Church in the Wilderness," from the early times of Christianity to the days of Peter Waldo—after which, history is abundant. These intervals do not at all hinder the continual succession of those churches, no more than the sun and moon do cease to be, when their light is eclipsed; though sometimes it has not been so visible to the eyes of men, it hath notwithstanding continued in a constant, uninterrupted succession, through all ages and generations.

—Robert Baird
Sketches of Protestantism in Italy, Past and Present, 1845

April 1460

FINALLY, A TARGET WORTHY of this once-in-a-lifetime opportunity. Andreas de Bonomo adjusted his hat, careful not to let it obscure his view of the regal ten-point buck that grazed on sparse blades of grass along the roadside. The deer took three timid strides onto the cobblestones and stood with its side facing Andreas.

Johan Lauras, his closest friend, tapped his arm. "You won't get a cleaner shot than that."

"He's too far." Andreas squinted into the light of the sun as it descended toward the towering Alps. He nocked an arrow and held the bow at the ready. A breeze blew over his cheeks, catching the edges of his neatly trimmed beard. "Just a few more steps."

"Take it as soon as it crosses the road. Aim a little above the shoulder."

Slowly Andreas raised the bow and pulled back the string. The world fell away. He anchored the string at the corner of his mouth, aimed, and breathed out.

A new sound rose—a distant yet steady clomping of boots on cobblestone. The playful squawking and chirping of birds ceased. The buck froze and looked down the road toward the swelling rumble.

Andreas released the arrow, sending it whizzing through the evening air. But in that sliver of time, the deer turned. The arrow grazed its hide and flew far past it in defeat.

The deer jumped and bolted, scampering off the road and into the thick forest beyond.

Johan pushed Andreas's shoulder. "How did you miss? That was a perfect shot!"

Bow still in hand, Andreas sprang into a run and crossed the road in search of the deer. Johan followed.

"There's no hope." Johan stopped, spread his arms, and nodded at the glowing horizon above the mountains. "He's halfway to Luserna by now, and it's too late to find a trail."

Andreas huffed and let the bow hang loosely at his side. "That would have fed my family for a week or more."

Down the road, the distant stamping drew together into a distinct march. Torchlight flickered over a rise as a vanguard of soldiers marched into view, carrying a crimson flag emblazoned with the white Savoy Cross.

There was no mistaking that banner. It was the same banner that proudly hung from the rafters of his childhood homes, the same noble emblem that sealed his father's official letters in wax, and the same symbol that was on Andreas's own signet ring, now stored away and almost forgotten. That red flag, rippling in the light breeze, pointed to his former life—when he was a prince of Savoy.

Andreas grabbed Johan and pulled him into a nearby thicket. He could never be discovered here, not after everything that had happened since his arrival in this humble valley he now called home.

Johan gazed down the road. "Savoyard soldiers, and they keep coming."

Bursts of laughter, discontented groans, and the continual clap of boots on cobblestone drew closer. The men were armed with short and long swords, lances, and crossbows. Most were armored in leather, but the man leading them wore heavy plate armor that glinted in the torchlight. The man was Philip, Andreas's younger brother.

Andreas swallowed a shaky breath. "They might be here for me."

"A hundred men-at-arms for you? You must be more important than I thought." Johan chuckled and nudged Andreas. "No, your family has forgotten you, and they're happy you've disappeared. Now they don't need to concern themselves with your inheritance or whatever else you nobles do with your riches."

"You don't understand my family. I have destroyed the prestige of the House of Savoy. I am an infidel no better than a Mohammedan for renouncing the Catholic Church. Now I'm a Vallense—a heretic in their eyes. I married my beloved Constanza without their permission and adopted twelve orphaned children. My home is a farm, my church is a small group of believers, and my vocation will be itinerant preaching. I'm a disgraced, rebellious son at best, and a raving madman at worst." A gust of wind caught the soldiers' crimson flag and unfurled it again. Andreas pushed back a lock of light brown hair that had fallen over his forehead. "The House of Savoy will confront me, or their honor will be forever lost."

"I once thought my life was complicated," Johan said.

"Do you see that armored man? That's my hedonistic, arrogant, self-centered brother Philip."

"Philip." Johan evaded Andreas's gaze. "He's the one who gave Gedeon Chanforan his noble title." He crawled backward into denser cover, keeping his head down. "I would rather not meet him."

"By now, he likely has a personal vendetta against me too, knowing we defeated his man Gedeon."

"We defeated Gedeon?" Johan brushed a hand through the leaves. "That was you and Constanza. If God hadn't opened my eyes, I would have fallen beside Gedeon."

"God used you nevertheless." Andreas nodded toward the head of the company. "May I also never cross Philip's trail. We'll head home after they pass."

As the vanguard marched in front of Andreas and Johan, an officer hurried to Philip and spoke to him. Philip raised his hand, and the column drew to a halt. "We will make camp here tonight," Philip announced.

Johan fidgeted and cast a wary glance at Andreas. "They'll find us here."

"If we move now, they'll spot us. We'll wait until there's an opening."

The standard-bearer drove the flag into the ground while the soldiers threw down their sacks, weapons, and leather armor. Some wandered into the surrounding forest with axes, probably in search of firewood. Five men, however, split off from the others, then converged. They passed Andreas and Johan's hiding place and walked off beyond it.

Johan leaned toward Andreas. "Deserters?"

"Most likely, and they'll be hanged soon enough." Andreas scanned the brush and open land between him and the growing encampment. "This is our chance. The soldiers are in front of us but not behind us."

"Except for those deserters."

"They won't harass us." Andreas stood and motioned for Johan to do the same. "Follow me."

Andreas carefully pushed the branches aside and crept out of the thicket. Johan slipped out after him. Once beyond earshot of the soldiers, Andreas quickened his pace and turned toward home.

A branch snapped in front of him. He froze, then ducked.

Twenty paces ahead of them stood a man in a dull brown cloak, his face shrouded by a hood. He looked directly at Andreas and Johan but didn't move. Had he seen them?

More branches snapped, and soon the five deserters joined the man with the cloak. They walked to an open area and sat together on a log.

Andreas tilted his head to one side and listened to the hushed voices.

"What are you doing?" Johan hissed.

Andreas held a finger to his lips. "I can't hear what they're saying."

"It doesn't matter. Let's skirt around them and find the path home."

"No, I'm curious now. That hooded man isn't a soldier, and I need to know why he's in our valley." Andreas knelt and crawled toward the men.

"Always so rash, my friend." Johan sighed, dropped to the ground, and followed Andreas.

The closer Andreas drew, the more distinct the voices became. He found a boulder to hide behind and peeked over the top.

"Meet me at the lakes of Avigliana seven days from now." Though hushed, the cloaked man's voice demanded attention. "At dawn, I will bring you the crown of twelve stars. Guard them with your lives, for next month in Thonon, all will come to pass exactly as the prophecy has foretold."

"What if Lord Philip isn't interested?" asked one of the deserters.

"He will be, for I have already ensured that."

Another deserter leaned forward to look past the other men seated on the log. "Philip still plans to join the king of France in the attack on Genoa. What if we can't meet you in a week?"

"There can be no delay. Thirty-one days remain before the day of the Lord." The cloaked man gazed toward the setting sun. "The sun will soon set on the House of Savoy. And that will be the dawn of the Ascendant Kingdom. By offering the twelve stars back to heaven, we will fulfill our sacred duty, purify the world, and usher in a millennium of peace." The man adjusted his hood. "If you cannot fulfill your duty, God will choose one of the truly faithful to assist me, His prophet."

"Forgive me, *ègal*, for I have doubted." The deserter's voice shook with reverence.

Johan tapped Andreas's arm and grimaced. "This is a waste. Forget about these madmen and go home to Constanza and your children."

The deserters' conversation suddenly ceased, and the cloaked man stood, peering toward the boulder. The soldiers drew their swords.

Andreas winced, ducked behind the boulder, and nodded at Johan. "Now we run." He bolted into the woods, and Johan followed close behind.

Shouts and hisses rose behind them, then a rush of footfalls in the brush.

Twigs scratched Andreas's cheeks, and a few concealed roots nearly caused him to tumble. But even in the darkness, he knew these lands better than those deserters. Before long, the sounds of pursuit disappeared. He and Johan crossed the road and entered the wooded foothills that formed the entrance to Val Angrogna—home.

Panting, Johan settled into a steady stride. "I was right. Listening in on those deserters and the madman brought us nothing but trouble."

"It was worth it. That cloaked man must be the leader of some fanatical sect, and the elder men will want to hear about it, especially since he spoke such things in our valleys."

"A crown of twelve stars. It sounds familiar, but also like something from a child's imagination." Johan lifted his hands and yawned. "It's been a long day, and my pillow is calling."

"Your pillow never ceases to call your name. 'Johan, don't go outside and work. Won't you stay here and rest?'"

"True, but if I had wielded the bow tonight, that buck wouldn't have finished dinner and pranced home to his wife. Now you both get to see your wives, except you haven't eaten."

"Were it not for me, Lord Addo would have never given us special permission to hunt on his lands."

"A single day out of the year, in September of all months. What kind of special permission is that? Almost worthless."

"I'll harvest far less grain than we need because of the blight this year, so every opportunity for more provision is a gift from God. You're the seasoned hunter. Do you know how seldom a lord grants his tenants permission to hunt deer on his lands? When have you ever been allowed to hunt deer?"

"Legally?"

Andreas shoved Johan in the chest. "Do you know the penalties for poaching?"

"I haven't done that in years." Johan pushed him back and pressed a finger into Andreas's shoulder. "Not since I met this monk."

A cool gust swept down from the peaks. Distant lightning rippled across the darkening sky. Andreas turned and peered far downhill at the soldiers' glowing campfires. If the cloaked man was right, then Philip and his men-at-arms were marching toward Genoa, away from Andreas's home and family. Andreas breathed a sigh of relief, but only a small one.

He couldn't hide in these mountains forever. As long as he breathed and was the son of the Duke of Savoy, then his beloved Constanza, the children, and all who so much as spoke a kind word to him were in danger. For the sake of his young family, Andreas would someday have to make peace with his noble heritage.

But today was not that day.

2

A well-matched couple carry a joyful life between them. . . . They multiply their joys by sharing them and lessen their troubles by dividing them; this is fine arithmetic.

—Charles Haddon Spurgeon
John Plowman's Talk, 1869

THE RAIN BEGAN the moment Andreas and Johan turned away from the soldiers' campfires. Though gentle at first, the late-summer shower soon swelled into a windy downpour. Andreas tilted his hat down, which did little to dispel the rivers running through his beard and over his chin like a waterfall. Walking beside him, Johan fared even worse, with no hat to shield him. They sloshed through mud and crossed once-calm streams the storm had transformed into torrents.

Andreas would face these trials daily when he became a Vallense barbe, if he was ever allowed to. Yet would an itinerant preacher declare a summer rainstorm a trial? Last year, while Andreas preached the gospel with the barbe Estève, those rainy days had made for hard travel. But such weather wasn't an executioner's sword, nor was it the forces of Satan fighting God's message—only water, mud, shivers.

At the main crossroads of Val Angrogna, Johan turned toward his house, a little cabin he had built with the help of a few Piedmontese men last month. Andreas turned right, then left, and walked along the hillside path toward his stone farmhouse.

Light poured from the windows, illuminating the nearby toolshed and barn. At this hour, the children would all likely be sleeping on their mats, but Constanza would certainly be waiting, either working at the loom or translating the Holy Scriptures by the hearth.

Andreas gave the door a light tap, unlatched it, and pushed it open. Laughter and the pitter-patter of feet met his ears as twelve children ran to meet him.

"How big is the deer, *Papà*?" Roberto asked.

"Are we having venison for dinner?" Zama bounded toward Andreas. "*Mamà* said I can help."

"How many points were on the antlers?" Ten-year-old Ezio puffed out his chest and tried to lower his voice. "Or was it a doe?"

The children clamored around Andreas, nestling under his arms, grabbing his legs, and hugging him around his chest.

He scooped up Alessia and laughed. "Why are you not sleeping? I don't want twelve snoring boys and girls next to me at the church gathering tomorrow."

Constanza rushed toward him from the hearth room. Andreas peeled Bino and Prospera from his legs and shifted Alessia to his other arm. He wrapped his free arm around Constanza's waist and whispered, "No deer today. The shot was perfect, but the deer heard something and turned away . . ."

Constanza smiled and put a finger to his lips. "I baked bread this morning."

Andreas leaned closer to her. "When we were on the ridge above San Jan, we saw soldiers—"

"Soldiers?" Ezio asked, loud enough for all to hear. "Where were they from?"

Andreas closed his eyes, chuckled, and murmured to Constanza, "We'll talk later."

"We already prepared the table." Constanza kissed Andreas on the cheek. "Everyone wants to hear your story about the great hunt."

Ave tugged on Andreas's tunic. "Papà, today when I was gathering eggs, Guido tried to scare me."

"Not your *fraire*." Andreas eyed nine-year-old Guido.

"He's already been punished." Constanza ruffled Guido's hair. "As has everyone else for a multitude of sins, ranging from lying to fighting to disobedience to—" She blew out a breath, but her eyes sparkled. "Pick any sin from the Scriptures, and it was likely committed here today."

"You must all honor your mamà." Andreas waited for the children's attention. "Let's recite what the Holy Scriptures say."

In unison they quoted, "*Honrea loteo paire elatoa maire.*"

"You're able to recite it well enough, but do you obey what it says?"

Alessia lifted her head from Andreas's shoulder. "I honored Mamà today."

"That's not true, Alessia!" Silvia put her hands on her hips. "You hit Umile today, and you said *non* to Mamà twice."

"You're a gossip, Silvia!"

Constanza leaned toward Andreas and mouthed, "From morning to evening."

Andreas set Alessia back on her feet. "Listen for a moment. 'But if ye bite and devour one another, take heed that ye be not consumed one of another.' I copied that verse from the Greek manuscript last night. Who said that?"

"Paul, in his epistle to the Galatians," Silvia said.

Andreas nodded. "Indeed, Paul, inspired by the Holy Ghost, but it's for all of us, in every time." He motioned for Constanza, and the children moved aside for her. Andreas held her left hand with his right and pulled her close. "We might be the most peculiar family in the valley, but one thing is certain—we will not bite and devour one another. We are a unified family, and we serve one another. When Mamà and I were married last spring"—he held her hand tighter and smiled—"we were two who became one."

"But we're not actually your children." Ezio moved his mouth as if he were trying to find the right words. "At least not from your . . . *euh* . . . marriage."

"That makes you no less our sons and daughters." Andreas looked at each child, one after the other. "Silvia, Fosca, Ave, Irene, Prospera, Zama, Alessia—you are our daughters. Ezio, Roberto, Umile, Guido, Bino—you are our sons. In God's eyes too, you are our children, and no man on this earth can change that."

"Will Mamà have a baby one day?" Umile asked.

Andreas caught Constanza's eye and winked. "Perhaps someday."

"I'm hungry," Zama said.

"Me too." Roberto grabbed Andreas's other hand and tugged him toward the kitchen. "May we eat, Papà?"

"To the table, children!" Constanza shooed them away. "One piece of bread for each of you."

Grasping Constanza's waist with one hand, Andreas lifted her hand and tenderly kissed it. Constanza touched his cheek and gave him a coy smile. "Should I have allowed that since you failed to bring home dinner?"

Andreas ignored the question and kissed her. "You have become a wonderful mother."

She threw her arms around him as he lifted her off the ground and spun her around once.

"And an enchanting wife."

Constanza giggled. "Your cheeks feel like my scrubbing brush, Andreas."

"I'll trim my beard after we eat."

Soon Andreas sat at the head of the table with Constanza at his side. Silvia and Irene brought the bread, sat on a bench, and joined hands with the rest of the family.

"This bread is a blessing from the Lord," Andreas said.

All responded as one. "And to Him we give thanks."

The youngest children leaped from their seats and tore off pieces from the barley loaf.

Silvia, always trying to be mother to the others, clamored for her own. "Mamà said one!"

"There's enough bread for everyone." Andreas tore off two pieces, gave the larger one to Constanza, and held her hand under the table.

Roberto fidgeted with his piece before taking a bite and gnawing on it. "*Madomaisèla* Elionor's bread tasted better." He grinned at Constanza. "I'm jesting, Mamà."

"Yes, Elionor was the better baker." Constanza's eyes misted as she slowly nodded. "Children, before we lay our heads down tonight, we should pray for Madomaisèla Elionor."

"I do miss her dearly," Silvia said.

"Tell us about the soldiers." Ezio turned wide eyes on Andreas. "Are they coming here?"

Andreas took a bite of bread. Barley might not be as luxurious as wheat, but it could fill an empty belly. He loosened his grip on Constanza's hand. "No soldiers will come here."

"Martino Pavarin said the Duke of Savoy's soldiers came to the valley once. They surprised the wicked priests, tore down their fortress, and chased them from the valley. They rescued you too, didn't they, Papà?"

"A bit of an exaggeration, but yes, Savoyard soldiers helped us once."

"Some soldiers are bad," Irene said. "I don't want to see any."

Bino crossed his arms and shook his head. "Neither do I!"

"You have nothing to fear with God as your heavenly Father," Constanza said, "and your papà as your earthly father."

Andreas placed both hands on the table. "I will never allow a soldier, a robber, or a priest to harm you." He focused on Constanza. "Not one of you."

Ezio threw the last bite of bread into his mouth. "Yes, because Papà is a swordsman!"

Bino gave Andreas a curious glance. "A real swordsman?"

Andreas leaned back and laughed. "I once showed Ezio a couple of stances and taught him how to block a stronger fighter."

"You never told me you can handle a sword." Constanza wrinkled her nose and playfully slapped Andreas's hand. "That might have proved useful once or twice."

"All noble sons are taught swordsmanship, but it's not as if I've used a blade in battle. I'm a farmer and a preacher now, not a noble. Besides, there's probably not a sword between here and Pinerolo that's worth carrying."

"Can you teach me, Papà?" Bino asked.

Umile shot up and ran to Andreas. "Me too!"

"Tomorrow, after the church meets, find two straight sticks."

"What tricks will you teach us, Papà?" Bino grabbed a spoon and swung it, but Andreas plucked it from his hand.

"Let's focus on the church gathering tomorrow. The Holy Scriptures offer protection far beyond what a steel sword provides. If you make the Bible your sword and your lamp, then I have taught you everything you must know."

"Perhaps you can be a barbe like Monsen Estève or Barbe Colletto someday," Silvia said.

Andreas pulled the sleeves of his tunic up to his elbows and looked at Constanza. "Indeed, someday."

After the children cleared the table and washed their faces, they begrudgingly snuggled into their mats. The boys slept behind one curtain, while the girls slept behind another. Rain pattered on the stone walls and created a rhythmic symphony, calmly reverberating through the house and muffling all else. Andreas sat on a rickety stool in the hearth room, where three sheep-tallow lamps cast a yellow glow on the walls.

The boys' curtain flipped open, and Constanza slid from behind it. Graceful steps brought her to his side. Andreas stood and offered the only seat in the room to her.

She gave him a warm smile. "No, I'd much rather nestle close to my husband."

Andreas stood, moved the stool aside, and walked to the blazing hearth. He grabbed the flax broom that leaned against the wall there and swept the dusty stones.

Constanza laughed as she tried to take the broom from him. "Ezio was supposed to sweep the floor today, but he must have had more pressing duties."

Andreas held the broom out of Constanza's reach. "You've worked enough today." He swept the dust into the fire, laid the broom aside, and carried a bench from the table to the hearth.

Constanza sat on the bench and tucked her skirts close to make room for Andreas. The lamplight made her dark eyes sparkle as she loosened her hair and let its chestnut waves cascade onto her shoulders. "Earlier you mentioned there were soldiers near San Jan this evening."

Andreas sat beside her and let out a long breath. "Yes, I think that's what made me miss the deer. I spied a hundred or so Savoyard soldiers marching east. At the head of their column, in a full suit of plate armor, was my younger brother Philip. They camped in the valley, but it seems they're leaving tomorrow."

"Remind me which brother Philip is."

"The one I would rather you not meet." Andreas brought both arms back to his lap and folded his hands. "After Amadeus and me comes Philip. He is more like my mother than the rest of us are, but he's also the one in constant conflict with her. I never heard him say a kind word to Mâre, nor she to him."

"And how many siblings do you have? You told me before. Was it twelve?" Constanza pointed at the small table near the hearth. "Would you hand me my hairbrush?"

Andreas passed the brush to her. "I have eleven living siblings—six brothers and five sisters—but my mother also gave birth to six more who did not survive past childhood."

A hush fell over the room. From the corner of his eye, Andreas glanced toward the children's sleeping places. Nearly a year had passed since Valeria had died from a fever. Since then all the children had been healthy, but sickness and death could come upon anyone, rich or poor.

With a steady hand, Constanza worked the brush through her hair. "Why do you think Philip is in Piedmont?"

"Knowing Philip, it's not for a noble purpose. He hates my eldest brother, Amadeus, because of his weakness, and though Philip is the third son, he thinks Savoy should be his. Amadeus's wife, Yolande, told me about it before she lent us her aid to purchase the Greek Bible manuscript last autumn." Andreas stood, walked to a nearby shelf, and lifted the bundle of parchment that lay there. "In return for this manuscript, you know Yolande required my loyalty to Amadeus should any man challenge his position. Philip is now trying to usurp him."

"That manuscript has proven immensely valuable to us." Constanza stood and placed her hand on the parchment. "In less than a year, we've made a copy of our own and compared it with our Romaunt Bible. Remember last week when we found an old copying error in the Romaunt?"

"'Peace, good will toward men' from Luke's Gospel—I remember."

"But our Romaunt translation said, 'peace to men of good will.'"

Andreas thumbed through the pages and soon found the line in Luke. "The Greek word here is *eudokia*, yet if it ended with an *s*, it would translate to what the Romaunt Bible says—'men of good will.' Without that *s*, as it is in this Greek manuscript, it means 'good will toward men.' It's an entirely different meaning." Andreas set the Bible back on the shelf and moved to the bench. "If we were able to find that in a single line, imagine what an educated doctor who fully understands both Greek and Romaunt could accomplish."

Andreas set the parchment down and took Constanza's hand. "Tonight Johan and I also overheard a man talking to five deserters from Philip's company—something about a prophecy of a crown with twelve stars, a kingdom, and the day of the Lord."

"In our valley?"

"If it isn't the Catholic teachings to contend with, it's a prophetic sect. I'll tell the men of the church tomorrow." Andreas guided Constanza back to the bench, and they both sat. "I'm more concerned about Philip, though. Surely he understands that I hold no ambition of becoming involved in his feuds with my parents and Amadeus. I want a simple life with you, our children, and our people."

Constanza rested her head on Andreas's shoulder. "And I wouldn't trade this life for all the flourishing barley, green pastures, and grand *chasteus* of Savoy. I'm content to be poor with you, though I would enjoy being a prince's wife for a day or two."

Andreas shook his head abruptly. "My pure, innocent, selfless Constanza—I would never wish that on you. It would only bring you misery, as it has my mother."

Constanza sat straighter. "What is your mother like?"

"Five years or more have passed since I last saw her, so my memory fails me. I do remember her light hair, which had a subtle red tint. She is from the island of Cyprus, a descendant of an old crusader dynasty that once ruled Jerusalem itself. She's known for her beauty, but that has been nothing but a vice to her." Andreas crossed his feet and sighed. "*Mâre* has been habitually unfaithful to my father, and for some reason he permits it. I am thankful to be here, far removed from the House of Savoy and its *machinacions*."

Sliding closer, he wrapped his arm around Constanza's waist and placed a hand on her side. A few moments passed in silence. Then Andreas leaned forward and stared at the fire. "I finally meet with the men of the church tomorrow. I already have a suspicion as to what they'll say, though."

"My papà thinks he knows too." Constanza laid her head on Andreas's shoulder. "I think we'll find out whether you both have the same guess."

"How are his goats faring with less grain?"

"No better or worse than ours. It's the same with Miquèl and Pèire and David and all my other siblings. The goats definitely give less milk, but Papà doesn't seem concerned. He says they had a more vicious blight before I was born, except that year there was a drought too. 'The LORD will not suffer the soul of the righteous to famish,' he always says."

"Last year's harvest was so abundant, though. A minstrel down in La Torre said the blight is because the moon will cover the sun on the fourteenth day of October—an eclipse. One of a thousand and one superstitions."

"Mercede and Patrizio are leaving the valley next week. There's not enough here to sustain them, they think."

"Another Piedmontese family leaving? That's three since the beginning of summer." Andreas scratched his cheek. "God will provide, but why did this blight choose to come after we had adopted twelve hungry children?" He closed his eyes for a moment. "*Perdon*, I didn't intend to complain."

Constanza lifted his hand from her side and kissed it. "I don't think those are complaints. They're weights that press down on you."

"And prevent me from fulfilling my commitments. I still want to be a barbe, and I know God implanted that desire in my soul. Yet how can I minister to others when I struggle to feed my own family?" Andreas gently guided Constanza's hand down to rest on her side again, holding it there as their hands found comfort together.

"When I was a little girl, I never imagined I would marry a man like you and have a family like ours. I still laugh when I remember I'm married to a prince."

"I forsook that life, and now I'm as poor as anyone in Piedmont." Andreas shook his head and chuckled under his breath. "I deemed the life of a monk to be humbling, yet that pales in comparison to being a mountain farmer, tending the land with a wife and a dozen children."

Constanza gave him a teasing smile. "How charming was I that I convinced a papist monk to break his vow of chastity?"

"*Per los cèus*, Constanza, that's not the truth!" Andreas held her close, his fingers entwined with hers. Youngest daughter of a Vallense farmer, dedicated student of the Holy Scriptures, industrious servant of everyone but herself, with a captivating grace and a radiant face more beautiful than all others—how much he adored her. "God saved me from that monastic life long before I dreamed of pursuing you. Since then, I've become wealthier than I had ever imagined."

Constanza lowered her chin at his admiration. "I'm content here on our rocky hillside farm in Val Angrogna and will follow you to whatever end, Andreas de Bonomo."

"You are aware that Bonomo isn't my actual family name, no?" Andreas stood and helped Constanza from her seat. "I invented that name to conceal my identity when I entered the Benedictine Order."

Constanza faced Andreas and met his eyes. "Then what is your true name?"

"Do you vow not to laugh?"

She gave him a knowing grin. "I don't make vows I can't keep."

Andreas leaned down and kissed her passionately. After a few moments, he touched her cheek and whispered, "Lord Andreas of Savoy."

"Which would make my title . . ."

"Lady Constanza of the goat pastures."

She eyed him playfully.

Andreas finished the title. "Wife of Lord Andreas."

"That's enough for me," she said, embracing him, "'wife of Lord Andreas.'"

Andreas helped Constanza snuff the lamps, and they withdrew to their humble room for the night.

3

The challenge is thus real, and was no different for the Waldensians. How were preachers to be trained without separating them from their flocks? We can surmise that persecution, a real threat hanging over all of them, gave them a common understanding which brought them together and kept the barbes firmly anchored in their community.

—Gabriel Audisio
Preachers by Night, 2006

THE DOORS OF THE MEETINGHOUSE swung inward at midday. In spilled the warm late-summer sunlight, and out poured the church who met there weekly. Andreas held Constanza's hand as they rose from the bench and gathered their children.

The youngest, Alessia, stood to Andreas's left and tugged on his sleeve. "What are we eating today, Papà?"

"I don't know, but if you follow Mamà and everyone else, you'll be sure to find out." Andreas lifted Alessia into his arms, tucked her dark hair behind her ears, and hugged her. "I'll join you soon, but first I must meet with your *papeta* Nicolaus and other men." He let her down, and immediately she ran through the open door.

Andreas and Constanza walked together until they reached the last bench.

"I'll be praying for you," Constanza said. "I know what this means to you . . . and all of us."

Alessia ran back inside, latched on to Constanza's arm, and pulled. "Come, Mamà, we're eating *poleta* today!"

Following Alessia to the door, Constanza turned and smiled sweetly. Then she went out.

Andreas positioned himself on the last bench and waited for the men.

"My brother!" Michele Pavarin slapped Andreas on the back as he walked past. "I'm heading down to Luserna tomorrow for a pair of breeding goats. I'll keep my eyes open for your deer. Johan told us the story this morning." He stopped and looked over his shoulder at Andreas. "Tell me, should I believe a story from Johan?"

A long trail of mistrust lay behind Johan Lauras after the previous year, when he had turned his back on the Vallenses for wealth and position. Worse was his stint of apostasy, though only Andreas, and to a lesser extent Constanza, knew the depth of that. Yet Johan had renounced that folly and returned to the faith of his childhood.

"It's all true," Andreas told Michele. "Perhaps God knows someone else needs the meat more."

Michele gave Andreas a parting nod and left through the doorway.

The gray-haired barbe Estève Malan sat on the bench in front of Andreas, and Bertran Arnaldi soon did the same. Estève crossed his arms, laughed, and gazed at the open door, where the sounds of playing children streamed from outside. "Overnight, a husband and the father of a whole flock of lambs."

Nicolaus Pavarin limped toward them and eased himself down beside Andreas. "Both of which he does as well as any man in this valley."

From behind, Barbe Colletto Corsone stepped over Andreas's bench and sat on his left. "The question is, can you also perform the duties of a barbe?" He put his arm around Andreas and tapped his shoulder. "*Mercé* for reading from the Holy Scriptures this morning, Andreas."

"*Amb plaser,*" Andreas said. "Paul's epistle to the Philippians is a favorite of mine."

Another barbe, Matteo Ghos, sat next to Bertran and faced Andreas. Etched on his clean-shaven face were years of both trials and triumphs.

"Matteo, how was your journey to the Dauphiné?" Barbe Colletto asked.

"*Excellente.* Believers are hungry for truth, despite threats from the king of France." His shoulders slumped, and his gaze sank to the floor. "I heard more rumors about that strange sect, though."

Andreas brushed his hand against across his cheek, feeling the coarse hair. "Odd, last night I encountered a sect outside San Jan."

Estève turned his head away in dismissal. "Yet another movement of imbeciles who believe they'll establish the millennial reign of Christ."

"This one feels different," Matteo said. "In Savoy, it's spreading like the plague, and now it's entered the Dauphiné—as close as Pragela."

"Pragela?" Bertran narrowed his eyes. "Isn't that village mostly made up of Vallenses?"

"It was a passing rumor, though it would be wise to verify it soon." Matteo tapped his fingers on the bench. "Now, what is the subject at hand? I'm famished and ready to eat."

Andreas folded his hands. These were men whom he aspired to be like one day, men of perseverance, sacrifice, wisdom, piety. Yet to them, was he still the same wandering, aimless monk they had first met? Not to Nicolaus, and Bertran also knew Andreas well, but what of the others? "I won't retain you for long. Last year I traveled with Monsen Estève, and I am grateful for his mentorship."

"My advice about women must have taken hold on you," Estève said. "You were a bashful young man standing before Madomaisèla Constanza last summer, but now you're married to her and have somehow gained twelve children in less than a year. That's a feat no other man I know can claim." He slapped the wood of the bench, grinning from ear to ear. "I shall lay claim to that accomplishment."

Andreas shook his head, a wry smile lingering. "I suppose you'll have a solution for me now too. I still want to be a barbe, and I believe that's God's plan for me. I committed myself to that soon after my conversion, and I hold to that commitment."

Matteo leaned forward, resting his elbows on his knees. "Who here has a wife and children?"

Andreas glanced at his father-in-law.

"He's not a barbe. Nicolaus, have you ever traveled more than a day's journey from our valley?"

Nicolaus shook his head. "Pinerolo is the farthest I've been from home."

Andreas shifted his weight and ran his thumb over his knuckles. This was how he had anticipated the meeting would unfold, but it still pained him. God had saved him and given him a desire to minister to Vallenses. How could he reconcile that with the present circumstances?

He looked at each of the men sitting across from him, then to Barbe Colletto on his left and Nicolaus on his right. "How can I still fulfill my commitment to God?"

Joyful sounds of distant laughter, chattering friends, and songbirds filtered through the open door. Bertran eyed the floor. Barbe Colletto tapped a finger on his knee. Estève wiped sweat from his brow. Matteo scratched his arm.

Nicolaus turned to Andreas. "My son, you've proven yourself to be both virtuous and courageous—a truly Christlike example. You chose a noble path by marrying my daughter and adopting twelve orphans, but that path brings commitments that can't be neglected despite your ambitions."

Every word Nicolaus said was true. How could it not be? No matter the hardships, Andreas loved his wife and children and the life God had given him. Why then did that unmistakable needle continue to prick his soul, not as an annoyance but as a persistent reminder that something was amiss?

"Your choices were noble, and I believe they were right," Estève said. "Yet you were somewhat rash too. I cannot recall a time when you sought counsel, especially concerning the children."

Barbe Colletto smiled faintly. "Alas, we could have discussed this months ago, before your wedding. I understand what you're feeling—I was similarly conflicted as a young man. Though I wanted to marry, I knew I couldn't be an itinerant barbe if that desire became reality. I chose a different path than you, preaching for five years before marrying and raising my children. Not until I was an old man did the flock here ask me to be their shepherd."

"I'm not as familiar with Vallense traditions as all of you," Andreas said, "but are there opportunities for a man like me to establish himself and serve a single congregation instead of taking months-long missionary trips?"

"If a church asked you, none of us here would oppose you," Barbe Colletto answered. "You're a wise man, qualified to teach the Scriptures, but though we've laid our hands on you, I've never heard of a Vallense church calling on a man with a young family."

"Those positions are for old men like me and Colletto, after the roads have worn our legs to threadbare strands of wool." Estève slapped his thigh and let out a burst of laughter. "But my legs are still as strong as fresh hemp rope, and I suppose they always will be!"

"Wait a few more winters," Barbe Colletto said, cackling, "and you'll watch the scant bit of youth left in you disappear like a mud puddle in a dry pasture."

"Not yet, old friend. I still feel as mighty as the River Po in springtime." Estève touched the gray hair behind his ears, brushed a hand through his tousled beard, and grinned. "Ah, I see . . . my appearance must be deceiving."

Andreas laughed at Estève, along with everyone else. Last year, he had spent many long days walking and talking with the old barbe. The days were so much different now—plowing, building, translating the Scriptures, learning to be an honorable husband and father. All good things, and yet . . .

Matteo straightened. "I think we are all in agreement about the matter—including you, Andreas."

"Responsibilities to your family always come first," Nicolaus said.

"Please understand," Bertran said, "none of us is holding you back. We want to help, but now is not the time for you to travel the world, even for the holy cause of Christ."

Andreas nodded. "I understand, though I still don't see myself as a farmer for the rest of my days."

"Perhaps that will change," Estève said. "Look how God has directed your path since you met Raimond Durand. You entered our valley to extinguish our beliefs, but now you fan the flames with the rest of us."

Matteo peered over Andreas's shoulder toward the door. Andreas turned, and there in the doorway stood Roberto. "Are you done, Papà?"

Andreas nodded toward Roberto, then turned back to the men. "I'm grateful for your time, and I value your wisdom."

"One moment," Matteo said, motioning for Andreas to remain seated. "I have an idea you'll appreciate."

Andreas slid farther onto the bench. "I thought you were famished."

"I certainly am, so I'll be brief."

Matteo looked first to Estève on one side of him, then to Bertran on the other, and last to Barbe Colletto. "What if Andreas took a short journey to Pragela to investigate this new sect?"

Andreas threw his head back and let out a short laugh. "I must be the designated monitor of obscure religious sects in Piedmont. The abbot at Sacra di San Michele assigned me a similar task two springs ago, to search out a group named"—he raised an eyebrow at Matteo—"Vallenses."

"This would be different entirely." Estève nodded. "The Vallense church in Pragela is a faithful congregation of believers."

Shaking his head, Andreas chuckled. "The abbot told me the same thing about the now nonexistent Catholic parish of Luserna."

"There are indeed some coincidental similarities," Barbe Colletto said, "but if I remember that story correctly, you were in a miserable and desperate state then."

"That's true. I was lost in a hopeless religion of tradition and idolatry until Raimond Durand patiently told me the truth. The Lord cleansed my heart, and since believing solely in Jesus Christ, I've become an entirely different man. If you wish me to go, I will."

"It's no more than a two-day journey to Pragela," Matteo said. "You have the Holy Scriptures, you can teach, and you know how to discover and combat error. The whole journey will take less than a week, so you'll be home with your family and your fields before the barley harvest."

"Tell me about this sect," Andreas said. "I wonder if it's the same one Johan and I encountered."

Matteo looked at Estève as if they held a mutual understanding. "We know very little, and what we do know leans toward unbelievable. I mentioned their interest in the second coming of Christ. That's something we also believe in, of course, but their interest borders on obsession—to the degree that they believe the millennial reign of Christ on earth can be established by human effort."

"They call themselves L'Asindinsa Divina," Estève said. "The Divine Ascendancy."

"It's the same one." Andreas slid to the edge of the bench and pointed at Estève. "That language is from Savoy."

"We don't know where this sect's teachings originated," Estève said, "but we assume it was somewhere in Savoy. They look to a man they call the Prophet, but we know nothing else about him."

"The Prophet—that's what the man we saw called himself."

"There's no need to investigate deeply." Matteo held up one hand. "Encourage the saints in Pragela, teach them something from the Holy Scriptures if they ask, and hurry home to your beautiful family."

"When should I leave?"

"As soon as you're able."

Barbe Colletto furrowed his brows slightly. "Though Pragela is not far, you still should not make the journey alone. There is much wisdom in our tradition of two men traveling together."

"I agree, but it's nearly harvest time," Andreas said. "Men need to sharpen their sickles, clear weeds, and prepare their granaries. I don't think I need help for this journey."

"Even the sharpest blade wears dull without the whetstone." Barbe Colletto rested his calloused hands on his knees. "Good friends keep our edges sharp."

Andreas pressed his lips tight and nodded, though the motion was likely imperceptible. "Who would be willing to go with me?" He eyed Bertran, then Estève.

Bertran sighed. "Monsen Estève and I are leaving for Lombardy in two days."

"Your partner doesn't need to be a barbe," Matteo said. "Any upstanding man in the church should be willing."

"Johan Lauras," Nicolaus said, almost in a whisper.

Barbe Colletto crossed his arms, Bertran cleared his throat, and Matteo glanced up at the rafters.

"Has he not proven himself faithful in recent months?" Andreas asked.

"After standing against God and his own people," Bertran said. "I don't doubt Johan's sincerity, Monsen Nicolaus, but I grew up with him. Even if Johan wanted to travel with Andreas—"

"He will," Andreas said, "and I think this trip is precisely what Johan needs. He's ashamed of what he did, and he wants to earn back everyone's trust."

Barbe Colletto scratched his beard. "Andreas, you are a good friend to Johan, and you are right—Johan needs a chance to serve alongside a steadfast man. Perhaps this is it."

"You have more patience and forbearance than I." Matteo shook his head but offered a reassuring smile. "That boy is well acquainted with mischief."

Andreas stood and offered a hand to Nicolaus. "I'll tell Constanza now. Johan and I will leave in the morning."

"And I will watch your farm for the week."

The men exchanged their farewells and joined the rest of the church outside. Even on this late-summer day, the sun beamed down like a flaming torch.

"Papà!" Zama bounded from behind the meetinghouse and ran toward Andreas.

Andreas wiped his brow, donned his hat, and hoisted Zama into his arms. "Before long you'll be too big for me to lift like this."

Zama threw her arms around Andreas's neck. "*T'aimi*, Papà."

"I love you too, Zama."

She broke the embrace and tapped her toes on his legs. Andreas set her down but held her hands and spun her around a few times. Dizzy and giggling, Zama stumbled back toward her friends.

Andreas scanned the open area outside the hamlet of San Lorenzo. Under the shade of a resolute oak, Abel Calmete sat talking to Paolo Stalliato, probably about the barley blight. Abel's wife, Gracia, gently rocked the infant cradled in her arms as other children played and ate about her. Of Nicolaus Pavarin's five daughters, Gracia resembled Constanza the most, sharing their mother's defined jawline and the deep, fervent eyes of their father.

Johan leaned against a fence post by himself, eating an apple. Andreas approached him and started to ask about the journey to Pragela, but before he could finish, Johan interrupted. "Pragela in Val Chisone? Of all the men in our valley, you asked me?" He grabbed Andreas's arm and gave him a nod. "I'll join you, though I would scarcely call it an adventure. I could make that journey in a day, and besides, the people in Val Chisone are practically the same as us. When are we leaving?"

"Tomorrow at first light, so we can return in time for the harvest."

"Dawn, at the crossroads." Johan shifted his weight from one foot to the other, his gaze darting into the distance. "I'll pack tonight, but if I'm not there, come shake me out of my stupor."

Constanza sat fanning herself in a grassy spot under the shade of a giant chestnut tree. Her soulful eyes and demure smile stole Andreas's breath. At least he wouldn't be parted from her for more than a few days. Quickly he recounted the meeting and told her about the upcoming trip.

"What a wonderful opportunity!" Constanza stood to face him. "My brothers would be happy to help with the farm while you're gone."

"Your papà already offered. Either he or your brother David will look in on you every day."

Constanza fixed her gaze on Andreas. "Imagine what Monsen Raimond would think of you now, heading out on your own with a Bible in hand."

"It's not as if we're barbes or anything akin to that. We'll be gone for only five days. And it's me and Johan." Andreas cracked a smile. "They must be desperate."

"I know what my papà thinks about you, and the other men certainly feel as he does."

"No doubt they all think the same about me—rash, highborn Andreas, taking in twelve young orphans as his own without asking anyone if it was wise."

"Rash or right?"

Andreas held Constanza's waist with one hand and touched her graceful nose with the other. "Am I allowed to be both?"

"I adore both." She flashed an elusive, mischievous smile and kissed him lightly on the lips. "And I pray that part of you never changes."

4

This is the true way to eternal life, which is found by so few, and walked by a still smaller number; for it is too narrow for them, and would cause their flesh too much pain.

—Jan Jans Brant, 1559

I N THE PREDAWN TWILIGHT of the next day, Constanza stood in the crisp mountain air and laid her head on Andreas's chest as his strong arms wrapped around her. *Andreas.* She uncurled her fingers and squeezed him tightly, pressing her hands against his back. How had six months of marriage passed so quickly?

"We won't linger there," Andreas said, calm and reassuring. "I'll be back here holding you before you remember I've left."

"I know." She stayed in his arms, holding him in this little place where God had woven two young hearts together, but ready to let him go so he would return all the sooner.

Andreas's hands slid toward her hips. Constanza lifted her head and took a small step back, allowing him to hold both hands there. She closed her eyes and let this quiet moment implant itself in her memory.

As his lips touched hers, a warmth spread through her, a sense of peace so real it felt as though she could hold it in her hands. Everything she had dreamed of as a girl God had given to her in this serene place, this tiny sliver of eternity.

How long they stood in each other's caress she didn't know. While it was still dark, Andreas's silhouette faded into the blackness of the forest. Constanza stood for a moment, gazing into the cool darkness, her heart still pattering. A shadow flitted in the corner of her eye, but when she turned, she found only a window curtain dancing in the breeze.

By the time she opened the door to the house, five-year-old Prospera sat awake near the hearth, wrapped in a wool blanket, her restless gaze aimed at Constanza. "May I eat now, Mamà?"

Constanza walked toward the hearth and unfastened a fresh kerchief from the drying line. "*Bonjorn* to you too, Prospera."

Disappointment dulled the usual brightness in Prospera's eyes as she tiptoed to Constanza. "Bonjorn, Mamà. There's nothing to do. Everyone is still asleep."

"Except you and me." Constanza wrapped the kerchief around her hair and, for the ten thousandth time in her life, tucked loose strands beneath it. She hugged Prospera, then retrieved a tallow lamp and ignited the wick with a candle. "I have something for you."

"Just me? No one else?"

Constanza held a finger to her lips. "Quiet."

"Is it honey?"

Constanza put her hand on Prospera's back and led her to the door. "No, it's in the barn."

Prospera stopped and crossed her arms. "In the barn?"

"You must work for it, as we all must to fill our bellies." Constanza coaxed Prospera to follow her again, but Prospera's steps were more hesitant now.

Outside, a brilliant red dawn simmered on the wooded heights above them. Though their valley was still cloaked in shadow, the sun already cast its first rays on the green pastures and rolling fields to the right.

Constanza set the lamp down, knelt to Prospera's level, and pointed at the rising sun. "It was a morning just like this."

Prospera leaned in, her interest obvious in the way she paused.

"'And very early in the morning the first day of the week, they came unto the sepulchre at the rising of the sun.'"

"What does that mean?"

"Three women, walking to the Savior's tomb at dawn. They didn't yet know that God had won His greatest battle that same morning. All they saw was the dawn. They were concerned about rolling away the heavy stone, but they hadn't seen that an angel had already rolled it away. When they saw the angel in the empty tomb, they were afraid."

"I would be afraid too," Prospera said.

Constanza pulled Prospera close, continuing to watch the sunrise. "'And he saith unto them, Be not affrighted: Ye seek Jesus of Nazareth, which was crucified: he is risen; he is not here: behold the place where they laid him.' I stop and remember that when I see the dawn."

A thump came from behind them, then a soft rustling in the thicket. Constanza retrieved the lamp and held it toward the barn, but all was still.

"The sun is up," Prospera said. "We don't need the lamp anymore."

"In the daylight, no, but the barn will still be very dark."

Prospera held her nose as Constanza unlatched the barn door. "It smells so bad."

"The animals probably think the same when we bring them into our house on cold winter nights." Constanza flung the door open as the goats and sheep bleated.

"Then they make our house smell like the barn!"

Constanza led Prospera to the far side of the room, found a stool, and placed it outside a pen. A goat and its kid bounded toward them. Constanza opened the gate and let the mother out.

"Why are we by the goats?" Prospera's hand still clamped her nostrils shut.

"You need to be around them more. Meet my lovely lady, Ròsa," Constanza said, petting the goat's back to calm it. "Now tell Ròsa your name."

Prospera tightened her mouth into a confused smile. *"Compreni pas."*

"You understand me." Constanza held Prospera's hand and helped her rub the goat's back. *"Avança't,* now tell her your name."

"Me dison . . . Prospera de Bonomo."

The goat stretched out its neck and bleated as Constanza smiled. "Ròsa is our friend. She doesn't need your family name."

Prospera raised her nose high, and her face brightened. "I like my family name."

"I do too." Constanza gave her a quick nod. "Sit on this stool now and keep petting her. Tell her what you're doing today. Be her very best friend."

Prospera took a step from behind Constanza and brushed her fingers over the goat's head. "Bonjorn, Ròsa. What's your baby's name?"

A bleat echoed through the barn, and Prospera giggled as she sat on the stool.

"Excellenta!" Constanza knelt beside Prospera. "Ròsa said, 'Luchino.'" She pulled a bucket from near the fence and placed it under the goat. "Now I can show you how to milk her."

Prospera raised her brows and pulled away from the goat. "Me? How? She's so big."

"First I reach under her like this. See how gently I hold her teats? You can touch them too, but very softly, yes?"

Prospera bobbed her head and mimicked Constanza. "Like this, Mamà? Like this?"

"Perfecta, now watch carefully as I squeeze ever so gently, like this." A stream hit the bottom of the pail. "Milk comes out. Now you try."

Without stopping to answer, Prospera looked under the goat again and replaced Constanza's hand with hers.

"Wait, let me guide your hand. Remember, be very gentle because she's our friend. Hold here and squeeze, almost like you're kneading dough. Yes!" Again fresh milk streamed into the pail.

"I did it, Mamà! I milked her!" Prospera wrapped her arms around the goat and whispered, "Mercé, Ròsa."

"That's barely enough for a day-old kitten, but I'll show you again another morning." Constanza laughed as she reached under the goat to finish the milking. "After I'm done, the first drink is yours."

The barn door suddenly creaked, and daylight flooded the room.

Prospera jumped up to look over Constanza's shoulder, kicking over the milk pail. She gasped. "Madomaisèla Elionor!"

Constanza stood and spun, wiping her hands on her apron. Standing before her was Elionor Janavel.

Constanza lifted her skirts and rushed forward. She and Prospera reached Elionor at the same moment, and both hugged her.

"Oh, Elionor! You surprised us! I saw you at the wedding and . . ." Constanza faltered, the words slipping from her like goat's milk through her fingers. Her chest tightened as she blinked rapidly, trying to hold back the rush of emotions.

"My dear friend Constanza." Elionor's voice was blanketed in a weary fog. "I'm so sorry. I . . . I have nowhere else to go, and . . . and I'm alone."

Constanza held Elionor's hands in hers at arms length. Elionor's light brown hair was tangled and unwashed, and her head covering was missing, but the faint glint in her eyes still reflected her kindhearted nature. "I've been praying I would see you again."

Bottom lip quivering and hands trembling, Elionor mouthed, "Mercé, Constanza."

Prospera buried herself in Elionor's skirts. "I missed you, madomaisèla!"

"And I've longed to see you, Prospera. Everyone else too."

"You just missed Andreas," Constanza said. "He's on an errand to Pragela, but he'll return in a few days."

"I know. I saw him . . . and you."

Constanza held a hand over her mouth, her cheeks warming.

"You two are so happy." Elionor brushed a tear from her eye. "And I am happy for you."

"It must have been you I saw this morning."

"I slept in the barn last night, and I tried not to disturb you . . ."

"Oh, Elionor, you didn't in the slightest." Constanza released Elionor's hands and shifted into a more upright stance. "You should have come inside. The house might be full, but we would have found a place for you."

"I arrived here late. It was . . . a long journey. I don't mean to intrude, and I know you have many bellies to fill"—she eyed Prospera—"but would I be a nuisance if I slept here for a time? I could clean the barn and feed the animals and perhaps wash the linens."

Constanza sighed. She and Elionor had been the closest of friends since they were young girls. They had tramped through the forest together, watching over their dolls like Miriam with her brother Moses or defeating the unholy Canaanites like Deborah. Constanza had cried on Elionor's shoulder well into the evening after hearing her brother Pèire had died in the avalanche. Just last year, they had both helped Luca and Vitòria Grimaldi and their thirteen orphans in Turin. And together they had wept when Valeria died from the fever. No, Elionor would not sleep on a cold, smelly barn floor.

But where had she been these months? Elionor's skirts were worn and muddy. Drawn, dark circles hung beneath her eyes, but it wasn't the kind of weariness that came from long days in the field. Something else was there—something Constanza couldn't see. Should she ask what was troubling her friend?

Constanza shook her head and smiled tenderly at Elionor. "My friends don't sleep in my barn."

"But Mamà, Ròsa sleeps in the barn, and she's your friend," Prospera said, grinning.

"Not like Elionor." Constanza offered her arm to Elionor. "Besides, I have five sons to clean the barn."

Tears glided down Elionor's cheeks as Constanza linked arms with her. Elionor said nothing, but her attempt at a smile told Constanza all she needed to know, at least until she could ask Elionor about her plight.

The hearth room bubbled over with excitement from the moment Elionor entered the house. At the Grimaldis' villa in Turin, Elionor had always been the one whom the children clamored around when she told stories of her mountain homeland. She was the first to discern when a child was sick and the last to leave that child's side at night. Constanza stoked the fire, then sat on a stool near the hearth, sipping a cup of steaming barley tea and watching the children pelt Elionor with questions.

Yet every one of Elionor's smiles seemed forced, her laughter short and obligated. *What burdens you, friend?* Constanza dropped a spoonful of honey and a pinch of the comb into her cup.

Silvia sat on the floor near Constanza. "Isn't it wonderful, Mamà? We've prayed for Madomaisèla Elionor, and now she's in our hearth room. How long will she stay?"

Constanza took a sip of tea, still holding the warm clay cup to her chin. "I don't know. A few days, at least."

Prospera sat on Elionor's lap. Zama stood behind Elionor, looking over her shoulder. Irene was on her knees, gazing up at Elionor. They didn't seem to see her dirt-smudged cheeks and tangled hair.

"Ezio, Guido," Constanza said to the two oldest boys.

They slumped their shoulders and frowned as they approached.

"Fetch the washtub for Madomaisèla Elionor and fill it with water from the well. The sun should warm it enough to be ready by midday. Don't forget to set up the curtain so she doesn't need to do it herself."

Ezio and Guido acknowledged her and plodded outside, heads sagging.

With Andreas gone, Constanza needed someone else she could ask for advice about Elionor. Was there something Constanza didn't know? Was Elionor disfellowshipped from the church?

Surely not—she had chosen to leave. She had told no one and simply left her seat in the meetinghouse empty. Sheltering her here seemed a kind act, but would Elionor temper the children's desire for the principles Constanza and Andreas were instilling in them? Unease settled in Constanza's chest. Papà would certainly offer wise counsel, but Mamà seemed like the better one to ask. Besides, she would be overjoyed to see Elionor.

Setting her cup on her lap, Constanza turned to Silvia. "Can you find *Mameta* and ask her to come down? Tell her we have a wonderful surprise, but no more."

"Yes, Mamà! I'm leaving right now!" Silvia jumped up and found her kerchief, wrapping it carelessly as she ran out the door.

Silvia, always eager to please me. Constanza placed dry mint leaves in her cup, then stirred the coals in the hearth and ladled hot water into her cup.

When she finished her tea, she had to peel the children away from Elionor to perform their duties: finish milking the goats, gather chicken eggs, wash linens, guide the sheep to a fresh pasture, clean the barn. But after each child allegedly completed a chore, he or she always returned to Elionor. The children told her varying accounts, often exaggerated, of what had happened at the cave last winter. One thread of truth remained in each account, though—their papà, the mighty hero who had defeated the cruel Lord of Luserna.

Dear God, give Andreas wisdom in Pragela. May he be salt and light.

As Constanza had hoped, Elionor's bathwater was almost warm enough by midday, but to spur the process along, she added a kettle of boiling water. The sun beamed down on her and Elionor as the children buzzed about them. Constanza handed Elionor a soap of lavender and lye. "Do you need a dress? I have one I could spare. It's worn"—she touched Elionor's sleeve—"but not like this."

"How can I thank you, Connie?"

"I'm baking bread this afternoon, and I could use your help there. Silvia is becoming helpful, but the others—"

"I know!" Elionor closed her eyes for a moment. "They're all just how I remember . . ."

Constanza turned Elionor toward the washtub and gave her a little push. "You can tell me later, but for now, soak as long as you want. Listen to the songbirds. Breathe in the clear mountain air. And nothing can compare to clean skin, washed hair, and a fresh dress."

Silvia's excited shout echoed down the hillside. "Mameta is here!"

All the children looked up, and a few cheered.

Elionor brushed her hands through her hair and rubbed her cheek. "Is there dirt on my face?"

"It's not a strong, handsome man," Constanza said, "only Mamà."

Elionor's countenance dropped, but it rose again when Mamà stopped and gasped.

Mamà lifted her skirts and jogged toward Elionor but stopped a few paces away. She glanced at the loose-fitting waist of Elionor's dress. Then she took the last few steps to Elionor, kissed her cheeks, and embraced her. "How did all this happen?" she asked between laughs and sobs. "How long have you been here?"

"Only since last night, *madòna.*"

Mamà smiled at Elionor. "Where have you been all these months? We've been praying for you and hoping—"

"I'd rather not spoil our reunion. I'm simply grateful I still have friends here."

"Why would you not?" Mamà asked. "The whole church will be thrilled to see you. Tell me, how is your mamà?"

After her husband, Lambert, had died fighting the crusaders, Elionor's mother had moved back to where her siblings lived in the Rorà Valley—a half day's journey from where they stood.

Elionor bit her bottom lip and peered up toward Mount Vandalino. "I haven't seen her in many months."

"Months? Magdalena gazes down the path as she weeds her garden, waiting for you." Mamà linked arms with Elionor and pointed downhill. "Go, Elionor. If you leave now, you'll arrive in the Rorà Valley before sundown."

Elionor untwined her arm from Mamà's and blinked a few times. "I will, but I'm not ready to see her yet."

For a few moments, the women stood looking at one another. A hammer clanged against an anvil in the distance. Bino and Umile sparred near the barn, using sticks as swords.

Mamà took Elionor's hands and offered a motherly smile. And nothing else was said about the matter.

While Elionor bathed, Constanza and Mamà fastened newly washed linens on the drying line. The children played in the field on the opposite side of the house, and a calm breeze glided down from the heights, rustling through the hung clothing.

Mamà squeezed a few drops of water from a doublet and fastened her eyes on Constanza. "Elionor is with child."

Constanza let out a disbelieving laugh and hung a stocking on the line. "No, she doesn't even have a husband."

Mamà pressed her lips together and gave Constanza a single nod.

"How do you know?"

"I've birthed eleven children, and I've assisted many other women. It's subtle, but the shape of Elionor's body doesn't lie."

"I . . . I don't understand. How could she be with child?" Her breath escaped her and her heart thumped. "She did enjoy the company of that Piedmontese man—Brando, I think his name was. Surely she wouldn't have . . ."

"You see the weariness, no? It may be from the child, but it's more than her body. Her spirit is drained."

"I don't know what I should do. I wish Andreas were here."

"Indeed, your husband will always be your best counselor. Your papà and I have been married for almost twoscore years. I seek his guidance now more than ever."

"But Andreas isn't here. I want to help Elionor, but what if she is a wrong influence on the children?"

"That's a question for you and your husband to answer. For now, I think you're right in letting her stay."

"Should I ask her about . . ."

"Let Elionor broach that subject. There's a reason she hasn't said anything yet, and until she does, let her see Christ in you." Mamà hung the last chemise on the line. "Let the words of your mouth speak truth, and allow the Holy Spirit to work on Elionor."

Elionor emerged from behind the curtain, drying her hair with a hemp towel. She wore a faded dark green dress that drew attention to her expectant form. Mamà was right.

*   *   *

The next day, Constanza brought the children to the place she would always remember as *la casa*. It took a little coaxing to convince Elionor to come, but with some gentle prodding from Mamà and a little more from Constanza, Elionor donned a kerchief and joined the Pavarin family for the evening meal outside, where they always ate unless it was raining.

Constanza's brothers, sisters, nieces, and nephews and her own children sat around two long hewn-stone tables as Papà thanked God for His provision. After the prayer, Constanza tore off a piece of barley bread and slathered on a lump of butter.

"Your sons are so tall," Elionor said to Constanza's oldest sister, Susanna.

"I'm afraid mine will be even taller." Another sister, Maria, shook her head as she held a cup of milk. "Both Papà and Stefano's papà have long legs."

"Mine will likely be normal height." Margarita was the most reserved of Constanza's sisters, but out of them all, she was the one Constanza confided in the most. "But with the blight this year, they all might lose a finger's width or two."

"Short or tall," Gracia said, admiring the baby cradled in her arms, "our children will still have these Pavarin eyes."

Maria glanced at Elionor. "Did you hear Theresa is expecting another? That will be her eighth. Soon she'll have as many as our youngest sister here."

Constanza gave them a genial smile. "I'm still very new to this . . . being a mamà. I can mend clothes and cook and teach them the Holy Scriptures, but I think that's a small part of being a mamà. Some days I feel as if I scold the children more than I hug them."

Her sisters nodded and voiced their agreement.

Margarita tore off a piece of bread and dipped it in berry jam. "You are learning, sister, and I think you're becoming a wonderful mother. What the rest of us have learned over years, you've had to learn in months."

"Then, just as you're becoming the mamà you need to be, here comes another child." Gracia shifted the baby to her shoulder and patted his back. She smiled slyly at Constanza. "When will we hear such news from you and Andreas?"

Constanza's throat tightened, and her cheeks warmed. She had been married for only five months, almost six now. It was too early to be concerned about such things. All seemed normal, though, so why wasn't she with child yet?

Susanna nudged Gracia and frowned at her—the same frown Constanza had received countless times from her older sister. "She became a bride only this spring. Give her and Andreas time."

Constanza smiled slightly at Susanna, and Susanna nodded subtly, her gaze flickering toward Gracia.

"Please pass the quail," Constanza said to Maria, who sat across from her, next to Elionor. Shifting in her seat, Elionor avoided everyone's eyes. Her face was flushed and her mouth downturned. It was no use asking Elionor what was wrong, especially in front of Constanza's sisters. *Lord, let me help her.*

Papà rose from the other table and walked toward them. His left leg, permanently maimed during Marco Spada's short-lived inquisition, forced him to a slow hobble. He held out his calloused hands for his newest grandchild, and Gracia placed the baby in Papà's muscular arms. He cradled the infant in his left arm and placed his right hand on Gracia's shoulder. "The new pond on the third terrace is ready. David helped me finish it last night." He motioned up at the sky. "Now all we need is more rain, then we'll be ready to plant the winter crops."

The best word Constanza could think of to describe Papà was *solide*—strong, yes, but so much more than that. Despite his age and his lame leg, Papà was still strong in body. But it was his soul the word *solide* belonged to. Papà and Mamà had raised eleven children, and despite her own shortcomings, Constanza thought they had raised them remarkably well. As Papà held his new grandson, she inwardly thanked God.

"Andreas and Johan should be in Pragela by now." Papà handed the baby back to Gracia.

"Yes, and he'll return in just two days." Constanza's heart leaped at the thought.

"Do you need help on your farm?"

"Papà," Constanza said, "you have enough to worry about here."

"You're right about that. Ever since that papist monk took my youngest daughter from me, I've been missing my shepherdess."

"Andreas is a prince." Constanza raised her head and put on a playfully haughty smile.

"He doesn't live like a prince—smells like goats the same as the rest of us."

Constanza and her sisters all laughed, and even Elionor chuckled a little.

Papà gazed directly at Constanza with those big, passionate Pavarin eyes. "Titles and other formalities mean nothing. Your husband is dedicated to God, to you, and to his children. That's what makes him a good man."

Forgetting all formalities herself, Constanza hurried around the table and wrapped her arms around Papà's chest. Nothing compared to hearing him say that about Andreas. "You are a good man too, Papà."

Constanza's sisters soon surrounded Papà too, some with tears in their eyes. They took turns embracing him, and after seeing the commotion, Constanza's brothers joined them. Mamà came and stood beside Papà.

A tear streamed down Elionor's face as she watched. Constanza left Papà's side and walked over to sit beside Elionor.

"I miss my papà," Elionor whispered, her chin quivering.

"Oh, Elionor."

"If he had stayed home like your papà that day . . ." Elionor fell onto Constanza's shoulder, sobbing. "I wish I could see him again . . . I want to tell him everything and listen to him talk."

Constanza held Elionor close, rubbing her back and weeping with her. Losing Papà—she couldn't imagine.

"Elionor." Papà's low voice brought comfort like a soothing arnica. "Your papà was the most selfless man I knew."

"And your mamà longs for you dearly." Constanza held Elionor's hands. "She needs to see you as much as you need to see her."

Elionor dried her eyes with her sleeve. "I need a few days . . . only a few."

"I can go with you."

Elionor touched her cheek. "Would you?"

"As soon as you're ready and Andreas is home."

Elionor hugged Constanza one last time and hinted at a genuine smile. Constanza couldn't help but smile back as the setting sun warmed the back of her neck. She sighed in contentment. God had already answered her prayer and shown her how to help Elionor.

5

Now, as in the days of the Apostles, God is communicating directly with his Elect; the reason for this is that the Last Days are at hand. By force of arms we must prepare the way for the Millennium.

—Thomas Müntzer, c. 1525

PESTILENCE, REVOLTS, PROPHECIES, TYRANNY, WAR —the rumors from Pragela grew more ominous the farther Andreas and Johan journeyed up the Chisone Valley. From the bustling trade center of Pinerolo to the quiet hamlet of Fenestrelle, adults and children alike averted their eyes at the mention of Pragela.

Lofty mountains, far higher than those near home, rose on either side of the winding trail that led deeper into the valley. On the left, towering above dark evergreens, the highest peak already displayed a blanket of snow. As the sun fell below the mountains, a shadowy twilight settled over the valley.

"It's so high up here," Andreas said, stopping to catch his breath. "How can crops grow?"

"They don't. The villagers probably import most of their food from farther downstream." Johan pointed at the ridge. "At least there's plenty of pasture for herding, and I imagine they harvest timber too, though they can't cut too much."

"Why not?"

"Avalanches. If there's nothing to hold the snow in place, it will move where it wills. This is the kind of valley where an avalanche can swallow your whole village. And you wouldn't even know it happened."

Andreas glanced up at the tallest mountain, thankful winter was still months away, though the wind blew into his nostrils and chilled his arms. *I should have packed a coat.*

Before them, on either side of the road, stood about twenty stone and wooden houses with steeply pitched roofs. A crudely written sign beside the road announced the end of their two-day journey: PRAJALATS.

"Must be the local dialect." Johan placed his hands on his hips and stared at the village.

"'Icy meadow,'" Andreas mumbled to himself. "And that's precisely what it looks like."

Below the village name, a symbol had been freshly carved into the sign: the moon covering the sun above a crown of twelve falling stars. Andreas traced the carving with his fingers. "Is this familiar to you?"

Johan angled his head to the side.

"Remember the cloaked man and the soldiers?" Andreas backed away from the sign. "He mentioned twelve stars too. But what does it mean?"

"Don't think too hard about it. They're sectarians who believe anything their leader tells them."

Gray smoke streamed from two chimneys, but no sheep bleated in the hillside pastures, no chickens clucked in the gardens, no hammer struck rock, and no axe felled timber.

Johan crossed his arms. "Does anyone live here?"

"If they do, they're not the type we would want to meet." Andreas removed his leather hat and brushed a hand through his hair. "We can't turn back now, so let's see if any Vallenses survive here."

Andreas and Johan passed three houses without doors or window curtains. Stepping over rotted wooden boards and shredded linen, they headed toward one of the houses with chimney smoke.

The distant howl of a wolf echoed through the valley, then another. Andreas scanned the slopes, but the walls of this narrow valley made it impossible to discern where the howls had arisen. "This is the kind of place older siblings frighten you with."

Johan chuckled. "I was that older brother."

Andreas approached another abandoned house and kicked the door lightly. It swung inward, creaking and cracking, until it lurched to a halt. He brushed away the cobwebs that hung over the doorway and entered. Birds flew out of a hole in the roof. The stale scent made Andreas's nose twitch. This place had been derelict for months.

He walked out, the floorboards creaking with each step.

One of the two houses with chimney smoke was the largest in Pragela. Light filtered through the curtains, and the fragrant scent of roasting meat drifted through the crisp air.

Johan smacked his lips. "I hope they're friendly in there, because that mutton or whatever is on the spit is making my stomach rumble."

Andreas was more bewildered than hungry. Why were all the other houses abandoned? Why were there no signs of livestock—or any other industry, for that matter? If disease was the cause, it would be foolish to stay and risk carrying the pestilence back home.

From within the large house, a cacophony of voices swelled into a rhythmic, melancholy chant lacking melody or harmony. Andreas and Johan stopped.

"What is that?" Johan asked.

Andreas turned an ear toward the house. "Latin?"

Johan sniffled and wiped his nose with his sleeve. "Papists."

"That's no Catholic chant. They're repeating the same line over and over. And listen closely. The tempo is increasing . . . the volume too." Andreas crossed his arms and repeated the chant in a whisper. *"Ecce lux prophetæ ducet nos. Ecce lux prophetæ ducet nos . . ."*

Johan shook his head. "I don't understand Latin . . . other than maybe *lux*."

"It means 'The light of the prophet shall guide us.'" The chanting continued to build momentum until it abruptly ceased. "I've never heard anything like it."

"It must be that sect. No Vallense in his right mind would chant something so *ridicule*."

The voices suddenly converged into a single phrase. *"Étoilembra delebit solem."*

"'Étoilembra will blot out the sun'?" Andreas raised his brows.

"Utterly senseless." Johan chuckled. "Étoilembra?"

"I don't know either." Andreas spread his feet and stared at the house. "Though I'm sure they won't be our friends."

"What are we supposed to do here, then? I don't see any believers to visit."

To the right, warm light poured from the single window in the smaller house and onto the cobblestone path leading to the door. "There. It seems far more welcoming."

"Is it too risky to knock?"

"Since when are you afraid of a few peasants, Johan?"

"You heard what I did. This village has gone mad."

"You're not a child or an old man." Andreas slapped Johan on the back. "We can still run if we need to."

"I've never run from danger," Johan said, puffing out his chest. "Always confront evil, and never hide from it."

Andreas cast a sidelong glance at him. "I'm certain the barbes would disagree with that. 'There are times for daring, and there are times for discretion,' Monsen Estève would say."

"What is it today, Andreas? Daring or discretion?"

Andreas didn't answer. He turned and walked toward the small house.

The door creaked open before he could knock. A man said, "You may not speak to my wife, nor my children." But the speaker didn't show his face.

"My name is Andreas de Bonomo—"

"Andreas?" The door opened farther, and a man about thirty years old walked out and shut the door. "Why are you here?"

"Was I . . . expected? Rather, is my presence somehow unexpected?" Andreas drew his head back. "Do I know you?"

"No," the man said, shaking his head, "but I know your name. You are famous in this village. Or infamous. Are you Andreas, son of Duke Louis of Savoy, disgraced monk of the Benedictine Order, and wicked Vallense convert?"

Andreas shuffled backward and tensed. His reflexes wanted to reach for a sword, but of course there wasn't one to reach for. "How do you know everything about me?"

"That's not important now. Did you see anyone else in Pragela?" The man peered over Andreas's shoulder. "Or did anyone see you?"

"Except my friend Johan here, you are the only soul I've seen, man or beast."

The man opened the door, bowed, and extended his hand, inviting them in. "I am Lorenzo Maridan, and tonight, my home is yours. Remove your boots, rinse your faces in the basin, and sit by the fire."

Johan looked at Andreas questioningly, but Andreas nudged him inside and closed the door.

Two young children sat on the straw-covered floor, playing with a puppy, while a woman sat in a chair, mending. A kettle hung over the crackling fire on the hearth.

"We are fellow believers, though only our enemies in this village call us Vallenses. The church here is gone, and we're all that remain." Lorenzo sighed. "Satan has conquered Pragela."

The woman stood, adjusted her kerchief, and bowed her head. "*Bonser, monsen.*"

"This is my wife, Dominica." Lorenzo's children rose at his gesture. "And my children, Giuseppe and Anna-Maria."

As Andreas and Johan removed their boots, Dominica grabbed a cloth, hurried to the fire, and lifted the kettle's lid. "It's not much, but it should fill you."

Andreas held up his hands and shook his head. He opened his sack and showed them a loaf of bread wrapped in a cloth. "Eat your food. We prepared for this trip, and you weren't prepared for guests."

Lorenzo handed Johan and Andreas each a wooden bowl. "We're always prepared for guests."

"And our food is yours," Dominica said, ladling a fragrant broth into each bowl.

Johan lifted his bowl to his lips and sipped. He grimaced, set the bowl down, and drew in a deep breath. "Perdon, it's hot."

The children cackled behind him, and Andreas was careful to let his bowl cool before attempting a drink.

Holding his own bowl of broth, Lorenzo sat next to Johan but turned toward Andreas. "We thought you were a legend."

Andreas coughed and narrowed his eyes. "I am a simple farmer from Val Angrogna."

"On top of everything I mentioned earlier. I'm only trying to understand why you're here in Pragela of all places."

"The barbes told us there were believers here." Johan blew gently on his broth. "They wanted Andreas to investigate a new sect here too."

Dominica drew back, her posture tense, and Lorenzo whispered, "The Divine Ascendancy."

Andreas took a small sip of the broth and let it sit on his tongue. The fragrant flavors of onions, carrots, and turnips filled his senses, blended with a mix of herbs and a hint of salt. It was far from the fare of his luxurious childhood in places like Château de Thonon, but it would satisfy his stomach. "We heard a little about them, and we heard the chants as we entered the village."

"I'm not sure why they chant or what it means," Lorenzo said. "Nor do I care to know."

Andreas took a longer sip. "The barbes told me there was a church in Pragela. What happened to it?"

"It would take all night to tell you. There's not one cause but many." Lorenzo looked at his wife, then at the floor. "Living in this valley has never been easy—rocky soil, short seasons, avalanches—but in the past hundred years or so, it has been pure misery."

"I met an old man two years ago," Andreas said between sips. "He was a Catholic priest who has since become a believer, but when he was young, he was part of what sounded like a crusade—"

"Back in 1400." Lorenzo nodded. "That year is etched into the memories of all Christians in Pragela. My grandmother told me the stories with tears rolling down her cheeks. She lost my grandfather and two of her children. Many mothers and their infants froze to death as they fled to the heights, but my grandmother found a cave and hid until the crusaders had done all the evil a man could fathom. That was only the beginning of our troubles."

Dominica placed a hand on Lorenzo's shoulder. "Last year disease ravaged us. Half the church perished."

"The other half left soon after, until only my parents, my family, and my sister's family remained. That's about the time the Ascendants found the village."

"Why did you stay so long?" Andreas took the last sip of broth, and Dominica promptly took the empty bowl and refilled it.

"This was our village, wrought from the rocks with our own hands. My parents refused to leave, even after the wars and plagues, and I would never leave them here with the Ascendants."

"Now you are here alone," Johan murmured.

"One more winter, Dominica and I thought, but I'm doubting my decision now. The Ascendants rule Pragela and don't fear anyone except their leader, the Prophet."

"The king of France rules these lands," Andreas said. "Why has he not stamped out this sect as the crusaders tried to do to Vallenses?"

"Pragela is far from Paris, and we are forgotten until the king marches his troops through our valley on his way to sack some distant Italian city. His armies slaughter our sheep, eat what little food we can grow, and take our women as their own. I doubt the king has heard about the Divine Ascendancy."

"Why did they settle here? Are they all foreigners?"

Lorenzo glanced at Dominica. "No. I told you my sister's family stayed here with us. The Ascendancy has devoured them."

"They proselytize, then?" Johan asked.

"More than I can believe. My sister always wavered in her religion, so when she finally was devoted to something other than herself, I listened to them." Lorenzo's daughter approached and sat in his lap. "I quickly discovered how evil their beliefs were, though," Lorenzo added. "I've tried to persuade her to forsake the Prophet's lies, but to no avail."

"How are they so convincing?" Andreas asked.

"Prosperity, power, meaning—peasants latch on to what they don't have, hoping for a life that would otherwise seem impossible. The poor will become rich, and the slaves will become the rulers. The Divine Ascendancy thinks they will install a new order in the world."

"Do they claim to be Christians?" Johan asked.

"Oh, they say they believe the Holy Scriptures as much as I do, but under the surface, they stand in stark opposition to our faith."

"Surely the Dominican friars have heard about them." Andreas leaned forward, elbows on his knees. "No bishop turns his back on these kinds of groups. Have you heard about a court of inquisition trying any of them?"

Lorenzo tightened his lips. "I'm only a poor shepherd trying to provide for his family. I know nothing about religious politics. As soon as we find somewhere else to live and have the provisions to take us there, we're leaving. I've lost a sister to these Ascendants, and I won't allow them to beguile my wife and children."

"When I introduced myself," Andreas said, sitting straight again, "how did you know my name and so much about me?"

Lorenzo looked both ways, as if he feared being overheard. "I heard your name for the first time last week, Andreas. A whole band of Ascendants tramped through here on their way to Piedmont, declaring the signs of the coming kingdom. As usual, it sounded like blather and noise to me, but when you introduced yourself, I remembered them saying your name. You are somehow a cornerstone of their prophecies."

"Andreas?" Johan let out a booming laugh and kicked Andreas's leg. "In a prophecy?"

Lorenzo's frown only deepened. "His family too."

"The Duke of Savoy and his family as the subjects of an end-of-days prophecy," Andreas pondered out loud. "Amusing."

"No, not the duke. It's you and your wife, but especially your children."

Andreas shot up from his chair. "My wife and children?"

"Twelve stars that form a crown, a woman with child, the sun, the moon—the Ascendants say it's from John's Apocalypse. As best I can tell, they seem to think they'll bring forth a new world like a woman brings forth a child."

"What do any of those things have to do with me and my family?" Andreas's fists clenched at his sides, his chest rising and falling with uneven breaths. Heat climbed his neck, and his jaw tightened so hard it ached.

"To them, your family is somehow the subject of that prophecy. With the casting down of the crown of twelve stars and the travail of the woman with child, the Prophet believes the old world will fall and he'll usher in the millennial reign of Christ."

Twelve stars. Does the Prophet think those are my children? "Who is this prophet? Is he here in Pragela?"

"No one knows where he lives. Some say he's among us, taking various forms, while others say he dwells among the most powerful men in the world, secretly preparing the way for his kingdom."

Andreas bowed his head in disbelief. How was his family, of all the ones on earth, the center of some faction's prophecies? "Who is the leader of the Divine Ascendancy in Pragela? I wish to speak with him so I can find the meaning of all this."

"They are all equal—men and women, old and young. Even the Prophet himself prefers not to be named their leader. The Ascendants call each other ègal and live under the same roof, sharing everything in common. But they won't talk to you unless you're willing to join them."

"They all live in that one house?" Johan asked. "Andreas, these people disturb me."

Andreas peered at the door and crossed his arms. He and Johan had traveled here to find believers. They had fulfilled that duty, but he needed to know more about the Divine Ascendancy. "Mercé for lodging us tonight," he said to Lorenzo. "We will leave for home tomorrow, but before that, I need to discover more about this sect. Are they a danger to us?"

"Only to the soul. I've never heard rumors of them being violent—not yet, at least. Though I'm not sure how they'll establish their prophet's kingdom without violence."

A sudden pounding rattled the door.

"You are not welcome here," Lorenzo shouted in that direction.

The knock came again. Lorenzo puffed out a breath, rose, and cracked the door open.

Andreas turned to the door and strained to listen.

"I do have a guest . . . No." The other voice spoke in a whisper, but only Lorenzo's voice was understandable. "What difference does it make? . . . I already said no." Lorenzo closed the door and threw down the latch. He sat across from Andreas. "They know you two are here."

Something rapped on the outside wall of the house, causing the children to run to Dominica. Again someone pounded on the door, this time harder. An unintelligible voice hissed through the door.

Lorenzo motioned his family toward the other side of the house. "They've never been like this before."

"Stay near your family," Andreas said. This might be his opportunity to meet an Ascendant. "Johan and I will answer the door."

Lorenzo nodded once and followed Dominica and the children.

Unlatching the door, Andreas sighed.

Johan gave him a half smile. "Rash and daring again, I see."

Andreas pulled the door open. Three men dressed in dull brown cloaks stood before them.

"The visitors," said the shortest man. "What business have you in Pragela?"

Andreas recalled a proverb Estève had taught him: *When the line between friend and foe blurs, guard your secrets closely.* "We are friends of Lorenzo and Dominica."

Another man took a step forward and sniffed. "I haven't seen you before."

"How long have you lived here?" Johan asked. "Lorenzo said you people arrived only last year."

The shortest man squinted at them. "Beware Lorenzo. He is faithless and does not heed the words of the Prophet."

Johan widened his stance and leaned away. "We don't—"

Andreas held a hand up to hush him. This was his chance to learn about the Ascendants, not verbally spar with them. "We're intrigued with this prophet. In truth, that's one of the reasons we made the journey to Pragela. Please, tell me about your prophecies."

The man's attention seemed to drift into another world. "The mysteries of the faithful are not revealed to the faithless."

"How can one be counted among the faithful?" Andreas asked.

"By heeding the words of the Prophet."

Andreas waved for Johan to join him. "Tell me more about your prophet."

Johan rubbed his temple and sighed but followed Andreas's lead.

Two more men wearing the same drab attire slipped from the shadows, their stances unthreatening but cautious. The shortest man smiled at the others, then glared at Andreas. "You are a Vallense barbe."

Andreas struggled to maintain his composure. "I am no such thing. What makes you suppose that?"

"While the faithful are prudent with their speech," said a man with a raspy voice, "the faithless prattle for all to hear. We know your name, Andreas of Savoy, Crown of the Twelve Stars."

"Already the stars have been reclaimed for the kingdom, and soon Étoilembra will blot out the sun," a new voice said from the shadows. "All will unfold as the Prophet has foretold. You will follow us now."

Andreas stepped back and wished there were a sword at his side.

Johan pulled him from behind just as a man sprang toward them. Andreas slammed the door and latched it.

Lorenzo hastened to them. "They're knocking on the walls."

"I guess we know now," Johan said. "They're dangerous."

Andreas searched the room. "Is there anywhere to escape?"

"The only way in or out is the door."

"I'm sorry," Andreas said to Lorenzo. "I've placed your family in danger."

Lorenzo shook his head vigorously. "All I ask is that you help us escape with you. There are safe villages nearby."

The knocking and tapping continued. Something blunt rammed into the door.

Andreas ran his hands over the plaster-coated wall. "If you're leaving with us, you don't need this house anymore, do you?"

"No."

"Johan, find a way through this wall. And try to be quiet." Andreas scanned the room for anything that might prove useful. The fire roared, but though torches might seem helpful, a flame would attract the eyes of their enemies. Tonight, stealth was their weapon.

Johan held up a woodsman's axe and ran his hand across its blade. "Duller than a wooden spoon."

"Alas, but at least you can scare them with it." Andreas slapped Johan on the back.

Johan listened at the wall for any intruders and started chipping away the plaster.

Lorenzo hugged his children, then snatched a sheathed knife from a wooden box on the mantel and handed it to Andreas. "We should head north toward Usseaux. It's safe there."

Andreas slung his sack over his shoulder. "The road will be too dangerous."

"There's a game trail on the other side of the river. If we can make it there undetected, we should be safe."

"Johan will escort you and your family away from the house."

"I'm almost through the wall," Johan said from across the room.

A hard thud splintered the door. Andreas gathered everyone near Johan. "Stay together and avoid confrontation. We're too few to best them in a fight, so we'll need to best them with speed and stealth."

Johan stood ready with the axe. At a nod from Andreas, Johan broke through the wall. He silently ushered Lorenzo out first, followed by Dominica, and the children last.

The door cracked open and fell to the floor in a dusty heap. Before the debris settled, Andreas lowered his shoulder and charged through the entry.

Someone grabbed his arm as he crossed the threshold. He flung the grip off and launched into a sprint.

Five men pursued him, while three more stomped into the house. They would discover Johan's path of escape soon, and Andreas needed to distract them.

He yelled out ahead, as if Johan and the others had fled in the same direction he had. Wheeling to the right, he scanned the house for movement.

Andreas's pursuers had almost closed the distance. He coughed. His legs begged for rest.

A man advanced into the road ahead, holding a rock. Andreas turned left, away from where Johan and the others had fled. He climbed a fence, ducked under low-hanging branches, and veered around boulders until he jogged breathless into a pine forest.

He slowed and wound a crooked trail through the forest until his lungs could bear no more. Sweat dripped from his brow, and his legs felt like lard. He leaned against a tree and listened for footsteps.

A light breeze rustled the pine needles in an airy chorus. High in the branches, an owl hooted. Andreas closed his eyes and relished the stillness.

At last he straightened away from the tree and started onward. He took a sweeping route around the village, discovered a shallow spot in the river, and crossed to the wooded slopes on the far bank.

As stars twinkled in the blackness far above the forest trail, light footsteps crunched pine needles beneath the dense pines ahead of him. Andreas walked faster but remained quiet in case he had happened upon more Ascendants.

Johan appeared on the trail five paces ahead of Andreas, arms crossed. "You'd be dead if I were your enemy."

Andreas balled his fist and hit Johan's shoulder in jest. "An enemy who talks too much, perhaps. Is everyone safe?"

Johan held his hand out toward the pines. "Yes, and Lorenzo is leading the way to the Vallense hamlet of Usseaux. Come, join us. It's been a quiet evening walk so far."

In a forest clearing on the far side of the pines, Andreas greeted Lorenzo and his family. "How far is the village?"

"We'll reach Usseaux by morning," Lorenzo said, scanning the trail ahead.

And the moment they reached Usseaux, Andreas was headed home to his family.

6

Tyrants generally find a reason for their tyranny, in the orders which they have received from their superiors in authority; this is for them a wide cloak, which can cover much evil. In the meantime they vent their anger, yea, rejoice in their wickedness, while the unoffending and innocent have to suffer.

—Thieleman J. van Braght
Martyrs Mirror, 1660

CONSTANZA PUSHED FEATHERY GREEN STEMS ASIDE and brushed away a layer of soil. "See this purple color, Silvia? It's deeper and livelier than last week. And these stems—they're starting to wilt." She grabbed the root at its head and slid it gently from side to side. "The soil is loosening too. These carrots are ready to eat."

"After we wash them." Silvia grabbed a carrot and inspected it as she had been shown. One of her eyes drooped slightly, and though she still felt insecure about it, she was learning to wave it aside.

"The boys can rinse them this afternoon." Constanza pulled up her carrot and held it at arm's length. "These aren't as long as I had hoped. Nothing grows as well as last year."

"God will provide, Mamà. You and Papà say it all the time."

Constanza nodded slowly then smiled as she yanked out another carrot. Silvia's father had died soon after she was born, and her mother died when she was only eight years old. Luca and Vitòria Grimaldi had just become believers when they found Silvia, and she was the first child they took into their home. Earlier in the summer, Constanza had shown her how to sew a simple kerchief, and Silvia now wore it every day. She was becoming a charming maiden.

"Mamà, we have no more butter," Ezio shouted from across the field.

Constanza let out a heavy sigh and shouted back, "There's only one way to make butter, and that means work."

"Prospera and I milked the goats this morning," Silvia said. "We have some milk from yesterday too. Ezio just doesn't want to sit and churn it."

Constanza dusted off her hands, shielded her face from the sun, and peered toward Ezio. "The churn is by the door."

Ezio's whole body seemed to droop at that simple statement of fact.

"It's your week to churn, no?" Constanza asked, walking toward him.

"My arms hurt every time, and they're still hurting from three days ago."

Constanza halted two paces from Ezio and put her hands on her hips. "You're a strong boy, the strongest in Val Angrogna, or so you've told me."

"Not for churning butter, Mamà. That's for children . . . and women."

Constanza pushed her tongue into her cheek. "Men don't churn butter?"

"No, Mamà, we don't."

"And you, ten years old, are a man?" Constanza stood beside Ezio, slipped a hand onto his shoulder, and pointed at the barley field. "Your papà plowed every row himself."

Ezio raised one shoulder and said, "We all helped him plant, though."

"That's the easy part. Next week when the grain is ready to harvest, he'll swing the scythe until every stalk is cut and lying on the ground. Have you tried to swing a scythe?"

"No, but I could."

"All day?"

Ezio nodded rapidly.

Constanza held Ezio's arm and squeezed the thread of muscle under his skin. "And churning butter makes your arms hurt."

Ezio's gaze fell to the dirt.

"When I was a girl, my papà would tell my brothers that there's no such thing as women's work. If a man can't do it, he learns it. He might not be the best at sewing or baking or washing or changing a baby's soiled linens or churning butter." She caught Ezio's eye. "But he needs to know how."

"Papà doesn't do any of those things." Ezio tilted his head inquisitively.

"That's because I want to help him. I want to free him so he can lift a beam into the roof of the shed or dig a well or do the many other things that need strong muscles or hours sweating under the hot sun. And Papà frees me so I can perform the duties I'm best at and enjoy. Our family needs both of us . . . and you."

Ezio's eyes brightened. "Just like a cart wheel needs spokes and a wheel to roll smoothly."

Constanza wrinkled her nose, studying Ezio with a flicker of curiosity. "I hadn't thought of it that way. I suppose that makes some sense."

Ezio looked past Constanza. "Who is that?"

At the edge of the forest, a tall man wearing a long dull brown cloak walked directly toward them at a methodical pace. She fastened her gaze on him and waved for Ezio to come closer. "Where is Madomaisèla Elionor?"

"With Silvia, washing the bedding at the creek."

"Run and find Papeta." She scanned the man for weapons but saw none. "Tell him a strange man is here."

Ezio blinked rapidly. "What about you?"

"I'll be at the creek with Madomaisèla Elionor."

"Who is that man, Mamà?"

"*Espècia-te*, Ezio!" Constanza pushed Ezio along, and he hurried up the hill.

Where are the children? Most would be near the house, but some might be playing near the barn or in the forest. She needed to gather them. This man was likely harmless, but Andreas would want the children together.

Hurrying toward the house, she found Roberto, Alessia, and Zama. "Follow me. We're going to the creek."

Behind her, the man still approached. Feeling safer with a few children, she called out to him. "I'm sorry, but my husband—" She caught herself. It would be foolish to tell him Andreas was away for a few more days.

The man halted and bowed slightly, saying nothing.

Constanza, holding Roberto's and Alessia's hands, took three paces toward the man. "Bonjorn, may I help you, monsen?"

The sun reflected off his completely bald head. Shallow wrinkles lined his brow, and deep, penetrating eyes locked on her and the children. Why didn't he speak?

Soon six more children gathered around her—three younger children from the house and three boys from the barn. Ezio had run up the slope to find Papà, so only Silvia and Elionor were missing. Constanza cautiously approached the visitor.

He gazed to the left, to the right, then back at Constanza. "Is this the home of Andreas de Bonomo?"

What accent was that? His voice was like water rippling over a smooth stone, but laced with an authority that sent a shiver down her spine.

"Andreas is my husband," Constanza said, her palms sweating against Roberto's and Alessia's.

The man reached into his cloak and removed a red flower. He smelled it deeply, then extended it to Constanza. "My gift to you, *Dama* Bonomo."

Constanza released the children's hands and accepted the flower. She returned to the children and lifted the flower to her nose. "What flower is this?"

"It is from my homeland, far over the sea. We call it *dianthus*—divine flower—but here its name is *ulit*. Perhaps you know it as *carnation*. Throughout the world, it is a symbol of the equality and fraternity shared by all mankind."

Roberto ripped the carnation from Constanza's hand and pressed it under his nose, bending the stem. "It smells like cloves."

Constanza pried the flower out of Roberto's hands and grasped his wrist. "This kind man gave us a flower. Ask before taking, Roberto." She bowed her head toward the man. "Perdon, my children often become excited—"

"Where is your husband, dama?" A deep frown accentuated the dark hollows under his eyes.

"He . . . he will be here soon."

"Will Papà return today?" Bino asked.

Constanza quickly pushed a wisp of hair under her kerchief. "As I said, soon." She motioned the children toward the house but kept her eyes on the man. As she fidgeted with the carnation, it slipped from her fingers and tumbled to the ground. She winced and bent to pick it up.

"Leave it." The man picked up the flower himself.

"I'll tell my husband you would like to speak with him. What is your name?"

He slanted his head downward and smirked. "I will be nearby." But he didn't acknowledge her question.

Constanza brought the children to the house, closed the door, and pressed her back against it. Her pulse raced. How could a man feel both good-hearted and frightening at the same time? She clasped her hands together and breathed deeply, but then came questions from every direction.

"Who was he?" Zama asked.

Umile tugged on Constanza's apron. "When is he coming back?"

"Where is Ezio?" asked Ave.

"Madomaisèla Elionor and Silvia too!" Alessia said, her lips pouty.

Constanza's answer was the same for everyone. "I don't know." Thankfully, Ezio would soon find Papà. And Papà would handle everything.

If only Andreas were here. Somehow he always chose rightly, then acted with confidence. But was that nameless man a threat to him? It certainly felt that way.

The children buzzed around her, some quarreling, others playing, and Roberto trying to jump onto her back. This house was too small for all these little feet, and Constanza needed something to do until Ezio returned with Papà.

She backed away from the door. "Let's walk to the creek and help Madomaisèla Elionor."

"May we play in the water too?" Guido asked.

"If you—"

The room erupted in elated claps and cheers. Constanza opened the door and led the clamoring children behind the house, but as they rounded the corner, a desperate shout interrupted their joyous parade.

Constanza froze. *Elionor.*

The children turned to her, their unvoiced questions begging for an answer. She held a finger to her lips and listened. Nothing.

Two men burst from the barley field, then others from behind the house. Constanza scanned the forest. More men rushed toward them.

The only place to flee was back to the house. *Please, Lord, let Papà come soon!*

Constanza swung Alessia into her arms, snatched Roberto's hand, and guided everyone toward the house. "Inside, everyone! Quickly!"

She stumbled into a sluggish jog. Nine-year-old Guido helped Prospera, while Umile aided Ave and Fosca.

The cloaked men converged on them from behind and either side. Another man appeared near the house.

But the house was too far. Already Alessia was slipping from her arm. Constanza stopped to set her down, then grabbed her hand and pulled both her and the whimpering Roberto.

Guido and Prospera reached the house first. Guido pushed the door open just as an assailant reached them. The man pulled a rope from his sack and stretched out his hand for Prospera.

"Guido!" Constanza shouted.

He charged the man and punched him in the stomach. Umile left Ave and Fosca and ran at the man from behind. The man buckled over, shielding his face from the boys' kicks and punches.

Three more men charged into the fray, all carrying lengths of rope. One of them lunged toward Prospera, gripped her by the arm, yanked her back. He wrapped the rope tight around her wrists before she could react. As she struggled, the second man seized the other two girls, one by the shoulder, the other by the waist, pulling them into a tight knot. The third man advanced on the boys, pushing Guido to the ground with a shove. Umile tripped over his own feet as he was forced to the earth, pinned under the man's strength.

A man's hand seized Constanza from behind and spun her around. She lost her grip on Roberto but still held Alessia's hand. Two men surrounded her, and others loomed nearby.

She pulled against the grasp and kicked, but the man was too strong. Constanza screamed and flailed. Another man ripped Alessia away.

"What do you want?" Constanza demanded. "Take anything!"

The man holding her forced her to the ground. Several children lay there too, cowering, crying, and shouting for their papà.

Andreas, where are you?

More children fell to the ground beside her. Someone grabbed her wrists, pushed her face into the dust, and stepped on her back. He pulled her hands behind her back and wound thick rope around them. Though every movement launched a new ripple of pain, Constanza kicked and tossed, rolled and pulled. But the rope was too tight and the men too strong.

Her family needed help, and there were other farms nearby. She screamed with all her might.

Someone pulled her to her knees while another man removed a thick cloth from a sack. She screamed again, but a hand covered her mouth and dampened the sound.

Constanza shook. She had been a captive before, but not the children. Those awful memories flooded her mind—the papist friar Marco Spada's devilish leers, the smug grin of Gedeon Chanforan. No matter what, she couldn't let these men harm the children.

She vaulted from her knees and lunged forward. Her feet caught her skirt. Hands bound, she fell face forward into the rocky dirt. A foot pressed into the small of her back.

Lying there in defeated silence, the children fell quiet, their cries fading one by one. The men sat her up again. Roberto lay in tears on her right, a gag in his mouth.

As she counted the children, someone threw a thick linen cloth around her mouth. She turned from side to side and tried to push the cloth out with her tongue, but the man jammed it into her mouth and tied it tightly. Her kerchief yanked her hair, loosened, and finally slipped to the dirt. She screamed again, but the wicked men around her were likely the only ones to hear it.

Constanza turned and leaned to find all the children, but Silvia was still missing, along with Elionor. And Ezio. *Please, God, let Papà come soon . . . and twenty strong Vallense farmers.*

Their captors signaled each other with nods, hand signals, and a word or two, but otherwise they remained silent. They varied in age, some with smooth, youthful faces and others with gray hair and deep wrinkles.

One of them held Constanza's arm and pulled her up. She swayed, and her back ached. The children all stood now too, and over a dozen men encircled them.

Hooves beat against the path behind Constanza, and her heart jumped. *Papà!*

She turned, and her hopes collapsed. The bald man rode a horse of nearly the same color as its rider's dull cloak. He galloped to them, pulled back the reins, and dismounted effortlessly. His boots hit the ground like a hammer's strike, and in his hand was the red bloom with a broken stem.

He commanded the men in hushed tones, then walked toward Constanza, giving short waves to his men and even the children as he passed through their midst. He stood before Constanza and stared down at her.

She stared back. "Let my children—"

But the gag muffled her words.

He lifted the red flower to his nose and sniffed deeply. Mocking her bound hands, he extended his hand and offered the bloom. "Again, my gift to you, Dama Bonomo." He tucked the flower into her apron, then stood back and frowned. "You may call me the Prophet."

Constanza tried to speak again, and the Prophet held a finger to his lips. A chorus of voices rose around her. "Ecce lux prophetæ ducet nos. Ecce lux prophetæ ducet nos . . ."

The Prophet raised his hands, closed his eyes, and beamed, relishing the eerie chants. When he lowered his hands, the chants ceased. "The day of the Lord is at hand," he said, his tone rich and lively.

What spawn of Satan were these men? The children's eyes latched on to Constanza, longing for answers, yearning for reassurance, begging for security. But she could offer none of those.

The Prophet remounted his horse and spurred it toward the creek. Someone pushed Constanza from behind. "Form a line and follow the Prophet. We stop when he stops, and we march when he marches."

The gag dammed up all Constanza wanted to say. The men pushed everyone into a line until they marched two abreast behind the Prophet.

Tears streamed down Constanza's cheeks. She gazed into the forest for a sign of hope, whether Andreas or Papà or one of her brothers or any man with a shred of conscience. Surely someone in the valley had seen these men, these—what were they? Who was this bald man they called the Prophet?

She plodded forward, praying, hoping, yearning for deliverance. They crossed the creek and walked through the forest Constanza knew better than these wretched imps.

Where were Elionor and Silvia? Maybe they had escaped and run up to Papà and Mamà's farm. Constanza peered back toward the creek, imagining Papà there.

But it was no imagination. Papà stood there gripping an axe, his countenance set like a boulder. Two of Constanza's brothers, David and Francesco, stood at Papà's side, one holding a thick stick and the other holding a spear. Riccardo and Patrizio ran up behind them, each armed with a wooden club. Ezio stood in the rear, obviously proud he had organized the rescue.

Constanza's heart soared. They weren't alone.

The Prophet dismounted and signaled his men. Half left their positions beside the children and hurried to the Prophet. Constanza stood on her toes to catch a better glimpse of what was happening. The Prophet unlatched a strap on his saddlebag and removed a number of knives. He gave one to each man, placing a hand on each man's shoulder and looking him directly in the eye. "For the kingdom."

A man still stood beside Constanza. But if a battle ensued, she and the children might be able to overwhelm their captors. She counted the men assigned to them—four, and none held a sheath as the others did.

Ten men fanned out ahead of her, knives drawn, and advanced toward Papà. The Prophet remained near his horse.

Beyond fallen limbs, tree trunks, and thick underbrush, Papà stood tall with the others. He held his axe as if he were going to fell an oak with one swing. Beside him, David and Francesco planted their feet shoulder-width apart. Patrizio and Riccardo stood with the same intensity, weapons raised, jaws set.

Constanza lightly kicked Guido's foot, mumbled through her gag, and turned her shoulder inward, signaling the children to move toward her. To attempt an escape, everyone needed to draw together. She wouldn't leave a single child with the Prophet and his vile followers.

Guido drew closer, and three younger children followed. Constanza gave them a subtle nod and eyed the others. These trees and trails were hers. Every rock and stump between here and the meetinghouse she knew. With a little help from heaven, they might escape.

Something stirred in the forest behind her, and grunts and mumbles accompanied the stirring. Constanza turned, and her heart sank.

Elionor and Silvia were bound and gagged, and two huge men prodded them forward. Elionor's hair blew freely in the wind, her sleeve was ripped, and mud covered her skirts. She must have fought like a fearless sparrow against a hawk.

Why had she ever come to Constanza's home for help? It had been only three days. If only Elionor had stayed away . . .

The men pushed Elionor and Silvia in with the rest and stayed nearby. *Pietat! Now six are guarding us, and two are giants!*

Silvia laid her head on Constanza's chest, and the children gathered closer. The creek was nearby, and once they crossed it, they could find help. At least four families lived along the creek, and more beyond it. Vallense men would be roused, their captors would be defeated, and they would be safe.

"Unbind my daughter and my grandchildren." Papà's firm voice echoed through the trees and warmed Constanza's soul.

The Prophet erupted in a sinister laugh. "The unfaithful cannot make demands of the Divine Ascendancy. The crown of twelve stars belongs to God alone, and none can stand against His faithful." He extended his hand, palm upward. "Join us, for the kingdom of God is at hand."

Papà advanced. "Who are you, and what do you want with my daughter and grandchildren?"

"The mysteries of the faithful are not revealed to the faithless." The Prophet waved his men forward, then reached into his cloak. "Resist the Ascendant Kingdom at your own peril."

"What is this kingdom you speak of? God alone will establish His kingdom when He wills it. No man knows the day nor hour, according to the Scriptures."

The Prophet turned to his men. "A man of the letter, as I have warned you. Without question, the Holy Bible is the Word of God, but is it the end of God's revelations?"

The men beside Constanza joined their companions in a haunting ensemble. "No. Ecce lux prophetæ ducet nos."

That had to be Latin, but what did it mean?

The Prophet turned back to Papà. "Does not creation speak the words of God to us? And have you not listened to that voice within, that enchanting spirit of experience and sensation? The spirit of the letter is for the basest of Christians, but God gives the spirit of dreams and revelations to his faithful Ascendants."

Constanza had never heard such teaching. It certainly wasn't Catholic teaching, and no Vallense would say such things. Was this the sect Andreas and Johan had heard about while hunting? Or the one they had gone to investigate?

Papà lowered his axe slightly. "I have some silver, or if you would rather we barter—"

"Naive soul." The Prophet shook his head. "Money is a tool of the powerful to oppress the weak. When the kingdom is established, all gold, all silver, all gems will perish in flames."

"What can I exchange for my daughter and grandchildren?" Papà loosened one hand from his axe. "I'll give you whatever you want."

"Reject your unfaithful ways, listen to the true spirit within, and accept the new age on earth, which His faithful servants will usher in."

"Then you would free my daughter?" Papà peered over the Prophet's shoulder at Constanza.

She readied herself for a sprint to the creek. *Lord, make us swift.*

The Prophet chuckled and advanced toward Papà until he stood only three or four paces away. "Your daughter and her children belong to the Ascendant Kingdom."

Papà planted himself a pace away from the Prophet, holding his axe with both hands. "They belong to our Savior, Jesus Christ. And my daughter belongs to her husband, Andreas de Bonomo."

The Prophet's shoulders rose and fell in long breaths. His followers stood behind him, poised and alert.

In a whirl, the Prophet feinted with his left shoulder. Papà flinched.

With an uncanny grace, the Prophet lunged forward. His knife emerged in a swift, decisive motion. And he drove it into Papà's chest.

Papà slumped to his knees.

Constanza screamed through the gag and burst into a sprint. Her bound arms, the cloth in her mouth, the evil men around her—none of it mattered. Papà needed her.

Turning, the Prophet took a white cloth from under his robe. He carefully wiped the blade, sheathed it, and nodded to his men.

An arm grabbed Constanza, but she squirmed away and stumbled toward Papà. Crude weapons clashed on the left and right. Men grunted and shouted.

Tears welled up in Constanza's eyes as she collapsed before Papà, who lay on his side with blood spreading from a wound under his collarbone. He stared over her, unfocused and unblinking.

She needed to roll him onto his back and find something to stop the bleeding. Twisting, pushing, and turning, she strained against the rope that bound her hands behind her back and slid closer to Papà. A man grabbed Constanza's wrist and pulled her away.

She jerked her shoulders, kicked, and shouted muffled screams through the damp gag. One of the man's hands came loose. She pulled against him with every muscle. Papà's empty eyes stared into nothingness. Could he see her? Was he—

An arm wrapped around her neck and squeezed her. "He's dead."

"Papà!" Constanza screamed, but all that arose was a guttural moan. Where were David and Francesco? She needed them now. She flailed against the viselike hold. Her whole body tensed and heaved as the man dragged her away. But Papà didn't move.

Clanging steel, dull cracks of wood, and whimpers from the children filled the air. Constanza's vision blurred behind tears she couldn't wipe away.

The man pushed her to the ground. A child fell onto her, then another, but she couldn't hug them. Her whole world collapsed as she lay in the dirt, sobbing.

A gentle touch rubbed her shoulder, but she didn't look to see who it was. Though her eyes were fastened shut, all she could see was Papà's eyes—the same eyes she had inherited, the eyes that had reassured her, taught her, loved her. Now they were lifeless, their spark snuffed out by that hateful, blasphemous Prophet.

The unrelenting surge of pain and emptiness brought waves of sobs. Someone pulled at her bound hands and drew her upward. She stood in an aimless daze, head hanging low, strands of hair stuck to her brow and cheeks, legs wobbling. Her wrists were untied, then bound again in front of her, but no struggle remained in her. A tug on the rope pulled her forward, but she kept her head down.

God in heaven . . . my Lord . . .

Her foot caught on a tree root, and she fell into a patch of dry pine cones and twigs. Her throat seized up, but there were no tears left. She couldn't surrender, though. Twelve children depended on her.

I don't want to die, Lord, but I feel as if I can't live either. I wish I could see Andreas and hug him and hear his voice.

Constanza forced a painful swallow and wiped her eyes on her sleeve. Gradually her vision cleared.

The Prophet offered her a hand. "Your sorrow will fade, dama."

Constanza winced and turned away. She wanted to throw something at him, but her strength had abandoned her.

Andreas would slay this false prophet, find her and the children, and protect them forever. But even more than Andreas, God would bring His vengeance upon all evildoers. In the end, He would destroy His enemies, including the Prophet.

From the corner of her vision, Constanza glimpsed Elionor. A lowered chin, a lingering blink, a subtle movement in her lips—in those silent gestures, she was a fellow traveler, one who understood Constanza's pain.

Constanza rose slowly and motioned for the children to follow. She set her sight ahead and started walking in a line with Elionor and the children.

7

God's eye was on you, blest and happy race!
God's hand was with you, holy men and true!
No common kindness smiled upon His face;
No common love was testified to you.
In your rude homes His presence oft ye knew;
And from the quiet of your valleys driven,
The rocks that glorious martyrdom did view,
That sealed the witness which your lives had given,
And changed the woes of earth for all the bliss of heaven.

—Robert Baird
Sketches of Protestantism in Italy, Past and Present, 1845

STIFLING FOG SATURATED THE PATH ahead of Andreas and Johan. Andreas took a bite of a freshly picked apple and picked up his pace. Home was just ahead. Soon he would hold Constanza in his arms while the children bustled around them. The barley would be ripe and ready for harvest, though the rain might delay that work for a day. *Lord, make the blight take less of the harvest than I think it will.*

Andreas turned to Johan and held up his apple core. "How far do you think I can throw this?"

"Not as far as I can." Johan wound his arm back and threw his own apple core. He shrugged when it fell near a rotten tree stump. "Cores are poor objects for a throwing contest."

Having seen Johan's core wobble in the air, Andreas nibbled more off the stem ends until his was evenly tapered. He threw it straight, and the core sailed a few paces past Johan's.

"Not fair." Johan grunted and continued walking. "If I'd thrown last, I would have done better."

Andreas tipped his hat at Johan and grinned. "I still won. We nobles are stronger than we appear."

A veil of misty rain shrouded the path, but the touch of it on Andreas's skin brought a cool, refreshing sensation. He breathed in the fragrant blend of damp hay, wild thyme, and woodsmoke. Spruces and pines covered the slopes on the left. To the right, ripe yellow fields, vibrant green pastures, and forest groves dotted the rising land. Without question, God had planted him in this valley. He had embraced the simple Christian religion of its people, suffered with its inhabitants, and married one of its daughters. Though he still yearned to teach, there was no better place in all the world to live, to build a home, and to nurture a family.

At the main crossroads of Val Angrogna, Andreas and Johan turned right, then left. Four recently built wooden houses flanked the trail, and the only sounds were a few clucking chickens and the drizzle of rain.

"All seems at peace here," Johan said as they approached Andreas's farm.

"At peace indeed." Andreas removed the sack from his shoulder and grasped Johan's arm. "Mercé, my friend. If not for you, Lorenzo and his family might have been harmed . . . or worse. It certainly wasn't the simple trip we expected, but we're home now."

"I enjoyed the extra excitement." Johan threw an arm around Andreas and slapped him hard on the shoulder. "You're a good friend, Andreas. No other man in the church would have chosen me. It feels good to be . . . remembered." He turned right, gave a short wave, and walked up the slope toward his house.

No smoke streamed from Andreas's chimney. The sun had been hot yesterday, so perhaps it was too warm to light a fire inside the house. The goats bleated furiously in the barn as he passed it. The sheep still lingered in their nighttime pen. He slowed down. It was past midday, and Constanza never forgot to usher the sheep up to the pasture. She must have assigned that duty to Silvia or Ezio, and they had forgotten.

The goats' loud bleating continued, almost as if their milking had been neglected. Andreas slung his sack over his shoulder again and jogged to the house. Where was the clamor of children cooped up inside on a rainy day? Why did no sound drift through the windows? He pushed the door open.

Two half-eaten bowls of soup sat on the table, flies buzzing around them. A pile of soiled clothes lay in the corner. Andreas breathed the lifeless air, and his pulse quickened.

He hurried to his and Constanza's bed, and though the blankets were folded, something was wrong. Not a soul had lived here for more than a day. The goats were unmilked, the sheep hungry, farm chores abandoned. The Ascendants' words from two nights before haunted him: *Already the stars have been reclaimed for the kingdom.*

Andreas spun and flew from the house. He glanced to the left, to the right, behind the barn, up the slope, at the field—nothing. The mist pelted his sweaty skin like ice crystals. He ran behind the barn, then back to the house.

"Constanza! Constanza!" He panted for breath. "Connie!"

Silence.

He ran toward the creek, his lungs ablaze. Was he simply mistaken, confused? Surely Constanza and the children were playing at the creek or washing clothes there and had forgotten about the goats and sheep. Soon he would see Constanza's warm smile, and the children would all embrace him. He would slaughter a chicken, and they would eat it tonight while he recounted stories from Pragela.

A flash of white on the ground caught his eye. He picked up Constanza's kerchief, squeezed his fingers around it, and held it to his chest. He shoved a hand through his hair, letting his hat fall to the ground. *Constanza, where are you?* Drawing the kerchief close to his face, he savored the remnants of her scent in the damp threads of linen. He folded the cloth and pushed it into his sack.

Uphill, chimney smoke trailed through the fog. That was Riccardo and Amalia's house. Surely they would know what had happened.

He bounded up the slope, wiping mist from his brow and forcing back tears. *Let them be safe, Lord. Please, let them be safe.* The barley and blight meant nothing as he sprinted through the ripe fields. Passing under the eaves of the grove, he ran toward the house he had helped Riccardo build last winter.

He pounded on the door and burst inside, not waiting for an answer. Riccardo's children sat on the floor, faces long.

"Where is your *babbo?*" Andreas asked in their native Piedmontese.

The oldest pointed to a curtain in the corner of the small room. Amalia slipped from behind it, mouth opening in surprise. "Andreas." Her voice broke. "My husband, he needs a healer. His wound is festering."

"Where is Constanza?"

"I don't know." Amalia's face tightened, and tears welled in her eyes. She covered her face with her hands. "My husband is dying." She broke down into sobs, and the children rose to gather around her.

This was the woman Constanza had witnessed to for weeks. In time, Amalia had believed the gospel, and her husband had soon after. They were part of the church now, and though the blight had wrought its harm on everyone this year, Riccardo and Amalia had remained faithful.

Yet Andreas couldn't stay here and torture her with questions. He placed his hand over his heart and nodded. "I'm sorry for what happened, Amalia. I will find help for Riccardo."

He rushed out the door and started downhill. The mist swelled to a steady rainfall as he followed the trail toward the Pavarin farm. Constanza's papà and mamà would know the facts. Perhaps his family was already there, safe and dry.

Andreas ascended the last rise below the farm. Outside the house, men, women, and children gathered in small groups. Andreas shouted as he ran, though at this distance few would understand him. "My family! Where is my family?"

A few people turned his way, but none ran to him in jubilation or called back in excitement. Estève walked toward him, no smile on his usually cheerful face.

No, Lord, please no. "Where is Constanza? Are the children with her?"

Estève bowed his head slightly.

"What happened at my farm? I need to speak to Nicolaus." Panting, Andreas stopped in front of Estève, bent over, and placed his hands on his knees.

"Nicolaus Pavarin . . ." Estève shook his head. "Nicolaus was murdered yesterday morning."

Andreas stiffened, his breath catching in his chest. His hands clenched at his sides, but Estève's words kept him rooted to the spot. "Constanza?"

"No one knows for certain. Nicolaus died trying to rescue her and the children from their captors."

Andreas's heart clenched, and his whole body tensed. He should have never traveled to Pragela. If he had been here, he could have prevented all of this.

Estève placed a hand on Andreas's shoulder. "We are all still in shock, Andreas."

"I went to Riccardo and Amalia's—"

Estève nodded. "Riccardo, David Pavarin, and Francesco Pavarin were all stabbed or cut. David and Francesco will survive, but Riccardo . . . there is nothing we can do except pray."

Andreas wanted to ask who had done this, but he already knew the answer. He unclenched his hands and gazed into the distance. Somewhere, Constanza and the children still drew breath. *Thank you, God.*

But what must they be feeling now? Had Constanza witnessed her papà's murder? Andreas yearned to hold her, to let her weep without reservation, to be her firm rock. Yet here he was, safe, while she and the children were in the greatest of perils.

From across the field, Armanda Pavarin rushed toward Andreas, two daughters and a son following her. Tears streamed down her cheeks, and her chin trembled. What could he say to the beloved wife of the fallen? She and her husband had been married for decades, but now his life was forever severed from hers.

Armanda embraced Andreas and pressed her face into his damp doublet. Her sobs came in heart-wrenching waves.

Andreas placed a hand on her head, and a few tears streamed down his face too. Anna and Gracia stood on either side of their mother, while Bartholomeo Pavarin solemnly stood behind them.

"I am sorry I missed the burial," Andreas said, barely able to form the words.

Armanda lifted her head, longing for something Andreas could not give her.

But there was something he could do, something that would bring hope to this ruinous hour. "I will find Constanza and my children, and I will not rest until they're safe again."

A spark of hope glimmered in Armanda's eyes. "I know you will, Andreas."

Gracia put her arm around Armanda and led her away. Andreas wandered under a beech tree and paced around it. Estève followed him.

Nothing felt real. Intruders had entered the valley. Nicolaus Pavarin was dead. A devilish sect had abducted Constanza and the children. The barbes needed to hear about what he and Johan had discovered in Pragela, but his family was more important.

Estève caught Andreas's arm, forcing him to stop pacing and look at him. "It was the Divine Ascendancy. The Prophet himself led them, according to David. He refused any offer from Nicolaus. Your family was his target, and Elionor Janavel was apparently caught in the tangle."

"Elionor?" Andreas scratched his beard. "She hasn't been seen in this valley for months."

"She returned a few days ago, and your wife offered her lodging."

Andreas closed his eyes for a moment, measuring his next words. "Does anyone know where the Prophet took my family?"

"Francesco said they were taken up the eastern slope."

That way was steep, heavily wooded, and seldom traveled. How could Andreas track them when they held more than a day's lead?

He shook his head in disbelief. "Why is my family the center of this prophet's supposed prophecies?"

"The news of your deeds has spread farther than you assume." Estève held up a finger. "Last month, I heard a weaver in Chambéry say your name. 'The disinherited prince of Savoy who overthrew a feudal lord.' It's rumored that the Bishop of Grenoble himself has named you the leader of the Vallenses." He let out a chuckle and placed the upheld finger on Andreas's chest. "Imagine thinking we Vallenses have such a hierarchical system and that we would name you, of all men, our leader."

Johan appeared from around the corner of the barn and ran toward Andreas and Estève. "Andreas, I heard what happened."

"I'm leaving now to find them."

Estève gripped Andreas's shoulder. "I understand this is all fresh on your heart, but you cannot be rash—"

"An evil sect has captured my entire family, monsen. I'm solely responsible for their wellbeing, even to my own demise. I have no choice but to fight for them."

Estève nodded, and his gaze softened. "Nicolaus must have been proud for such a man to marry his daughter."

Andreas braced himself. "I'll run home to pack a few supplies, then start up the eastern ridge. From there, God alone knows my path."

Estève gave Andreas a quick embrace. "May the Lord guide your steps and bring you home quickly. I'll tell the church, and we'll all be praying that you and your family return soon. But be wary, Andreas. The forces of darkness are at work, and we don't yet know the depths of their evil. If you leave, you might never return."

"You won't be going alone." Johan strolled out of the fog and stood beside Estève, arms crossed.

"This is my burden," Andreas said. "Your home is here, and I won't let you risk your life for me."

"Do you know how to track? And if it comes to it, do you know how to fight?"

"I'm a son of nobility, so of course I can hold a sword."

"I'm not staying here and waiting for you to return with your family and tell me about your triumphs. I've walked the paths up the eastern slope since I was a boy." Johan gave Andreas a half smile.

Andreas looked back to Estève for advice, but the older man bore no expression to indicate which choice was right.

"I'm traveling light," Andreas said. "I don't know where or how far I'll journey, and I might lose my own life before this is finished."

"Now that's the kind of adventure that befits me." Johan extended his arm and pointed at Andreas. "Pragela was too dull . . . and mysterious. I'm ready to meet this Prophet face-to-face. When do we leave?"

"We?" Andreas shook his head as he knelt to pick up his leather hat. He couldn't risk Johan's life—not when Johan's presence would only slow him down. Constanza and the children were at stake, and he couldn't afford to rely on anyone else. "No, Johan, this time I'm going alone."

"You think you can do everything by yourself." Johan let out a low, humorless laugh, barely more than a breath. "Let me come. I'll help you find your family, and I'll face any man who stands between you and them."

"It seems you won't accept my refusal." Andreas smiled in resignation, put on his hat, and lowered its brim. "Gather supplies for three days and meet me at the crossroads."

8

He that is down needs fear no fall;
He that is low, no pride;
He that is humble, ever shall
Have God to be his guide.

—John Bunyan
The Pilgrim's Progress, 1678

T HE FORESTED SLOPE SPRAWLED in every direction, thick with oaks seemingly as ancient as the rocks themselves. Rainwater dripped from the leaves in soft patters as the afternoon sun peeked through the gray clouds behind Andreas. The damp earth underfoot grew muddier with every step.

"This is the place." Johan squatted near a fallen tree and examined the branches. "Many little feet stamped around this area. Big ones too."

Andreas stepped over the log and bent to Johan's level. "I don't see anything."

"Pull your eyelids apart and look around you. Signs are everywhere, some small and others glaring back at you." Johan held up a stick and pointed at a bend in it. "Broken twigs—they're everywhere here, and finding them isn't hard."

A thin branch snapped under Andreas's feet. A day ago, Constanza had been here. This was where she had resisted her captors, where she had watched the hope of rescue dashed, where she had witnessed her papà's death. Had she lost hope, or was she still resisting? Were the children unhurt, or was Constanza tending to gashes and bruises?

Andreas took the branch from Johan and fiddled with it. "How do you know it's not deer or some other animal?"

"Deer are graceful when they walk through the forests. Does any of this look graceful?" Johan shifted to one knee and brushed his hand through the rotting foliage. "These leaves are either strewn about or stamped into the mud. There was a crowd here, and if you keep those eyes of yours open, you'll find where the crowd marched off." He cocked his head slightly, closed one eye, and pointed straight up the slope. "My friend, that is our trail."

As they moved up the hillside, the scent of damp moss mingled with the crisp aroma of fallen leaves in an earthy fragrance. Pines and spruces grew more numerous, standing like royal guards watching over the valley far below. Andreas stepped over and around the snaking, gnarled roots as he followed Johan.

"The trail is faint," Johan said as they approached the ridge crest, "but thankfully these Ascendants weren't concerned about our following them. They didn't leave a patch of mud undisturbed, and they snapped nearly every twig from our starting point to here."

Something gray interrupted the otherwise green and brown undergrowth. Andreas left the trail and picked up a single waterlogged shoe.

It was Roberto's. He had outgrown his old shoes, so Constanza had gathered scraps of sheepskin and crafted them into two imperfect shoes. They were meant for wearing in the barn and fields, not for long journeys. And now Roberto was tramping through the twisted forests with one shoe. Andreas opened his sack and dropped the shoe inside. Roberto would need it.

"*Perfecte*, you're using your eyes." Johan settled beside Andreas and scrutinized the ground and branches. "It looks like they rested here, which is what I need to do now too." He sat on a log and gazed in the direction they had come from.

"We can't rest when we can still follow the trail. The sun will set soon, and we'll be forced to rest anyway."

Johan slapped the log and motioned for Andreas to sit. "They're a day ahead of us, so a brief rest won't make much difference. We need a few moments to rest our legs, and I need to eat something before I fall over." He rummaged through his sack, removed a green apple, and chomped into it.

Shaking his head, Andreas went on searching for snapped twigs and bent branches himself.

"Come, sit for a moment or two. I don't want to carry your bony mass back down the ridge when you sprain an ankle, or worse, tell everyone you collapsed because you refused to stop and eat. I'm not following that trail until you sit and eat a piece of bread."

How could Johan rest when the trail was still warm? Andreas halted and turned in a slow, deliberate motion. "I can't sit on a log while those I love suffer."

"If you don't sit on that log, you'll have no strength to relieve them of their suffering." Johan took another bite of his apple and nodded toward the log. "I didn't eat for three days after my papà died. My soul was cut in a hundred places, and I refused to let God heal those wounds." His voice softened as he stared into the distance. "I tried to forget about God, and for a time, I did. Now I regret those foolish actions . . . and I'm not going to watch you take a single step down that path."

Andreas closed his eyes for a moment and inhaled deeply through his nose. Though he might not be turning his back on God, he certainly was trusting in his own strength. His shins and knees ached, while his thighs were on the verge of cramping. His arms weighed on his shoulders, and a steady throb pulsed in his upper back.

He walked to the log and sat on it, surveying the grand vista in the direction he and Johan had come from. The skies above had slowly cleared, allowing marbled sunlight to flare through the canopy of clouds. The whole Luserna Valley spread out before him like a scroll, cutting a tapering gap in the mountains. Below lay the narrow valley he called home—the place he had labored to make fruitful, peaceful, and secure.

"A year ago, I hated living down there." Johan sat next to Andreas, pulled another apple from his sack, and tossed it to him. "I thought all the excitement was elsewhere. 'Vallenses waste their lives in poverty and moralistic religion,' I thought." He rubbed his temple. "When you became one of us, I was in disbelief. Why would a man of the world turn from his merry life and join himself to such dull people?"

Andreas wiped the apple with his doublet and motioned toward the trail. "It's as if you pulled your eyelids apart, looked around, and discovered what you had overlooked."

"God opened my eyes . . . and you did too. When you refused to play Gedeon Chanforan's games and showed what it meant to be a true follower of Christ, I saw my error. I wasted a year or more chasing whatever I felt was right, but I never found satisfaction." Johan nodded toward the valley below. "But God and His people remained where they'd always been."

"Raimond Durand once told me believers like us live in other lands too." Andreas took the first bite of his apple and chewed. "I'm not talking about a place as near as Pragela either, which is still well within the Vallense sphere. Far beyond these mountains, in lands so distant they feel like a rumor, there are redeemed men and women who meet in the darkness. They recite the Holy Scriptures in a language foreign to us, sing spiritual songs of their own tradition, and gather in what they may or may not call a church."

"Do you mean to say we're not the only ones who follow the Holy Scriptures?" Johan's words carried a touch of sarcasm.

Andreas chuckled with his mouth full. "I would like to meet a foreign church someday—one that might not have heard the words *Vallense* or *barbe*."

"Let's wait until we find Connie and the children. We can talk about other adventures later."

After finishing his apple, Andreas rose, threw the core into the undergrowth, and stretched. "What can we do when we find them?"

"That's your decision, *mon amic*. I'm following the trail, but I have no grand plans for when we overtake them."

"Then let's focus on the overtaking part." Andreas turned his palm outward, motioning for Johan to follow the trail ahead.

Cresting the ridge, he turned and gazed to the west one last time. The fading daylight cast long shadows across the valley floor, but just above the majestic peaks on the other side, the sun shone with the brilliance of a thousand gemstones. Scents of pine and wildflowers permeated the mountain air, and the bells of grazing sheep clanged in the distance. Quaint hamlets nestling among green pastures, terraced fields showcasing the labor of generations, paths winding from creek to barn to meetinghouse—he took in as much as he could.

Would he see this place again?

Yet many valleys offered the same sights, sounds, and smells. In truth, what made this valley so memorable was its brave, faithful, resilient people. As Andreas turned away, he tightened his jaw and squared his shoulders. *I will bring my family safely back.*

Darkness fell upon him and Johan as they descended the other side of the ridge. With no moonlight to guide them, the trail dwindled into blackness.

"If we walk in the dark, we'll veer off the trail and never find it again." Johan loosened his belt, sat on a boulder, and removed the sack from his shoulder. "We should camp here tonight."

Andreas removed a flintstone and iron from his belongings. "I'll build a fire, at least."

"The sun will rise before you ignite anything. The wood is too damp."

"I've built a fire in worse conditions."

"Do as you please." Johan brushed away wet leaves to make a bed and lay down in it.

Andreas gathered the driest sticks he could find and set to work. The firewood soon popped and cracked in a fury as Andreas prepared a comfortable place to lie down, then curled up and closed his eyes.

A loud pop startled him awake. Glowing embers and a wispy stream of white smoke were all that remained of the fire. He gazed at the black canvas above, where each twinkling star told the story of God's unfathomable creative power. No opulent castle or rich château could match the glory of His handiwork.

Amid the expanse, a solitary streak of brilliance tore through the heavens. Perhaps Constanza had seen the same falling star. *Lord, remind her of Your nearness.*

9

It is not our way to ask each other: Where are you from? or what is your name? for we well know our blood is much sought.

—Claes de Praet
Confession before the Bailiff of Ghent, 1556

ANOTHER NIGHT ON THE COLD EARTH loomed over Constanza. A man shoved her to the ground next to the children, who huddled around her and moaned through their gags. She couldn't understand their muffled words, but their movements and expressions spoke instead: thirst, hunger, weariness, pain. Countless questions filled their eyes. *Where are we? Who are these wicked men? What happened to Papeta?*

In some awful sense, the gag relieved her of the anguish of answering.

As she lay on her back amid the harsh silence of the forest, her thoughts felt as if they had swallowed her. Her gaze absently drifted upward to the sky. Twinkling stars, normally a comfort, seemed so distant, so unreachable.

A sudden shimmer cut through the darkness. Constanza's breath hitched. The shooting star's fiery tail painted a hauntingly beautiful trail, a reminder of passing hope in an evil place.

From the shadows, three men appeared and nudged the children with their feet. "Up," one of them said.

Nearby, other men built a campfire, and one motioned for Constanza, Elionor, and the children to join them.

She wanted water for the children and bread to soothe their hunger and something to cover her head, not hollow gestures from devils. But it would do no good to resist.

As the captives rose, the men loosened the knots on the children's gags and lifted the cloths over their heads. The children smacked their lips, and then all that had been dammed up for two days and a night burst out.

"Mamà!"

"I'm thirsty. Please may I have water?"

"Where are we going, Mamà?"

Cries and sobs filled the night air like a springtime thunderstorm, drowning out their questions. The children gathered around her, while Elionor sat nearby, tears streaming down her cheeks.

One by one, the men unbound everyone's hands. The instant Constanza was free, she wiped her dirty hands on her skirts, unstuck tangled strands of hair from her face, and wiped away tears—both old and new. Another man handed her a waterskin, but she immediately passed it to Alessia, who poured the liquid into her mouth.

The children all drank some, but when the skin reached Elionor, not a drop remained. A man handed her another skin, but she held it toward Constanza. "You drink first."

Constanza shook her head. "No, I need only a little." She passed a knowing glance at Elionor's abdomen. "You need it more than I."

Elionor brought the water to her lips and drank in silence.

When Constanza at last held the skin and tipped it upward, the cool water brought a rushing relief—first her lips, then her tongue, and finally her throat. After every drop was gone, she bowed her head. *Thank You, Father, for visiting the earth and watering it.*

A man unpacked pieces of stale bread and handed them to everyone. They took their time, nibbling at each crumb and relishing every bite. Constanza used her skirts to wipe dirt from Bino's cheeks. Elionor ran her hand through Zama's knotted hair. Silvia helped with the younger children, fixing their shoes, wiping their noses, and offering warm smiles.

"Roberto only has one shoe," Silvia said to Constanza.

"I lost it yesterday, Mamà."

Constanza pulled Roberto close and hugged him. Shedding more tears seemed impossible, but somehow more still fell.

"Will Papà find us?" Roberto looked up at her, lips quivering. "I want to go home."

Constanza buried her face in Roberto's hair. Her tears dripped onto the fine strands. Fosca, Prospera, and Alessia joined them in one embrace, their sobs shattering the quiet.

But she couldn't let sorrow overwhelm her. The children needed a soothing presence, not the hopelessness that plagued her. God was still in their midst, shepherding their hearts and working through His providence. They still breathed, and they weren't seriously wounded.

Memories of Papà's death washed over her. The wicked Prophet and Papà's shocked eyes and the blood-spattered leaves—

She breathed in deeply, holding back the swelling horror. *No, God, I don't want my mind to go there. Papà lives in the eternal realm with You now.*

As she released the children and brushed her hands against her apron, the foul red flower nestled in its pocket jostled her memory. Constanza ripped out the carnation, stomped on it, and threw it into the nearby brush.

Fingers gripped her shoulder, but not a man's rough, inconsiderate hands. She rubbed her eyes, turned to the side, and blinked rapidly. Elionor wiped a tear from her own soft, caring eyes. "The ache will lessen, Connie."

"How? I watched Papà die." Constanza's chest tightened, and her jaw shook. "Every time I think about something else, those awful thoughts race back."

"I felt the same when my papà died, but in time, they relent." Elionor leaned toward Constanza's ear. "Who are these people and why are they concerned with us?"

"I don't want to think about it. Could they want us as slaves? I've heard about that before, but I thought only Saracens and Turks did such things." Constanza rubbed Alessia's back until the girl's muscles relaxed.

"They targeted us."

"Me and the children, not you."

"That might be true. Silvia and I were washing clothes in the creek when a few men approached us. They thought I was you and didn't believe me when I said my name was Elionor."

"I'm sorry you have to endure this too."

"Now that we can speak, do you think we could approach their prophet?"

Constanza tensed and shook her head.

"By now, he must know I'm not you, so he might release me. I can find help."

Before Constanza could stop her, Elionor quietly walked toward one of the men who guarded them. "May I speak to your prophet?"

Firelight flickered off the man's smooth skin as he sat still, watching her. "No one approaches the Prophet uninvited." The accent was oddly reminiscent of Andreas's, though less refined.

"Please tell him I have information he'll find useful, and that it's urgent news about"—she held a finger to her lips—"the Ascendant Kingdom."

The man leaped up from his seat and hurried toward one of the campfires without another word.

"Pietat, Elionor!" Constanza hissed. "Are you mad? We don't know anything about their kingdom."

Elionor shrugged and brushed a hand through her hair. She sat across from Constanza and leaned back on her hands. "I heard the Prophet say something about it back in the valley, so I thought it might stir these Ascendants up a bit."

"Is that what they call themselves?" Constanza asked.

"From the mouth of the Prophet himself."

Leaves rustled and sticks snapped behind Constanza. Fearing the Prophet, she clenched her fists and turned. But it was Ezio, scampering as fast as a squirrel through the darkness.

She sprang up but held her tongue. Ezio was faster than any of these Ascendants. To keep from drawing attention to him, she brushed off her skirts and returned to her seat.

The camp erupted in shouts and swishing cloaks. Footsteps pounded after Ezio.

"Let me go!" Ezio's voice echoed through the forest. "My papà will find us, then kill all of you."

His grunts and complaints drew closer until two Ascendants dropped him in front of Constanza.

Someone appeared from the shadows and stood over her. "Don't lose your children, Dama Bonomo."

Though his face was shrouded in blackness, that horrible voice was unmistakable. Bowing her head and shivering, she prayed for him to leave.

"Don't touch my mamà, you . . . *diable*!" Ezio leaped to his feet and stood face-to-face against the Prophet.

"A devil? Is that what you think I am? No, God has ordained the Divine Ascendancy to vanquish the devil, wherever he may be found, whether in a Catholic cathedral, a Vallense home, or a château of Savoy." The Prophet pushed Ezio aside and bent to Constanza's level.

She clamped her eyes shut, refusing to give him the slightest glance. The Prophet's warm breath crawled over her cheeks, an invasion that carried the stench of malice and hatred. Two fingers lifted her chin. Still she kept her eyes closed.

"If you obey me and my men, this will be a much more comfortable journey."

Heart racing and skin tingling, Constanza turned her face away from the sickening presence. Relief washed over her as he stepped backward. She opened her eyes but refused to look in his direction. Roberto, Fosca, Prospera, and Alessia clung to her and trembled, while murmurs of fear resonated among the other children.

"Why have you taken us?" Elionor's firmness demanded an answer. "What do you want?"

"Your submission and cooperation," the Prophet answered. "And the news you mentioned to my men."

"I . . . have no news."

"A lying wretch, as I expected." The Prophet caught sight of Elionor's abdomen, and his mouth opened slightly. "Oh, I see your news. 'And she being with child cried, travailing in birth, and pained to be delivered.'"

Elionor gasped and turned her head away.

John's Apocalypse. Why had he recited that portion of it?

The Prophet turned back to Constanza and regarded her with a twisted calmness. "That man in the forest—he was your father, I assume. It is a pity he attacked me."

"He did no such thing." Constanza could take no more. "My papà was the kindest man on earth, and I promise you, he's never attacked a soul."

He glared back at her. "The little bird speaks now. Such acute words from so delicate a creature."

Constanza shuddered. She glanced to the left, then the right, where forest surrounded them. If she outran the Ascendants, she might find someone nearby who could help.

But she couldn't leave the children. She flicked the thought away and focused on the Prophet again. "My husband won't stop until he finds us. He'll track us down and . . ."

Words lodged in her throat. When Andreas found them, what could he do? He couldn't raise an army to fight these Ascendants, and his only allies were peasant farmers. Her lip twitched as confidence drained from her.

The Prophet moved toward her, his lips curling in amusement. "Then may Andreas de Bonomo arrive quickly, for I have desired to meet him for many months."

"My husband has no ill will toward you. We are simple people who want nothing except to live in peace and worship God freely." A tear of desperation wound its way down her cheek. "Please let us go. Please, monsen."

"The prophecies are already in motion, and your purpose is predestined."

"My purpose? My children's purpose? We are innocent!"

"Ah, innocence—such an abused, misunderstood word. No, your destiny is woven into something far grander than you understand." He gazed at his followers and swept his hand toward the surrounding campfires. After a few whispers to the nearby men, he marched off to the other side of the camp.

Soon ten or more Ascendants surrounded Constanza, Elionor, and the children, blocking any chance of an escape. One built a little fire near the children, but when tenderhearted Silvia tried to thank him, he ignored her.

Outside the perimeter of the encampment, the trees rustled with a fervor, the night concealing its secrets among the leaves and branches. What was this place? They had traveled hastily, continually poked and prodded to walk faster, until the familiar mountains near home faded into distant gray silhouettes. For the most part, they had walked through forests and fields, and they hadn't passed through a single village.

How would Andreas find them in these unfamiliar lands? Had he even returned home from Pragela yet? Constanza prayed rage wouldn't consume him when he discovered their abduction, but at the same time, she asked God to give him strength and determination.

The night wore on, and the Ascendants remained tight lipped, their intentions veiled in shadow. The campfires dwindled, men snored, and the children slept soundly around Constanza. At least she still had them and Elionor. But the

Prophet's voice, his eyes—each time she drifted to sleep, that man and his disciples haunted her dreams.

At some late hour in the night, or perhaps near sunrise, another light whisked through the heavens. Constanza gazed in wonder. Then another star fell.

Alessia nestled closer. "Did you see it, Mamà?"

"Yes, a shooting star, a wonder of the heavens."

"Have you seen one before?"

A soft smile tugged at the corner of Constanza's lips as she traced the glittering pathways. "Many times." Her mind wandered back to the summer nights spent in the high pastures, sitting on Papà's lap while he pointed out the patterns in the starry sky. The memory brought back the sounds of bleating sheep, the fragrant scent of clover, the echoing hoots of *chòtas*.

Oh, how she longed to relive those moments with Papà—to feel the warmth of his embrace, to hold his large hand again as he guided her up the terraces, to listen to his teaching about the marvels of God's creation.

Papà's words echoed through the pastures in her mind. *Look, Connie, we have visitors tonight. Shooting stars, but they're not ordinary travelers. They're like whispers from God, dancing across the sky to remind us of the beauty and mystery of His works. Each one carries a story, a promise as it pierces the darkness.*

"What's wrong, Mamà?" Alessia kissed Constanza on the cheek.

Constanza sniffled and wiped away a tear. Papà had changed from a spectator of the sky to an active participant in the worship of God. "I miss my Papà."

Alessia laid her head on Constanza's shoulder and held her hand. "I wish my papà were here."

"I do too."

"When are we going home?"

"Soon, I pray. Your papà will find us, and when he does, all will be well again."

"Papà is very strong. And he fights with a sword!"

"He can, but his true strength lies elsewhere. He trusts in God, and that's where all of us need to find strength."

"Me? I'm still little."

"'Seek the LORD, and his strength: seek his face evermore.' Remember when we learned that?"

"I forgot already."

"Then let's practice right now."

"At night?" Alessia yawned. "I'm tired."

"We'll practice tomorrow, then."

"Will they put that rag in my mouth again?"

"I hope not, but even if they do, God will guide us through it."

Alessia snuggled close and yawned again. "*T'aimi*, Mamà."

"*T'aimi tanben*, Alessia." Constanza closed her eyes and drew in a long breath. So much had changed in less than a year. Now a child, one of twelve, called her mamà and said "I love you."

*   *   *

A sharp tap on her arm pulled Constanza from the haze of sleep. "Up, everyone up."

The hollow whisper jostled Constanza back to the present as she peeled her eyes open. The sky above was still dim with the pale gray of dawn. The scent of damp earth and crushed grass filled her senses, and the ground's chill seeped through her chemise. Children yawned and groaned as they rose from their beds of dirt and leaves.

Constanza stood and stretched, and a blunt ache pulsed from her lower back to her shoulders. To sleep outside on soft grass was one thing, but the hard forest floor offered just enough nighttime comfort to make the rest of the day uncomfortable.

Her stomach rumbled, and her parched throat yearned for relief. Some of the Ascendants knelt near fallen trees or boulders, heads bowed, faces covered with both hands, lips moving in silence. Their religion was false, but they were devout. There she stood, a believer in the true religion of Christ and His apostles, and she hadn't offered a single word to God. She closed her eyes. *Thank you, Lord, for rest . . . and the promise of eternal salvation.*

Soon the Ascendants bound Constanza, Elionor, and the children's hands again, but thankfully, none were gagged.

"Will we eat anything this morning?" Elionor asked one of the men. "Or do you at least have water for the children?"

"Midday," the Ascendant said.

"We're all parched." Constanza closed the distance between them. "We can't go without food and water until midday."

He turned away without a reply, and the march began. Onward they plodded, with the Prophet leading atop his horse. The forest thinned into a sheep pasture, and the familiar scents lent Constanza a trace of refreshment. The rising sun flooded the field with warm light and cast long shadows at its far edge.

But those shadows were not of trees or hills. They were of men. Many men.

Scores of leather-clad soldiers stood two deep at the edge of the field, some bearing shields and all holding weapons. Red banners on long poles snapped in the morning breeze. That standard—it was the same one the Savoyard soldiers had carried when they stamped out the crusade two years ago and helped free Andreas from the inquisitor. They were saved!

Hissing commands to his Ascendants, the Prophet wheeled his horse to the side and flung a hood over his head. Though heavily outnumbered, he still rode tall and confident.

A gray horse galloped across the field, bearing a rider in a long red cape. He unsheathed his sword as he pulled back on the reins. His thick golden locks swirled in the wind, tousled by the sporadic gusts. The rider turned toward Constanza.

Her breath caught in her throat. The pronounced jawline, the straight nose, the strong neck—it was Andreas and yet . . . not. He had to be one of Andreas's brothers.

An Ascendant pushed Constanza to the ground. "Remain here."

The children gathered around her.

All at once and in perfect cadence, the soldiers advanced. Three Ascendants remained with the captives, but the Prophet pressed most of them into a ragged line, blocking Constanza's view of the soldiers and the rider with the red cape. She stood and peered past the Ascendants, but someone shoved her back to the ground from behind.

Men shouted and grunted. Metal slammed against metal. Four soldiers broke through the line of Ascendants, swords arcing right and left. They slew one Ascendant, then another and another. Constanza gathered the children closer and mouthed a prayer for protection and deliverance.

The ground beneath her thrummed with a horse's steps. She looked up.

The Prophet gave her a measured look and nodded once. In his hand he twirled a broken red carnation. "Until our destinies entwine once more, Dama Bonomo."

He cued his horse and galloped away. In what felt like an instant, the Ascendants were gone. Constanza stood and gazed at the wide field, the lofty peaks, the vast blue sky. They were free. Soon they would be home, cooking, milking goats, washing clothes. The children stood around her and cheered.

Elionor sighed deeply at the fast-approaching Savoyard troops. "Is this Andreas's doing?" She smiled at Constanza. "How convenient to have a noble lord as a husband."

"Yes, but it's the Lord of heaven who has delivered us." Constanza beckoned the children closer with a nod. "See what God has done? Look around. Do you see any more evil men?"

"Who are these soldiers?" Guido asked, looking around.

Constanza sighed and softly said, "Our rescuers."

The soldiers approached and soon surrounded them. One with wavy deep brown hair drew a knife and freed Constanza's hands. "Bonjorn, dama. I am Lugotenent Elias Renaud. You're safe now."

The rest of the soldiers followed his lead, using swords and knives to cut the other ropes.

"That was the Divine Ascendancy." The lugotenent's voice was hushed yet kind, and his accent reminded her of Andreas. "They've spread through the realm like *la pesta*." He dropped the ropes, sheathed the knife, and brushed off his hands. "Why did they hold you hostage?"

"I don't know, Lugotenent. They mentioned something about a prophecy, and it might have something to do with my husband."

Elias worked on Guido's bonds next, but Guido stared at the sheathed sword at the officer's side. "Is that real? My papà knows how to sword fight, but he doesn't have a sword."

"Is he a man-at-arms like me?" Elias gave Guido a jesting smile. "Or a common criminal?"

"No, monsen, Papà is the son of the duke."

"The son of the duke?" Elias chuckled and pointed at the red-caped rider galloping toward them. "Lord Philip is my commander. He's also the son of Duke Louis."

The rider guided his horse into their midst and dismounted effortlessly. No man in Val Angrogna could ride like that. He held his head high and walked with the haughty grace only a true nobleman must be capable of.

Constanza bowed and motioned for the children to follow her example. "Mercé, my lord. Those men captured my children and me, as well as my friend. They are murderers, and they killed—"

"Who is this?" the caped man asked one of the soldiers behind him.

"My lord, I am not familiar—"

"Then ask her!"

Zama reached for Constanza's hand and held it.

Constanza rose from her bow, keeping her hands clasped tightly at her waist. "My name is Constanza de Bonomo of Val Angrogna."

Philip tugged at the girth strap and patted the horse's mane. "You are my brother Andreas's lover, then?"

"Lord Andreas of Savoy is my husband."

"I've heard rumors, but now I see her with my own eyes." Philip laughed with his mouth closed and shook his head. "What is your name again?"

"Constanza, my lord."

Philip's sharp gaze swept over her. "A true shepherd girl, as I had guessed. Thank the Blessed Virgin I found you before those madmen did who knows what to you." He flipped a lock of his hair back and tucked it behind his ear.

Constanza laughed inwardly. *Qual pretié, what a dainty man who's never seen the back of a plow.*

"The Bishop of Turin himself approached me last night about the mob marching through the countryside, and it so happened my men and I were on our way to—" He shifted his weight to one leg as a smile played on his lips. "As you can observe, divine providence has allowed our paths to cross."

"As I said, mercé for freeing us."

"Indeed . . . freeing." Philip eyed the ground, then waved one of the soldiers to him. "Bring food and water for Constanza and this other peasant woman—"

"Elionor, my friend."

"Indeed, but do not interrupt me." Philip turned to the children. "What are all these wretches?"

"My sons and daughters. Silvia, Ezio—"

Philip let out a hearty laugh. "All yours, are they? Shepherdesses do start young. Did Andreas accept them all as his own? Or perhaps a few are his illegitimates too."

Constanza wrinkled her nose but held her tongue. How could a man who so resembled Andreas be so brash and vulgar? If she weren't related to him, she would slap both of his smooth cheeks. "May I be dismissed now, my lord?"

"I was only jesting with you. Of course you may be dismissed." Philip briefly tightened his fingers on the horse's reins. A knowing smile formed at the corners of his mouth. "But first you will be my guests for a short time in Thonon upon Lac Léman."

"We are going home, where Andreas surely awaits me."

"Oh, he won't stay there for long. I hear my father, the duke, has sent numerous commands to Andreas, but your . . . husband has answered none of them."

"Andreas holds no ill will toward you or any of his family, but he wants no part of the intrigue and backstabbing. He surrendered his position and cares nothing for riches or power."

"Yet he allies himself with Amadeus and his French witch, Yolande." Philip's nostrils flared. "Was it not Andreas who overthrew Gedeon Chanforan, the man whom I appointed as the Lord of Luserna? Don't tell me Andreas has forsaken his noble lineage. He is as conniving as ever." Philip called out to his men. "Feed the women and children. Afterward, rebind their hands."

"Wait!" Constanza advanced toward Philip, but a soldier blocked her path. "We've done nothing to offend you!"

"I mean no offense to you personally, Constanza, but Andreas has taken sides against me. Your presence will be necessary for me to achieve my desires. I need Andreas to follow me, and your family will be the bait."

"Release the children, at least . . . and Elionor. They have nothing to do with this."

"A peasant woman commands me?" Philip spat on the ground, then recoiled at the sight of the children. "I do despise whelps. They are nothing but loud, disgusting, inquisitive attention seekers. Taking them across the mountains will wear on my patience, but I doubt you would agree to leaving them alone here with those mad heretics roaming about."

"If you ask Andreas, he'll give you what you want."

"My desires lie on the shores of a faraway lake, and with your cooperation, Andreas will assist me in gaining those desires." Philip flashed a crooked smile and gave a small wave of his hand. "Or else he will never again gaze upon his mistress and her brood."

"I am Andreas's wife." Constanza flicked a tear from her cheek and scowled at Philip. "And an honorable woman."

Philip spun from her and motioned for one of his men. "Feed and water them but keep them in the center as we march. I can't have any of them thinking escape is an option."

The children whimpered and wept as soldiers wrapped ropes around their hands again, but none resisted. These soldiers were all broad shouldered and well armed. Resistance would be foolhardy. The dark-haired officer, Lugotenent Renaud, gently bound Elionor's hands but said nothing to her.

A hundred or more soldiers soon formed into rows of four, then into a column. As Philip had commanded, Constanza, Elionor, and the children were directed to the center and surrounded. They marched out of the field and into a thin birch forest. Through the foliage, sun glittered off a broad body of water.

Elionor parted her lips in amazement and gazed at the expanse. "Have you ever seen so much water in one place?"

The lugotenent answered her without turning. "Would you believe that's a small lake, dama?"

"I am . . . unmarried, monsen."

"Then where I'm from, I'd call you *Demoisèla* . . ."

He paused as if waiting for her name. Elionor tugged at her bodice and didn't finish his sentence.

"I hail from Thonon," the lugotenent said. "It sits on a cliff above a lake so vast that whether you look left or right, you see only blue water."

As they came out of the forest, Constanza stared at the water and couldn't picture a lake more vast. Truly, she had seen only a pinch of this immense world. But the familiar places were drifting farther and farther away, and before her lay foreign lands and strange tongues and men of unknown reputation.

Scores of tents covered the open land near the lake. Trails of smoke rose from dwindling campfires, and the scent of roasting mutton made Constanza's mouth water. The soldiers guided the women and children to a campfire and untied their hands.

Elionor sat next to Constanza and shook her head. "At least they're more hospitable than the Ascendants."

"Still, Lord Philip binds us with these ropes. I pray Andreas finds us soon, because this tramping around Piedmont is wearing on us."

As she spoke, a soldier brought them a pail of water and a ladle. "Fresh from the stream."

Another set a steaming pot near the campfire. "This will be all you eat until tomorrow, and we're not carrying it with us."

Constanza widened her eyes at the delicious sight and brushed her hands on her skirts. "Children, let's wash our hands in the lake and come back quickly."

"No, that's not allowed," said a stout soldier, glowering across the fire at them. "Stay here."

Constanza held her hands out toward him. "We slept on the ground for two nights, and this same dirt has been on our hands for three days."

"Let them go to the lake," Lugotenent Renaud said from behind them. "There are a hundred of us, Jòrdi. Or are you afraid they'll outrun you?"

Jòrdi huffed and heaved himself up from the ground. "Follow me, then."

Splashing the cool water onto her face gave Constanza a refreshing breath of life. She scrubbed her forehead and vigorously rubbed her hands together, then helped the children wash their faces and hands. With everyone somewhat cleaner, she ushered the children back to the campfire.

After Constanza offered thanksgiving for their food, she and Elionor served the children. No one complained about the lack of salt or the slimy fat or the chewy gristle. They emptied the pot of meat, chewed the remnants from the bones, and drank every drop of the broth.

Meanwhile, most of the soldiers packed tents and belongings into sacks, but a few stood guard nearby. "How old do you think the shorter one is?" Jòrdi asked another soldier, pointing his nose toward Elionor.

"Twenty, I'd say. She's fresh and plump too."

"Seems another man found her first. See her belly?"

Elionor had picked up a piece of lamb, but her hand froze midway to her mouth. Shame surged to her cheeks and stained them crimson. She bowed her head and picked at the morsel.

Constanza rose, hardening her gaze as she fixed it on Jòrdi. "How dare you speak to an honorable woman like that!"

"An honorable woman, you say?" Jòrdi scratched his scraggly beard, shifted his weight to one leg, and pointed at Constanza. "What does that make you, woman?" He looked to the other soldier. "I can't figure it out, Antonin—how could *na bela petiòta* like this one birth such a brood as we see here?"

Constanza's cheeks warmed, the satisfaction of the meal dissolving in an instant. Ezio moved in front of her, fists clenched.

"The mother certainly is a pretty one." Antonin sauntered toward Constanza.

"See her?" Jòrdi asked. "She acts shocked, as if she's never heard a compliment."

"My husband is the only man who can compliment me like that."

Antonin turned from side to side, mocking her. "I don't see a husband anywhere."

"He'll meet you soon enough, and when he does—"

"Now the mother makes threats," Antonin said. "Don't fret, dama. I would never steal another man's wife. But your maidservant—I heard her say she has no husband."

Constanza took small steps backward, and the children clustered around her. "Elionor is my friend, not my servant, and if you dare look at her—"

"What will you do?" Jòrdi said. "None here would stand against me."

"I would." A kind and familiar voice rose from behind the soldier. Lugotenent Renaud threw a sack off his shoulder and dropped it on the ground. Jaw set, he gripped his sword hilt and strode toward Jòrdi and Antonin. "I'll slice your throats if you say another word to these women. Slink back to your place in line."

"Lugotenent Renaud, always spoiling our bit of jesting," Antonin said. "I'd wager he bears his tale to Lord Philip too."

Jòrdi faced the lugotenent and sneered. "Philip's lapdog."

Lugotenent Renaud stared back and revealed a sliver of his sword. "Insubordinate swine."

"Mind your neck, Lugotenent." Jòrdi snarled and followed Antonin toward the band of soldiers forming nearby.

Lugotenent Renaud watched the men leave, then turned to the women. *"Je suis désolé, les djanas."*

Elionor gave him a curious look. "I don't know that phrase, Lugotenent."

"Ah, it's from Savoy, from where I hail. I mean to say, I'm sorry, *bones femes.* I don't know how you say that in Piedmont."

"Mi dispias in Piedmontese," Elionor said, averting her gaze from the lugotenent.

"But we're from the mountains," Constanza said, "and there we say *sèi desolat,* similar to your Savoyard."

Elionor bowed her head toward Elias. "Mercé, Lugotenent—"

"Elias Renaud."

"Earlier you asked my name. It's Elionor Janavel of Val Angrogna."

"Val Angrogna," the lugotenent said, slow and pondering. He walked back to his sack and heaved it onto his shoulder. "Jòrdi and Antonin won't bother you again. If others behave like weasels, I'll be nearby." He tipped his head toward them, but his gaze lingered a little longer on Elionor.

Commands were shouted out to break camp, and all the soldiers obeyed. With tents packed and lines formed, the troop set off. Philip galloped up from the rear and placed himself in the lead. They skirted the shores of the lake, then passed an even larger one. The sun's rays warmed Constanza's face as the column entered a deep valley. Far to the left, perched atop a tall mountain, stood a haunting Catholic church.

Andreas's stories flowed into her mind—a gray monastery overlooking a sweeping valley, towering mountains surrounding it on all sides. That must be

Sacra di San Michele, where Andreas had once been a monk. Its dark silhouette against the skies was so unlike the man she loved. God had truly saved him from that empty life and had made him a new man.

Thank You, Lord, for my strong, loyal husband. Guide him to us, but keep him safe.

10

But I dare to say, for it happens to be true,
That all the popes there have been since Sylvester until the present
        one,
And all the cardinals, and all the bishops, and all the abbots,
All these together do not have enough power
To be able to forgive a single mortal sin.
God alone can forgive, since no one else can do so.

—*The Noble Lesson*, lines 410–415

THE WINDING TRAIL LED ANDREAS AND JOHAN through moss-covered forests and foggy glades. Other than the squirrels, rabbits, and birds, no other life showed itself in these wild, hilly woodlands.

"Where are we?" Andreas asked as they crested a rise. "If this hilltop were not so crowded with trees, I might be able to discern our whereabouts."

Johan stopped and stuck his walking stick in the earth. "I've never walked through these woods until now. When I was a boy, there were tales about what lay over the eastern slopes—everything from man-eating giants to papist monks. Of course, the monks scared us most." He winked at Andreas and pointed left. "If you want to spy out the land, we might find a break in the woods over there."

"No, we can't lose this trail. How far ahead of us are they?"

"We haven't seen a campsite yet, so they must have marched through the night."

Andreas puffed air out of his nostrils. "Are we gaining on them in the slightest?"

"I'd guess we are. How fast can twelve children, two women, and a few crazed sectarians march?"

Andreas gazed ahead, hands on his hips. "Faster than I had expected."

Up rocky knolls, across shallow creeks, and around bends in the landscape, he and Johan trudged through the rugged hills until they overlooked a narrow valley dotted with houses and ripe fields. Andreas placed one foot on top of a rock and tightened his boot.

"Feels like we were just here." Johan sat on a boulder and gazed down into the valley.

"That's because we were. On our way back from Pragela two days ago, we followed the Chisone River down there." Andreas tucked the leather strap into the boot and dropped next to Johan. "Yet it seems like a year ago."

"We should've just camped down there a few nights and waited." Johan leaned forward on his elbows and chuckled. "Can you imagine the sight, Andreas? We set up camp for the night, knowing next to nothing about prophets or Ascendants, and down the path walk a score of them, carrying your Connie and the children somewhere."

"Then I would have wished for a sword, shield, and crossbow."

"Which you don't know how to use."

"*Bensur!* Of course I do."

"Show me." Johan leaned over, found a crooked stick, and tossed it to him.

Andreas grabbed the stick, twirled it once in his hand, and threw it into the brush. "I know we need rest, but this is certainly not the time for play." He stood and pointed to the trail heading downhill. "Their footsteps are still here."

"Excellente, you're learning—slowly, but you're grasping it."

The trail switched back and forth down the steep slope, crossed a pasture of grazing sheep, and ended at a cobblestone path that followed the river's course.

"Left or right?" Andreas reached for a stone and threw it into the river.

"Either, or they could have just as easily crossed the river."

White water churned into itself and cascaded over jagged rocks with no sign of a ford in sight. "I doubt they tried to cross here."

"Then it's either up the valley toward Pragela again or right toward Pinerolo and Turin."

Andreas peered left, where layers of ridges rose higher and higher into the distant west. "Pragela would make the most sense, but it's a desolate hamlet." To the right, the valley emptied out into the rolling Piedmontese plains. "They might have turned toward Pinerolo, and from there, anywhere else east or north of here." He removed his hat and ran a hand through his hair. *Dear God, where am I supposed to turn?* "Can we find their trail on the cobblestone?"

"Impossible. Scores of feet plod down this path every day, and we won't see the difference between your family's and anyone else's."

The morning fog dissolved into wisps that soon vanished, but the distance between Andreas and his family seemed no smaller than yesterday. Left might be the right choice, but how would he know if the Ascendants had veered off over a narrow mountain pass or continued on the same road into the Dauphiné? If the Ascendants had turned right, choosing the road to Pragela would send Andreas in the opposite direction. He couldn't rely on his instinct, not when his family's lives were at stake.

"Johan, I don't know where to turn."

"Then it's across the river and into the face of that cliff ahead." A pinch of sarcasm laced Johan's words. "Didn't Solomon say 'Turn not to the right hand nor to the left: remove thy foot from evil'?"

Andreas's lips twitched as he tried to hold back a smile. "That was perhaps the worst application of the Scriptures I've ever heard, and I say that as a Savoyard prince raised in popery."

"You're the one who won't decide." Johan threw his hands up. "You don't want to return home, do you?"

"God alone knows the path." Andreas knelt on one knee and bowed his head. Johan knelt beside him, and together they prayed for guidance. Andreas stood and brushed off his knee.

Someone nearby was bound to have seen a score of brown-cloaked men tramping past with two woman and twelve children. Far more valuable than the word of a stranger, though, would be information from someone who had an interest in the realm's comings and goings. Andreas turned right and nodded downriver. "Miradolo."

"What's Miradolo?"

"One of my family's summer residences."

"'One of my family's summer residences,'" Johan said, bobbing his head from side to side as he playfully mocked Andreas's accent. He punched Andreas's shoulder and cackled. "Only a spoiled noble boy would say that. Who among us can say *summer residence*, let alone one of a number? Meanwhile, we peasants are perfectly content with God giving us a roof and a little hearth."

"And gathered around that hearth, a wife, sons, and daughters, listening to you recount the parables of Jesus Christ." Andreas closed his eyes and sighed, then opened them. "I wouldn't trade my life in Val Angrogna for all the lands and castles in Savoy."

The spirited gleam in Johan's eyes softened, giving way to pensiveness. His lips settled into a thoughtful line, and the corners of his mouth relaxed. "You're the best man I know, and I do look up to you."

Andreas looked toward the horizon and sighed. "This is all because of me and the past I cannot escape. I warned Constanza that marrying me could bring danger to her, but how could I guess a mad sect would abduct her? When we chose to adopt the children, we did so because we loved them and because it was our duty as Christians. They were the ones the world had cast aside, the ones whom no one wanted. Yet my being their papà has placed them in far graver danger than they were in before. Have I been too rash, even selfish?"

"No, and you're a fool for thinking it." Johan grabbed Andreas's shoulder and waited for Andreas to look up at him. "Yes, you might sometimes dart ahead like a falcon chasing its prey, but I admire that, as every good man should."

"Then to Miradolo it is." Andreas pulled the last good apple from his sack and took a bite from it before slinging the sack back over his shoulder.

Johan picked up his sack more slowly. "Does the duke live there?"

"No, my brother Amadeus, firstborn and heir to the duchy."

"Yes, Amadeus. Gedeon Chanforan used to grit his teeth whenever someone mentioned that name."

"Powerful men despise Amadeus." Andreas's boots scuffed against the uneven cobblestone. "Much like my father and mother, Amadeus is seen as weak and controlled by his wife, Yolande. True as that might be, there's more to it than what the commoners see."

"Doesn't Amadeus live near Turin?"

"I heard Moncalieri is under renovations, so Amadeus and Yolande are living at Miradolo until the work is complete."

"Moncalieri, Miradolo, Montefrolico—all for our wealthy rulers' pleasure and funded by us peasants."

"Montefrolico?"

"It sounds like a lord's residence, no?"

"Be kind to them, Johan. Without Yolande's gold florins, we would have never found the Greek New Testament. And don't forget, it was Amadeus's soldiers who rid our valley of inquisitors."

Johan's scraping footsteps slowed. "Those are days I'd rather forget. So many tears . . . so much suffering."

"There are days when I wish I could forget too." Andreas waved Johan closer and gave him a hard slap on the back. "Today we need wisdom we don't possess. Amadeus and Yolande will have heard about the Divine Ascendancy, and they might point us toward my family."

Two other faces entered his mind as he spoke. "I also have friends there who can help."

* * *

The castle's silhouette loomed against the backdrop of rolling hills. The formidable structure, composed of sturdy stone walls and two circular towers, stood proud and commanding. Though it didn't possess the grandeur of Moncalieri, Miradolo Castle exuded an aura of impregnability akin to a younger brother striving to assert himself over the elder. A straight path guided Andreas and Johan closer and led them to an imposing gatehouse where armed guards stood vigilant.

Nearing the entrance, Andreas scrutinized the intricate stonework. Etched and carved into the facade above the narrow, arched windows were symbols of the House of Savoy: the quartered shield of its coat of arms, the cross of the Knights of the Holy Sepulchre, the drops of blood that symbolized courage in battle. He set his shoulders and pushed his chin forward, but the sense of pride fled as swiftly as it had entered. Though Savoy was in his blood, it was no longer who he was.

Sounds of industry emanated from inside—the clang of metal from the forge, the distant murmur of servants attending to their duties. Life bustled in Miradolo's walls more than ever, likely because the heir of the Duchy of Savoy had planted himself there.

Johan held out his hands and eyed his garments. "They'll let us enter looking like this?"

"I think so, but if not, I can show them my—" Andreas slumped his shoulders. "I forgot my signet ring at the house. Someone here other than Amadeus and Yolande is bound to know us, though."

"What about that French soldier friend of yours?"

"If Yolande is here, Basile will be standing at her side. Convincing the guards to let us close enough to see even Basile, much less Amadeus, is what makes this challenging." Andreas removed his hat and walked toward the gatehouse.

A guard blocked the path five paces from the gate and studied him. "Hail, stranger. What business have you here?"

Andreas's first tactic was to speak in French, seldom spoken in Savoy other than among the nobility. *"Je requiers une audience avec Monsieur Basile Halphen."*

The guard who stood in the path waved the other guard forward. "Do you speak French, René?"

"No, but Basile—"

"That's who this man is asking for." The guard took a step toward Andreas, keeping an eye on Johan too.

"I can speak Romaunt if you wish. I'm here to see Basile Halphen. Please tell him that Andreas de Bonomo is here to see him."

"No one sees anyone from the court or their servants unless summoned."

Andreas threw back his shoulders and pointed at the guards. "If Basile or Princess Consort Yolande or even Prince Amadeus himself knew I was here, they would command you to give me entrance."

"You're nothing but a vagrant." The guard chuckled, spat on the ground, and turned back toward his post.

Johan reached out and grabbed the guard's shoulder. "Monsen, my friend here is Lord Andreas of Savoy, and he's here to see his brother, Prince Amadeus."

Cringing, Andreas gazed sideways at Johan. Did he have any sense of formality or respect? No peasant would mention the names of his lords so flippantly.

The guard looked twice at Andreas and smirked. "I've never heard of a Lord Andreas. You two are mad. Now step back from the gate before I jab you with my sword."

"My friend isn't lying, and I will prove it to you, as long as you're permitted to carry a message to the princess consort herself." Andreas caught himself bowing his head. What could be less convincing than that? And his words certainly hadn't sounded like a lord's, for nobles never asked—they commanded. That life seemed so far away, though. He wasn't ready to act like a haughty prince.

The guard gave Andreas an odd look. "René, come here."

The other guard scurried forward and stood straight beside the first.

"I'll throw you in the cesspit if you're lying," the guard said to Andreas. "What's your message for the princess consort?"

It was risky, but there was one thing that would easily spark Yolande's curiosity. "Simply tell her I seek the pearl of highest price. My name isn't necessary—she will know."

Long moments passed before the guard returned to the gatehouse. With deliberate precision, he grasped the iron handle, his calloused hands betraying years of service. He was the type of servant every lord coveted. "You weren't lying, my lord. Forgive me for having troubled you."

Andreas gave him a short nod. "You performed your duty well enough."

The gates, adorned with a labyrinth of metalwork, creaked ominously as the guard applied pressure. With practiced motion, he eased the heavy doors ajar, revealing the inner courtyard, bathed in the soft glow of the setting sun. The guards ushered Andreas and Johan past a bubbling fountain and under a stone arch.

"Humbert, *merci* for escorting them." Yolande slipped from behind a bush of yellow roses and nodded toward the guards. "You are dismissed."

"My brother." Amadeus stood nearby under the canopy of an exotic tree. He set a pair of shears on a stone bench, brushed his hands on his coat, and walked toward Andreas. Though his skin was still pale, it carried more color than it had last spring.

Andreas bowed low as Amadeus approached. "You look well, brother."

"My wife and everyone else in the court inform me otherwise."

As Yolande approached, she held her right hand out toward Andreas. After kissing it, Andreas motioned for Johan to do the same.

"I have to do that?" Johan whispered, but loud enough for them all to hear.

A light laugh rose from Yolande. "Customs among us nobles, I'm afraid. If I were a peasant, how would you greet me, Monsieur . . ."

"Johan Lauras of Val Angrogna . . . my lady." He cleared his throat, wiped his forehead, and fidgeted with his cloak. "You're a lady, so I would bow and say *bon vespre.*" He did exactly that as he spoke.

"That will suffice, Johan Lauras of Val Angrogna. If you are a friend of Andreas, you are welcome in this house."

Loud footsteps echoed through the courtyard, and from the back corner emerged a middle-aged man. Basile Halphen marched to Yolande, shoulders set and jaw firm. "*Ma maîtresse,* I heard you allowed a guest—" He caught sight of Andreas, and his countenance lifted. "The guards let everyone into the castle this time of year! Andreas, it's a pleasure to see you!"

Basile embraced Andreas and gave him a few hard slaps on the back, then held him at arm's length while he inspected Johan more intently. "*Bonjour à nouveau,* Johan Lauras. The last time I saw you was with a crossbow. That was a risky shot with all those people around, but a necessary one."

Andreas spread his feet to shoulder width. "Unfortunately, I'm not here for the niceties of a reunion. My wife and my children were abducted from my home two days ago."

Amadeus furrowed his eyebrows, then released them. "Who would do such a thing?"

"The Divine Ascendancy. Do you know of them?"

Amadeus's usually quiet voice rose. "I became acquainted with that group only yesterday. An informant appeared here and told us about intruders wandering through the countryside, heading north toward Val di Susa."

"They're not the only intruders in Piedmont, I'm afraid." Basile scratched the top of his head and glanced at Andreas. "Your brother Lord Philip is in Piedmont now, with a hundred of the duke's best men-at-arms."

"I know. Johan and I saw them a week ago in the Luserna Valley."

"Directly under our noses. We didn't know they were in the principality until they had already camped here for three days. *Apparemment,* they were marching for the king of France to pay the doge of Genoa a visit . . . and take the city. I don't believe it, though. I am convinced Philip means to sack us here at Miradolo. He wants Amadeus dead so he can be named heir."

Amadeus picked a rose and held it to his nose. "Except that yesterday Philip and his troops marched past Miradolo, heading north. Bishop de Romagnano met him outside the gate, and for once it seemed Philip was cordial."

"He stays in Piedmont for a week, then he leaves?" Andreas stared off into the distance for a moment. "Why does he march north?"

"He wouldn't say, but after the bishop told him about the marauders, he vowed his troops would scatter them."

Andreas's breath caught, and his heart lifted. "If Philip overtakes them, he will save my family. Where were the Ascendants last seen?"

"Bishop de Romagnano would know." Amadeus peered toward a pear tree and slid his tongue under his top lip. "Odd, he was here with us before you entered the gardens."

"He said he had matters to attend to elsewhere," Yolande said, reaching into a pouch at her waist.

"*Effectivement étrange,*" Basile said to Andreas, tapping his foot on the ground. "You and the bishop always had a kind of friendship, and he should have wanted to see you."

Johan scratched the back of his neck and shook his head. "Something's crooked."

"Where would Bishop de Romagnano have scampered off to?" Andreas asked Basile.

"The tavern in Pinerolo, most likely."

Andreas nodded to Johan. "Then that's where we go next."

"I will accompany you," Basile said, stepping forward. "I need to know when there are traitors in our midst."

Andreas bid adieu to Amadeus and Yolande, then led Basile and Johan out of the garden.

Yolande caught Andreas's arm near the gate. "Wait." She placed a booklet in his palm and closed his fingers around it. "This belongs to you."

Andreas opened the front cover but already knew what it was—the tattered Bible that Raimond had given him before the barbe's martyrdom. "No, it's for you to read, Yolande."

"I have read most of it," she whispered. "Some might call me a heretic for reading it, which is why I have spoken to no one of its existence. It seems so *étrange* to me—the Word of God in the common tongue. I have many questions, and perhaps someday we could speak of such things."

Andreas discreetly placed the Bible in his sack. "The Greek manuscript . . . I still have it."

"Your people may return it when they are finished with it."

"Merci, Yolande. Merci."

"I pray you soon find your *belle épouse*."

Andreas bowed his head toward her one last time before turning away. Johan and Basile followed him through the gate and onto the cobblestone road that led to Pinerolo.

* * *

Andreas crossed the threshold of the tavern doorway, a familiar creak of wood underfoot as he entered. The air hung thick with the scent of sweat, ale, and hearth smoke, which swirled around him as he scanned the dimly lit room.

"How does anyone suffer it in here?" Johan stopped beside him, blinking rapidly and sniffling.

"Ah, the sensation of stale ale burning your tongue and throat," Andreas said. "In time you leave the same way you entered, whether you stumble out or the innkeeper throws your drunken body into the muck." Across the room, the innkeeper filled a cup to the brim. "Wine is undeniably a mocker. I miss the taste on occasion, perhaps even the dulled senses. But I'm in Christ now, and old things have passed away."

Basile crossed his arms. "I don't see him."

Andreas looked from one corner to another, searching for the bishop's stocky figure amid the clusters of locals and travelers. The raucous voices and thudding wooden cups reverberated against the rough-hewn walls, creating an atmosphere tinged with camaraderie and merriment. A fire crackled in the stone hearth.

Two hooded figures were nestled in the far corner, their whispers inaudible over the tavern's din. Andreas elbowed Basile and subtly pointed his nose toward the corner.

With measured steps, he navigated the maze of tables. Uneven floorboards tilted and shifted under his boots, while the tavern's rhythmic pulse coursed through his feet.

Johan tapped Andreas's shoulder and pointed at two patrons who ate steaming bowls of hearty soup at a nearby table. "After we find this bishop, that's what we're doing. We haven't eaten a hot meal in a week."

Andreas let out a short laugh, but by the time he glanced back at the corner table, one of the hooded men had vanished.

The lingering aroma of roasted meats and vegetables mingled with the scent of damp wood, invoking memories of his last visit here. Over two years had passed since that providential day. The tavern and its ale had seemed so welcoming after the humiliating trial in the abbey and the resulting banishment from the Benedictine Order. Then, on his way to spy on the Vallenses, he had selfishly ignored a family of needy refugees, which had brought an overwhelming sense of guilt he had planned to wash away with a few drinks of a strong ale. He was thankful now that his plans had been interrupted.

A thickset man approached the innkeeper at the edge of Andreas's vision. Andreas turned.

There stood Bishop de Romagnano, near the same spot he had been two years ago. That night, Andreas had evaded the bishop, not wishing for his family to discover his banishment from the monastery.

But now Andreas strode toward him with his chin up, his gaze locked on the man clad in unmistakable ecclesiastical garb.

The bishop widened his eyes and shifted his posture. Unease flickered across his face. He edged away while maintaining the facade of casual conversation with the innkeeper.

Johan's and Basile's footsteps rumbled behind Andreas. A hush fell over the tavern. The bishop shuffled backward and scanned the tavern's periphery.

Basile moved to the door and stood before it like a marble wall, while Johan swung to the left to block any attempt at escape.

Andreas moved to within arm's length. The bishop's hand trembled as he made the sign of the cross. "Andreas, my son . . . I heard you were at Miradolo." He leaned in for an embrace, but Andreas sidestepped him.

"Why did you leave so soon, dominus?" Andreas crossed his arms. "I heard you met with an informant and my brother Philip yesterday."

"Indeed, it was a small matter of court politics." His gaze wandered over Andreas's shoulder toward the door. "The Feast of Our Lady of Sorrows is today."

"I wasn't aware." Andreas curled his fingers.

"There is a Mass I must attend—"

"First I have a few questions."

The bishop tried to step around Andreas, but Basile pushed forward to block his path. "You're staying here until we're finished."

"You have no authority over me, Basile Halphen. I'll tell the princess consort—"

"What? That you would not answer the questions of her loyal servant, who places her every interest above his own?"

Again the bishop tried to pass, but this time Andreas's sidestep obstructed him.

"I am the Bishop of Turin, with power bestowed by the Holy See itself. I demand you—"

Andreas shoved him into the wall. His family's lives were at stake, and he couldn't waste words with this man. "I thought we had an understanding."

"You are both a madman and a heretic, Andreas of Savoy."

Still holding Bishop de Romagnano against the wall, Andreas scanned the room. Most of the laughter had ceased, and all eyes were on him and the bishop. They had drawn far too much attention. He could hear the rumors now: *A heretic Vallense pinned the Bishop of Turin to a wall and threatened him.* Gradually Andreas loosened his hold.

Basile took his place, grabbing Bishop de Romagnano by his cassock and dragging him through the door. "This is business of the House of Savoy," he shouted to the onlookers. "You need not worry about your bishop's safety."

Once outside, Basile heaved the bishop into an alley. Dimly lit lanterns cast a soft amber glow, illuminating the cobblestone streets and casting shadows along the walls of the nearby buildings.

"By the Blessed Virgin, what is the meaning of this?" the bishop asked.

Andreas pushed him against a stone wall and clenched his right fist. "What do you know about my wife and children?"

"By striking me, you would place yourself at the mercy of the Holy Church of Saints Peter and Paul."

Standing beside Andreas, Basile shoved the bishop's shoulder. "And betraying the crown prince of Savoy would be sentencing yourself to death."

"The pope would never permit it."

Andreas yanked the bishop from the wall, then threw him back against it and held him there. "I will not waste my time prattling with you, dominus. Whatever I must do to extract your secrets, I shall do it."

"Yesterday . . ." The bishop bit his lip and recoiled from Basile. "I swear, I remain loyal to the House of Savoy."

Basile grunted. "That remains to be proven."

"What do you know about the Divine Ascendancy?" Andreas asked.

"It is a millenarian sect."

"I know that." Andreas lowered his fist. "What do they want with me and my family?"

"There are rumors. I heard them a month or more ago. Their prophet is a power-hungry subverter. He clings to a prophecy from the book of Revelation about a crown consisting of twelve stars. When the stars are reclaimed and the crown is cast down, then he says his kingdom will ascend." The bishop stared at Andreas. "Do you see the resemblance? Twelve stars, twelve children?"

Andreas loosened his hold on the bishop. "How do you know all of this?"

"As I said, there are rumors, and it is my duty to know all the various religious factions and dissenters in this diocese. I had almost forgotten about it until an informant appeared at Miradolo."

"Who was this informant friend of yours?" Basile asked.

"It is a matter of the Holy Catholic Church and is of no concern to the House of Savoy."

Basile reached into his coat, brandished a knife, and held it to the bishop's throat. "Speak, Bishop."

"He . . . he is only an acquaintance."

"Name?"

"I do not know." The bishop pushed against Basile's arm, but to no avail.

"An acquaintance whose name you do not know. How cordial." Basile flung the bishop's arm aside. "Tell us everything, or all of Pinerolo will mourn your death tomorrow."

"The Ascendants . . . he said they had captured Andreas's wife and twelve children."

"And why did he tell you this?"

The bishop shot a glance at Andreas, then at the ground. "So Lord Philip could rescue them, which he likely has by now."

Andreas closed his eyes and let out a long breath. *Thank You, Lord, that they are at least alive.*

"Now, may I please excuse myself so I can make my way to the cathedral?" The bishop shuddered.

"So many lies," Johan said from over Andreas's shoulder. "Don't let him go, Basile."

Andreas leaned close to Bishop de Romagnano. "You're saying that if I wait here, Philip will return with my family?"

"This is a complicated matter, Andreas, and one that would take all night to explain."

Basile smirked. "My blade and I can wait that long."

"First assure me of my safety."

"That's for the House of Savoy to decide," Basile said.

"Please, can you at least sheathe your knife?"

Basile pressed the bishop tighter against the wall and lowered his knife. "Tell us everything."

"Philip is a capable leader—more than the duke, and far more than Amadeus. Savoy has become a weak duchy with inept rulers, and I would have it restored to the glory your grandfather built, Andreas."

Basile leaned closer and whispered, "Traitor."

"Tell me what has happened to my family." Andreas clenched his teeth. "Politics are not my concern, dominus."

"Politics are indeed your concern. They concern everyone, from the pope in his palace to the peasant in the poorhouse. As a son of the duke, you do not have the privilege of being unconcerned." The bishop thrust out his chin. "By now, your wife and children are probably in Philip's custody."

"In his custody? I thought he was rescuing them. Where are they?"

Bishop de Romagnano's eyes met Andreas's, a flicker of apology shimmering within their depths. His brows furrowed slightly, and a subtle downturn formed on his lips. "Thonon."

"Thonon. That's a half-month journey, most of it through the highest mountains in Europe." Andreas's thoughts drifted back to his evening of hunting deer with Johan a week ago—the cloaked man, the deserters, the crown of seven stars. The hooded man was the Prophet. What had he said? *Next month in Thonon, all will come to pass exactly as the prophecy has foretold.*

The Prophet had told some of Philip's soldiers to meet him at the lakes of Avigliana in seven days. Andreas counted back the days. *Today is seven.* At least Andreas knew where his family was headed. But why would the Prophet abduct Constanza and the children only to give them to Philip?

"Lord Philip wants your family as a ransom," the Bishop said. "He means them no harm, but until you forfeit your rights to the duchy and back his own claims, he will keep them in Thonon."

"You concocted this entire scheme when you heard Andreas's family had been captured?" Basile's voice grew tense. "Instead of simply rescuing them from these Ascendants, you advised Philip to take them as hostages. What a virtuous man you are."

"No, it was the informant's idea. I only relayed the plan to Lord Philip."

"He's not lying." Andreas drew his brows together. "Bishop de Romagnano isn't intelligent enough to craft such a plot."

"If you want to find your family, meet Philip in Thonon. This should be a simple matter—"

"I could have done all that here in Piedmont. Why does my fool of a brother insist on dragging my family across the Alps to make me sign a few pieces of parchment?"

"He wants to be named your father's heir, and that cannot be done in this backwater principality. His legitimacy lies at the duchy's heart, and that is where he needs your assistance."

"Philip is the third son," Andreas said. "Before him is not only me but also Amadeus. What hope does he have of becoming the duke?"

"Lord Philip needs your support against your mother, against your father, and"—he flicked a wary glance at Basile—"especially against Prince Amadeus and Yolande."

Basile seethed beside Andreas. "You'll be hanged for sedition."

"You promised me safety."

"I did no such thing, nor would I for a thousand-thousand gold florins." Basile seized the bishop's arm and pressed the knife against his neck again. "I should cut you here and let you bleed out like the *poulet* you are."

"I need to find my family." Andreas held Basile back, eyeing the bishop. "Which path is Philip taking over the mountains?"

The bishop's rueful gaze bore a sincerity that begged for Andreas's forgiveness. "Lord Philip should have found your family this morning near the lakes of Avigliana. From there, he will likely take the pass at Mont Cenis, or perhaps he'll traverse one of the passes of Saint Bernard. Your pursuit is precisely what he wants, though, for he knows you will seek your family."

Andreas's heart leaped. His family was only a day ahead of him, and he could close that distance quickly. "We leave tonight."

Johan replied with a quick nod.

"And tonight," Basile said, "the bishop will be thrown into the holding cell below Miradolo." He pulled Bishop de Romagnano from the alley and led him onto the road.

Andreas followed Basile. "We could use your expertise . . . and your sword."

"I must remain here to protect Prince Amadeus and my maîtresse. Besides, if I stood face-to-face with that *usurpateur* Philip, he would no longer have a head atop his neck. But I will certainly pray for your quick success, *mon ami*."

After a parting adieu to Basile, Andreas and Johan slipped through the shadowed alleys of Pinerolo. The hushed murmurs of the town gradually faded, and the cobblestone streets, still warm from the day's sun, now cooled beneath the moonless sky.

Pinerolo's silhouette receded behind them, and the distant shadow of the Alps loomed ahead as if awaiting their arrival. As Andreas walked beneath the landscape of countless stars, the sounds of night surrounded him—the howl of a wolf, the rustle of leaves stirred by a gust of wind. Guided by bright Polaris, he and Johan pressed northward into the night.

11

There is many a thing which the world calls disappointment; but there is no such thing in the dictionary of faith. What to others are disappointments are to believers intimations of the will of God.

—John Newton
The Works of John Newton, 1820

AFTER A SHORT NIGHT OF REST somewhere north of Pinerolo, Andreas and Johan set off again. With Constanza and the children only a day ahead, Andreas could overtake them within two or three days—so long as he and Johan made haste. They passed through sleepy towns and hamlets as they followed the shadow of the western foothills. The sun warmed Andreas's cheeks, and a few drops of sweat beaded on his forehead.

In an open field, Johan discovered signs of horses, then a few brown cloaks and, under them, decaying bodies. This must have been where Philip confronted the Prophet and his followers. At least Andreas could negotiate with Philip rather than battling the raving cultists himself. But why would the Prophet plan his own defeat at the exact time and place he had predicted?

At midday, Andreas gazed over the first of the lakes of Avigliana. Three women washed clothes in the shallows, and ducks sat atop the calm surface of the water, dipping their heads underwater for a meal. Pine-covered mountains rose to the left. Far beyond them, through the fading haze, stood lofty gray peaks that scraped the clouds.

"Is that Mont Cenis?" Johan asked, blocking the sun with his hand.

"I don't know its name, but it's not Mont Cenis. First we'll round these green mountains on the left, and after a day of journeying through Val di Susa, we'll climb the pass at Mont Cenis. Yet I pray we'll find Philip before then."

Skirting the edge of the lakes, Andreas and Johan passed through the village of Avigliana and turned left into Val di Susa. In the distance, bathed in afternoon light, Sacra di San Michele stood like a sentinel atop Mount Pirchiriano. Its presence dominated the expansive valley, its towers reaching toward the heavens as a silent testament to centuries of religious ritual.

The abbey reminded him of his former life—a life of empty works, of unforgiven sin, of unquenchable fear. But God had saved him, forgiven him, and set him on a new path of Christian service. The sun, at his back now, cast its warm rays across the fertile valley and pointed Andreas and Johan on toward Mont Cenis, which came into view at the head of the valley.

"Do you have anything to eat?" Johan asked as they plodded down the cobblestone road. "I ate my last piece of bread this morning."

"I have an apple with a few rotten spots on it, but there's a village up ahead where we can buy more provisions. A day's worth should be enough."

"How many ducats did you bring?"

"None, only two grossi and thirty quattrini."

"Couldn't you have asked your wealthy brother back at Miradolo for a few coins? Or you could've swiped some from the bishop when you had him pinned against the wall."

Andreas looked down his nose at Johan.

"*Era una blaga, tranqui!* It was a joke, so relax."

The bustling streets of Saint Ambrogio throbbed with life. Stalls teemed with goods, and animated chatter filled the air. With Johan at his side, Andreas walked into the village square, trying to blend into the crowd and staying alert for any sign of recognition.

Johan squinted at Andreas and swiveled his palms upward. "Why are you so vexed?"

"I see too many familiar faces here." The memories of raucous nights at the tavern haunted Andreas—nights when he drowned his guilt and fear in red wine. "I was the drunken monk from the abbey, and the whole village knew it."

"No robes, no shaven spot on your head, no smooth cheeks." Johan tightened his lips and shook his head. "No one will recognize you."

Yet the shame of the past he so desperately wished to leave behind still gripped Andreas. He ducked away from faces and refused to meet anyone's eyes. A hushed conversation here, a pointed gaze there—any interaction might hold rumors of his sinful history. "I can't stay here, Johan. We should have skipped Saint Ambrogio and searched for food in the next village."

Johan placed a hand on his shoulder. "We all have sins we wish we could forget—I as much as anyone."

"Why do I still feel so guilty? God has forgiven me of my sins, but I wish He would cleanse my mind of those memories." Sighing, Andreas gazed far up the cliffs, where the abbey loomed like a monstrous *gàrgola*. "At the time it was all merriment and laughter, but now I see through the haze. I was a wretched sinner."

"In need of a Savior," Johan said. "'For all have sinned and come short of the glory of God.'"

"'Being justified freely by his grace through the redemption that is in Christ Jesus.'" Andreas finished the thought from Paul's epistle to the Romans. "'Whom God hath set forth to be a propitiation through faith in his blood, to declare his righteousness for the remission of sins that are past, through the forbearance of God.'"

"Mirabell!" Johan nodded along. "I learned those words as a child, but where did a papist like you memorize them?"

"A month ago, while Constanza and I were checking the Romaunt Bible with the Greek one, we learned that portion together."

"She already knew it and was being kind."

"You're probably right." Andreas peered through the haze at the distant gray peak. Were Constanza and the children crossing the mountains now? Or perhaps they were in the same valley, only a short distance ahead. He itched to confirm they had passed through here.

He moved carefully through the market, still hiding his face. Familiar men stood near the stalls: the baker who delivered bread to the abbey, the butcher whom Andreas had drunk with at the tavern, the wineseller who procured barrels from the monastery vineyards. Johan could easily ask about his family in his stead, but then Andreas remembered something the barbe Raimond had once told him.

Andreas stopped. "We might have a friend in Saint Ambrogio—someone who's not one of my old tavern friends."

Johan slackened his mouth, eyeing Andreas curiously.

"I've never met her personally—"

"What are you thinking, my friend? A woman's home?"

"A widow . . . I don't recall her name, but she's a fellow believer." Andreas waved Johan out of the bustle of the market. "Follow me."

The widow's house stood apart from the market, its weathered exterior nudging Andreas's memory toward that life-altering moment over two years ago—the scoffing onlookers, the two black-clad inquisitors, the accusations. He hesitated before knocking, uncertain of what to say.

The door creaked open. The aged widow seemed to sense his urgency before Andreas could open his mouth. *"Bon-a sèira, viandanti,"* she said in Piedmontese. "What brings you to my doorstep?"

"I am Andreas de Bonomo, and this is my friend Johan Lauras. Once I knew Raimond—"

"Please, come into my house, please." The distinctly Piedmontese way she formed the sentence highlighted her graciousness. She guided them to a sitting area and smiled at Andreas. "I am called Lidia. Your name precedes you, Andreas. I have heard much about you, including how Barbe Raimond left you sleeping on my doorstep once." She beamed. "For many years, I have prayed for the monks at Sacra di San Michele, and at last, here standing in my home is God's answer to my prayers."

Andreas swallowed hard. "I'm . . . honored, *madama*."

"A barbe passed through here a few weeks ago—Bertran. Do you know him?"

"Indeed, Bertran is a good friend from the same church as Johan and I."

Lidia pointed to a pair of chairs, inviting the men to sit. She rushed to a table, picked up a loaf of bread, and tore off pieces for them.

"*Nò*, we didn't mean to disturb your evening." Andreas remained standing. "Johan and I simply wanted to ask if you had seen Savoyard men-at-arms marching through the valley in the past day."

"*Sì*. Soldiers, only this morning. They were marching west."

Andreas's heart skipped a beat. "Were there two women with them . . . and children?"

Forehead creasing, Lidia paused. "Nò, I only recall seeing soldiers. I was gathering eggs when they passed and didn't pay them much heed." She slumped her shoulders and shook her head. "Always, men march through our valley, off to fight another war for their emperor or king or duke or count."

"My wife and children march with that army. I'm trying to reach them, though they're probably at Mont Cenis by now." Andreas offered her a bow before walking to the door. "*Mersì*, Lidia. I wish Providence permitted us to visit longer—"

Lidia hurried to a chest and grabbed five or six ripe pears, two loaves of bread, and a small wheel of cheese. "Take these, and don't let me keep you any longer. I shall pray for you, and when you're on your way home with your precious family, don't hesitate to stop here, whether you're in need of a meal or a night of lodging. *La mia ca 'l'é toa*. My house is yours."

Andreas helped Johan pack the provisions and led the way to the Via Francigena, the valley's main westward road. Somewhere beneath the shadows of the looming mountains ahead, his family awaited him.

*　*　*

Andreas's muscles strained with each step the next morning. The ascent into the pass demanded unwavering determination as the narrow path wound its way up the mountainside. The air, thin and biting, stung his lungs as if the Lord Himself sought to test his resolve.

Johan followed in silence, his boots crunching on gravel and loose stones. The towering cliff cast shadows that altered with every shift of the billowy clouds. The trickle of a nearby stream blended with the cry of a hawk circling high overhead.

Traders hauling everything from wooden furniture to wine casks to barrels of olive oil navigated the challenging descent as Andreas and Johan ascended. Near the midpoint of the path, a rugged figure guided a mule cart up the winding path. The creaking wooden wheels reverberated through the quiet as the mules strained against the load of heavy salt sacks. The driver, weathered by wind and sun, gripped the worn reins with calloused hands, squinting against the glare of the intense sunlight.

Panting, Johan raised his hand. "I need to rest. The air . . . I can't breathe in enough of it."

"We still have quite a distance to the top." Andreas turned and walked back to Johan. "Keep moving. Don't stop."

"How many times have you crossed here?" Johan sat on the stony ground, raised his knees, and laid his head on them.

"Here at Mont Cenis?" Andreas unslung his sack and set it on the ground. "I suppose seven crossings, the last when I committed myself to the Order of Saint Benedict and journeyed to the abbey. There are other crossings too, some less challenging than others. To the north are the two Saint Bernard passes, and to the south is Montgenèvre, which is the easiest pass but the least direct."

Johan lifted his head and picked up a rock, then tossed it up and caught it. "You think we'll find them before sunset?"

"I can't imagine not overtaking them today. This ascent has been difficult enough for us, so think how it must be for Alessia and Roberto or even the older children. Constanza and Elionor can't carry all of them." He peered ahead at the trail that continued to snake higher. "They might be up there right now."

"What will you say to your brother?"

"Whatever I must to see my family safe. Does he want me to forfeit my rights? I'll do it. If he needs my allegiance, for whatever that gains him, I'll grant it. These courtly intrigues are of no interest to me. To kiss my wife, to embrace my children, to harvest my fields—that's all I want." Andreas picked up his sack and helped Johan to his feet. "I'll give Philip what he wants, then go home to my hearth and my church."

After a deep breath, he fixed his gaze ahead and set off. The trail, carved by the ancients but worn by time and weather, revealed the wild beauty of the Alps. A relentless wind poured through the mountain gaps, carrying tales of travelers who had not survived this passage.

The higher he and Johan climbed, the more treacherous the terrain became. Narrow ledges clung precariously to the steep slopes and challenged Andreas's balance. The air grew thinner and colder with every breath.

The trail switched back and forth eight more times before it finally crested onto a wide plateau set amid snow-covered summits. A lake of clear, brilliant blue dominated the center of the plateau, and several small stone buildings flanked the lakeshore.

Andreas turned toward the path he had just finished. The ascent had taken half the day, but they had done it. As he turned back to the lake, a smile played at the corners of his lips—the reunion was mere moments away.

A red banner flitted in the breeze. His limbs lightened, and the weariness drained from his body. "Look, Johan, next to that hospice up ahead."

Johan sighed. "Water."

"No, the flag and those soldiers. We've found them!" Andreas waved Johan forward and sprinted toward the lake, searching for Constanza's light blue skirts, her billowing white sleeves, her white kerchief. With no immediate sign of her, he scanned the shoreline for evidence of children.

But all he saw were five Savoyard men-at-arms, likely the column's rear guard. One soldier stood and shielded his eyes from the sun as Andreas approached. The man picked up a spear that leaned against the hospice wall and held it with both hands. "Hail, traveler!"

Breathless, Andreas halted three paces from the soldiers and slumped over, clutching his knees for support. *"Bon après-midi, messieurs."*

"It's two quattrini to cross Mont Cenis." The soldier held out his hand.

Andreas stood straight, and his head lightened. "Lord Philip of Savoy . . . your commander . . . I must speak with him."

"Philip is a usurper, and if you've seen him, we would like to know."

"He should have passed through here today . . . with a hundred men-at-arms . . . and a woman and her children."

"Impossible. We've been stationed in this wasteland for six weeks, and I've seen no force greater than ten."

Johan stumbled up next to Andreas and struggled for breath. "Are they here?"

"We've seen only pilgrims and mule carts today," said the guard. "No soldiers, no women, no children."

The alpine landscape spun around Andreas in a mocking dance of gray and white. His fingers tingled as the blood drained from them, and his legs shook. As his vision blurred and his senses dimmed, the urge to sit overwhelmed him. But the ground offered no respite, only unforgiving gravel. Constanza—

Gradually, his eyelids flickered open, and a clear blue sky unfolded before him. He lay upon the ground, fine gravel molding around his body.

"Andreas." Johan sat beside him and offered a piece of bread. "You fainted."

"I did?" He propped himself up on his elbows. The sky tilted above him. "I don't think that's happened to me before. How long have I been here?"

"Not long, though I think we shouldn't keep going today." Johan pointed his nose at the stone structure to the left, where a half dozen soldiers sat on stools, carrying on a boisterous conversation. "The hospice has room for tonight."

"We can't. Constanza and the children—"

"They're not here, Andreas, and they never were. We guessed wrong."

"Lidia back in Saint Ambrogio—she saw soldiers marching west."

"We never asked how many there were. Whoever she saw must not have been them."

Andreas surged upright and gazed at the lake. The late-afternoon sun sparkled off its surface, yet he felt none of its warmth as he sat in the gravel, shivering.

"I'm a fool. I assumed Philip would cross here, and I've based every shred of evidence since Pinerolo on that." Andreas bowed his head. "We've lost at least a full day."

Johan spread his arms. "We can still catch them, even if it takes a bit longer."

"If we retraced our steps out of Val di Susa, we'd still have to brave one of the other passes. The closest is at least a four-day journey from here, and they all carry the same chance of failure. But I can't stop now." Andreas pulled himself to his feet, but the mountains spun again.

Johan grabbed his shoulder with one hand and offered him bread with the other. "Bread, water, rest—that's what you need now. We've barely stopped in three days."

"At least we know where Philip is taking my family." Andreas took the bread from Johan, then a waterskin. "The journey to Thonon will take a *quinzèna*—fifteen whole days and nights. You should return home, Johan. I can manage the rest of the journey on my own."

Johan let go of him and backed away. Andreas dropped the waterskin and wobbled on his heels. Johan caught him. "What were you saying?"

"It's the air up here—"

"I see that. It makes your legs weak and your mind weaker." Johan helped Andreas back to the ground and opened his sack again. "But do you know what's stronger than ever? Your stubborn, foolish will." He broke off a piece of cheese and tossed it in Andreas's direction.

Andreas snagged it with one hand and swiftly placed it in his mouth. The blend of salty and creamy flavors left him craving more.

"Besides, I don't go backward." Johan tossed Andreas another piece of cheese. "Only forward."

"Mercé, Johan. I can't promise an easy journey, but Lord willing, we'll be gazing over Lac Léman before the leaves fall." Andreas finished his piece of cheese and looked up at the towering peak to the right. "Thonon awaits us."

12

I shall temper so justice with mercy.

—John Milton
Paradise Lost, 1667

THE COOL MOUNTAIN BREEZE BRUSHED Constanza's cheeks as she plodded down the trail, so narrow that soldiers, women, and children walked in a single snaking line led by the haughty Lord Philip. Not once since the lake had he so much as acknowledged her or the children. Instead he rode atop his steed like a king who disdained his subjects.

The scent of pine mingled with the crisp air. Constanza's worn boots crunched on the pine needles strewn across the path, each step a reminder of the arduous journey she, Elionor, and the children had endured over the last ten days—five marching to the mountains and another five crossing the pass.

At a sharp curve in the ever-switching trail, Alessia stumbled and grabbed Constanza's skirts. "Umile keeps pushing me, Mamà."

Constanza turned slightly and caught Umile's sheepish smile.

"Alessia is too slow," he said, "and Guido is pushing my back too."

She peered farther back in line and, for what felt like the thousandth time, counted the children. But she couldn't stop walking, or the whole line would stop. The soldiers would curse at them or shove them from behind or yank them forward.

Alessia, Umile, Roberto. She looked back but nearly tripped over a tree root. Bino, Fosca, Ezio, Irene, Ave, Silvia. A forward glance realigned her footsteps. Zama, Prospera, Guido. And bringing up the rear of the line was Elionor. Silently Constanza repeated the same words she had prayed for the past ten days. *Thank You, God, for bringing us this far. Preserve us in the day ahead.*

Despite the long, treacherous crossing of the Great Saint Bernard Pass, God had protected them. Two days ago, at the crest of the mountains where the air was thin and cold, they had even been blessed with a full night indoors—the Hospice of Saint Bernard, the soldiers called it. Philip, of course, had taken the best room in the monastery, but Lugotenent Renaud had secured a room with plenty of pallets, warm blankets, a roaring hearth, and enough steaming vegetable stew to soothe all their bellies.

Now, as Constanza descended the washed-out trail, memories of the frigid heights faded, replaced by the sight of a long, fertile valley unfolding below. It was a welcome change from the unyielding rocks and sparse trees. A distant town with smoke streaming from its chimneys was nestled into the head of the valley. Were they almost to Thonon? That question had plagued everyone since the soldiers had abducted them.

But Constanza couldn't dwell there. The answer might drag her soul down into the mud again.

The path widened, and before Constanza realized it, a child held each of her hands. Though the trail still descended, the bends were no longer as numerous nor as steep. She breathed in deeply, taking in the fresh air. It felt different from home—purer, but also wilder.

Elionor lagged behind, struggling to keep pace. Children clamored around her, but her eyes remained dull and her face was traced with sadness. Constanza slowed to walk next to her. "How can I help you?"

Elionor brushed her fingers against the rough bark of a tree and steadied herself. "I need to eat something . . . and sit for a moment."

"Can you walk a little farther?"

Elionor nodded.

"How long have you felt like this?"

"I think it started last week, not long before the Ascendants came."

Constanza touched Elionor's shoulder and smiled. "I still have a few pieces of bread from the hospice, if that would help."

"Please, if you could spare a little. I always feel stronger when my belly isn't empty."

Constanza opened her pocket and gave a piece of bread to Elionor. As she fidgeted with the fringe of her bodice, she eyed Elionor's abdomen. What should she say? She had wanted to say something for days now but could never find the opportunity. The children had begun chasing one another along the trail and gathering odd-shaped stones. Constanza took a deep breath and cleared her throat. "I know, Elionor."

"What?"

"I know you're with child."

Elionor cast her gaze down. "I was planning to tell you." She pulled at the front of her dress and whispered, "I felt the quickening for the first time the day after the soldiers found us, and it's continued ever since."

Constanza's breath hitched. Elionor's form bore witness to the fact, but to hear it confirmed from her own lips made Constanza's pulse quicken. "When will . . . the child be born?"

"In the spring, I think." Elionor tapped her belly lightly. "I never thought it would be like this, you know. Remember when we were girls and we pretended to be mothers?"

Constanza nodded. "I always wanted the most children—fifteen, if I recall."

"It seems you're well on your way." Elionor formed a subtle smile and nodded toward the twelve children walking ahead of them. "But we always pretended to have husbands too."

"Yes, a handsome man who could plow the fields with strength that rivaled Mount Vandalino and would love God with all his heart and carve love notes into the oaks and whisper promises of forever."

"You still remember that?" Elionor chuckled, but with little mirth. "That was a wonderful dream. And I know God has fulfilled it for you." She looked straight at Constanza. "I've sinned and have done so in the most horrible way you can imagine."

Constanza blinked rapidly. She had warned Elionor about her waywardness last summer, but what had Elionor done? Run away, forsaken Christ, and only the Lord knew what else. Constanza sighed and nodded toward Silvia, who held Prospera's hand a few paces ahead of them. "She saw how you romanced Brando at the market," Constanza said, barely opening her mouth. "Is he the father?"

Elionor hesitated, then nodded.

"Are you married?" The words came out with more of a hiss than she intended.

Elionor closed her mouth and shook her head.

For the past two weeks, Constanza had tried to envision this conversation, but that hadn't prepared her for experiencing the truth. Elionor Janavel—her dearest friend, her trusted confidant, the woman who was near a sister—was an unmarried mother.

"I was in love with Brando," Elionor said, "and I thought he was in love with me. When I left your parents' home last autumn, I stayed with my mamà for a time. But I was restless. I felt like I was letting my life slip away into meaninglessness."

"You should have told me how you felt. You could have talked to your—"

"Papà? He was dead, killed in a pointless skirmish with the inquisitors. The man I loved the most in this world wasn't there when I wavered . . . and fell."

The raw wound from her own papà's death suddenly tore through Constanza. Was Papà truly gone forever? She wouldn't find him on the terrace pruning fruit trees. He wouldn't finish building that new fence in the upper pasture. God had given her a husband to confide in, but Elionor didn't have even that.

"You have always been so good, such a righteous Vallense girl." Elionor stared into the distance. "I tried, and for my whole life I've wanted to be like all the other girls. But my blood, the sins of my parents and grandparents and probably further back than that, haunted me." She rolled her sleeves to her elbows. "I didn't go to Brando immediately—I wasn't that bold. I journeyed to where I was from, to the village where Monsen Raimond found me sixteen years ago. I wanted to see who I actually was, to find the people who knew me before I came to the mountains."

"Where did you go?"

"Chivasso, which is down the River Po from Turin. I searched for the few places I could remember. The barn where I used to sleep is gone, as well as the old villa nearby. My aunt's house is occupied by someone else. The tavern was the only place still the same." Elionor dipped her head. "No one there remembered me or cared who I was. No one knew my father or my mother. I was nothing to them, the same as when I was a miserable child begging for a morsel of bread. I left and soon returned to Val Angrogna. That's when I heard you and Andreas were to be married."

"I saw you there, but you left before I could greet you."

"You were so happy and in love." A tear streamed down Elionor's cheek. "How could I interrupt the moment you had dreamed about? I saw your smile when Andreas draped the pure white ribbon over your shoulder. Without a doubt, he's your man who plows the fields with the strength of Mount Vandalino, loves God with all his heart, carves love notes into the oaks, and whispers promises of forever."

Those simple, girlish words nearly brought Constanza's heartbeat to a halt. Andreas was all of those things, and oh, how she wished he were here. His strength would have carried her through the mountains; his will would have inspired her forward; his love would have sacrificed all for her. From what Philip had said, she would see Andreas soon. But when? When could she wrap her arms around him, pour out all her sorrows about Papà, and weep with the man she had given her whole soul?

She gave Elionor a long look. "Why did you leave Brando?"

"He already had a wife, Connie." Elionor's voice, layered with guilt, drew the eyes of curious children in their direction.

"Silvia, Guido, mind the path," Constanza said.

Elionor drew closer until her elbow touched Constanza's. "I didn't know Brando was married. I met him secretly for several weeks, waiting for the day he would ask me to go before a priest with him. I was ready to marry him, ready to raise our child together. When I told him about the child, he became belligerent. 'My wife . . . she lives in Bibiana,' he said. 'I already have a son, and if my wife heard of you or this child—' From there he denied the child was his, and then he left me."

A tear traced a solitary path down Constanza's cheek. Would it not be so easy, so natural, to condemn Elionor for her actions? A twinge of guilt gnawed at her conscience as unbidden thoughts of her own self-righteousness surfaced. *I'm a sinner too and need God's mercy just as much.* "I'm sorry for what he did to you, Ellie."

"There's no need for you to apologize, and I'm not worthy of your pity." Elionor brushed her cheeks with her sleeve and sniffled. "My relationship with Brando—it was as much my sin as his. He might be a lying scoundrel of the vilest sort, but in the end it was my choice. I could have resisted the temptation, but I surrendered to my lust. I've confessed my sins before God a hundred times and know He's forgiven me, but I'll bear the results of my actions for the rest of my years. Last week, I came to your home because you were the only one who I knew would take me in."

"Me?" Constanza's throat seemed to squeeze shut.

Elionor puffed out air through her nose. "I'm a fornicator, maybe even an adulterer too. Unlike so many other sins, this is one I can't hide." She held her abdomen and revealed a little smile. "I can feel his flutters. This child, I already love him, but everyone will know me as the fornicator with a fatherless child. But you'll always see me as more. You are more tenderhearted than anyone, Constanza de Bonomo."

Constanza closed her eyes, not feeling as tenderhearted as she should. Elionor had confessed her sin before God, and Constanza knew the Holy Scriptures. *He is faithful and just to forgive us our sins, and to cleanse us from all unrighteousness.* Still, Elionor had ignored all the warnings and, worse, the Holy Spirit. She had known better.

To see Elionor how God sees her—that's what I need to do. Constanza opened her eyes. *I need to submit to the Spirit instead of these feelings.*

"When we're back in Val Angrogna, I'll provide for myself." Elionor held her chin high, though her pleading eyes belied her resolve. "After the baby is born, I could build a small place next to yours, but with Andreas's approval. I can bake, I can sew, I can wash linens, I can do anything. I never want to be a burden to you or a blotch on your family."

"We'll worry about that when Andreas rescues us from Lord Philip." Constanza touched Elionor's shoulder as they continued the march downhill. "Until then, I will be at your side, and this child of yours will be welcomed when he arrives."

Elionor wiped away tears and tried to speak, but the emotion must have overwhelmed her. Risking a brief halt, Constanza hugged her and wiped tears from her own eyes. This world was surely overflowing with the sorrows of sin, but Christ was not only the great Savior. He was also the great Forgiver—the shepherd of lost sheep and a father to the prodigal.

* * *

Elionor sat on the ground outside an old barn and watched Ave and Fosca play in the farmyard. The six-year-olds smiled, laughed, and skipped as if nothing were wrong in the world. The sun had fallen behind the tall mountains some time ago, bathing the valley in twilight.

The flutters came again, and Elionor touched her belly. So small this child must be, so innocent, so fragile. Oh, she wanted to rejoice in the life growing within her, but every time the thought brought a little smile or a touch of expectation, thoughts of the child's father seized her. How could she have been so foolish and naive?

Her sickness had faded with the day. Every morning she prayed for strength, and even when it seemed to falter, God reminded her He was near—a singing bluebird, a smile from a child, a kitten the same color as Rosmarin, her own childhood cat, curled up near a house.

Constanza sat near a roaring fire with the other children, handing them pieces of bread and dried meat. How could Elionor ever regain her friend's trust?

Soldiers surrounded them. It seemed there was never a fleeting moment without at least one man watching them. Such dirty, loud, crude men they were, all led by the arrogant Lord Philip on his gray horse.

One soldier was kind, though. Wherever they marched, sat, or slept, the lugotenent maintained his vigil over them. Even tonight, after Lord Philip and two of his officers had found a castle to lodge in, Lugotenent Renaud had arranged for Elionor, Constanza, and the children to sleep in the barn. And only the women and children, thank the Lord.

Elionor leaned back and rested her head on the barnwood. Many years had passed since she had last slept in a barn. Memories surfaced from the depths of her mind—Damiano's barn with the sheep, her old bone necklace, and the cat, Rosmarin. Elionor had always preferred a barn's roof and warm hay over sleeping outside, and tonight was no different.

Three soldiers appeared from around the corner of the barn. Two walked a stumbling, crooked path toward her, while the other stood in a stupor, rubbing his messy beard. She had seen these three before but hadn't bothered to remember their names.

One sank down beside her and leaned his shoulder against the wall. "Where do you hail from, demoisèla?"

Elionor shifted herself away from him.

"I'm Humbert." The soldier's breath smelled of ale and other foul things. "A good, honest man I am." He hiccuped and pointed away with his thumb. "These other men are rogues."

"You're as drunk as anyone." Elionor rose to her feet and edged away, refusing to look at him. Near the barn, two girls chased each other, and Elionor hurried toward them. "Ave, Fosca, time to lie down for the night."

Ave bounded toward her and stopped a pace away. "Already?"

"We only started playing," Fosca said, halting next to Ave, her breathing heavy.

"Go ahead, demoisèla," Humbert said from behind. "I can wait. Tuck the girls into the hay so we can talk alone."

"Not alone." Another smelly soldier slipped next to Elionor, wiping his nose. "I'd like to know this one better too."

Blood pulsed through Elionor's wrists. Her palms sweated. Why were men such vile creatures?

Silvia walked out of the barn and headed toward the fire, her wispy hair blowing in the breeze.

"Look there, it's Crooked Eye!" The first man's shoulders rose and fell with coarse laughter. "Can you see straight today, little Crooked Eye?"

Silvia cast her eyes down, her face reddening.

Humbert staggered toward her and mockingly crossed his eyes. "Is this how you see the world, *filha petita*?"

Elionor clenched her fists. Back at the orphanage in Turin, the other children, especially Guido and Ezio, had playfully mocked Silvia, and Elionor had often been the one to shield her from their cruelty.

The soldier at Elionor's side hacked and spat on the ground. "Watch out, men! Crooked Eye is walking about. She'll veer off course and knock you from your feet."

Elionor placed her hands on her hips. "Do you find joy in tormenting her?"

"I heard a lazy eye is the sign of a lazy soul," said the soldier with the messy beard. He pointed at Silvia. "Is that true, filha petita?"

Humbert stooped toward Silvia and curled his lips. "I say she's bewitched. You can't trust a girl who won't even look you in the eye."

"That's enough!" Elionor said. "Silvia is a child of God, and if you think you can—"

"You're powerless here, demoisèla. We can do as we please." Humbert took a step toward her, a smirk on his ugly face, and placed his hands on her arms. The others snickered.

Her whole body recoiled, but Humbert's grip was too strong. He reached for her mouth with one hand and whispered, "Don't scream."

In the menacing silence, a crisp melody of metal met the cool night air. "Take your hands off her, or trade them for bloodied stumps."

There stood Lugotenent Renaud, his jaw set and the tip of his blade at Humbert's shoulder. His eyes bored into Humbert, challenging him.

Humbert withdrew his hands.

Elionor sighed in relief. Silvia embraced her first, then Ave and Fosca.

"Can't you see, Lugotenent." The bearded soldier shifted on his feet. "We were just playing with her. We meant no offense."

Lugotenent Renaud remained in place, feet spread wide and blade pointed at Humbert. But he said nothing.

Humbert hiccuped and grimaced. "You won't always be in command, Elias Renaud. Very soon, men like you will serve us and grovel on your knees."

The lugotenent stood unyielding. "Go back to your tent. If you glance at her again, I'll take your eyes."

The soldiers exchanged looks, pulled back, and staggered into the shadows.

Lugotenent Renaud sheathed his sword and faced Elionor. "That was my fault, and it won't happen again. I promise you."

"Mercé," Silvia said, smiling up at him. "Are you an *èroe*?"

"A hero? I've never been called that."

"My papà says you can tell an èroe from everyone else by how he cares for women and children."

"Your papà is a wise man." He looked back at Elionor, but she avoided his gaze. "I was in Saint-Pancrace on a brief errand." He reached into his doublet, fumbled a moment, and extended his hand. "These are for you."

Elionor gazed down at the delicately wrapped bundle in the lugotenent's large, calloused hand. Intrigued, she unfolded the cloth to reveal two beautifully embroidered kerchiefs. The intricate patterns spoke of a craftsmanship that must be unique to these foreign lands.

A soft gasp escaped her as she realized the kerchiefs were a gift. "I . . . don't know what to say." She gave Lugotenent Renaud the briefest of glances but quickly focused on the kerchiefs again. "Mercé. They are lovely."

He fidgeted with his sword belt. "I overheard you and Dama Constanza yesterday . . . talking about your heads being uncovered."

"Embarrassing, but it's been a week since I lost mine. I was beginning to forget." She removed two pins from a fold in her chemise sleeve and fastened the fresh kerchief to her hair. "Now I'll feel like a true woman again."

"It's no trouble."

Why was he so much different from the other soldiers? His strength and military bearing surpassed most, but unlike the rest of the men, the lugotenent radiated kindness.

Realization flooded over her like a torrent. While soldiers like Humbert boldly pursued women, men like Lugotenent Renaud seemed compassionate and virtuous but swooped in to scavenge like hawks.

A year ago, Brando had been the same way. Though he had never believed the gospel, he was always gentle and kind. But in the end, he had left her like a carcass to rot under the sun.

Dear God, let this misery end. I wanted a safe home for me and my child, and I still do. I want peace, Lord, and to be shielded from evil.

"Your kindness is genuinely appreciated, Lugotenent." Eyes downcast, Elionor finished with the kerchief, excused herself from the lugotenent, and moved toward the fire. She had repented of her sins, and she would not allow herself to be scavenged and picked apart.

13

The true love of Christ shall not destroy the enemy; he that would be an heir with Christ is taught that he must be merciful, as the Father in heaven is merciful. Christ never accused any one, as do the false teachers of the present day; from which it is evident that they do not have the love of Christ, nor understand His Word.

—Felix Manz
Admonition to his fellow brethren, 1526

Twelve days of navigating mountain paths, conquering steep ridges, and wandering through ancient forests brought Andreas and Johan to the final stretch of the journey. Two more days of walking, and Andreas would enter Thonon, seat of power for the House of Savoy. Hopefully, Constanza and the children would have already arrived, and Andreas could negotiate a settlement with Philip and put an end to this whole venture.

"There's a hamlet on that ridge," Johan said, shielding the morning sun from his eyes. "We're out of everything, even those bitter berries you picked yesterday."

"We have five quattrini left. Two should be enough to buy a loaf of bread and leave us with some for the return trip."

Johan burst into laughter. "Three quattrini to feed sixteen people?"

"We can find a farmer near Thonon and help him harvest his crops for two or three days. That will give us enough."

Andreas and Johan ventured down a sloped sheep pasture and into a dark forest of pines and spruces. The distant murmur of a stream reached Andreas's ears. Soon the forest thinned and revealed a meandering watercourse, its clear waters reflecting the dappled sunlight. Dragonflies frolicked above the surface as Andreas and Johan followed a narrow trail beside the river.

The path wound up the slope until it swept left into a cluster of rustic dwellings. In the center of the hamlet stood a church that seemed as old as the mountains surrounding it, but oddly, no cross stood atop the steeple. Children in drab attire played in the open areas between the houses. Outside the hamlet, the land had been stripped bare, leaving a desolate expanse littered with tree stumps. A rotted signpost read LA COUTA.

"This is a poor village if I've ever seen one," Johan said. "Look at those children. If I had bread or coins to give them—"

"Indeed, they'll appreciate what little commerce we offer. I doubt there's a bakery here, but there will be a widow or young mother willing to spare a loaf for a few quattrini."

Three children stared at Andreas as he approached one of the houses. Chickens clucked and pecked at the ground and fluttered away as he passed. "Bonjorn," he said to the children in the Savoyard tongue.

Their eyes grew wider, but their mouths didn't budge. Did they speak something other than Savoyard? No, that couldn't be, for they were deep in the realm of Savoy. Ever since Andreas and Johan had crossed at Mont Cenis, Savoyard had been the prominent language. Andreas had spoken it since boyhood. It was similar enough to Romaunt that Johan could understand most of it, and Piedmontese speakers usually had little trouble with it. Why did these children look at him as if they didn't understand?

Andreas tried French instead. *"Mes jeunes amis, savez-vous parler la langue française?"*

Their expressions were even more confused, perhaps afraid. The children carefully rose from the ground and disappeared around the corner of the house.

"I haven't shaved in a week." Johan scratched his chin and turned a palm upward. "Maybe I scared them off."

"I wonder how often the people here in La Couta see visitors." Andreas scratched his beard and knocked on the door.

A wrinkled, gray-haired woman of about sixty years opened the door halfway and smiled. "Bonjorn, amis," she whispered in Savoyard.

"We are traveling to Thonon and need bread for the day." Andreas fumbled in his pocket, reaching for two quattrini but grabbing three. Under normal circumstances, three quattrini was too much, but these people needed it.

The woman shuffled backward and held her hands up, palms out, as if forming an invisible barrier between her and the coins. *"Nou,* I won't take those. We don't trade in La Couta."

"We don't seek alms," Andreas said, "only a fair exchange for your grain and labor."

Her lips parted, and she hesitated. One hand twitched at her side before she met Andreas with a searching look. "All belongs to God, and in the kingdom, we shall all share the bounty of labor."

Something tingled at the base of Andreas's neck. *Those aren't her words.* He balled his hands. Surely the Divine Ascendancy hadn't spread to these lands too. Johan's wide eyes showed he had arrived at the same conclusion.

But curiosity pushed Andreas to unearth more. "Indeed, all belongs to God." His mind jolted back to Pragela and its chants, and he repeated the Latin phrase he had heard there. "Ecce lux prophetæ ducet nos."

"*Ègal!*" Her face immediately shone with joy and anticipation. She reached out and embraced him. "You must be a novice in the kingdom. Forgive me for scolding you about the coins. It takes time for us to cast off the shackles of our former lives."

Andreas accepted her hug but gave her only a tight tap on the shoulder in return.

"I am Ègal Sidonie," she said.

Ègal—that meant "equal." Lorenzo of Pragela had said the Ascendants called each another that.

"Welcome to La Couta," Sidonie added. "Here we serve God and His appointed prophet as you do."

His family—the crown of twelve stars, apparently—was part of the sect's prophecies, so he wouldn't give her his real name, not even his first name. Instead he modified his surname and used that. "I am Ègal Bonome." Andreas motioned to Johan, and Sidonie embraced him too.

Johan's eyes bulged, silently begging for relief.

Andreas chuckled at him. "And that is Ègal Johan."

Sidonie released Johan, then gazed up at the sky and smiled. "The day of the Lord is at hand!"

Trying to follow her train of thought, Andreas tightened his lips and gazed with her. "Yes, the day of the Lord." How long could he sustain this awkward pretense? Surely he would accidentally declare something blasphemous.

She opened the door farther and invited them inside. "Please, come in, ègals."

Five other women sat at a round table, all wearing the same style of brown cloak. They varied in ages, the youngest about twenty and the oldest near the age of Sidonie.

"We've been waiting for news of the kingdom for weeks," Sidonie said. "Tell us, has the crown of twelve stars arrived in Thonon?"

Andreas glanced at Johan for an answer but found none. "Euh . . . yes, in Thonon."

"As the Prophet has foretold." The youngest woman blinked rapidly, her fingers curling into her palm. "On the fourteenth of October, just ten days from now, the Prophet will offer the crown back to heaven, and the Ascendant Kingdom will be established. Étoilembra will blot out the sun over Thonon, and we faithful will gather in triumphant jubilee to offer our holy sacrifice."

Johan exchanged glances with Andreas, a subtle mixture of disbelief and wariness etching lines on his face. No matter the occasion, Johan never concealed his thoughts.

Andreas nodded once toward Sidonie. "We are both novices in these . . . divine prophecies. Can you remind me what *Étoilembra* is?"

"She is the giver of knowledge, the oracle of the Divine, the voice of God," said one of the women. "Every month she waxes and wanes, showing us her ever-changing yet constant nature."

"The moon?" Johan blurted out, furrowing his brows.

Andreas threw him a stern look and mouthed in Romaunt, *"Jòga amb ieu. Play along with me."*

"Moon is what the unfaithful call her." Sidonie picked up a small basket from the table and handed it to Andreas. "And novices in the Ascendant Kingdom."

Andreas unwrapped the cloth and pressed his fingers against the crust of the bread. Its warm, nutty, slightly sweet scent surrounded him, invoking memories of the grand feasts of his youth. This wasn't the barley or rye bread of peasants but the wheat bread of the wealthy. How these peasants had obtained wheat, he didn't know, but this was a treat beyond imagination. *"Merci bôcô."*

"All things belong to God," Sidonie said. "Freely we give, and freely we receive."

Andreas almost tore off a piece of bread right then, but it could wait until midday.

Johan peered around the room, then back to the door. "Where are all the men of the hamlet?"

"Like you, our husbands and brothers serve the Prophet," said the young woman. "The women and children tarry here until the day of the Lord."

Those same husbands and brothers might be the men who had abducted Constanza and the children. "How do they serve the Prophet?"

"Whatever he asks, they do. What are your assignments, ègals?"

Andreas scratched his beard. Blurting out a blatant lie might breed suspicion. Neither did it seem morally right.

Sidonie's countenance hardened as she shifted her weight to the other leg.

"Whatever the Prophet demands." Johan stood tall, proud of his act.

"A mystery!" The young woman rose. "My husband is also on a covert assignment."

"My brother is with the Prophet himself," said another woman. "They are bringing the crown of twelve stars to Thonon."

Andreas's breath caught in his throat. The crown, the Prophet, the day of the Lord—what was this offering? *How strongly do these Ascendants hold to their beliefs?* "I bear grim news from Piedmont."

A hush fell over the room.

"Lord Philip of Savoy found the Prophet and killed him."

Unperturbed, the young woman shook her head. "Impossible. The Prophet can't be defeated."

"Have you lost your faith?" Sidonie asked, drilling a hole into him with her glare. "How could you believe such lies?"

Johan held his hands up. "Remember, we're novices with this Étoilembra . . .
I mean, Divine Kingdom."

Andreas leaned toward Johan and whispered, "Ascendant Kingdom."

"You are unfaithful." The young woman strode toward them, the rest close
behind. "And spies!"

"From the House of Savoy," one woman said.

Sidonie faced Andreas, unflinching. "Or from the Poor of Thonon."

"True, we are poor," Johan said. "That's why we knocked on your door and
asked for bread."

Sidonie waved the other women closer. "We will bring you to the Prophet."

"No you won't." Johan let out an amused laugh.

Andreas stuffed the loaf of bread in his sack and pulled the door open. He
and Johan backed out, but the women followed.

"I'm not fighting them," Johan said in whispered Romaunt. "They're all mad.
What if they bite?"

"Then we run."

"As long as you don't tell anyone I ran from six women."

Andreas and Johan spun and fled down the winding path. Their pace steadied
as they neared the bottom of the hill and walked along a ravine. Dark, brooding
clouds gathered overhead, and their ominous presence cast shadows across the
rugged landscape. The snowcapped peaks in the distance took on a muted,
foreboding tone. A shift in the air heralded a coming rainstorm. Behind them,
the same eerie chants as from Pragela seeped out of the hamlet.

Was this entire valley filled with Ascendants? More than women and children
might occupy the next hamlet. And the Ascendants had spread farther than the
Vallense barbes had guessed. The Prophet's followers had infested both Pragela
and La Couta, and likely more hamlets and villages.

"Was a free loaf of bread worth all that?" Andreas asked, tearing off a piece of
the loaf.

Johan swatted the bite from Andreas's hand and, in the same motion, ripped
the whole loaf away and threw it into the ravine. It tumbled down the slope and
settled in a slow-moving stream. "Ascendant bread. Eat that, and we'll catch
whatever madness they have."

Andreas threw his hands into the air. "That was wheat bread, Johan, and we
haven't eaten anything since yesterday!"

"Wheat or barley, I'd rather eat a rock than Ascendant bread."

Andreas shoved Johan hard, knocking him onto the path. "If you didn't want
to eat it, you could have saved it for me."

"And when I walk into Thonon tomorrow, I would have to tell Constanza you
died from eating Ascendant bread." Johan rose and dusted himself off, laughing.
"As I said, I'd rather eat a rock." He motioned for Andreas to walk beside him.
"Come, let's find your family."

14

His purposes will ripen fast,
Unfolding every hour;
The bud may have a bitter taste,
But sweet will be the flower.

—William Cowper
Light Shining out of Darkness, Olney Hymns, 1779

Elionor held Roberto's hand as the column marched single file along a winding trail perched high above a wild, rushing river. Since yesterday, the gray mountains had given way to low foothills emblazoned with a spray of autumn colors.

Lugotenent Renaud marched three paces ahead, Prospera riding atop his shoulders. She stretched her arms high to touch the branches arching over the trail. He turned halfway toward Elionor, though he continued to walk forward. "Tomorrow we arrive in Thonon, my home."

Despite Elionor's best efforts to ignore his goodwill, the lugotenent still tried to lift her spirits. But not only hers—the children's too, and Constanza's. The kerchiefs for her and Constanza were a kind gesture that had brought a sliver of normality to their plight. Elionor could at least show him a little courtesy.

She hurried her pace and moved within comfortable earshot. "Tell me about your home."

Lugotenent Renaud's face brightened at the invitation. "It wouldn't be home without my family."

"Do you have any children?"

"No children. It's me, my *pâre*, and my *mâre*. They're aging, so my income supports the three of us. My sister and her family live near us."

The cloak of mystery seemed to fall ever so slightly from him. "Why do you show us kindness, Lugotenent?"

He turned to look at Elionor. "You can call me Elias."

"No, I prefer *Lugotenent*."

"As you wish." He slowed his steps and shortened his stride until he walked beside her, though he maintained a comfortable distance. His stalwart presence warmed her, but she kept her eyes locked on the trail. In the periphery of her vision, however, he silently drew her attention.

"I follow Lord Philip faithfully," the lugotenent said, edging closer, "but there is something that I share with you. I dare not say it now, though."

Elionor glanced at him tentatively and traced the lines of his profile. The darkness of his hair framed a face that defied her attempts to remain indifferent. He was undeniably handsome, though the acknowledgment came reluctantly.

Prospera waved at Elionor. "See how high I am? Monsen Renaud is even bigger than my papà!"

Elionor couldn't resist a quiet smile as Prospera bounced on the lugotenent's shoulders. Elionor's gaze drifted back down to his face. He didn't quite smile but offered a single nod.

"Don't fret," he said. "I won't allow any harm to come to you."

His promise, though surely meant for all the captives, seemed to settle most on her.

The column halted at midday on a grassy knoll overlooking a valley. Elionor, Constanza, and the children sat in the soft grass and awaited a few morsels from their captors.

The air, burdened with moisture, carried the scent of damp pine needles and the promise of rain. Once alive with the rustle of wind through the evergreens, the forest now stood silent before the coming shower. No one wanted to be wet again, though. Their clothes would be soaked and wouldn't dry until after a day of sun.

Elionor took a piece of bread from a soldier, and after making sure no one watched her closely, she devoured it.

Bino held his bread out to her. "Are you very hungry, madomaisèla? You can eat mine."

That will be Bino's one meal today. I can't take it from him.

Bino continued to push the bread toward her. "I'm not hungry."

"Mercé." Elionor took his offering, pulled him close, and kissed the top of his head. "You're a kind boy, Bino."

As she ate the bread, a drop of water fell on the tip of her nose and dripped down to her lip. Another fell on her hair, then a few on her arm. The sprinkles became a shower, and the shower a roaring deluge. Her clothing clung to her under the relentless assault. The green landscape disappeared behind a curtain of mist and raindrops. Elionor rose and joined Constanza and the others in the shelter of the forest.

A sudden wave of sickness gripped Elionor with a gnawing intensity. The alpine air, once light and fresh, now fought against her. Her stomach churned.

She placed her arm against a tree and stared at its scaly bark, but the distraction didn't work. The scent of wet earth and raindrops deepened. She couldn't let everyone see her like this.

Constanza's hand touched hers. "Take heart, Ellie. All will be well."

Elionor breathed in deeply, and her hand instinctively went to her abdomen. *This child will undo me!* "I need a few moments."

She rushed downhill toward the thick forest, but a soldier stopped her. "Stay with the others. We're leaving soon."

"I need a moment of privacy, monsen." Elionor held her hand up as she hurried past him.

She pressed farther into the pine trees until she was alone. At last she relieved her raging stomach.

As the bout subsided, she steadied herself against a tree, her breaths coming hard in a desperate attempt to regain her composure. The acrid taste lingered on her tongue, but the river was just down the slope.

She moved downhill from tree to tree. Strangely, no soldiers were nearby. Every other time she had needed privacy, soldiers stood guard in the background. It was almost as if she'd escaped without trying.

Elionor moved farther downhill until she stood on the riverbank. She tucked herself behind a thick tree trunk and observed the tangled landscape. None of the children could escape by themselves, and Constanza would never leave them. If anyone might be able to escape, it would be her. She knew how to fend for herself and had traveled alone, to Chivasso, to Brando—

I'm unworthy of Your mercy, Lord. Forgive me of my sin.

She bowed her head, and droplets of water fell from her forehead. Her hair had succumbed to the rain, clinging to her scalp beneath the new kerchief. *As far as the east is from the west, so far hath he removed our transgressions from us.*

God had already forgiven her. She didn't need to keep asking.

But she did need to find a village somewhere in these hills. From there she could discover where she was and hopefully get help. Would she find anyone she could trust? If she stumbled into a house, soaked, disheveled, and with rounded belly, wouldn't the owners refuse her? Or worse, whoever she found might take her back to the soldiers.

But would she find a better chance to flee? She had to try.

The river roared between its banks, swollen by the downpour. Flat rocks, still visible above the torrent, offered a fleeting opportunity to cross. Elionor moved away from the tree and crept forward.

A rough hand grabbed her arm from behind and spun her around. Lugotenent Renaud looked down at her with his dark eyes. "Don't try it."

"Unhand me!" She pulled against him with all her might, but he was too strong. "I need to cross!"

"You're a captive, Demoisèla Elionor." He moved his hand to hers and began pulling her back up the hill. "Believe me when I say this—you don't want to wander here. Evil people live in these hills."

She jerked her hand away, slipping from his moist grip, and stared at him. "I thought you were kindhearted, but now I see how wrong I was." *I'm always wrong about men.*

"I wish I could tell you everything, but not here." The lugotenent grabbed her wrist, but gently. "As I said earlier, I won't allow any harm to come to you. Please trust me, Elionor."

She lifted her gaze to meet his. Somewhere beneath his sternness, there lingered something that tempered the hard edges of his expression. She relaxed, and he released her wrist.

"Follow me." He began the trudge uphill. "And please don't try that again."

Amid the drumming of rain and the tumultuous roar of the river, a muffled shout rose from behind Elionor. She turned, but white water and tree branches obscured the opposite bank.

*　*　*

"Elionor!" Andreas shouted from the depths of his lungs toward the opposite bank of the river.

Johan cupped his hands around his mouth. "Elionor!"

No answer came. Elionor followed the Savoyard soldier—judging by his red cape, an officer—up the opposite slope and beneath the dense pine branches.

"Elionor Janavel!" Andreas waved his hands and charged down the slope toward the river. The last time he had seen Elionor was at his and Constanza's wedding, where Elionor had watched from the shadows, then disappeared.

The river crashed with the fury of a thousand thumping drums. Yet Constanza and the children were almost surely on the other side. If he waited for the flood to subside, he might lose their trail. He had to cross.

Johan stopped at the riverbank next to Andreas and leaned over, panting. "Are you sure that was Elionor?"

"It was her, and my family must be with her." Andreas took a single step into the river. The current pressed against his ankle with all its might, but his other foot, still on solid ground, held him steady.

His sack was still slung over his shoulder. He couldn't bring it across—it held Raimond's Bible and a change of dry clothes. Andreas threw the sack against the base of a towering tree.

"Are you mad?" Johan shouted over the pounding river and falling rain. "We can't cross here."

"It's shallow." Andreas took another step into the river. "And it's not even up to my knees."

"This is a real torrent, not a little stream for washing your clothes. It'll sweep you off your feet before you're halfway across."

Andreas took two more steps into the rapids. Though the icy current tugged at his legs like unseen hands, he maintained his footing. "Come, Johan! We can do this."

His family was just up that opposite slope. Once he waded through this torrent, he could climb up there and find them. Andreas continued to push forward as Johan took careful steps through the river a few paces behind him.

Each step was a struggle against the advance of the water. Andreas's foot tapped a boulder near the midpoint of the river. Instead of stepping over it, he took two steps left and passed it.

The current smashed into his legs the instant he stepped from the rock's shield. One foot slipped, then the other. He fell backward.

The rapids swirled around him like a storm, twisting his arms and legs in the bubbling tempest. His head was still above water, though. He pressed his legs into the riverbed and extended an arm.

Johan grabbed it and helped Andreas back to his feet. "The current is too savage. If your family is up that slope, they won't go anywhere tonight with this weather. We'll try again tomorrow."

Andreas shook his head and coughed. "No, I only lost my footing. You can swim, no?"

"Of course, but white water like this doesn't know the difference between a good swimmer and a bad one."

Waving him off, Andreas shuffled from behind the boulder again, this time with more care. Again the force of the current nearly swept his feet out from under him.

Johan was a pace behind, arms stretched out above the water for balance. Andreas did the same. Slowly and methodically, they made their way toward the opposite bank.

The water rose above his waist, and the angry waves lapped as high as his chest. The rapids plunged downstream to the left. To the right, granite boulders stood like mocking sentinels, laughing at Andreas's feeble attempts to conquer the river. Yet conquer it he must.

He staggered from behind the shelter of a rock cluster. The seething flow tugged at him from all sides, seeming to weave around, beneath, and through him. He strained every muscle to keep himself upright.

The shore was near. A few more steps, and they would be safe.

Andreas turned his shoulder and lifted his right foot for his next step. His knee buckled. His left foot slipped. And the river trounced him.

In a whirl, the current threw him into Johan, sweeping them both away. The river tossed and whipped and shoved Andreas like a champion fighter throwing all his fury at him.

The water roared in his ears, a thunderous echo when he was lifted above the surface, muffled when he was submerged below. Each gasp for breath became a desperate struggle. He surfaced, fighting to fill his lungs with air, only to be driven under again.

The current flipped him over and pummeled him. He desperately swung his arms and legs in search of stability, but each grasp was met with a smash or a scrape. The unyielding turbulence pulled him farther and farther from the opposite bank.

Something crashed into his head. The water's vicious clamor waned into a blunted whisper, then a high-pitched ring. Water seeped into his mouth, but he couldn't spit it out. He swallowed, but his mouth continued to fill.

He shot his legs outward and found solid stone. The jolt radiated up his legs and into his torso. Loose gravel scraped his arms as the river tossed him one more time and relinquished him into a gentler flow. His knees and hands found the rocky riverbank, and Andreas struggled ashore.

The roar fell to a distant murmur as his vision spun. He gasped for air, but the water in his lungs demanded release. He coughed and hacked until his lungs could take no more.

Rolling over, Andreas lay on his back and faced the vast gray sky. Raindrops fell on his face, a fresh, soothing cadence after his battle with the white water. Time seemed to pass in slow drips that wavered between dream and reality. He turned his head, and his gaze fell upon the river, an impenetrable wall still separating him from his family. All that strife, and he hadn't made it across. He turned away from the tumult and stared into the dark forest. *I will never swim again. Never.*

The thought of Johan nudged him upright. An overwhelming wave of exhaustion engulfed him, and the back of his head pulsed with a burning throb.

He wiped water from his eyes and looked upriver. Nothing but the unceasing rapids. Downstream revealed only water and rocks veiled in mist.

Dear Father in heaven, I can't lose Johan. Let him be safe, I beg You.

Movement in the forest caught his eye. He rose to his knees, then his feet, but as he straightened his legs to stand, his muscles surrendered. Back on his hands and knees, he searched through the downpour.

A hulking figure appeared from the somber depths of the forest. A long, untamed beard obscured much of his weathered face and mirrored the color of his shoulder-length gray hair. A plain linen headscarf, tightly wound around his head, accented his ruggedness.

"A bad day to swim in the Dranse, I'd say." The man reached for Andreas's hand and helped him up. "Take my arm."

"My friend Johan—he was with me."

"Johan?" The man linked arms with Andreas and walked him toward the forest. "We've already met. He's in my cabin now by the fire, eating through all my stores."

Andreas sighed. *Thank You, Father.*

"And you'll be there soon too, *jeune seigneur.*" He slapped Andreas hard on the shoulder. "I'm Claude Montagnard, steward of the duke's forests along the Dranse."

"My name is Andreas." He peered across the river. "I need to get across."

"The nearest bridge is halfway between here and Lac Léman, and the Dranse will be impassable for days. You're staying with me until you regain your strength."

"My family, though. They're on the other side."

"You'll have to wait until tomorrow. If you try to cross that torrent again, I'll be burying your body instead of lending you a bed."

Perched atop a rise, a cabin of roughly cut logs looked out over the river far below. The modest dwelling, encircled by majestic pines, seamlessly harmonized with its sylvan surroundings.

The old door creaked as Claude pushed it open. Inside, Johan sat wrapped in a woolen blanket, sipping a steaming drink by the fire.

"*Bienveunue*, Andreas," Claude said. "Warm yourself at my hearth and take what bread your friend here hasn't already eaten."

Andreas undressed and wrapped himself in a blanket, then slumped onto the wooden floor by the fire. Tomorrow he would find a way across the river. But for now, he offered thanks to God for warmth.

15

To every thing there is a season, and a time to every purpose under the heaven: a time to be born, and a time to die; a time to plant, and a time to pluck up that which is planted.

—The Holy Bible
Ecclesiastes 3:1–2

SOFT ORANGE LIGHT flickered from within a cluster of homes along the trail, teasing Constanza with their inviting warmth. She, Elionor, and a dozen children huddled beneath the saturated canvas of a tent that barely accommodated them. Just outside the tent, Lugotenent Renaud had built a small fire for them. It crackled and sputtered, spitting small embers that the wind quickly consumed. The constant rainfall muffled the steady breaths of the children, who, even though they were uncomfortable, had managed to fall asleep.

Constanza shivered under a damp blanket that did nothing more than shield her from the wind. On the other side of the makeshift tent, Elionor sat up, wrapped her arms around her legs, and stared into the black, rainy night. She extended an arm to the edge of the awning. Water dripped into her palm, and she brought her hand to her lips.

Constanza stood and carefully stepped over and around the sleeping children toward Elionor. "I can't sleep either." She sat and breathed into her hands.

"What a man of quality Lord Philip is, suffering in that warm house while we're treated like royalty out here in the muck." Elionor stared at the light that glowed from a window in the house.

"Philip is nothing like Andreas." Constanza's words came out louder and sharper than she wanted. "They walk differently, they talk differently."

"Why did he drag us over the mountains?"

Constanza sighed as she stared blankly at the log house. "A few times since we were married, Andreas said his past might catch up to him. But I don't think he guessed something like this." She gestured toward Lugotenent Renaud, who lay on the ground with only a fallen log for protection from the rain. "At least we're not him."

Due to his rank, Elias Renaud was assigned a tent, but since their first encounter with Lord Philip, the lugotenent had generously allowed them to shelter under his tent each evening, save for the one luxurious night at the Hospice of Great Saint Bernard.

Elionor pointed her nose at the lugotenent. "What do you think about him?"

"Lugotenent Renaud? He's the only bright star amid the blackness of the other men. He seems to favor us"—she looked directly at Elionor—"and you most of all."

"Please, Constanza. I've learned from my sins and won't make the same foolish choices again."

"There's something different about him—something deeper than what we see."

"He's not a believer, though. Once I saw him cross himself like a papist."

"Surprising." Constanza shifted her shoulders, and her fingers curled involuntarily. "I had thought better of him. Have you seen that he doesn't gamble with the other soldiers?"

"Yes, and I've never heard him swear or curse God's name, not even once."

Constanza turned and revealed a half smile. "You do pay attention to him."

"Not as you imagine. I appreciate his generosity, and that's the end of it. Whatever his intentions are, they're nothing to me." Elionor shook her head. "Even if he were a true Christian, which I doubt he is, we both know what he would think when he discovers—" She touched her abdomen. "No decent man will give me his devotion. And I've accepted that. I'll bear the results of my sin alone."

Constanza opened her mouth to reply, but what could she say? That Elionor was wrong? That the right man might see beyond her shame? It felt useless, like trying to stitch a wound with frayed thread. She let the silence linger instead.

The lugotenent shifted from one side to the other. He repositioned his ragged hat and settled back into a reclining position.

"Besides, I don't think Elias—" With a quick gasp, Elionor covered her mouth. "I mean Lugotenent Renaud. He's not as bright a star as he seems. When I felt sick earlier, I almost escaped to the other side of the river."

"I wondered what took you so long."

"No one was around. I had a clear path to freedom and finding help, but just as I started across, the lugotenent grabbed me. If he were on our side, he would've let me escape. Instead he told me I was a prisoner and pulled me back up the slope."

"What if another soldier had caught you alone like that?" Constanza set her jaw as the weight of Elionor's words pressed against her chest. "Escape isn't an option for us, and I've told Ezio and Guido many times already. The next time you try to escape, it might not be Lugotenent Renaud who finds you."

Elionor sighed deeply. "Maybe it was foolish. I just needed to help somehow. But why did he bring me back here? My guess is that he's Lord Philip's spy, pretending to be friendly to keep us passive until we're in Thonon."

"To what end? What will happen to us then? Will Andreas be there?" Constanza hugged her legs tighter. "I've prayed every day for this to end, but it continues. I only want to be with my husband again and sleep in my own bed. And then there's another thing . . ."

The words caught in her throat. Could she even say it aloud? The idea felt fragile, too uncertain to share. What if it was just her imagination?

Elionor straightened, her curious gaze urging Constanza to continue.

Constanza took a long, nervous breath. "There are signs, though maybe I'm mistaken. These fifteen days or however long it's been . . . I've certainly eaten less. And walking every day up and down mountains, barely stopping to rest . . . and at night, I can hardly sleep." She paused, her voice faltering. "I don't know, Ellie, but I might . . . my mamà once told me . . ."

"Are you with child?"

"I don't know, but that's what I'm wondering." Constanza wet her lips. "How did you know for sure?"

"The signs don't all come at once. I was certain when I felt the baby move."

"When does that come?" Constanza touched Elionor's arm.

"For me, two weeks ago."

"When did you first guess you were with child?"

"Nine weeks ago, I think."

"I wish I knew for sure. Maybe at the end of next month, I'll feel the baby." A visible puff of breath escaped Constanza's mouth, lingering for a moment in the cold, damp air. "Oh, I can't wait to tell Andreas—if it's the truth."

"I do hope it's true." Elionor, disregarding her damp attire, leaned over and embraced Constanza.

Constanza sighed and held Elionor's shoulders at arm's length. "How will I care for a baby along with the rest of the children? And what if we're far from home for a long time? I'll never have the strength to cross the mountains—not as you have."

"The Lord will guide your path." Elionor formed a little grin. "At least that's what you've been telling me this whole journey."

Constanza gave Elionor's arm a brief, firm squeeze. They sat next to each other and watched the rainstorm gradually ease its ferocity. The air, once heavy with the scent of damp earth, began to clear, and the pounding rhythm of droplets became a sporadic tap.

Lugotenent Renaud remained in his earthen bed against the log but periodically raised his head to scan the surroundings. If Andreas were in the lugotenent's position, he would be just as watchful. But who was this riddle of a man?

16

In the eyes of the inquisitors, and the judges more generally, one feature distinguishing a suspect as a member of the Waldensian community, and thus a sign of heresy, was the fact of receiving the barbes in one's home.

—Gabriel Audisio
Preachers by Night, 2006

THE RHYTHMIC *pink, pink* of pinson birds and the savory aroma of fried meat stirred Andreas from slumber. The warmth of the cabin wrapped around him, and as he peeled his eyes open, flickering firelight danced on the rustic walls. His clothes hung on a leather strap near the hearth, where crackling flames extended an invitation to the new day.

Andreas sat upright and stretched his arms toward the ceiling. Massive timber rafters vaulted upward to a steep peak, their rugged elegance framing the heart of the cabin. The back of his head still throbbed, and when he reached back to feel it, he touched dried blood.

Johan lay on the far side of the hearth, still curled up in a blanket and breathing deeply. Shafts of morning light filtered through small, weathered windows and cast a glow on the rough wooden floor.

Andreas's sack sat within arm's reach, damp but intact. He narrowed his eyes and pursed his lips. *I thought I left that upstream against a tree.* He crawled over, opened the sack, and removed his spare clothing. But it was still drenched.

"Bonjorn." The deep, resonant voice from behind startled Andreas. "You can hang those once the others are dry."

Andreas turned. On a weathered wooden chair sat the man who had brought them here—Claude, if Andreas recalled. The man held a block of wood in one hand and a knife in the other, carving the wood with deliberate strokes and turns of the knife. Shelves behind him displayed dozens of carved symbols and figures—saints, icons, crucifixes, a squirrel, foxes, a pair of golden eagles.

"I picked up your packs on my walk this morning." Claude nodded toward a table in the corner. "I cooked some pork belly too. It's not much, but I normally don't house guests." Within the veil of his gray beard, his smile emerged, a worn expression with lines of wisdom, strength, and kindness. "Other than me, you and your friend are the first to sleep under my roof in years . . . many years."

With the blanket still wrapped around him, Andreas rose and felt the clothes above the fire. A touch of dampness still lingered, but they were dry enough to wear. He removed them from the strap, draped them over his arm, and turned to Claude. "How can I repay you, *bon homme*? A few quattrini is all I have left."

"Don't bother." Claude set aside the knife and wooden block, then stood and walked to Andreas. "Let me see your head."

"It's only a—"

Claude grabbed Andreas's shoulder and turned him around. Parting Andreas's hair with his rough hands, he said, "This needs to be cleaned and bandaged."

"I can do that after I put these clothes on."

"*Và!* Those will be more useful than an old blanket."

Claude had placed another chair in front of his own by the time Andreas finished changing into dry clothes in the corner of the room. The wooden floor yielded to Andreas's weight with a gentle creak, each step resonating in harmony with the humble yet firmly built cabin. He sat on the chair in front of Claude and gazed toward the fire.

"These are yours." Claude reached around and gave Andreas a wooden plate with eight thick slices of pork belly. "Save a couple for your friend, though."

As Andreas ate, Claude used both hands to examine the back of Andreas's head. "Your accent tells me you're from here, but not your friend."

"Indeed, I am Savoyard, though five years have passed since I last lived in this realm."

"Your lilt points to a nobleman."

Andreas's neck tensed, and his hands froze. With all the Catholic symbols Claude had carved, Andreas shouldn't reveal too much about his faith—not yet, at least.

"My pâre was . . . is an influential man in the duchy."

"Hmm, I might know him. What's his name?"

"Louis."

Claude grunted. "I know of at least five nobles with that name who live within a day's journey of here. Is he a lord? A bailiff? A bishop?"

Andreas shifted in his chair, exhaled slowly, and relaxed his shoulders. Claude had shown him nothing but kindness. Why shouldn't he know the truth? "Louis, Duke of Savoy." The name felt foreign on Andreas's lips, yet somehow familiar, like something he could never fully escape.

Claude pressed a warm, wet cloth against the wound and carefully wiped it in small circles. A sharp sting radiated from the back of Andreas's head. "Your *gran-pâre* was a far better duke than your pâre."

Andreas turned to Claude, his chest loosening a little. "You believe me?"

Claude groaned, grabbed Andreas's head on both sides, and turned him back around. "Without a doubt, seeing how you think you can do whatever you want here—trying to cross the Dranse during a rainstorm, insisting on trying again, spinning your head about while I try to clean it. Yes, you're the son of the duke."

"Do you know him?"

"No, though I saw him once years ago in a parade through Genève."

"Yesterday you said you're the steward of these forests."

"Upriver to Morzine and downriver to Lac Léman. Since I was about your age, I've lived in these hills, tending its pines and firs and spruces, its beeches and oaks." Claude blew on Andreas's wound and wiped it once more. "This is the House of Savoy's forest, and that includes every living creature within it." He let out a long sigh. "Though your mâre and her lover have made my work difficult lately."

"My mâre?" Andreas leaned forward and turned to Claude again.

"Forgive me, I didn't mean to be so forward."

"Do I appear shocked? Because I'm not." Andreas frowned. "Unfortunately, she's held that reputation for many years."

"This lover is from the island of Cyprus, like your mother. Lucien Bouchard is his name. The duchess oversees Savoy's affairs from Thonon, but it's Monsieur Bouchard who holds the reins. Meanwhile, your pâre, the duke, crafts ballads within the same château, ignoring his own wife's indiscretions. Enter your brother Philip, who conjures up schemes to unseat your mother and her Cypriot court. Oddly enough, should he succeed, he might bring an element of dignity back to Savoy."

"How do you know all this?" Andreas asked.

"Rumors from friends who also hate Monsieur Bouchard. I deal with that man all too often. The duchy's lumber orders come through him, but he tries to tell me how to steward this forest. More, always more lumber, but with fewer good men."

"You oversee the logging too?"

"Not the actual work, but I tell the men where to cut and how many trees to take. This autumn and winter they'll be logging near a hamlet called Bellevaux. Good, hardworking, honest men they are too. They listen to what I tell them. You can't clear-cut a whole forest. Let the younger trees grow a little taller and wider before you chop them down. Use the whole tree, not just the trunk. All these simple rules that some don't bother to heed."

As Andreas sank his teeth into the succulent pork belly, a burst of rich flavors overwhelmed his tongue. The crisp exterior melted in his mouth before he swallowed. "Johan and I happened upon a village recently, and all the surrounding trees were hewn down."

"La Couta. My parents raised me near there. It was once a pleasant place to live. Last year that prophet came and spread his lies. His followers have been a needle in my foot ever since, destroying this land and its creatures and undoing years of stewardship. They poach the deer and boars, they tear the forest apart with their lazy logging, they leave the fields fallow. Everything they do is careless."

"I told you, Andreas." Johan sat up, stretched, and yawned. "It's a good thing we didn't eat their bread, because it probably would've killed us."

"You're a wise man," Claude said to Johan, laughing. "I wouldn't eat their bread either."

"It was tempting, I admit," Johan said, "especially after crossing the Alps."

"From Piedmont," Andreas said. "This is our seventeenth day since leaving Val Angrogna."

As Johan walked toward a more secluded corner of the room with his dry clothes, Andreas recounted their journey—from the abduction of his family and Philip's intervention to the encounter with the Ascendant women at La Couta.

Claude ripped off a long strip of linen from a bedsheet. "Those Ascendants are cut from the strangest block of wood. The husbands and wives—as soon as they become part of that sect, they sever their bonds and live in separate houses. Marriage and everything that comes with it is forbidden."

"We saw children, though," Johan said from the corner of the room.

"All from before they 'ascended.' You won't see their women having any babies. And do you know what I say? That's how the Prophet controls his followers. He conjures up the wildest teachings and prophecies and uses them to convince the weak-minded that he's some kind of messenger from heaven."

"They're like the Cathar Perfecti from centuries ago," Andreas said.

"I've heard far worse about them—illicit rituals in the dark of night, praying to evil spirits, offerings of crowns with seven stars."

Andreas's skin chilled. "Twelve."

"Ah, that's it, twelve stars. How did you know?"

"Rumors, the same as you." Andreas tried to cast the thought from his mind. "As much as I hate that my brother is using my family, I'm thankful he rescued them from the Prophet."

"I would be too, though I wonder why the Prophet had such an interest in them." Claude wrapped the linen around Andreas's head three times. "When I saw you wade into the river yesterday, I almost thought you were one of his followers."

Andreas chuckled. "No, I'm happily married."

"And I plan on having a wife someday!" Now wearing his dry clothes, Johan walked to Andreas and grabbed the rest of the pork belly strips.

Claude tightened the bandage and adjusted its position. "What are you two? Something tells me you're not Christians—at least not the kind I am."

"We are certainly Christians." Andreas glanced at the window, then the fire again. "Many call us Vallenses—or Vaudois in French, Waldensians in English, and Waldenser in Teutonic. But we're the same, no matter what we're called."

"I've heard of them. In fact, I met one many years ago. He called himself a barbe."

"One of our preachers," Johan said. "He must've been visiting other believers in the area when you met him."

"I believed what he preached—the corruption of the Roman Church, how all true believers are saints, salvation by faith, good morals."

Andreas pointed at the carvings displayed along the wall. "Yet these are all Catholic."

"I don't know what I believe. That barbe disliked icons and images, I remember. But that's the only kind of Christianity, no?"

Andreas shook his head. "I've separated myself completely from that religion."

"A son of the Duke of Savoy, a heretic? What a time to be alive." Claude paused, holding the bandage in place. "Since you're heading down to Thonon, you should try meeting some of the Poor."

"Do you see us?" Johan threw his head back and laughed. "We're the poorest in all of Savoy."

"No, not that kind of poor. They don't call themselves the Poor, but everyone else does. Finding them might prove hard, though."

"Are you sure they're not just followers of the Prophet?" Johan asked.

"The Ascendants hate the Poor more than they hate anyone else, I hear. From what I've experienced, the Poor are humble and industrious people. The Ascendants aren't. Remember those woodcutters I mentioned? I think most of them are Poor." Claude tied the bandage behind Andreas's head. "Keep that on today, and I'll wash it again this evening."

"No, we must reach Thonon by tonight."

"You're not my prisoner, but I think you should stay here for another day."

"I am grateful for your help, Claude, but this is my burden alone."

"Alone?" Claude wiggled the bandage, and Andreas winced. "Then I suppose I should have left you on the riverbank. No, you need others."

Johan pulled his tunic over his head, adjusting the loose fabric around his waist. "I've tried telling him that for the last month." He shoved Andreas's shoulder. "But he's more stubborn than a mule with its ears clamped shut."

Andreas shook his head and chuckled, then rose and moved toward the hearth. "Philip captured my wife and children, and they're heading to Thonon. I'm leaving now, and I won't rest until I find them."

"*Asse sie.* So be it." Claude handed Andreas his sack. "This is still wet, but since you're in a rush—"

"Your generosity is enough for legends, mon ami. We won't forget you."

17

I cannot thank and praise the Lord sufficiently, that He so comforts me in my tribulation, and that my mind is still fixed to fear the Lord with all my heart all the days of my life, according to my weak ability.

—Clement Hendrickss
Written from his prison in Amsterdam, 1561

"ARE WE REALLY GOING TO BE THERE TODAY?" Ezio's shoulders sank in exaggeration as he held Roberto's hand and walked beside Constanza.

Roberto looked up at Constanza with longing eyes. "My feet hurt."

"And I'm hungry!" Alessia said in her whiniest tone.

Constanza answered everyone at once. "I pray we're almost finished, and hopefully today." The journey had worn on all of them, and all were ready to be rid of the constant walking, scant food, and restless nights under the black sky. But they had heard nothing since yesterday about a journey's end. The soldiers, even Lugotenent Renaud, remained tight lipped, and far ahead atop his gray steed, Philip was as aloof as ever.

Oaks, beeches, and maples, coated with a frenzy of colors, wrapped the trail on all sides. Since midday, the landscape had transformed from dark pine forests and rocky slopes to glades of blazing leaves and rolling farmlands.

Constanza hurried to catch up with Elionor, who held Ave's and Fosca's hands several paces ahead. As Constanza reached them, the road turned sharply left onto a long stone bridge. The river they had followed for the last several days—the Dranse, as Lugotenent Renaud called it—flowed through a shallow gorge in a wide, lazy course, drastically different from the raging rapids farther upstream. To the left, green mountains rose in the distance, but to the right, not even a knoll rose amid the line of trees.

"Are we almost to Thonon?" Elionor asked, breathing heavily. "I don't mean to sound like a child, but my head is spinning, and my stomach is turning."

Constanza reached into her pocket and handed Elionor a piece of bread.

"You don't have to keep saving your bread for me." Elionor smiled with one side of her mouth and glanced down at Constanza's abdomen.

"Ave, Fosca, walk with Silvia for a few moments." Constanza released the girls' hands and gestured for them to leave. "Madomaisèla Elionor and I need to talk about something."

The girls frowned but hurried ahead toward Silvia.

Constanza gazed into the woodlands on the opposite bank of the river. "Oh, I wish I knew for certain, Ellie. I can't stop thinking about it."

"Wait until you're as far along as I am, because then you'll feel unpleasant things you can't stop thinking about." Elionor traced the edges of her kerchief with her fingertips. "But never as much as I do. My regrets run so deep."

Dear friend, why did you have to stray? Constanza silently pleaded. *I warned you and tried to help. My papà and mamà warned you. The Holy Spirit warned you. If only you had been more like me—*

In the privacy of her thoughts, a voice whispered, chastising her for her own self-righteousness. *How can I think I'm better than she is? Father, forgive my pride and pharisaical heart.*

The soldiers came to a halt. Far ahead, Philip said something to the tollman sitting on the last length of a bridge parapet, and the marching continued. The tollman tipped his hat to Constanza as she walked by, but he didn't stand up.

The forest thickened, and the tree branches formed a canopy of pretty reds, oranges, and yellows over the road. Sunlight sparkled through the leaves and cast frolicking shadows across the forest floor. Through the foliage on the left, a deer with a mighty rack of antlers stared curiously at them before bounding deeper into the forest.

Soon the trail expanded, changing from dirt to cobblestone and from cobblestone to hewn stone. Constanza's footsteps echoed against the smooth surface as the band crossed the threshold of the forest into a vast open space. The crisp breeze chilled her skin, but the bright, descending sun ahead of them warmed her cheeks. Remnants of the grain harvest lay on the field to the left, while rows of grapevines stretched across the fields on the right.

The road curved gently toward a stone structure that soared above the landscape. Its seven octagonal towers stood in a straight line like tall guards, and a low stone wall surrounded it on all sides.

"It's a castle, Mamà!" Ezio's eyes were as vast as the sky above him. "Are we going there?"

"We're staying there?" Silvia asked. "I thought only nobles lodge in castles."

Ezio straightened his neck. "We are nobles . . . in a way."

"Papà!" Bino said from behind. "He's a prince."

"Yes, and that's why we're allowed to stay here," Ezio said.

The closer they drew to the castle, the more the children buzzed with questions and unending movement. Had they finally arrived at Thonon? Would Andreas be here, ready to take them home? Constanza's heart fluttered. Maybe even today she would be in Andreas's arms. She didn't want to recount the journey nor complain about Philip and the soldiers nor speak about the Prophet and Ascendants—only to hold Andreas, to weep into his chest, to remember Papà, and soon to tell him about the baby.

"Thonon," she whispered. "Lord, please let Andreas be here . . . or let him come soon."

At the gate, Philip dismounted and spoke to the four officers, including Elias Renaud. Soon a wave of voices carried across the light evening breeze. Some of the soldiers hugged each other, while others simply walked away. Before long, almost the entire force had dispersed across the field, leaving Philip and his officers standing alone in front of the gatehouse.

Philip himself waved Constanza and Elionor toward him.

"Come, children," Constanza said, motioning for them to stand and follow her.

Philip crossed his arms and frowned as they approached. "No whelps."

"These are my children, and they stay with me."

"Leave them where they are and come to me alone. I have no patience to speak over their whining."

"I want my friend with me, at least." Constanza nodded toward Elionor.

Philip dropped his shoulders and shook his head, then motioned sharply for them to approach. Next to him, Lugotenent Renaud gave Elionor a subtle nod as if saying *Don't worry.*

Constanza took five steps toward Philip and the officers, then planted her feet. "Where is my husband?"

"My scouts spotted him yesterday along the Dranse. He should arrive soon."

"Yesterday?" Constanza let out a little gasp. "You're certain?"

"No one can mistake Andreas's plain face, though I hear he has grown a beard." Philip snickered, grabbing his smooth cheeks in mockery. "How rustic, blending in with you peasants as if whiskers could mask his inadequacy."

Three of the officers cackled with Philip, but Elias remained straight faced.

Constanza composed herself and lifted her chin. "Andreas is thrice the man you are, my lord."

Philip exchanged glances with the other officers, but as soon as he looked back at Constanza, Lugotenent Renaud hinted at the slightest of smiles.

"You won't see a single strand of Andreas's hair until he gives me what I want, *Constanza.*" Philip sniffled. "Until then, you will remain here at the château."

"As your prisoners." Constanza held his gaze, unflinching.

"I prefer *guests*, but you may call yourselves what you wish." Philip brushed his hair back.

"Why are you so cruel? I'm married to your brother, so is it possible for you to show us a pinch of kindness?"

"Who rescued you from the cultists? Who has fed you, your friend, and your brood for half a month? Who has freely offered you a comfortable place in my château?" Philip swung his cape behind him. "Be grateful I am not as dishonorable as you imagine."

"Can you at least explain why we're all here?"

"Peasants." Philip threw his head back in contempt. "So naive about the intrigues of a noble house. My family is a disgrace to our once-reputable lineage. My pâre is a weak and impotent fool; my mâre and her Cypriot courtiers squander our wealth on frivolity. Her lover, Lucien Bouchard"—he uttered the name as if filth had been dropped on his tongue—"he is the worst of them. I despise that man with every fiber of my being." He turned slightly and peered into the distance. "My oldest brother, Amadeus, and his French wife are no better, perhaps worse than my parents. As for me, I wish to restore our realm to the glorious duchy it once was under my gran-pâre."

"And you plan to do that by declaring yourself the duke." Constanza crossed her arms and glared at Philip. "How noble of you. Meanwhile, you abduct your own brother's family and force them to follow you across the mountains."

"Andreas is the only sibling who could convince my father to abdicate. Once that's arranged, declaring Andreas illegitimate should be easy, given his rejection of the Holy Catholic Church. Bringing you here was the only way to compel my brother to Thonon."

"Whose wise idea was this?"

"That is of no concern to you. As soon as I am declared heir instead of my brothers, you will be free to leave, but until then, you will be treated cordially. Your rooms will be warm, your food will be exquisite, and you will be safe—all at my expense, I might add." Philip placed his hands on his hips and stared at Constanza.

"Are you waiting for me to say mercé?" Constanza's voice cracked under the weight of her exhaustion. "Yes, mercé for rescuing us from cultists while you forced us on your ploy over the Alps. Mercé for letting us sleep in the cold while you slept in comfort. Mercé for your hospitality, my lord Philip." She held back tears that yearned to be released. Elionor drew closer.

Philip turned his back to Constanza. "Lugotenent Renaud, escort them inside and give them to the steward. Tell him that the children are to be kept far from my quarters." He pulled his red cape around him and marched through the gate with the three other officers.

Constanza, Elionor, and the children followed the lugotenent through the gate and into the cobbled courtyard, surrounded by buildings ringing with the evening bustle. The wind carried a mixture of scents—the earthiness of the gardens, the mustiness of ancient stone, the distant fragrance of ripening grapes from the surrounding vineyards.

The castle's sand-colored facade basked in the warm glow of the setting sun as Elias approached an arched wooden door. His firm yet polite knock sent an echo through the courtyard. A stern man, his cheeks sagging with age, swung the door open.

"These are Lord Philip's guests. Treat them well." Elias motioned toward the children. "The lord also ordered that the children be kept far from his rooms."

Huffing, the man ushered them in and slammed the door behind them, leaving Elias outside. "The cesspit smells better than all of you." He snatched a candle from a shelf and mumbled as he walked them up a flight of stairs.

At the top, he handed them off to an old woman. "Take them to the west wing." He sniffed and grimaced. "Throw some water on them to rinse away the filth too."

Constanza took a deep breath. *We don't smell that bad.*

The hunched old woman grumbled more than the steward as she led them deeper into the castle. The dimly lit hallway, decorated with tapestries depicting both papist and noble symbols, offered them little welcome. The woman pressed against a heavy wooden door that refused to move.

Constanza came up alongside her and helped, and soon the door creaked open. The woman glowered at Constanza and coughed. "Don't leave this room unless I say so. And keep the children's mouths shut too, for Lord Philip demands peace and solitude."

Constanza forced herself to use a kind tone. "I am Constanza de Bonomo, and this—"

"Do you think this is pleasant for me?" The woman wiped her nose with her sleeve and coughed again. "I already have too much work within these walls to worry about you. I do what my lord tells me and no more."

The children gathered around Constanza and Elionor with questioning eyes.

"In," the woman said, pointing her crooked nose into the musty room. "The door will be locked behind you, so don't try to leave."

Guido stepped toward the door. "It's cold in there."

"I could arrange for you to sleep with the dogs if that suits you better." She flashed a toothless grin at Guido and shoved him inside. The rest of the children fell in line and entered, and once Elionor and Constanza crossed the threshold, the door slammed with a resounding thud. A moment later the lock clicked. Aside from a few stray glints of sunlight filtering through the window, darkness covered their surroundings.

Constanza drew in a steady breath and scanned the gloomy confines. *Dear God, please grant us rest here, especially Elionor—she needs a place to lay her head. And we all need patience, Lord.*

*   *   *

The heavy door burst open as the last rays of the sun dwindled into shadow. A new glow bathed the room with warmth and painted the walls in shades of amber as the darkness retreated before a lantern.

Constanza, nestled in the corner with the four youngest children, shielded her eyes and blinked against the intrusion of light. Gradually her vision adjusted to the radiance that now revealed a slender silhouette.

In the soft glow, a woman stood like a heavenly angel, her features illuminated by the gleam of the lamp. A white linen headscarf, tied in a loose knot below one ear, concealed most of her dark hair. Beauty and kindness seemed to pour out from her.

Constanza and Elionor both rose and motioned for all the children to follow.

The woman offered a warm a smile and curtsied. "*Bon vêpre.* I am Madeleine Dupont, and from now on I'll be caring for your needs here." She entered the room and hurried toward the fireplace with light footsteps. "*Ché pa bon*, it's not good. This room is so dreadfully cold." She set her lantern on the mantel, bent over, and peered up the chimney. "I don't know when someone last lodged here. I'll start a fire for you, and for now I'll bring blankets and make tonight as comfortable as I can. Tomorrow I'll make sure you're more comfortable."

With Alessia latched on to her hand, Constanza approached Madeleine. "I am Constanza de Bonomo, and these are my children." She nodded toward Elionor, who held Prospera's partially finished braid. "Except for her, of course. Elionor Janavel is my dearest friend."

Again Madeleine curtsied. Her large, round eyes, pools of gentleness and care, met Constanza's, and a soft smile graced her lips. She took a step toward Constanza, spread her skirts, and crouched to Alessia's level. "And what's your name?"

Alessia touched Constanza's skirts.

"Tell her." Constanza prodded Alessia to step closer to Madeleine.

"Alessia," she mumbled.

"Alessia—what a beautiful name! You may call me Dama Dupont. How old are you?"

Alessia held up four fingers.

Madeleine grinned and held her hands out. "I have a daughter the same age as you. Her name is Clarisse."

"Does she live here too?" Alessia asked.

"Oh no, Clarisse and my older children stay with my family in the village during the day. But Henri, my youngest, is in the servants' quarters right now, sleeping. I bring him to the château so I can feed him."

"How many children do you have?" Elionor asked.

"God has blessed me and my husband with five beautiful, healthy children—two girls, Hélène and Clarisse, and three boys, Florian, Aymon, and Henri." Madeleine rose, bent slightly at the waist, and placed her hands on her apron. "Now, the rest of you, tell me your names."

One by one, some more timidly than others, the children introduced themselves to Madeleine.

Elionor looked up at Madeleine as she tied Prospera's braid and draped it over the girl's shoulder. "What happened to the old woman who brought us here? Not that I'm asking for her back . . ."

A small laugh fell from Madeleine's lips. "Zéphérine was glad to be assigned other responsibilities." She pushed her tongue into her cheek. "It was arranged that I should care for you instead."

"Was it Lord Philip?" Constanza asked.

"No, not the lord. He is occupied with . . . other matters tonight." A touch of discretion crossed Madeleine's countenance. "For now, be assured that you are safe at Château de Ripaille."

"Château de Ripaille? I thought this was Thonon."

Madeleine shook her head. "No, Château de Thonon is the duke's own residence. It's in the town of Thonon, on the other side of the forest, and it sits on a cliff overlooking the lake. While we're close to the town here, Château de Ripaille is merely a hunting retreat, one that Lord Philip has claimed as his own."

That look in her eyes—I've seen it before. Without question, Madeleine's bright presence in this dark room felt like God Himself had sent her to dispel the shadows.

Madeleine extended her hand toward the fireplace. "Usually it is my chore to maintain the lamps and candles of the château, so I'll arrange a fire for you." She drew a finger to the corner of her lips. "I need to carry the firewood up here first."

"Silvia, Ezio, and Guido can help you carry it." Constanza waved them forward.

"No." Madeleine raised both hands, palms facing outward. "It would be unwise for me to bring them outside this wing of the château. I don't even bring my baby out of the servants' quarters. Lord Philip despises children, and I fear his reaction if he hears yours, especially while he's occupied."

"These three are older and know how to be quiet." Constanza caught herself and shot a playful glare at Ezio. "At times."

"I can't risk it. Lord Philip would be angry, and I fear for my employment here if he discovered I had allowed them out of the room. Merci for thinking of me, but I'm accustomed to work." Madeleine offered a quick bow and exited the room. A short time later, she returned with a bundle of logs and tossed them beside the fireplace.

"I can light the fire!" Guido grabbed the lantern from the mantel.

Ezio reached for it too and ripped it away from Guido. "I'm older!"

"Shh!" Madeleine held a finger to her lips. "You must be quiet, children, or Lord Philip will hear you."

Ignoring her, the boys continued to tussle over the lamp. Constanza pushed her way into the fray and tried to pry the boys apart. The lantern flew from Ezio's hand and crashed to the floor, its metal clanging as it rolled across the wooden planks. The light winked out, and darkness filled the room.

Constanza clenched her hands into fists and held her breath. A floorboard creaked near the window, and the smell of smoke laced the air.

"Ezio did it," Guido said, breaking the silence.

Foolish boys! Constanza scowled in their direction, but the room was nearly black, and her vision hadn't adjusted.

"For all our sakes, don't cause any loud disturbances in the château." Madeleine's voice was quiet and subdued. "Lord Philip might not be the most honorable man, but he is a reasonable master—as long as he forgets children are under his roof." She drew closer to the hearth. "I'm aware of your plight, and I will do my best to make your stay here both short and comfortable."

"I'm sorry," Ezio said. Guido echoed him.

Madeleine picked up the lantern, then rushed away and returned swiftly with a new flame. She lit the fireplace and placed the lantern back on the mantel. Constanza waved the children toward the fire, and everyone huddled together near it.

"You are famished, no?" Madeleine asked, hands on her hips. "Dinner was already served, but we have plenty left over. I'll bring it up."

Rubbing her hands together near the fire, Silvia glanced at Madeleine. "Why does the lord hate children so much?"

"I'm not entirely sure." Madeleine flashed a mischievous smile. "Perhaps because he's still somewhat of a child himself."

Giggles erupted across the room as Madeleine hurried off again and shut the door.

"The Lord answered my prayer," Constanza said to Elionor. "I was sure that other woman would be our host."

"Madeleine is as pleasant as can be." Elionor sighed heavily. "I just want this all to end. I would much rather sit at Madeleine's house and eat with her family than be locked in this cold place." She swept her hand across the room. "Though this is much better than sleeping outdoors."

Madeleine made numerous trips to the room—food, water, fresh linens, a mound of blankets, more firewood, and even three straw mattresses. "There are more beds in the storehouse, but if you can wait until tomorrow—"

"We're already blessed," Constanza said, "and I could never give you enough thanks."

"And you and your children have brought life and goodness to this château when that had all seemed to disappear." A smile adorned Madeleine's lips, a subtle curve that carried true joy. Her eyes glistened with tears, but she quickly wiped them away.

Before long, blankets covered all the children as they lay next to the fireplace. Its soothing pops and crackles serenaded them as they fell asleep. Lacking a real bath, Constanza rinsed her face, neck, and hair, then lay down on one of the mattresses and drifted into a heavy slumber.

18

They were pious of life and conduct; they embraced a faith which the lords and princes could not understand.

—Steward of Winnick, 1558

THE SUN HAD LONG SINCE SET by the time Andreas and Johan reached the walls of Thonon. Directly above them, the growing moon hung in the night sky, not seeking attention but shining a steady light on the slumbering town. Andreas's boots clapped on the paved thoroughfare that led through an open gate and meandered gradually downhill into the town.

Andreas gazed toward the distant citadel with a single lit lamp glowing from its pinnacle. "We won't be permitted to enter the château at this hour. Another night in the dirt for us, it seems."

Johan tipped his nose up at the citadel. "Do you think your family is in there?"

"That's probably where Philip took them."

"I thought he was trying to usurp your father. How could both of them live in the same place?"

Andreas slowly shook his head. "My own mâre is unfaithful to my pâre in the same château, so why can't my rebellious brother also live there?"

"And I thought my family was odd." Johan winced.

Andreas and Johan made camp and lit a fire under an oak with most of its leaves still intact. Andreas curled up next to the fire, closed his eyes, and prayed until he fell asleep.

Before dawn, roosters startled Andreas awake. While Johan still snored, the sun rose over the mountains they had descended three days earlier.

Church bells tolled, cart wheels clattered, and hammers clanged, while scents of baking bread and burning wood filled the air. Andreas gazed above the line of trees to the distant hills. *Dear God, I need wisdom today. Help my brother to be reasonable, and if I must speak with my parents, give me compassion and patience. Most of all, let me be a faithful witness of Your Son.*

Andreas nudged Johan once, then again. "The cow needs to be milked and the wood chopped. Time to awaken, Johan."

With his eyes still closed, Johan rolled over, yawned, and smiled. After a light kick from Andreas, Johan sat up and stretched. "Yes, Papà, I'll do my chores, but not before I eat."

"From what I remember about your papà, he would've thrown a bucket of cold water on your face by now."

"No, two buckets by now." Johan stretched his arms to the sky again, then sighed. "I miss him every day, Andreas. As much as I dishonored him, he was always patient with me. I wish he could see me now—I'm a different man than I was two years ago. Maybe he'd even be pleased with me."

"He would." Andreas nodded and gave Johan a brotherly slap on the shoulder. "Today you might have the opportunity to meet my pâre, though I think you'll find him quite unimpressive."

"The Duke of Savoy himself?" Johan stood, placed his hands on his hips, and twisted from side to side. "You act as though that's nothing."

"Today, Johan Lauras, in the grand Château de Thonon upon Lac Léman, you'll quickly discover how petty, inept, and foolish your rulers are."

"Oh, I've always known that, but today I guess I'll see it for myself."

Bustling activity greeted Andreas and Johan as they entered the outskirts of the town. Merchants haggled over goods along the street. The scent of exotic spices and fresh wheat bread mingled with the clean aroma of the nearby lake. Its calm waters glittered, reflecting the golden hues of the morning sun as fishing boats glided across its surface. Lac Léman—years had passed since Andreas had last laid eyes upon the pearl of the Alps.

Yet despite the vibrancy of Thonon, an underlying tension hovered in the air. Shadows seemed to linger a moment too long in the narrow alleyways, and whispers of half-heard conversations hung on the breeze. An uneasy feeling settled in the pit of Andreas's stomach.

The flagstone road wove through Thonon, passing houses of varying size. The mostly wooden structures, their roofs a reddish hue that caught the sunlight, reflected the passage of seasons and generations. Each roof was subtly different from the others—a steeper pitch, a darker color, a more intricate pattern, evidence of the ways Thonon had grown and adapted.

The old château's citadel towered high above all the roofs. The facade boasted intricate detailing, with arched windows and decorative stonework that reflected the elegant tastes of the House of Savoy. A high stone wall, anchored by four stout towers, encompassed the château and its citadel.

As Andreas led the way toward the entrance, three guards wearing full suits of plate armor took positions in front of the open gate and blocked it with their spears. Before any of the guards had a chance to speak, Andreas raised his hand and waited for a response.

"Who are you?" asked one of the men. "Do you expect us to bow before you?"

"I am Lord Andreas, son of Duke Louis and Anne of Cyprus. Allow me to enter."

All three guards burst into laughter. One bowed low and pretended to remove a tiara from his head. "And I'm the pope." He held out his hand to Andreas. "Kiss my ring, Lord Andreas."

Andreas took another step toward the gate, lifted his chin, and tried to recall his noble Savoyard accent. "Allow me to enter at once, or I shall have you all drowned in the lake."

One guard shuffled his feet, and the other thumbed his ear.

"If I must prove myself, you would not be the first to be chained to a stone and thrown in."

One guard crossed his arms and drew a steady breath. "Who are your siblings?"

Andreas leveled a disdainful look at him. "I shall be granted entrance to my residence immediately, or your final breath shall be not fresh air but the water of Lac Léman."

A blacksmith's hammer clanged repetitively from inside the walls as the guards stared at each other. Andreas pushed aside the spears and marched through the gate and into the expansive courtyard.

"What was that?" Johan asked after they had passed the guards.

"'A noble never asks, and he never proves—he only commands.' That's what my mother taught me."

"You didn't do that back at Miradolo."

"I'm finished with the frivolities. I want my family back."

"Couldn't you have just named your brothers and sisters and been done with them?"

"If I had answered, the guards would have doubted me. Even acknowledging their demands would have been unlike a prince of Savoy."

"But I've never seen you treat men like such dogs."

Andreas half smiled over his shoulder at Johan. "Wait until you meet Philip. Then you'll see what it means to treat men like dogs."

In the courtyard, the murmur of bubbling fountains mingled with the nickering of horses from the nearby stable. A well-tended garden, featuring carefully manicured hedges and symmetrical flower beds, added to the pretentiousness of the castle grounds. The castle never used to look this extravagant. Yet five years had passed since Andreas had last walked through this courtyard.

Andreas walked up the citadel's broad stone stairs. The massive oak door, bound with iron straps and studded with black nails, stood three times the height of any man. He knocked, and an unfamiliar, dark-complected steward answered. "Duke Louis is unavailable until later today."

"I am not here for my pâre but for my brother, Lord Philip."

The steward's face stiffened. "Lord Philip the usurper? Who are you?"

"Must I continue to answer the same question?" Andreas strode past the man and motioned for Johan to follow. "I am your lord, Andreas."

"Ah, the heretic Andreas—I've heard much about you. Allow me to find the duchess, for she desires to speak with you."

Andreas took a long breath. Was he ready to see Mâre after all these years? So much time had passed, and so much had transpired. "I need to see Philip first."

"All in due time, monseigneur." The steward's crooked smile twisted at Andreas's patience.

Andreas extended his hand, palm outward, then flicked his wrist sharply downward. *"Allons, fâs-le."*

As soon as the steward was out of earshot, Johan asked, "What does *allons, fâs-le* mean?"

"'*Proceed, do it.*' The servants hear that phrase more than all others. It was probably the first sentence I learned as a child—allons, fâs-le."

The steward returned within moments and bowed slightly. "Please follow me, my lord."

The castle buzzed with activity as the steward ushered them through the halls. Servants clad in finely embroidered attire moved gracefully through the corridors, attending to the needs of the household. The halls resonated with the plucked melodies of courtly music, while the smell of roasted meat drifted into Andreas's nostrils and stirred him to hunger.

"You shall remain here," the steward said to Johan near the entry to the great hall.

Johan complied, and Andreas followed the steward into the hushed grandeur of the hall.

Tall, arched windows framed with intricate stone tracery allowed slivers of daylight to dance on the polished marble floor. Overhead, immense wooden rafters soared like the ribs of a mighty whale. Each beam bore the scars of centuries, etched with the marks of countless winters and summers. The air carried the rich scent of burning hearthwood, creating an atmosphere both regal and welcoming. The steward led him deeper into the chamber, its high ceiling supported by sturdy pillars. Ornate carvings adorned the walls, depicting tales of valor and heraldry: the Savoyard crusade to Constantinople, the glorious victory at Gamenario, Amadeus the Peaceful, and even Pâre. Andreas lifted his chin a little higher. This was all his family, his blood, his heritage.

At the far end of the hall, upon a raised dais, sat Duke Louis of Savoy and Duchess Anne of Cyprus—Pâre and Mâre. A tall man clothed in a gold-trimmed deep crimson robe stood behind Mâre. Sunlight reflected from his smooth scalp as he caught Andreas's eyes and swiftly moved forward.

The man placed his arm across his torso and bowed slightly. "Lord Andreas." His clear voice resounded like the deep pluck of a lute. "I am Lucien Bouchard of Cyprus. It is a pleasure to finally be in your presence."

Andreas acknowledged him with a curt nod and approached the dais. How could Pâre allow his own wife's companion to stand in the same room with him? He bowed to his father. "Pâre."

"What at last brought you to Thonon after so many summonses?" The duke leaned back in his ornate chair, his fingers drumming against the carved armrest.

Andreas turned to his mother and kissed her hand. "My brother Philip. I must speak with him now."

"You must seek him out yourself, then," Mâre said, her voice weaker and raspier than when Andreas had last seen her. "Most of the knights and soldiers and several lords have sworn allegiance to him over your pâre and his heir, Amadeus, Prince of Piedmont."

Deep within her was still the same motherly warmth Andreas remembered. Memories of boyhood, sitting by Mâre's side as she recounted tales of her homeland across the sea, flooded his mind. He blinked rapidly and refocused on the true reason for standing here. Now was not the time to dwell in the past. "Where is Philip?"

"Château de Ripaille." Bouchard drew closer behind Andreas with slow but sure steps.

Andreas turned to Bouchard. "Ripaille, the hunting lodge?"

"Why do you seek Philip?" Pâre asked.

"He has my family in his custody."

Bouchard looked down his nose at Andreas. "Then I suppose your family is there."

"His family?" Mâre sat straight in her chair and let out a shallow laugh. "We are his family. I heard about the peasant girl, and whoever she is, she is not his wife." She stared directly at Andreas, her warmth vanishing behind a freezing stare. "To think otherwise is simply delusional. Who are her parents? Whence does she hail? What land does her family hold?" She held a white cloth to her pale lips and coughed.

"Her name is Constanza, and she is my wife." Andreas's pulse and breathing quickened. "I am no longer entangled in this house's affairs and am no longer subject to the whims of the nobility."

Lucien Bouchard withdrew from Andreas, took his place behind Mâre, and patted her shoulder.

Andreas raised his hands as though he could ward off the sight before him. "Pâre, how can you allow this man in your court?"

"Lucien is a wise man, and your mâre deeply values his counsel."

Andreas shook his head and scanned the room. "Look at this great hall. When my grandfather was duke, we were a powerful house, esteemed by all

Christendom. Now it has fallen into decadence ushered in by Mâre's Cypriot courtiers."

"Have you been listening to the gossip in the streets?" Mâre leaned forward in her chair. "You dare to enter my hall and repeat Philip's lies in my presence. I am ashamed of you, Andreas."

Tense quiet stretched out, broken only by the rustle of wind outside the windows. Pâre's voice broke the lengthening silence. "The abbey did not suit you, I hear."

Andreas took a deep breath. "I have come to understand the Holy Scriptures and have even read the New Testament from beginning to end."

"A heretic nonetheless." Bouchard tightened his mouth as if he'd tasted rancid boar meat.

"We already have too many heretics in our lands—the Poor, the Vallenses, and this new sect with their prophet." Pâre sighed and stared off at a corner of the room. "But to hear my own son has left the tender embrace of the Church of Saints Peter and Paul . . . I am very disheartened."

Andreas dropped his gaze, struggling to find the right words. He taught his own children to honor their father and mother, as the Holy Scriptures commanded, but the same applied to him. Despite observing little in them to honor—only faint memories of years gone by—he must still submit to God's order. "I should have obeyed your first summons, and for that I ask your forgiveness. But I am fulfilled in my new life. To you, I may seem mad, but God has filled me with His Spirit—"

"You speak blasphemy." Bouchard clenched his teeth and sneered.

"I know only what the Holy Scriptures tell us. 'What? know ye not that your body is the temple of the Holy Ghost which is in you, which ye have of God, and ye are not your own? For ye are bought with a price: therefore glorify God in your body, and in your spirit, which are God's.' God is my Savior, and the Spirit lives within me."

"If a priest were here," Pâre said, "he would also name you a blasphemer for quoting the Scriptures in the vulgar tongue."

Andreas allowed himself a smile. "I see no priest here."

Pâre and Mâre both offered restrained laughs, but Bouchard remained silent.

"I don't mean to depart so swiftly, but I must find my family, and as we speak, my brother holds them against their will. You said Philip is at Château de Ripaille?"

"He seized it in the spring," Mâre said, "which is a sore tragedy, for Ripaille was my most beloved retreat."

"Then I must go there to free my family."

"Don't you see?" Bouchard extended his hand, palm upward. "Philip is using you against us. As we speak, his forces gather, intent on overthrowing your father and mother. All he needs is legitimacy. If you give him that by forsaking your title, his path is clear."

"Then send soldiers to free my wife and children."

Pâre rubbed his cheek, and his countenance sank. "We do not have the power to overcome him."

"Then I shall do this without any help, and my only recourse is to negotiate. I didn't choose to come here, but I'll do what I must for those I love."

As Andreas gave his parents a parting kiss, he wished his relationship with them were as loving as Constanza's had been with her parents. Riches, prestige, pride—they were each a poison that choked true familial love.

He met Johan outside the entry and briefly recounted the meeting. Together they walked into the courtyard, through the gate, and back into the town, heading toward the nearby Château de Ripaille.

* * *

"I'm still disappointed I couldn't meet the ruler of the whole duchy." Johan gazed through the forest as he walked, occasionally stopping to watch deer feed on the undergrowth.

"You didn't miss anything," Andreas said. "My father is weaker than before and my mother more decadent while she entertains the Cypriot that Claude mentioned—Bouchard. Perhaps Philip would show himself a more capable ruler than anyone who resides at Château de Thonon."

"No, he wouldn't. Remember how he installed Gedeon as the Lord of Luserna? Philip had the old lord poisoned so his man could steal the title."

"But that was for power. I don't believe Philip had specific designs against Vallenses."

"Either way, do you want the man who abducted your family to be your duke?"

"Johan, it's of no concern to me who the ruler of Savoy is. As I've said a number of times, the politics of this realm don't concern me. I simply want to find my family and head back to my farm."

A buck stared at them through the brush, and Johan observed it intently. "Do you see that? Twelve points on that rack. If I had a bow right now—"

"If you shot that deer, you'd rot in a dungeon. See all this around us? It's the prime game reserve of the duchy, and you would never be granted permission to hunt here."

"Look at it, though—standing there and waiting for me to kill it." Johan gave Andreas a devious grin. "You're a prince. Couldn't you grant me permission?"

Andreas sighed and shook his head as he continued to march through the forest.

The sun had risen almost to its apex by the time they passed through the gates of Château de Ripaille. Without a second glance, the guards allowed them to enter, saying Philip was expecting Andreas.

The expansive yard, nestled between the outer walls and the château itself, hummed with anticipation, its air tinged with music and the scent of freshly cut grass. Andreas drank in the sights unfolding around him. Banners billowed overhead, their vibrant colors contrasting with the weathered walls of the castle. Whatever event would soon occur here was certain to be grand.

His heart raced at the thought of seeing Constanza and the children again. He almost expected them to barge through the door, run to him, and plaster him with hugs and kisses.

The door of the château opened, but instead of Constanza and the children, Philip sauntered out with his arm wrapped around a scantily dressed woman. "Brother!" He kissed the woman on the lips, whispered something in her ear, and dismissed her.

She walked past Andreas and Johan toward the gate, batting her eyelashes, but Andreas kept his eyes locked on Philip. "Where is my family?"

Two armed guards filed out from the door and flanked Philip, one with dark, wavy hair and the other short but muscular.

Philip scanned the landscape as if Andreas was beneath his notice. "Constanza and your children and that other woman—Elionor, I think her name is—they are all well cared for here."

"Thank you for rescuing them from the Ascendants." Andreas managed to speak without sarcasm, though it still simmered under his words.

"Oh, it was a simple matter. That band of rebels might have seemed daunting, but I have over a hundred men-at-arms who are loyal to me. We killed a few of the cultists, and the rest fled."

Andreas curled his toes in his boots. "Allow me to see my family."

"Andreas, making demands of me?" Philip snickered. "Do you imagine me as your servant to command? No, brother, I hold the power here, and you are nothing but mud on my boots."

"What do you want from me? I'm willing to give what I'm able."

"Time presses against me at the moment. The afternoon's entertainment will soon begin here. You should join me, for then we can discuss your family—and our dear pâre and mâre."

Andreas drew in a slow breath, steadying himself, and stiffened his back. "Philip, I don't have the patience for a play, a dinner, a joust—nothing. Tell me what I must do to see my wife."

"Indeed, you are at my mercy." Philip grinned and motioned for the dark-haired officer. "Lugotenent Renaud, take my brother and his guest to my viewing platform. Have the servants bring them the finest cuts of meat, and fill their goblets with the most superior wine. I will join them shortly." At that, he turned and reentered the château.

The officer motioned toward the right. "Follow me."

Andreas trailed the lugotenent, and Johan fell into step beside him. "Constanza, my children, Elionor—they're here, Johan." As they walked, Andreas quieted his voice to a murmur, barely audible above the flutter of activity in the yard. "Somewhere in this place, they wait for me. Yet as near as I am, they're still distant."

"I wonder if we could sneak in and find them."

Andreas shot Johan a sharp, silent warning.

The officer turned and smiled at them. "Don't try it."

He led Andreas and Johan around the seventh tower and into a field of neatly cut grass. Ahead, the stage stood as a centerpiece, its curtains drawn like a veil, awaiting the moment to reveal the wonders behind them. A mix of nobles, courtiers, and members of the Savoyard elite, each adorned in elaborate dress, congregated in small groups near the stage. Animated conversation and laughter, punctuated by the occasional rustle of silk and the clink of goblets, flowed through the yard.

The smells, the sights, the sounds—they all washed over Andreas like a familiar melody, one he had once sung with youthful abandon. But now his song had deepened with the harmony of life, its notes richer and more resonant, a new song far more meaningful than anything he had known before.

He and Johan followed the officer onto an elevated platform that commanded the best view of the stage. "Your seats," the officer said, motioning with his right hand. He turned and left without another word.

Johan sat, crossed his legs, and reclined in his chair. "So this is what it's like to be a rich noble? To think that all this luxury came from the labor of poor farmers and simple craftsmen."

"An injustice, isn't it?" Andreas said. "Philip is no better than my mâre, as you can see."

Philip appeared from the opposite side of the yard, waving, smiling, and laughing as he passed through his admirers. A new young woman held his arm, undoubtedly enjoying the attention of the gawkers.

Nodding once toward Philip, Andreas whispered, "And he seems to be just as loose with his morals too."

Two guards escorted Philip and the young woman onto the pedestal and left them standing near two chairs to Andreas's right. Philip introduced his guest as Élisabeth, daughter of a minor noble near Chambéry.

As Andreas bowed slightly toward Élisabeth, Philip sat next to him and pointed toward the stage. "*The Misadventures of Pierre and Jacques*, it's called. I know you shall enjoy it. Perhaps it will also remind you of your humble new home in Piedmont."

Andreas ignored the quip. "Where is my family, Philip?"

"They are safe in the château and perfectly content in their quarters." Philip didn't bother to look at Andreas.

"When will I see them?"

"Look, it's starting." The curtain opened, and the crowd erupted in applause—all except Andreas and Johan. Old tapestries hung in the background of the stage, depicting a rural village complete with quaint cottages, winding streets, and a rustic marketplace. Props including wooden barrels, stacks of hay, and rustic furniture added to the scene, while colorful costumes alluded to the charm and whimsy of what was to come.

Andreas clenched his fists, eager to end this ordeal before the last descent of the curtain. "I saw Pâre and Mâre . . ."

"So I heard." Philip remained focused on the stage. "Did you also meet that conniving Cypriot Lucien Bouchard?"

A wave of applause swept through the crowd as two actors dressed as peasants stumbled onto the stage and bowed low. Slurring, Pierre mumbled his name first; then Jacques shouted his after a hiccup.

"Monsieur Bouchard was there, standing behind Mâre," Andreas said.

"You saw the rot of our noble house, then. Why did I provoke you to come to Thonon, you asked? Exactly for that reason—to see for yourself what Savoy has become. If it were not for Bouchard and his Cypriot courtiers, I would not have been forced to take action as I have. Pâre has always been unwilling to rule, and Mâre has thus ruled him. But with Monsieur Bouchard, the whole court has fallen into decadence. Mâre spends every ducat she finds on parties, sculptures, and jewels. The Duchy of Savoy has become the subject of all jests in Europe . . . and I wish to put an end to that."

Andreas dropped his shoulders and sighed. Perhaps Philip was right in his judgments, but why should this involve Andreas?

On the stage, Pierre and Jacques entered the marketplace, their expressions alight with anticipation. A young peasant woman stood behind the counter of a flower stall, arranging bouquets with practiced skill.

"Jacques, mon ami, look! There she is, our Isabelle, fairest flower in all the land!" Pierre's grin was wide with excitement.

Glancing toward the sky, Jacques said, "Ah, Pierre, you never tire of singing her praises, do you? But be careful, lest your songs wilt her vibrant roses!"

Philip laughed and held a hand up to Andreas. "Listen, for this will make even you laugh, Andreas."

Isabelle noticed Pierre and Jacques approaching and greeted them with a smile. "Bonjour, Pierre! Bonjour, Jacques! What brings you to my little stall today?"

"Ah, Isabelle!" Pierre bowed gallantly. "It is not *what* brings us, but *who* brings us, for we have come to offer you the prettiest blooms from the fields of our affection."

"Prettiest blooms indeed." Jacques signaled the audience. "More like wilted weeds from the roadside."

Laughter bubbled up from the crowd, but Andreas leaned back and crossed his arms. Johan watched with a trace of levity on his face.

Amused, Isabelle said, "How kind of you, Pierre! And what of you, Jacques? Do you bring me flowers as well?"

"Flowers, Isabelle?" Jacques beamed. "No, I bring you something far more precious—the wisdom of a poet's heart and the wit of a jester's tongue."

"Ah, Isabelle, don't be fooled by his clever words," Pierre said with a chuckle. "For it is I who truly cherishes you."

"Merci, Pierre. Merci, Jacques. Your words bring light to my day, as bright as the summer sun itself."

As Pierre and Jacques exchanged a triumphant glance, a sudden gust of wind, helped along by a few silent stagehands, sent Isabelle's flower cart careening out of control, scattering blooms in every direction.

Pierre rushed in to help. "Oh, Isabelle! Allow me to assist you!"

"Fear not, fair Isabelle!" Jacques said.

Pierre inserted a crude remark, and the audience's laughter faltered. But not Philip's. Andreas shifted in his seat and frowned, while Johan's expression darkened at the dishonor shown to Isabelle.

Jacques chuckled at Pierre's inappropriate comment and nudged him with an elbow. "Even in chaos beauty blooms eternal."

The curtain dropped. Philip and his companion rose to their feet and applauded.

Johan showed a tight smile and shook his head at Andreas. "You nobles find this funny?"

Andreas itched to march out of this vile gathering, but he couldn't until he was finished with Philip.

As Philip sat again, a servant approached and filled his goblet to the brim. Philip took a long drink and leaned over to Andreas, his breath smelling of strong wine. "Nothing can bring mirth like this. Do you ever miss it, Andreas? The comforting minstrels, the luxurious dinners, the beautiful women? Surely you do at times." He took another gulp.

"I am happier than ever, brother—at least I was until you took my family." Andreas lowered his voice and looked directly at Philip. "What do you want from me?"

"Declare yourself illegitimate."

"I can't do that, and you know it. Besides, it would be a lie."

"Don't we all lie to get what we want?"

"Not everyone in this world sees sin as a light matter."

Philip's jaw tightened briefly as he flipped up his hand in dismissal. "Did the monastery do this to you—make you such a holy . . . whatever you are?"

"God changed me from the inside. I am not the man I once was. It wasn't the Church, and it wasn't even the Vallenses—"

"Indeed, the heretics of Piedmont. How you've evaded the Inquisition, I don't know, but you can't hide in those mountains forever. The Church will find you, take all you now hold dear, and burn you."

"I'm not hiding." Yet as Andreas voiced those words, he questioned the truth of his claim. For months, he had skirted confrontation with his past, evading the weight of his noble family and his lineage. Regardless of how much he denied it, no matter how far he ran from it, the truth remained—Andreas was a prince of Savoy, ordained by God to fulfill a purpose in that role far greater than himself.

Should he side with Philip against his weak pâre and frivolous mâre? Or would it be best to side with his parents and the natural order, opposing Philip's pride, debauchery, and rebellion? Either way, he must free his family first.

Andreas sat straight in the chair. "I can't declare myself illegitimate—only Pâre can do that, and even then, the Church would have to confirm it."

"You must help me convince Pâre. I have obtained letters from before you were born that imply Mâre's infidelity—"

Andreas grimaced and let out a harsh puff of air. "A liar and a schemer both. That's what you are."

"You want your wife and children returned to you, no?" Philip turned to his companion and pointed his thumb at Andreas. "My brother must not care for his woman as much as he professes."

"Stop with this madness, Philip. Are you so naive as to believe that other realms will accept you as the ruler of Savoy? Even if Amadeus and I declared ourselves illegitimate and relinquished all our claims and Pâre named you his heir, Savoy's neighbors would see this as weakness. The king of France might intervene and claim the whole duchy for himself."

"I have the dauphin's backing. He despises Mâre and her Cypriot courtiers even more than I do."

"The dauphin's sister Yolande is married to our brother Amadeus, the true heir to Savoy. As much as the dauphin might despise Mâre, he won't allow a rogue like you to upset the natural line of succession. France arranged the marriage of Yolande to Amadeus to their advantage, and the House of Valois will not stand aside and let you steal Savoy."

Philip leaned toward Johan, chuckling. "Did you know Andreas was so shrewd? I almost forgot what it was like to be his brother. Now this is the older brother I was seeking, not the one I met before the play."

"He's wiser than any man I know," Johan said. "You'd find it best to heed him."

Philip let out a puff of air and locked his eyes on Andreas. "Constanza—I admit she is charming. No harm will come to her, and I promise you that. The children . . . I wish I had left them in Piedmont, but they're here now, and I will not hurt them."

"At least let me see them."

"I need your cooperation first. Perhaps there is a better way than saying you and Amadeus are illegitimate—whatever it takes to rid Thonon of that wolf Lucien Bouchard and all his Cypriot friends. Mâre is very sick and will likely die soon, and Pâre is waning too. Neither will last more than a year, and when they are gone, will Amadeus rule next? He has no interest in being duke. Instead of Cypriots managing the realm as they do now, Yolande and her cheese-eating French attendants will. Foreign powers will conquer us, and our noble house will be forever ruined if we don't save the duchy. This is our divine calling. Do you not see it?"

"Our calling?" Andreas raised his brows. "We're not saving the duchy, and I'm not your hound dog. How can I trust you while you hold my family hostage?"

"It lured you here, did it not? It was the only way."

"Then I'll make another way by myself." Andreas stood and motioned for Johan. "Bonjorn, Philip."

Philip held his goblet toward the stage. "Won't you stay to see the next act? It's starting now."

As the curtain rose, Pierre and Jacques appeared from behind a cart. They faced the crowd and raised their voices in unison. "Ecce lux prophetæ ducet nos."

Laughter rippled through the audience, and a smattering of applause followed. Andreas opened his mouth and nudged Johan. "Did you catch that?"

Johan reared his head back and squinted at the actors. The play commenced with more of Pierre and Jacques's antics, and everyone from Philip to the servants at the periphery watched in delight, not seeming to have noticed the actor's declaration.

"Curious," Andreas said. "They might have simply been mocking the Ascendants, though it has nothing to do with what they're acting out now."

He nodded toward the exit and waved for Johan to follow. Philip raised his goblet toward them but otherwise devoted himself to the play. Once Andreas rounded the tower, he meticulously examined the weathered walls of the château. Thick tendrils of ivy clung to the stone and plaster, creeping upward around the windows like determined mountain climbers. Behind those aged windows lay his Constanza and the children, imprisoned because he was a prince of Savoy.

Andreas took a deep breath and straightened his shoulders. He would not pass this wall again without liberating them.

"I don't trust Philip," he said to Johan, "not in the slightest."

"Now I can see why he chose Gedeon as one of his lackeys. Philip is a viper."

"Which is why I'm going to free my family myself."

"How?"

Andreas half smiled as he walked past the guards and through the gate. He did not answer.

19

The Savoyard shore of Lake Geneva, with its feudal ruins, evokes a past rich in memories. This region, with such picturesque charm, retained the princes of Savoy at a time when the future of their house on the other side of the Alps was not yet defined. One of the House of Savoy's favorite residences was Ripaille, whose important constructions can be seen near the lake between Thonon and Dranse.

—Max Bruchet
Le Château de Ripaille, 1907

MOONLIGHT BATHED the outer wall of the château as Andreas pressed himself against the rough surface, his heart pounding in his chest. Lush ivy rustled and crackled beneath his weight, a fragile tether in the darkness. Just a little higher, and he'd reach the pinnacle of the wall. Johan held one of Andreas's feet with both hands while Andreas searched for a foothold with the other foot.

"Higher," Andreas whispered.

"Grow taller then, because I can't push you any higher." Johan's grip tightened.

Andreas grabbed a spray of ivy and tested its strength. Too loose. He wiped his sweaty palm on his breeches as he fought to maintain his balance against the unforgiving stone.

"Don't do that!" Johan hissed.

Andreas found a deep gouge in the wall and wedged his right foot into it. With one leg sturdy now, he grabbed the vines with his left hand, tugged, and pulled himself up. Straining every muscle, he raised his left foot out of Johan's hands and struggled for a foothold.

The vines snapped and shifted. Desperation clawed at his chest as he jammed his foot into the ivy and the wall beneath. The ivy held, barely.

"Almost there," Johan whispered from the ground.

Only a forearm's length of wall separated him from the top. One more push, and he'd be over.

Andreas released his left-handed grip and, with a final surge of strength, reached for the ivy above. His muscles burned as he hoisted himself upward, his weight suspended by sheer willpower.

The vines on top of the wall loosened and fell, but not enough to make him do the same. He took a short breath, rocked from side to side, and swung his right hand over the edge of the wall.

The corner of the wall dug into his wrists. His arms trembled with fatigue, and his grip loosened. But he couldn't falter now, not when Constanza and the children needed him.

After a long breath, he pulled himself over the edge. His breathing came in short, ragged gasps as he collapsed on the battlements. The night air filled his lungs with each gasp. He lay on his back and stared up into the sky. *Thank You, Lord.*

Andreas rolled over. Warm light poured from the arched windows of the château and into the courtyard. Each of the seven towers standing in a straight line before him held a small semicircular balcony. If he reached one, he could enter through one of those doors and hopefully into the room where Philip had imprisoned Constanza and the children.

At the front entrance of the château, one guard stood at attention, and two others sat near a sputtering fire. Andreas rose to his hands and knees and crawled to the outer edge of the battlements. Far below, Johan clung to the ivy, not more than a few feet from the ground.

"Wait for me on the ground." Andreas dropped his sack down to Johan.

"I'm not letting you go alone."

"I'll handle this by myself, Johan. Besides, you can't make it up without someone giving you a foothold from below."

This had been the plan all along: Johan would help Andreas over the wall, and Andreas would rescue his family by himself. Never again would someone die so he could gain what he desired. The memory of courageous Victor, who had helped Andreas find the priceless Bible manuscript only to lose his life, still haunted him. The faces of Victor's widow and son were still etched into his conscience. He would not allow Johan to be a casualty like Victor.

"Stay here so you can help everyone down. I'll return soon."

He crept across the wall to the roof of a shed and lowered himself onto it, keeping an eye on the yard. Laughter and music wafted from the far end of the château, stirring memories of childhood visits to Ripaille. If he recalled, the chamber reserved for the lord and lady sat directly above the principal hall. That would be where Philip resided. The guestrooms and servants' quarters, however, were in the opposite wing. *And that's likely where my family awaits me.*

A guard traversed the yard between the shed and the château. His gaze swept the grounds with practiced efficiency. Andreas waited until the guard veered back toward the front entrance before he sprang from the shed and darted through the shadows toward the building.

He pressed his back against the ivy-clad stone. The balcony floor loomed within arm's reach, a far more manageable ascent than the outer wall.

Andreas hugged the shadows as he crept along the facade, his movements as silent as the blackness itself. He flicked his eyes to and fro, vigilant for any sign of patrolling guards.

One man guarded the entrance. His silhouette stood like a sculpture against the moonlit yard. Andreas held his breath and waited for the guard to turn his back. As the sentry turned, Andreas scurried up the ivy and onto the edge of the balcony.

His senses sharpened, attuned to the slightest sound or shift in the air. He pulled himself over the railing and crouched behind its cover.

Save for the distant murmur of revelry, the courtyard below lay silent. Andreas exhaled a measured breath. He was one step closer to Constanza—one step closer to Silvia, Ezio, Guido, and Umile; to Irene, Fosca, Ave, and Bino; to Roberto, Prospera, Zama, and Alessia. *Dear God, help me find them.*

He pressed his ear against the balcony door and listened. Nothing except his heartbeat drumming in his ear. He unlatched the door and swung it open.

Not a chair, not a tapestry, not even a lone crate occupied the expansive room. His first step inside made the boards creak. Andreas froze in place, then sighed with relief.

Step by careful step, he moved to the opposite side of the room. After a brief pause to listen, he pulled the door open.

Lamplight flickered in the long, tapestry-adorned hallway. A lute, singing voices, and a scattering of many footfalls echoed through the château from far to the right. To the left, anchoring the end of the hallway, stood a resplendent suit of Savoyard armor, a relic likely harking back to the valorous days of King Richard of England's crusade to the Holy Land. Gleaming under the hall's subdued light, the ensemble boasted a meticulously crafted chain mail hauberk. Atop it rested a conical helmet, and nearby, a pristine shield evoked the courage of its bearer. A sword, nestled in its sheath, stood at an angle and silently spoke of deeds long past.

Andreas turned left, walked heel first down the hallway, and listened for the laugh of a child or the gentle melody of Constanza's voice. Light flitted out from under the last door in the hallway. His breathing quickened. *They must be in there.*

He turned his head from side to side, then crept to the door and listened. A fire cracked and popped. Someone whispered, but it wasn't Constanza. Elionor?

A tingling unease crept into his arms, and his mind raced in a hundred directions. Once he found his family, how would he lead them to safety? The reunion would bring a flurry of joy and excitement, but they couldn't linger here.

After the balcony, crossing the open yard would prove the most difficult. But they could do it.

Another whisper arose from the room, then an answer. Andreas pushed at the door and found it unlatched. His soul swelled with anticipation as he opened the door.

Seven men huddled around a table lit by a single candle. Their armor and weapons stood propped against the nearby wall. All their attention fell on him.

"Are you joining us?" one man whispered. It was Pierre from the play, or at least the man who had portrayed Pierre. Jacques sat next to him.

Andreas tensed and hunted for an answer. "Joining? Euh . . . yes."

Jacques rose, wearing a long dull brown cloak, the same as the others. "Who are you? I've never seen you here."

The rest of the soldiers—no, Ascendants—rose from their chairs, their strides measured as they approached Andreas, curious smiles mingling with sinister frowns.

Andreas stepped backward, grabbed the door, and pulled it shut. The floorboards shook at the men's pounding feet as they rushed toward the door. The ceremonial sword nearby was probably dull but better than nothing. He grabbed the sword and scabbard, then bolted down the hallway with no destination in mind.

A door opened in front of him. From it stepped another soldier—no, an officer. It was the same one who had escorted Andreas to Philip earlier, and he now held a sword and scabbard of his own. "Halt!"

The Ascendants from the room now stood abreast in the hall behind Andreas. All paths of escape were blocked.

"Lugotenent Renaud," Pierre said. "We . . . we found an intruder."

The officer narrowed his eyes, but not at Andreas. "Yes, an intruder. I'll handle him." He drew his sword and pointed it at Andreas. "You're outnumbered. Surrender. You can't win this fight, especially with a dull sword that doesn't belong to you."

"It belongs to my family." Andreas unsheathed his sword and pointed it at the lugotenent. "And I would be careful before making such a boast."

The corner of the officer's mouth turned slightly upward. "We shall see. Stand back, men."

The stale air of the hallway hung heavy around Andreas as he squared off against the lugotenent. He tightened his grip around the sword, and his pulse quickened. The officer's stance was poised, every movement precise. Andreas rolled his shoulders back, steeling himself for the clash.

The officer lunged forward, his blade slicing the air with deadly precision. Andreas deflected the blow with a deft parry. The clash of metal reverberated through the corridor like a thunderclap. *Parry and parry again—if I wear him down, I'll win.*

The swords danced in a frenzied blur of steel. Each strike sent tremors rippling through Andreas's arm. He fought to hold his ground, but this officer was too skilled.

Yet Andreas would not yield. Constanza waited behind one of these doors, and he would rescue her. With every sinew, he pushed back against the onslaught. But the officer's attacks came with relentless speed.

The walls closed in around Andreas. He could almost feel the Ascendants breathing down his back. Sweat beaded on his brow, and his breaths came in gasps.

"Are you finished?" The lugotenent pressed forward, his attacks coming one after another.

A sudden, deliberate strike brought Andreas to his knees. His chest heaved as his sword clattered to the floor.

A mixture of admiration and regret flickered within the officer's eyes. "Well done, Lord Andreas. Well done." He kicked the sword aside and spoke to the other men. "I'll take the intruder to Lord Philip. Thank you for your help, men. You may return to your quarters." He reached down and offered Andreas a hand.

Andreas's hands shook as they splayed atop the floorboards. If he couldn't defeat this lugotenent with the sword, he would best him in hand-to-hand combat. Who else would save his family?

He accepted the lugotenent's hand but pulled down with all his might and brought his opponent to his knees.

Barely flinching, the officer pivoted to Andreas's side, slid an arm around his neck, and squeezed. "Stand and do as I say." He released his grip and pulled Andreas to his feet, then grabbed Andreas's sword and scabbard. "Straight ahead, my lord. Or I'll squeeze harder next time."

Andreas sighed and took a compliant step forward. He had journeyed all the way to Thonon, and still he had failed his family.

The lugotenent grasped Andreas's shoulder and led him to the lower level. At the bottom, however, they continued straight through the front entrance instead of turning toward the hall.

Andreas jutted out his chest and tried to pull his shoulders back, but the officer's hold was too firm. "I know who you people are, and now I know Philip is in league with the Prophet."

"Silence," the officer said. "You're a prisoner. Behave as one."

*   *   *

The clanging outside Constanza's room stopped. Men talked briefly in the hallway. Then all was quiet except the children's breaths and the crackling hearth. Alessia sat on Constanza's lap and stared at the door. The tension ebbed away, and the children's restless movement slowed. Constanza wiped the sweat from her palms.

"I think it was a sword fight." Umile swung his hand as if he were holding a sword.

"No, it wasn't," Bino said. "It was over too fast."

Umile shrugged. "Maybe it was the soldiers practicing."

Ezio rose from the hearth and walked back to his spot on the floor. "Why would soldiers practice sword fighting in the hallway?"

The door creaked and swung wide as the latch was released.

"What was that noise?" Philip stomped in, his gaudy attire disheveled and his light, wavy hair lying in every direction. "Speak up!"

Constanza grabbed a kerchief and haphazardly covered her hair. "It wasn't us, my lord."

Philip huffed and twitched, then pointed at the nearest child. "Tell me, boy!" He marched to Guido, his face flaming red.

Guido held his hands up but stood his ground.

Snatching Guido's slender arm, Philip swung him around and dragged him toward the hearth. He grabbed a poker and threw it against the stones. "That is precisely what I heard."

Elionor shook her head and mouthed, "No, it wasn't."

"What?" Philip tossed Guido aside and stared at Elionor. "You dare question me, woman?"

Constanza lifted Alessia off her lap, stood, and placed herself between Elionor and Philip. "We heard the clanging too. It sounded like men were fighting in the hallway."

"Impossible. Only you and soldiers are lodged in this wing, and the soldiers know better than to spar indoors."

"We were sleeping in here, I—" Constanza almost let her tongue slip to add *I swear*, but Papà's instruction had taught her otherwise. *But let your communication be, Yea, yea; Nay, nay: for whatsoever is more than these cometh of evil.*

"Did you swallow your tongue?" Philip cackled as he walked toward Constanza with a slight wobble in his step. "Would you guess who I saw today?"

Constanza couldn't resist responding. "Who?"

Philip shifted his weight to one foot and placed a hand on his hip, taking an almost feminine posture. "My brother, Lord Andreas of Savoy."

"My husband?" Constanza gasped. "He's here?"

"He left without so much as giving you a wave or a nod."

"You lie."

"Say what you will, but I know Andreas when I see him. We watched a rather amusing performance in the yard this afternoon—Pierre and Jacques. Have you heard of it?" Philip tilted his head back with a chuckle. "Alas, I know you have not. You are too primitive and prudish."

Constanza dismissed the comment and peered toward the door behind Philip. Andreas had tracked them all the way here, and he wouldn't surrender. Soon they would all be free and on their way home. But one obstacle still seemed to stand between them. "Andreas will never kiss your ring, Philip."

"Kiss my ring?" Philip laughed. "I demand no such thing. All I need is for Andreas to convince my father to name me heir instead of Amadeus. It is not a complicated matter, yet Andreas seems to think it so. Instead of negotiating your release, he stormed off."

Constanza's throat tightened into a knot. "Where is he?"

"I don't know." Philip shook his head. "He is no different from when we were children—determined, yet so weak and distractible."

She scowled. "You're a coward."

Philip clenched a fist at his side. "You should avoid insulting your lord."

Ezio stood up and rushed to Constanza, fists raised. "If you touch my mamà, I'll make you cry!"

A patter of footsteps echoed from the hallway and grew in volume. Madeleine peeked around the corner of the doorway, her reassuring expression shining light into the shadowy room. "My lord Philip, your guests await you."

"Tell them I shall return in a moment." He snatched the poker, threw it against the hearth again, and addressed all the children. "If I hear that noise again, I will hand you back to the Ascendants and their prophet. We all know what they think of children."

Constanza opened her mouth a little, then bit her bottom lip. *No, we don't all know.*

"Please, my lord, I'll manage them." Madeleine hurried to the hearth, grabbed the poker, and stirred the fire. "It would be best if you attended to your friends."

Swinging his cape around, Philip marched out and slammed the door behind him.

"He's so cruel," Silvia said as soon as Philip's footsteps waned.

"There are certainly more virtuous men in the world." Madeleine sat at the hearth next to Alessia, pulled her close, and rubbed her back, all while focusing on Constanza. "May I ask what sent him into a rage?"

"We all heard it—metal clanging in the hallway. But it wasn't us."

"It couldn't have been the soldiers either. Most of them were relieved for a few days, I heard."

"Philip said some were lodged in this wing."

Madeleine lifted an eyebrow. "Odd, I've heard nothing about that."

Silvia sat on the hearth at Madeleine's other side. "Why did you not go home to your family like last night, Madòna Madeleine?"

"*Madòna.* That's your Piedmontese tongue, no?"

"Except for me, none of us speak Piedmontese," Elionor said. "It's Romaunt."

"I've heard of Romaunt, and I wish I knew it." A flash of longing passed through Madeleine's eyes. "Your accent—it's so lovely." She sighed and brushed a wisp of hair off her cheek. "You asked why I remain here so late. It is Lord

Philip and his party. He asked all the servants to stay, though I pray it will be over soon so I can return to my family."

Silvia's face brightened. "Do you have a husband?"

Madeleine smiled gently. "Jean is my husband. He's a hardworking man and is away right now in the forests, cutting wood for the duke. We seldom see him during the woodcutting months, but next week, all the woodcutters' wives will meet our husbands at their encampment, L'Ermitage. It's such a joyous gathering!" She drew in a deep breath as she smoothed the fabric of her sleeve. "That day can't come soon enough."

"Madeleine," Constanza whispered, "Philip said something about Ascendants and children—"

"We should not speak of such things, not with tender ears nearby."

"Speak of what?" Silvia tilted her head.

Madeleine nodded toward the other side of the room, laid Alessia on the floor, and covered her with a blanket. Constanza and Elionor met Madeleine near the window.

"You know about the Ascendants too?" Elionor asked.

"More than I wish to know," Madeleine whispered. "They rose like a blight from right here in Thonon a few years ago, and their prophet has ensnared many with his teachings."

"Last month," Constanza said, "before Lord Philip found us, the Prophet and his followers abducted us from our homeland."

Madeleine dropped her jaw. "You've seen the Prophet?"

"He killed my father three weeks ago." Constanza's breath caught. The reality stung like a venomous serpent sinking its fangs into her soul.

Madeleine drew a hand to her mouth. "I'm so sorry."

"The Prophet is more evil than any other man I've met—and I've encountered a few."

"I still can't believe you've seen him. Everything about him is secretive, and I was sure no one except Ascendants had actually seen him."

"Why do people follow him if they haven't seen him?" Elionor asked.

"I don't know much about these things. As I said, the Ascendants are secretive, and most of what I've heard is rumors." Madeleine crossed herself as Catholics did. "When Philip mentioned the children, he was only throwing an empty threat at you. He does that. Lord Philip might seem strong, but he's actually a weak man. Don't fret over his words." She folded her hands and nodded to the door. "I must hurry back now. Henri is hungry, and I need to fetch my other children. I'll return tomorrow with breakfast. Sleep in peace tonight, *sâre*."

Constanza sank onto her pallet. What did that word mean? It almost sounded like *seror*—sister. Why would Madeleine call her that? Even though she had shown the sign of the cross, there was a sparkle in Madeleine, a light Constanza had glimpsed only in true believers.

20

We may consider that the medieval Waldenses had enjoyed the great religious and cultural privilege of being able to see, touch and listen to the "little books" which the barbes carried with them, and which they brought into the homes of men and women, illiterate laypeople, who were able to hold them in their hands and even leaf through them under a cherry tree in the company of others.

—Marina Benedetti
A Companion to the Waldenses in the Middle Ages, 2022

Andreas and the officer crossed the grassy yard until they reached the gate. A chuckle escaped from the sentry who guarded it. "Found yourself a rat, Lugotenent Renaud? No room in the dungeon?"

"A common thief pilfering weapons, no doubt to hawk them for a mug of ale." The officer waved dismissively. "I don't have the patience to lodge him here."

With a contemptuous spit, the sentry marked his disdain on Andreas. Lugotenent Renaud steered Andreas onto the path that led into the dark expanse of the forest, but the moment the path curved away from the château, he let go.

"My name is Elias Renaud," he said, his frame rigid with urgency. "There's much I need to tell you. But first you must trust me."

"Trust you?" Andreas spun and faced Lugotenent Renaud. "You are a traitor and loyal to Philip, or worse, a follower of the Prophet."

"*Que ridicle!* If I were an Ascendant, I wouldn't be freeing you."

"Then why did you stand between me and my family? Are you that loyal to my usurper brother?"

"You can't rescue your family—not by yourself. But I know where to find help."

Andreas fixed a hard look on the lugotenent and clenched his fists. "This is my burden and no one else's."

But the words pierced his heart before he could say more. For the past month, save for Johan's help, he had shouldered every task and chased every clue on his own. And where had it gotten him?

His breath caught in his lungs, a tremor running through him as he met the officer's steady gaze. The fire that had driven him for so long revealed the weariness he'd tried to bury. The burden was too great, and his stubbornness had only made it heavier.

Swallowing, he unclenched his fists. The words were bitter on his tongue, but he forced them out, each one a surrender to the truth he had fought to deny. "Where do I find help?" he whispered.

Elias Renaud motioned for him to follow. "Come with me."

From the shadow of the forest, Johan ran onto the trail and faced Elias. He held a thick stick with two hands, his face lined with determination. "Let him go, or I'll fight you."

"Does it look like he's my prisoner?" Elias shook his head and pointed to the side of the trail. "Throw your stick in the brush, mon ami. I'm on your side."

Andreas raised his hands and showed them to Johan.

"What is this?" Johan asked. "Is it a trick?"

"It's no trick . . ." Elias looked at Andreas.

"Johan Lauras. If I need to trust you, you need to trust him." Andreas nodded once at Johan and waved him over.

Johan threw his stick into the forest and handed Andreas's sack to him. "It looks like you got caught."

"I must have been close, but I picked the wrong room to enter, it seems. It was full of Ascendants, including Jacques and Pierre from the play."

"Enough chatter." Elias kept his eyes locked on the trail and continued his march.

"Where are we headed?" Andreas asked.

"I still can't believe I'm bringing you, but I must. Things are happening faster than we had guessed."

"Is it far?" Johan asked.

"Not far. But you must remain discreet. There are too many prying eyes in Thonon these days."

"Do you know anything about my wife and children?" Andreas asked.

"Later." Elias turned onto a new path and quickened his pace.

Johan lifted his hand in confusion. "This isn't the way to Thonon."

"Do you live here, mon bon homme? No."

After a short descent, the forest's edge parted and revealed a narrow trail that wound its way alongside a vast body of water. Lac Léman shimmered under the fragile glow of the moon, its surface rippling with reflections of silver and shadow. Water lapped onto the rocky shore, where docked fishing boats swayed on the waves, and a mild breeze carried the scent of damp earth and decaying leaves. In the distance, the silhouette of Château de Thonon loomed high atop a cliff, its towers and spires rising against the star-filled sky.

At the city wall's lakeside bastion, Elias turned left onto another narrow trail that ascended the steep hill along the shore. The trail led to a cluster of wooden houses that surrounded a stone well. Andreas exchanged a glance with Johan, but Johan's expression mirrored his own uncertainty.

"Stay here," Elias said, then he left Andreas and Johan in the shadows.

Johan leaned over to Andreas. "What if this man is an Ascendant? Didn't those women in La Couta say their husbands were in Thonon?"

"His name is Elias Renaud, and he isn't an Ascendant. I think he shielded my family from harm at the château."

Elias appeared behind Andreas, startling him. "Follow me and keep your heads down."

Andreas and Johan complied as they trailed Elias through an alley. They soon arrived at a modest dwelling nestled in the heart of Thonon. The soft glow of candlelight filtered through its windows and illuminated the path. Elias paused at the threshold, his hand resting lightly on the door as if seeking permission before entering.

With a light push, he opened the door and ushered them into the warmth of the house. Scents of woodsmoke mingled with the aroma of vegetables and herbs. A flickering fire cast a parade of shadows across the worn wooden floors. A middle-aged man and woman sat on simple stools by the fire, while a few children played on the floor behind them.

The man rose and bowed his head, his features weathered by time and toil.

Elias turned to the man. "May I introduce Andreas de Bonomo and Johan Lauras." He smiled and grasped the man's shoulder. "This is Antoine Renaud, my pâre."

Andreas moved in to grasp Antoine's arm. "Bon vêpre, monsieur. I am Andreas de Bonomo, and this is my friend Johan Lauras."

"*Frâres.*" Antoine greeted them with a warm smile that reached his tired eyes. "Thank you for coming to our home."

Elias motioned to the woman beside Antoine. "And my mâre, Marie."

Her calloused hands reached out in greeting. "Frâres."

Frâres. That meant "brothers," a peculiar title for strangers. Why did they use that word?

Marie pointed toward the playing children. "These are my daughter's children, whom we often watch during the day." She walked to the hearth, grabbed a towel, and lifted a kettle from the fire. "I made plenty of stew for tonight, so two more guests won't make a difference. There will be plenty for everyone."

"Everyone, dama?" Andreas stood taller, lifting his chin slightly. The children behind her surely wouldn't eat much.

"It's Monday night. Soon our frâres and sâres will arrive, and then we will sing and pray."

"Come, sit at the table." Elias pulled out a chair. "I have much to explain and little time. I must return to Ripaille soon."

Andreas leaned his sack against the wall, sat in the chair, and faced Elias. "My family—have you seen them? Are they safe?"

"I saw them yesterday, and they are well—Constanza, your twelve children, and another young woman, Elionor." At that last name, the corner of Elias's mouth turned upward.

Andreas sighed and closed his eyes for a moment. *Thank You, Lord, for protecting them.*

"I've been with them for over fortnight, since Piedmont," Elias said. "It was a hard journey, but they're strong."

"If you're a friend, why did you stop me from rescuing them?"

Elias let out a brief chuckle. "A valiant effort, but you wouldn't have made it, especially not with those men you found."

"Were they soldiers?"

"New recruits."

"But I think they were Ascendants too."

Antoine approached and sat next to Elias. "In Lord Philip's army?"

"I've suspected it for the last few weeks," Elias said, "but after tonight, I'm certain."

Andreas shifted in his chair. "Is Philip in league with the Prophet?"

"Philip is about as far away from an Ascendant as you can imagine. He and the Prophet aren't allies."

"Who are you?" Andreas rubbed the coarse grain of the chair's wood. "And why are you helping me?"

"My son says we share something." Antoine motioned for Marie to sit by him, then held her hand. "Our common faith."

Andreas slid his chair closer to the table. "Are you Vallenses?"

Elias shook his head. "I've heard that word. What does it mean?"

"What makes you think we believe the same as you?"

"I noticed it when I met Dama Constanza and Demoisèla Elionor—even your children. Then I saw how they prayed and how they treated each other. They are true followers of the Savior."

"And tonight others will meet us here," Marie said. "Will you join us?"

"I can't. Philip is holding my family hostage—"

"And they will remain that way until he gets what he wants." Elias stood and motioned for the children to follow him.

Andreas rose from his seat. "Can't you help them escape?"

"Not when Ascendants have infiltrated the troops. Do you know why they were in that room when you opened the door, Andreas? They're the Prophet's spies—I'm sure of it now."

"Does Philip know?"

"He doesn't care. As long as he has soldiers to help him overthrow the duke, he's satisfied."

"Then why have you joined Philip, Lugotenent? You call yourself a believer, yet you align yourself with a usurper."

Elias glanced sideways at Andreas. "You know nothing."

"Elias never wanted to be a woodcutter like me," Antoine said. "From the time he was a boy, he aimed to become a sword-wielding, standard-bearing man-at-arms for the duke."

Marie grinned. "He's an officer now, with threescore men under his command."

"I was always loyal to the duke," Elias said, "but when Lord Philip said we would fight beside the king of France to sack Genoa, I couldn't resist the call. That was early last month. I knew Philip was rebellious, but it wasn't an open rebellion. It still isn't. Not a drop of blood has been shed during his spat with the duke."

"Why not leave Philip, then? Go back to the duke and renew your service to him."

"And leave your family with no one to protect them?"

Andreas breathed in deeply. Elias seemed to be a good man, and he had launched himself into a heap of danger by helping Andreas. If Philip discovered Elias had caught Andreas sneaking into Ripaille only to lead him to safety, Philip would undoubtedly execute Elias.

"I'll return as soon as I can." Elias grabbed the door handle and turned to Andreas and Johan. "This is the home of my pâre and mâre, and their safety depends on your caution. Don't be careless walking about, and trust no one outside this home." He gathered the children, then opened the door and led them outside, leaving Andreas and Johan with his parents.

While Antoine stoked the fire at the hearth, Marie placed wooden bowls and cups on the table. The husband and wife moved with ease from hearth to table, from storeroom to kitchen, showing their hospitality through their humble gestures.

The door creaked open, and people of various ages slipped inside, their movements cautious yet purposeful. The men, all older than Andreas, wore rough-spun tunics and breeches, patched and faded from years of labor. The women were draped in long dresses with sturdy bodices, their skirts gathered at the waist with simple cloth belts. The children's clothes, though worn and threadbare, bore the marks of loving resourcefulness. Neat stitches lined the mended tears, and the cuffs and hems were creased where they'd been let out to fit growing limbs. If these people lived in Piedmont and wore a little more wool than linen, they could pass as Vallenses.

"Bienveunue, bienveunue," Antoine said to each newcomer. "Please come and sit with our frâres from afar. Elias assured us they are safe." One by one he introduced Andreas and Johan to the guests, even the children. Frâre Andreas and Frâre Johan, he called them.

Marie's kindhearted smile illuminated the room as she placed a steaming pot of stew and a loaf of bread on the table. "Sit, sit. There's plenty for all."

Fifteen people crammed onto the chairs and benches around the table, while the children sat on the rough wooden floor. In unison, they prayed, "We give You thanks, our Father, for the resurrection which You have shown to us through Jézu, Your Son. And even as this bread which is on this table was formerly scattered abroad and has been made compact and one, so may Your church be reunited from the ends of the earth for Your kingdom. For Yours is the power and glory forever and ever. *Âmin.*"

Andreas exchanged a glance with Johan. It certainly sounded like more of a Catholic prayer than a Vallense one, but these people prayed with a devotion few Catholics displayed outside convents and monasteries. Andreas's heart swelled with gratitude for this little place of refuge. Of all the sights in Thonon, this was not one he had imagined.

But were these people true believers, or were they simply devout Catholics? Worse, they could be another strange sect like the Divine Ascendancy. They might call each other frâre and sâre, but were they genuine Christian brothers and sisters?

As Andreas took the first spoonful of Marie's stew, the warmth overwhelmed him like the embrace of a long-lost friend. The rich aroma of savory broth and slow-cooked vegetables wafted from the steaming bowl, mingling with the earthy scent of herbs and spices. Tender chunks of lamb melted in his mouth and released bursts of flavor complemented by the soft texture of carrots and turnips. He hadn't tasted anything like this since home.

Home. The little stone house in the mountains of Piedmont seemed like another world—the smell of the crisp alpine breeze, the children fighting and frolicking around the hearth, and Constanza. Her tender smile, her warm embrace, and the softness of her lips were engraved in his memory, yet they felt so distant. To hold her again and kiss those lips—if it meant standing against Philip, the Prophet, or his own pâre and mâre, he would do it.

An old man tipped the pot and ladled stew into his bowl. "Where do you hail from, frâre?" he asked Andreas.

Andreas laid his spoon on the rim of the bowl and stared at the broth, hesitating. Could he trust these people? Perhaps Antonie, Marie, or one of the elder men could lend him a little knowledge, as Claude had along the Dranse. He spooned some of the soup from the bowl. "From the mountains of Piedmont."

"What brings you to the shores of Lac Léman? Trade?"

"My family." While the pot emptied spoonful by spoonful, the whole room listened to Andreas's account of the journey, starting in Pragela and ending in Thonon, through tangled forests, over high mountain passes, and down a raging river.

Antoine shook his head in disbelief. "The son of Duke Louis himself in our midst. And he's a true believer. The providence of our God is a wonder."

"Âmin," responded five or six others.

Marie took the empty bowls from the children. "Frâre Andreas, what are your plans?"

"I wish I had a good answer. My family is trapped, and Philip says the only way he'll free them is if he is named heir. If I could make that happen, I would, but only the duke has that power. I think my next step is to approach him without my mâre and her lover present."

"Where are you and Frâre Johan lodging?" Antoine asked.

"A tent outside the town."

"No, you won't sleep there. The cold is bitter tonight, and you are Christian frâres. Tonight and for as long as needed, you will stay here with us."

Andreas held a finger up to object, but Johan elbowed him. "He's offering, Andreas. This is the most pleasant place we've seen in weeks."

"Only be careful as you come and go," Antoine said. "We have many enemies in Thonon, and if they knew who we are, they would have us dragged before an inquisitor."

As Marie placed the empty pot next to the hearth, a hush settled over the room, punctuated only by the soft crackle of the fire. Antoine's hum rippled through the silence, the single note streaming through the air like a thread of melody waiting to be woven.

Then, as if drawn by God Himself, the others joined in, their voices rising in a harmony that seemed to fill the room with light. From the youngest girl to the oldest man, each voice added its own color to the chorus. The melody swelled and wove its way through the home until its notes coalesced into words.

> Come, faithful frâres, who love the Lord,
> Who taste the sweetness of His Word,
> Who taste the sweetness of His Word,
> In Jézu's ways go on;
> Our troubles and our trials here
> Will only make us richer there,
> Will only make us richer there,
> When we arrive at home.

Their voices blended into a patchwork of harmonies, a sound distinct from any Vallense song yet far removed from the cadences of a Gregorian chant.

> The glorious time is rolling on,
> The gracious work is now begun,
> The gracious work is now begun,
> My soul a witness is;
> I taste and see the pardon free
> For all mankind as well as me,
> For all mankind as well as me,
> Who come to Christ may live.

The melody faded, leaving an echo of unity in the corners of the Renauds' abode. How could these people not be believers? The words they sang, the joy on their faces, and the beauty of the melody all pointed to the true faith of the Holy Scriptures.

The guests bowed their heads in prayer, and Antoine began. "We thank You, our God, for bringing Your servants, Frâres Andreas and Johan, to join us in worship tonight. Frâre Andreas needs Your wisdom, his family needs Your protection, and he needs Your help. May we all serve him with our prayers and deeds. Grant him patience to endure temptation and wisdom to see Your divine ways. And may we soon see a glorious victory over the enemies of Your Son, Jézu Christ."

When Antoine finished, men, women, and children prayed aloud for guidance and strength. As Andreas listened to the hushed words, something stirred within him—peace in Christ, comfort in the Holy Spirit, and strength from the Father that transcended trials and circumstances. Strand by strand, the tension in his soul unraveled, replaced by a sense of contentment and belonging. How often had he neglected his worship and service to God in the past month? Now God blessed him with the fellowship he needed.

The youngest child, her head bowed in quiet devotion, lent a purity to the atmosphere. Her whispered petitions pointed to the Spirit who dwelled within them all.

As the child prayed, Andreas offered his own prayer. *Dear Father, forgive my sins of pride and self-reliance. Again I trusted in my own strength instead of Yours.*

With bowed heads, the congregants concluded their prayers. Yet as they finished, they each made the sign of the cross like any sincere Roman Catholic. Antoine rose from his seat and faced everyone. "*Dóminus vobiscum.* The Lord be with you."

Everyone but Andreas and Johan responded with the same—the ancient Latin blessing of the Catholic liturgy. Who were these people, and what faith did they practice? Were they Vallenses, Catholics, or something else entirely?

Antoine walked to the hearth and placed three more logs on the embers. Andreas could simply ask what Antoine believed about the important doctrines, but that seemed too forward, and the evening had been too pleasant to introduce a contentious subject now.

Marie placed her hand on Aline, the young mother who sat next to her. "I will come to your house tomorrow to help around midday. Does that suit you?"

"You are more than a blessing, sâre. I forgot what it was like without Françoise here every day."

"I feel the same," said another young mother. "I'm thankful Vincent has work, but these months with only me and the children are trying."

"Where do your husbands work?"

"Mine labors in the forests above the Dranse." Aline nodded toward the other women. "All of theirs do the same."

"And Jean, my daughter's husband," Marie said.

Andreas nodded. "A few days ago, Johan and I met Claude, the steward of the forests, and he held a high regard for some woodcutters." He scanned the men and women in the room—perhaps these were the ones Claude called the Poor.

"Ah, Claude, and a good friend he is!" Antoine rubbed the palm of one big, calloused hand with the fingers of the other. "I was once a woodcutter too, but those days passed long ago."

The older men nodded or voiced agreement.

"Almost all the woodcutters along the Dranse are frâres in Christ," Antoine said. "Since the days of my *papi*, in the days of your grandfather's grandfather, the lords of Savoy have hired our men to cut their lumber."

Johan placed both arms on the table and leaned forward. "You're such a small group, though."

"You're looking at only one of twenty or so assemblies along Lac Léman. Here in Thonon, there are four, and there are others in the surrounding communities, though we try to remain ignorant about each other."

"Because of the parish priests?"

"A few of them suspect we meet, but we try to be discreet by attending Mass, baptizing our children, and observing the holy days."

Andreas's heart sank. "You're still part of the Roman Catholic Church."

"Yes, in some ways we must remain attached to the parish."

"Your songs, though, your prayers, the way you call yourselves frâre and sâre, your gathering here—the Church has long forbidden those practices."

"Which is why we meet in secret," Antoine said. "You're from Piedmont, and Elias said you believe as we do. Tell me, Frâre Andreas, how does your family worship God?"

"We gather together like this, we sing, we read the Holy Scriptures—"

Antoine's gaze sharpened. "You read the Scriptures? How?"

"Long ago, men translated the New Testament into our language, Romaunt." Andreas stood, walked to his sack, and reached inside. "Here's a copy, though it is quite worn."

Silence fell upon the room as every man and woman gazed at the booklet. Andreas returned to the table and handed the little Bible to Antoine. "A barbe, Raimond Durand, gave me that before Dominican friars martyred him."

Antoine opened the Bible and thumbed through its pages. "I've always dreamed of hearing God's Holy Word."

"You can now." Andreas pointed to the words on the page.

"I can't read it," Antoine said. "I doubt any of us can."

"No, look. The language isn't so different from your own."

"It's not the language." Antoine tugged at the collar of his tunic. "None of us can read or write anything other than our names."

Andreas stood straighter and crossed his arms. True, many peasants never learned to read or write, but the only peasants he had spent time with were Vallenses, who were peculiar in that respect. "Have you heard the Word of God spoken in your own language—not Latin, but the tongue you speak in, the one you pray in, and as my friend Estève says, the language you sin in?"

Antoine shook his head in bewilderment. "No. I had heard rumors of such things but always doubted them." He offered the Bible back to Andreas. "Would you read a portion to us?"

"Oh, I've never preached by myself."

"We don't need you to explain anything. Just read the words."

Andreas reached for the small, weathered Bible and opened it. On the first page were the words he had read countless times: *Copied by Constanza Pavarin and Elionor Janavel.* His fingers brushed against Constanza's familiar handwriting, each delicate stroke of ink carrying her memory.

He flipped to the Gospel of John and read from the very beginning. "*Lo filh era al comenczament . . .*'"

"I have never heard something so beautiful." Marie blinked rapidly. "Jézu is the eternal Word of God. He created all things, and He shines His light to all men, even in darkness. Who wrote the words you read?"

Andreas smiled at her question. "John the Apostle, one of Jézu's closest disciples."

"Can you read more?" Aline asked.

Andreas continued until Antoine held up his hand after the words "even to them that believe on his name."

"We have received Him and believed on His name—all of us." A fervent look crossed Antoine's face. "We believe that Jesus Christ is the Son of God, and only through His death and resurrection are we saved."

"What makes you different from the rest of the parishioners in Thonon?" Andreas asked.

Everyone looked to Antoine for guidance, and he answered. "We're poor Christians who want to follow the religion Jézu gave His disciples." He nodded toward the Bible. "Not the traditions of Rome, but the religion of the Scriptures."

"Yet you have no copy of your own." Andreas's words were more an acknowledgment than a question.

"The clergy keep the Bible from us—they never read it, and they never teach it. We practice what we believe is true, and the rest we follow as the Spirit of God leads."

"I've seen you make the sign of the cross, you recited the Latin salutation, you allow the priest to baptize your children—"

"Are those things not in the Scriptures?" Marie's gaze was guileless, and she leaned forward as if eager to learn.

Andreas shook his head. "None of them."

"I've always wondered about baptism." Antoine scratched his earlobe and smiled slightly. "Since my papi's days, we haven't believed the priests can transform the bread of the Eucharist into the body of Christ."

"How did you come to that belief?"

"A hundred or so years ago, a traveling minister visited Thonon and taught from the Bible. He showed my papi and others that the Church of Rome is not God's true church. Since then, we've known the priests are unworthy of their vocation and there are only two sacraments—baptism and the supper of our Lord—instead of the seven taught by the priests. And those sacraments aren't the means of grace, but a symbol of Christ's grace."

Andreas's jaw dropped as he listened to Antoine. It must have been a barbe who had preached to them those many years ago. All they lacked was the full truth of God's Word. "If you could learn more of the Scriptures, you would hear from God Himself what a true church is."

"Will you teach us?"

"As I said earlier, I'm not accustomed—"

"Have you read all the Scriptures?" Antoine asked.

"I've read the New Testament in Romaunt. As for the Old Testament, I've read much from Jerome's Vulgate."

Marie reached over and squeezed Antoine's hand. "For years we've prayed for another preacher to teach us the Holy Scriptures."

"We want to learn . . . the other congregations nearby do too," Antoine said. "As you can see, we're ignorant of so much."

Andreas scanned the room of humble believers. Something tugged deep within, pulling him down a path he was not yet ready to tread. "Though I appreciate your trust, my time here is too short. Tomorrow, as soon as the sun rises, I'll seek an audience with my pâre, and from there I pray he comes to an agreement with Philip. Besides, there are others far better suited to teach you—men with more experience and wisdom."

Antoine extended both hands, smiling. "You're the only wise man I see here, Frâre Andreas. I believe God has sent you to us, and I, like my son, will do whatever I can to help you."

The mothers with children departed first, and the older couples soon followed. A white-haired widower left last, and Marie made sure to stuff a sack full of bread for him. When the door closed for the last time, Andreas rose and stretched.

"I doubt Elias will be home tonight." Marie blew out the candles at the table and wiped its surface. "His pallet will be free, and we have another left from his sister. It's been many years since she slept under these beams."

Johan picked up the pot from the hearth. "I saw the well outside. Is it clean?"

"I'll fetch the water for you." Antoine grabbed the pot from Johan and walked to the door. "Just in case there are prying eyes outside."

Andreas scratched the back of his neck. "Do you have enemies? The Church seems to overlook your meetings."

"They certainly don't overlook us." Marie sat on a stool near the hearth, picked up a chemise, and held it toward the fire, examining a hole in the sleeve.

"The clergy and many of the commoners call us the Poor," Antoine said, "though we never call ourselves that."

"What do you call yourselves?"

Antoine tightened his lips and spread his arms wide. "Christians? Frâres and sâres? Our enemies are the ones who insist on giving us names. It's not only the Poor we're called, but also Donatists and Cathars. I don't even know what those words mean."

"It's all slander. The Church calls my people, the Vallenses, the same." Andreas slid his gaze toward the ceiling and chuckled. "From what I've heard, the Church created the name Vallense too, though we have taken to calling ourselves that now."

"God has used our men's work in the forests as our greatest shield." Marie threaded a needle with practiced precision. "The House of Savoy values their skill and hard work, so even when we're accused of heresy, the clergy and magistrates are often lenient."

"Less so recently." Antoine set another log on the fire and sat in a chair nearby. "The Divine Ascendants hate everything about us and accuse us whenever they can."

"The teachings of their prophet have ensnared some of our neighbors," Marie said somberly. "For years we've tried to invite them to our meetings, but they never listened. Then one day last spring, they told us about this prophet and his teachings."

"They're convinced that the end of days is near." Antoine shook his head and stared into the fire. " 'If you follow the divine revelations of the Prophet,' they say, 'you'll rule with Christ when He returns to earth.' But that doesn't seem right to me."

"And my family seems to be the centerpiece of his prophecies," Andreas said. "He distorted a portion of John's Apocalypse that says a crown—"

"Of twelve stars?" Antoine frowned at the realization. "Your children—they're the crown?"

"That's why he stole my family from me, I believe."

Antoine nodded once. "Ah, he's dead now, according to what you told us about the Ascendants' defeat in Piedmont. I hope they fade away here in Savoy soon."

Marie pulled another garment from a basket and tore off a piece of cloth. "Last summer, a family who attended our gatherings was accused of sorcery."

"And who accused them?" Antoine sighed. "Their Ascendant neighbors across the way. The court of inquisition tried the whole family. The magistrate sentenced the mother and father to drowning, and the children were taken to Genève to be cleansed of their so-called heresy. That's one case of many that the Ascendants have stirred up in the last few years."

"Yet God is merciful to us and has preserved us through trials and persecutions." Marie smiled and nodded as she wove the thread through the patch and chemise. "In the end, God will defeat His enemies, whether they be pope or prophet."

"I mean no offense," Andreas said, "but without the Holy Scriptures to guide you, how do you know God will defeat His enemies?"

"We've passed our songs down through each generation," Antoine said. "Some of them contain the Scriptures, we think, and we savor that little bit we have. One of our favorite songs tells about God's vengeance on behalf of martyrs and how the Lamb, Jézu Christ, will be victorious."

Andreas nodded. "That sounds like John's Apocalypse, though I doubt you twist God's words like the Ascendants."

"Can you read it for us?" Marie asked.

"I know one part by memory, because my wife taught it to me last year. 'These shall make war with the Lamb, and the Lamb shall overcome them: for he is Lord of lords, and King of kings: and they that are with him are called, and chosen, and faithful.'"

"Called, chosen, faithful." Antoine's mouth slackened. "Is that what God calls us?"

"It's so wonderful," Marie said. "To hear the very words of God, to know that the Lamb will overcome Satan—it brings something to my heart I can't fully explain."

After a few silent moments, Andreas leaned forward, the chair creaking under him. "What is Étoilembra? I heard the Ascendants mention it at least twice."

"They call her an angel," Antoine said. "They believe that on the day of the Lord, she'll blot out the sun."

Andreas furrowed his brows. "An eclipse? I heard a minstrel in Piedmont say one would happen in October, but I can't remember which day. Maybe the fifteenth or perhaps the fourteenth?"

"Yes, the fourteenth. They believe God will establish their kingdom on the day Étoilembra blots out the sun. They will cast down the crown of twelve stars and the woman in travail." Antoine traced a finger along the edge of the table. "The Ascendants seem to be planning something. Strange men have always passed through Thonon, but in the last ten days, they've stayed—the stables are full, the taverns are busy, and strangers lurk in the market."

The Prophet had abducted Andreas's family. Philip had coincidentally rescued them with apparent ease. The duchy was in turmoil. Ascendants had infiltrated Philip's army. And an eclipse was coming. Today was the sixth of October, so only eight days remained before the eclipse. A flicker of unease crept into Andreas's heart. "Do you truly think this is all about my family?"

"Your wife and children are safe at Château de Ripaille." Marie offered a tender smile. "Lord Philip hates the Prophet."

"But there are Ascendants there too. I saw them this evening."

"My son will protect your family," Antoine said. "There's no man stronger or more loyal in all Savoy than Elias Renaud."

"Still, if these rumors have anything to do with us, I need to take my family far from Thonon as soon as I can." Andreas stood and grabbed his sack. "I'm going to my pâre in the morning."

Johan yawned. "Enjoy your visit. It must be past midnight, and I'm going to enjoy this warm home as much as I can."

Marie pointed to the corner of the room. "Your pallets are behind that curtain. If Elias comes home in the morning, he can sleep by the fire. I think he prefers that anyway."

21

Wash me throughly from mine iniquity, and cleanse me from my sin. For I acknowledge my transgressions: and my sin is ever before me.

—The Holy Bible
Psalm 51:2–3

ELIONOR SHIVERED UNDER HER WOOL BLANKET and turned toward the window, where the faintest embers of sunlight streamed through gaps in the wooden shutters. The occasional creak of the floorboards beneath her and the distant chirping of birds were the only sounds that broke the stillness of the room. No matter which way she turned, whether on her back, belly, or side, nothing gave her sleep. *How long have I been stirring like this?*

Between Elionor and the hearth, six-year-old Fosca breathed steadily. Beside her, Ave slept curled up like a little kitten. Elionor's heart lightened at the memory of her old cat, Rosmarin, who had brought so much comfort and joy when Elionor was about their age.

Her mind drifted from mountains to valleys, from towns to farms, but still her eyes remained open. The children would awaken soon, and finding sleep then would be near impossible. *May as well stoke the fire now.*

As soon as she sat upright, her head reeled like a spinning wheel set loose. The morning air, heavy with the scent of damp stone and old wood, only aggravated her nausea. With a hand pressed against her stomach, she willed the churning to flee.

The little life within Elionor fluttered. *God, I'm a sinner, and I know You've forgiven me. Please use me in spite of my mistakes. I would give anything for Constanza and these children. And my baby too.*

Summoning all her strength, Elionor swung her legs over the edge of the pallet. The rough wooden floor pressed into her feet, and she clung to the hope that the discomfort would soon pass and the promise of new life would outweigh the trials.

As she made her way to the window, new slivers of light peeked through the shutters and illuminated the chamber with a golden glow. She cracked open the shutters and peered into the world outside. The morning mist, like a Vallense bride's delicate ribbon, settled over the landscape, softening the edges of the château's shadow and casting a dreamlike mood over the surrounding yard and gardens. Servants bustled about below, guards loitered near the gate, and a lone falcon soared against the backdrop of the endless sky. The world stirred to life, oblivious to her silent struggle.

The odor of cooking wafted from the kitchen below, blending with the musty scent of the room's worn tapestries. Elionor recoiled at the mere thought of breakfast. To feel the free, crisp air against her cheeks, to stand in the sunlight unbarred by stone walls—those were the comforts she craved, not the heaviness of food her unsettled stomach refused to bear.

By the time she turned from the window, half the children were sitting up, stretching, and chattering. Constanza picked up the poker to stoke the fire, but Ezio intervened and finished arranging the firewood. Soon the hearth roared with flames, and the rest of the children awoke.

Constanza waved for them to gather around her and, as she had every day since their capture, recited the Lord's Prayer with them. Curly-haired Zama climbed onto Constanza's lap as they finished the prayer. "What does 'kingdom come' mean, Mamà?"

With a tender smile, Constanza beckoned the children closer. "'Thy kingdom come' is a prayer for the coming of God's kingdom on earth." She gestured toward the window, where the dazzling sunlight streamed in. "It's a prayer for a world where our Savior will reign and where His words will conquer all evil. His justice will prevail, the hungry will be fed, and the oppressed will find refuge."

"When is His kingdom coming?" Silvia asked.

Guido leaned over Constanza's shoulder. "I wish it were today!"

All the children voiced their agreement.

"We don't know when He will come again." Constanza reached over and smoothed Zama's hair. "The Holy Scriptures say, 'But of that day and hour knoweth no man, no, not the angels of heaven, but my Father only.' Just as the Hebrews awaited their Messiah, we do the same. Until then, we trust His promise that 'the Lord himself shall descend from heaven with a shout, with the voice of the archangel, and with the trump of God: and the dead in Christ shall rise first.'"

Zama hugged Constanza, and Alessia rushed over to do the same. Elionor smiled at the love and honor these twelve children showed to Constanza . . . their mother. It still felt strange to think that. Constanza, her faithful, forgiving, compassionate friend—suddenly a mother of twelve orphaned children. They weren't orphans anymore, though. They had the best mamà and papà any child could ask for—except for Elionor's mamà and papà.

She drew her lips together, and her throat tightened. It had been over fifteen years since Papà and Mamà had taken her in as a filthy, scrawny, lice-ridden outcast from Chivasso. They had bathed her, clothed her, and given her a new name. From her first wintry day in their comforting arms, Lambert and Magdalena Janavel had called her *filha*—daughter.

If only Elionor could give her child the same kind of home Papà and Mamà had given her. But how would that be possible? She had committed the gravest of sins, and she had to endure the penalty. *Yet please, Lord, for the sake of the baby, have mercy on me.*

A knock sounded at the door, not loud, but insistent. Madeleine never knocked, so it must not be her. The knock came again, and Elionor said, "You may enter."

The door swung open, and Lugotenent Renaud stood at the threshold, the sunlight from the window casting a shadow into the hall behind him. He shut the door and strode into their midst while Elionor reached for her kerchief and fastened it to her hair. She hurried behind the children, trying to avoid Elias's intense gaze.

"Did you hear the fighting last night?" Elias asked.

Constanza stood. "I heard clanging metal . . ."

Umile's face radiated excitement. "It was a sword fight, wasn't it, Lugotenent?"

Silvia pushed Umile's shoulder. "Don't be a fool, Umile. No one—"

"It was." Elias didn't smile. "Your husband tried to rescue you, Dama Constanza."

Constanza gasped and placed a hand on her heart. "Andreas was here?"

"He's a valiant fighter, but I could tell he hasn't held a sword in years."

"How do . . . how did you know that?"

"I fought him. I defeated him too, but he's unhurt."

"No you didn't!" Bino said in disbelief, but with a tinge of despair. "Papà is the best swordsman in the world."

Elias cracked a smile and let out a puff of air.

Constanza curled her fingers at her side. "You laugh?"

"Andreas is safe."

"Then did you come here to gloat?"

Elionor wove through the children to stand by Constanza. Her heart beat faster as she brushed past Elias and turned to face him. "Lugotenent Renaud, you act as though you're our friend, but whenever we find a spark of hope, you pour cold water on it."

"I am your friend." Elias squared his shoulders and extended a hand, palm open. Yet as he looked at Elionor, a hint of sorrow fell over him, like the fleeting shadow of a cloud passing over a sunlit valley. "And I pour no cold water on your hope."

Elionor shook her head and blinked rapidly. "I could have easily crossed that river and escaped."

"I saved you from certain death by drowning or capture."

"May I remind you that it was you who held me captive."

"Better Lord Philip than the Divine Ascendancy. Those forests we were in—Ascendants lurk in every hamlet. They know who you are, and they know Lord Philip took you, Dama Constanza, and all the children from their prophet. If they had recaptured you—"

"You were only doing your duty, no?" Constanza's chin trembled. "That's why you didn't let me see my husband."

"If I hadn't crossed swords with Andreas, he would be dead by the hands of Ascendants. As I speak, the Prophet's men watch this door." Elias's neck muscles tensed. "They probably think I'm here by Lord Philip's command. No, I'm here by my own choice. I'm your frâre in Christ, and you're in far more danger than you realize."

Constanza tugged at the sleeve of her chemise. "Frâre?"

"Yes, 'brother.' I know you're Vallenses, and from what I've seen in you, our beliefs are the same. In Thonon, we are called the Poor, but among one another, we are simply frâres and sâres."

"But you're one of Philip's officers." Elionor struggled to steady her breathing. "You helped him take us over the mountains, from our homes, from our people. You took Constanza from her husband."

"And I protected you the whole journey. From the moment I met you, I saw your faith. You are godly women, the children are obedient, you are chaste . . ."

Elionor tensed at that word—*chaste*. Perhaps at one time she could have been called that, but not now. Did Elias not see her? Was he so oblivious to her growing belly?

Elias continued. "I am loyal to Lord Philip, but if I could have found a way for you to return to your homes, I would have. Now I regret not doing so."

Constanza studied him, but she relaxed her arms. "How do we know you're not bluffing . . . or mocking us?"

"From the time I can remember, my pâre and mâre have instructed me in the true Christian religion, not the pope's."

Elionor locked eyes with Elias. "We saw you, Lugotenent. You crossed yourself like a devout Catholic, and one Sunday on our journey, I saw you enter a parish church to partake in the filthy Mass." Though her heart longed to reach out to him, to bridge the chasm that separated their worlds, she refused to succumb to the draw of her emotions. She had fallen into a chasm like this once, and she wouldn't again.

"Maybe we don't know as much about true religion as you." Elias offered her a brief smile, as if masking the vulnerability that lay beneath his stoic facade. "All we have is what little is in our songs, Elionor."

Her heart skipped a beat at the sound of her name escaping his lips. For one passing moment, she savored the sweetness and strength of Elias Renaud's voice.

"I must depart before anyone becomes suspicious." Elias gave them a courteous bow, his eyes briefly meeting Elionor's again before flickering away. "I've arranged for you and the children to enjoy the outdoors this morning. A servant will meet you shortly. Though you might not see me, I'll be nearby."

A pang of longing flittered through her as she struggled to mask her feelings. "God be with you, Elias."

Elias bowed his head slightly, this time only to her. "And with you, Elionor."

As he closed the door, Elionor's gaze lingered on the threshold where he had stood. The echo of his parting words resonated in the air.

Soon after his footsteps faded, Madeleine rushed into the chamber, carrying a pail of water. "Come, children, clean your faces, wash your hands, scrub your feet." She smiled at Constanza and Elionor. "I'll bring a fresh pail for you two soon."

Elionor helped the four youngest children wash, but the two boys among them needed some encouragement. "No, take your shoes off too."

"It rained before we came here," Bino said.

Elionor placed her hands on her hips. "That doesn't clean you."

He lifted his arm and sniffed it. "I smell the same as I always do, madomaisèla."

"And that's why you need to wash." Elionor grabbed his arm and forced it into the water. "You're not finished until your mamà or I say so."

Bino giggled and splashed water at her.

"No playing!"

But that didn't stop anyone. Before long six of the children splashed and played.

Constanza yanked the two instigators away from the pail. "Do you want to sleep in a puddle tonight?"

Both shook their heads.

Madeleine appeared again, linen towels over her shoulder, struggling to carry a larger pail than the first one.

Elionor walked toward her. "Let me help you."

"No, you should be lifting no such thing." Madeleine heaved the pail onto the floor away from the children. "This is for only you and Dama Constanza." She reached beneath her apron, removed a small linen-wrapped package, and handed it to Elionor. "This soap is the best I could find in the château."

In time Constanza joined them, her sleeves rolled up to her elbows and strands of hair falling from her kerchief. "The children are nearly washed." She glanced toward them and shook her head. "And there's little water left for them to wet the floor with."

"I understand," Madeleine said. "My children would do the same."

Elionor touched the water in the pail. "Thank you for warming the water and for the soap."

"As soon as I'm able, I'll arrange a secluded place for you to wash. Not today, but perhaps tomorrow."

Elionor offered the soap to Constanza, who unwrapped the linen and lifted the soap to her nose. "I can't remember smelling something so wonderful."

"One of Lord Philip's . . . friends left it here."

"Friends?" Constanza raised an eyebrow. "Why did you say it like that?"

"Lord Philip is not a moral man. It seems a new woman passes through Ripaille every other day. He uses his position and wealth to lure them, then throws them aside."

Elionor dropped her gaze to the floor. How could a man be so debauched? And to lodge under the same roof he did—would he burst through the door and threaten her or Constanza next? "Has Philip tried to approach you, Madeleine? You're so beautiful."

Madeleine laughed. "Lord Philip has seen my husband and fears him. I've known the lord for a few years now and have noticed he preys on girls without a strong man behind them." She nodded to Constanza first, then Elionor. "And you have nothing to fear from Lord Philip, for you also have strong men behind you."

Elionor shook her head in gradual dissent. Papà was dead, and the father of the child growing within her had abandoned her. No strong man stood behind her.

As if reading her thoughts, Madeleine clasped Elionor's hand with both of hers. "I've seen how Lugotenent Renaud treats you, Elionor. He sees the treasure in you that any virtuous man would see."

"No, no, you're mistaken. The lugotenent is kind, very kind. Constanza and I are both thankful for him."

"For as long as I've worked near him, he's been considerate, more than any other soldier. But not until I saw him with you have I seen him so . . . thrilled." Madeleine locked eyes with Elionor. "He adores you."

Elionor's heart wavered. How could Elias adore her? He was an honorable man. She traced the contours of her rounded belly, and the regrets of the past thundered back. What if she had remained chaste? Perhaps then she could consider his affection, but not now.

Madeleine gave Elionor a warm smile and squeezed her hand. "Don't doubt love when you see it." She let go and turned toward the door. "Bread, butter, and milk will be waiting for everyone at the table in the gardens."

"You can wash first," Constanza said to Elionor after Madeleine left. "I'll make sure the children are ready to go outside."

With slow, deliberate movements, Elionor dipped the fragrant soap into the water and watched it dissolve into a frothy lather. The scent of lemons and mint mingled with the steam, infusing the air with a delicate fragrance. As she plunged her hands into the warm water, tendrils of steam rose to caress her skin.

Though Elias had declared himself a fellow believer, she couldn't allow herself to long for him. Maybe he hadn't seen her pregnancy, that increasingly pronounced declaration that her path had diverged from the course of a truly moral woman. How could she entertain love when her very form bore witness to her unworthiness?

Elionor dabbed her face, arms, and hands with a towel, then watched the children bubble with excitement around the other pail. After Constanza washed herself, all the children clamored near the door, awaiting their release into the open air.

Two servants led them through the hallway and down the stairs to a side door. As soon as the door opened, a wave of brisk air greeted Elionor, carrying with it the fresh scent of woodsmoke and newly fallen leaves. The children sprinted onto the grassy lawn, but Elionor relished the sunshine that hadn't touched her skin in two long days.

In a small garden to the right, under the yellow shade of enormous chestnut trees, stood a small wooden table and three chairs. Two steaming loaves of bread sat atop the table, and next to them, a slab of butter and a pitcher rested on a wooden board.

"Children, don't forget to eat!" Constanza shouted.

The children ran to the table, tore pieces from the loaves, spread them with the butter, drank a few gulps from the pitcher, and returned to their play, bread in hand.

Half a loaf remained when the table cleared of children. Constanza sat first, and Elionor followed. She tore off a piece of bread and eyed it. It was still warm, and its crust glistened in the sunlight like polished amber. "I'm hungry, but I'm afraid it will come back up if I eat it."

"I haven't seen you do that yet."

"I did a few times in the forest a week ago. I pray this ends soon."

Constanza buttered her piece, set the knife aside, and smelled the bread. "I haven't felt sick yet, but the signs are still there."

Elionor grabbed the pitcher of frothy milk, drank a few sips, and returned for more. As she wiped her mouth with her fingers, she gazed at Constanza, seeking answers to the questions that fluttered in her soul, hesitant to take flight.

"Ellie, unless my heart deceives me, the lugotenent seems to have taken an interest in you. Perhaps you could consider that possibility."

"How? I've already accepted the fact that I'll live in shame. Lugotenant Renaud doesn't know me. He doesn't see who I truly am. Does he think I'm a widow? Has he noticed I'm with child?"

Constanza reached out and touched Elionor's hand. "The grace of God is boundless and everlasting. We've been taught that since we were girls, but now

He wants to show us. Maybe Lugotenant Renaud doesn't see your flaws but instead sees the beauty of God's grace."

"How can you say that? I'm not the innocent girl I was."

Constanza's lower lip trembled. "I admit, I didn't want to forgive you at first. But God convicted me of my own self-righteousness. In His eyes, you're more than your shortcomings. Since that's how God sees you, that's how I should too."

Elionor looked away to hide her tears. The breeze whispered through the leaves above, and the sounds of children playing in the grass floated through the crisp air. Her gaze wandered through the garden. Behind a shrub about twenty paces away, two soldiers watched them and the children. On the other side of the garden stood two more soldiers. Their presence cast a shadow over the otherwise peaceful scene. A flicker of unease ran through Elionor's chest.

But then, like a ray of sunlight breaking through clouds, Elias moved confidently among the trees. Elionor's pulse slowed, and her fears fled. Their eyes met for a moment, a silent understanding passing between them.

Constanza smiled at Elionor and nodded toward Elias. "God has given us a good man inside the château to protect us and one outside it who works to free us." She poured a few drops of milk onto her bread and lifted it to her mouth. "Knowing Andreas is nearby gives me every reassurance I need. While we sit here eating our grand breakfast, I know he's fighting for us."

22

The history of Savoy, during the second half of the fifteenth century, offers an example of the degradation into which a country can fall when its destiny is abandoned to the inadequacy of men or the caprice of women.

—Victor Flour de Saint-Genis
Histoire de Savoie, 1869

ANDREAS STOOD in the reception chamber of Château de Thonon and awaited the appearance of his father, Louis, Duke of Savoy. Tapestries that had once been vibrant depictions of valor and glory now bore the marks of time, their colors muted and their threads frayed with age. The wall frescoes, once clean and vibrant, were cracked and stained with neglect. Flickering candles cast long shadows across the room, their light failing to penetrate the musty gloom.

The wooden door squealed open on the opposite side of the room. The duke entered without an escort and pulled a chair from a table near an arched window. "Come, my son, sit with your pâre." His raspy words slurred together.

Andreas approached Pâre and embraced him. The stench of strong wine hit him immediately as he pressed his hands against the black robe. "I have missed you, Pâre." But was that the truth? How often he had tried to forget about these courts and their intrigues, pushing them to the edges of his memory and focusing only on the new life God had given him.

Pâre sat first. Andreas followed, but the wooden chair shifted and wobbled under him.

"I am sorry," Pâre said. "That chair is old—probably crafted when my pâre was the duke. It needs to be replaced."

Andreas shook the armrests and shifted his weight to one side. "I believe it will hold me."

"Am I not a failure? Your gran-pâre made our duchy the envy of all Christendom. He expanded our borders, he won prestige in battle, he founded the knightly orders. I have done nothing except let the realm fall into decadence."

A servant entered from the same door as Pâre, carrying a bottle of wine. He set a goblet before Pâre and filled it to the brim. With an unsteady hand, Pâre lifted the goblet, sloshing the purple wine over the rim and onto his robe. "A cloth," he said to the servant.

The servant pulled a square of white linen from his pocket and dabbed Pâre's robe. "My lord, if you would allow, I can wash out this stain."

"Later. You are dismissed for now."

This pale, long-faced noble gazing at Andreas was not the man he had once been. Pâre had been vigorous and youthful in Andreas's childhood, not dull and helpless. Perhaps this was where riches and fame could lead. While the Medici dukes of Florence or the Hapsburg emperors of Austria projected their power and expanded their realms, other nobles dwindled into dependent children. When Pâre died and his title passed to Amadeus, the House of Savoy would be in no better hands.

But Andreas wasn't here to dispel the rot within the house. "Pâre, I came here this morning to talk to you about Philip alone."

"Without your mâre. I understand. I understand completely." Pâre glanced over his shoulder at the door he had come from. "One of your mâre's Cypriot courtiers likely listens as we speak, and before you depart, she will know everything we discussed."

"Why do you allow her to rule in your stead? It wasn't like this before, when you maintained the reputation of our noble house and ruled the duchy yourself."

"Is it so obvious?" Pâre took a long drink of wine and set the goblet back on the table. "I am old and weary. I would much rather pray and write verses of poetry than rule."

"You're not yet fifty years old. Don't waste your life on wine and passivity."

"My own son, telling me the truth I already know." Pâre picked up the goblet and stared into it. "Our enemies and allies both think I'm a failure—Louis, the duke who is ruled by his wife. Yet she is still kind to me . . ."

"Mâre is unfaithful to you."

"Name a duchess, countess, queen, or empress who isn't the same. The Holy Catholic Church preaches virtue, but few nobles follow it. Even the Church's own priests are unchaste."

Andreas folded his hands on the table. "I don't want to be here, Pâre, but I am. Philip holds my family hostage and won't release them until he takes what he wants from you. I believe in the true line of succession—you, Amadeus, and eventually his son, Charles. To name Philip as heir would only bring shame on Savoy. But I also must see to my own family. The Divine Ascendants seem to have some sway over Philip, and they mean to cause harm to my wife and my children."

"Yet you also follow their heretical teachings."

Andreas shook his head vigorously. "I have no connection to the Divine Ascendancy and their prophet. I am—" He bit his tongue. Would he incriminate himself before the ruler of Savoy?

"I raised you in the Church of Saints Peter and Paul, and you committed yourself fully to serve her. Yet you broke your vows and joined one of a hundred heretical sects between here and Asti. All who oppose the one true Church are the same—apostates, heretics, abominations."

Andreas opened his mouth to retort but caught himself. Two years ago, he would have said the same. The Spirit of God whispered the words of the Holy Scriptures to his mind, a portion he had learned in his journeys with the barbe Estève. *But sanctify the Lord God in your hearts: and be ready always to give an answer to every man that asketh you a reason of the hope that is in you with meekness and fear: having a good conscience; that, whereas they speak evil of you, as of evildoers, they may be ashamed that falsely accuse your good conversation in Christ.*

"Pâre, what is the true, undefiled religion of the apostles?"

"It is the tradition entrusted to the Catholic Church by the apostles. You already know this."

"I do believe God bestowed the truth upon His churches, but not by man's traditions, which can misinterpret and distort the truth. Rather, the Almighty has given us eternal, infallible truth in the Holy Scriptures."

"The followers of the Englishman Wycliffe and the Bohemian agitator Hus have said similar things, I hear." Pâre held his goblet up toward Andreas. "Do you not see how much turmoil they have caused—poverty, calamity, death? It's what this Divine Ascendancy desires too. Their prophet preaches that God will overthrow us nobles and that heretics will rule in our stead."

"I can't answer for the Prophet or anyone else, but I can tell you that true Christians honor the authority God has placed over them, including you. We tend to our little plots in the mountains and pay our dues in harvest season."

"You have become a peasant." Pâre rubbed his forehead and chuckled. "And you come to me, begging to have your peasant wife and orphans back." His words softened into a gentle tone of understanding. "I would almost be enticed to assist you if it were not for your mâre."

"If you offered Philip a little land or gold, then perhaps this conflict would end."

"My hands are chained in these matters." Pâre shook his head and sighed. "I have no gold to give Philip, and to give him land, I would be forced to take it from other landholders, who would then revolt."

"Pâre, you must take charge. Rid your household of Lucien Bouchard and these Cypriots, assert yourself as Duke of Savoy, and show your subjects the leadership they yearn for. Your strength will not only secure your legacy and that of your rightful heirs but also inspire loyalty and reverence among your people." He locked eyes with Pâre. "Including me."

"It's too late for me, my son," Pâre murmured. "I am but a vessel weathered by storms of my own making, too far adrift to chart a new course."

Andreas let out a long sigh. "What must I do to free my wife and children from Philip's grasp?"

"Talk to your mâre."

"She's the one Philip despises most."

"Yet Anne knows Philip best." Pâre struggled up from his chair and called for a servant before glancing back at Andreas. "I wish I weren't such a shame to everyone."

Andreas's chest tightened. This was his father, not simply the eroded and beleaguered Duke of Savoy. How much different his relationship was with his parents than Constanza's was with hers. Yet Louis and Anne were still the parents God had given him.

Pâre had once been his pillar of strength, the man who had taught him how to hold a sword, ride a horse, and display a chivalrous spirit in all his endeavors. Andreas approached his father with careful steps and tenderly embraced him. "You are not a shame to me. You are a father, a leader, and though you may be burdened, your worth endures." His voice trembled. "I am here for you, as you were for me."

As Andreas backed away, the door squeaked open, and a servant entered. Without a word, Pâre bowed his head toward Andreas, then followed the servant out of the room.

Andreas couldn't leave Château de Thonon without an answer. When the steward returned, Andreas demanded an audience with the real ruler of Savoy. He was escorted directly into the great hall.

The sound of hammers and chisels echoed off the walls. His eyes widened at the sight before him—one that had not been there yesterday. Masons labored tirelessly over freshly cut stones, stacking them with precise, almost reverent care. The structure extended wide, but its form remained obscured by the workers' movements.

Mâre sat alone on the dais in an ornately carved chair, smiling as Andreas approached. She held a white cloth with a few stains of blood. "My son."

As anyone did when standing before the duchess, Andreas bowed low. "Mâre, we must speak about Philip."

She motioned to the right. "There is no need to bow, Andreas. Come sit in your pâre's chair and tell me your plight."

Andreas followed her instruction. The chair's polished wood gleamed in the flickering candlelight. Intricate carvings depicting the heraldic symbols of the House of Savoy adorned its armrests. As he sank into the plush cushions, the fabric yielded beneath him, rich and heavy, an indulgence far beyond simple comfort. His fingers traced the delicate embroidery, each stitch whispering of ancient hands that had labored over it, the very threads woven with the history of his powerful lineage. The scent of aged wood and musty fabric filled his nostrils, and the quiet creak of the chair seemed to echo with the authority of those who had sat here before. He felt it—a presence, as though the air itself carried the weight of centuries past, pressing down on him, urging him to recognize his place in the House of Savoy.

He turned to the figure seated beside him. Mâre's gown, fashioned with the finest silks, cascaded in rich folds of deep blue adorned with delicate silver-threaded motifs that shimmered in the candlelight. Her golden locks fell in glossy waves, swept into an elaborate coiffure held by a crown of gilded leaves.

Yet her features carried the marks of suffering, her skin pale and drawn, her movements slow and labored. She reached over and touched Andreas's arm, and despite her weakened state, her touch still carried the gentle warmth of a mother's love.

"Many years have passed since a man of your stature sat in that chair." Her breathy voice barely rose over the hammering of the masons.

"When I was a boy," Andreas said, patting the armrest, "I would sit here and pretend to be the Holy Roman Emperor."

"Dethrone the Hapsburgs, would you?"

"Every noble son dreams of being higher than his station allows."

"Except for your pâre and your brother Amadeus." Mâre sat back in her chair and took a long, labored breath. She coughed into her cloth again and again until a servant arrived with a goblet of water and a fresh white cloth.

Mâre closed her eyes and slowly shook her head before leaning on the armrest and staring into the vast hall. "I am dying, Andreas. The physician says I won't survive to *Dies Natalis Domini*."

The words hit Andreas like an overladen pushcart. "Are they treating you with anything? Is there a cure?"

"I have phthisis, called consumption by some. The priests say it is a divine punishment, but I think it is bad air. The physicians say it is incurable."

"Can anything be done?"

"Other than my leaving the House of Savoy in better condition than when I first joined it? No." She lifted a frail hand toward the masons at the center of the hall. "It will be beautiful, will it not?"

Andreas squinted at the table-like structure, trying to guess its purpose. "The château already has a dining room, no?"

"It is to be the foundation of a glorious monument to our noble house. These are the most skilled craftsmen, I am told, almost as talented as those in Florence. Within the week, they will finish the display table."

"What will it hold?"

"We will decide once the foundation is complete—perhaps a sculpture of your gran-pâre, Amadeus VIII."

Andreas scanned the spacious hall and its obvious decay. While the murals on the walls faded and dust collected on the window ledges, Mâre had chosen to install a sculpture in the center of Château de Thonon's great hall.

"Why now, Mâre? How does this grant prestige to the House of Savoy when Philip seeks to overthrow it?"

"How else will I be remembered? Will I forever be known as Anne of Cyprus, the duchess who ruined Savoy? The people already blame me and my Cypriot advisers for all the woes in the land, from failed crops to dead children. Or perhaps I will be entirely forgotten to history except for this glorious monument."

"Of all the places in Thonon, why demolish the floor and build a statue here?"

"My adviser, Monsieur Bouchard, said this would be the perfect place."

"Why do you listen to him?" Andreas's breath quickened, and his cheeks warmed. "What has he done for you?"

Mâre folded her hands and frowned. "Lucien loves me more than anyone, and I trust his wisdom. You probably think the same as everyone else, though—Anne, the debauched Duchess of Savoy. Yet that is not the whole tale. When I was but fifteen years old, I was forced to marry Louis. At first, he loved me deeply, and I was faithful to him. Soon after you and Philip were born, however, he was declared duke. Savoy became more important to him than me. It was he who left me, not I him." Mâre lifted the cloth to her mouth and coughed again. "Now I bide my time until Azræl, the angel of death, takes me."

Andreas swallowed hard, his breath catching for a moment, hands flexing at his sides. Mâre was dying. She might have lived in impropriety for most of Andreas's life, but he still loved her, just as he did Pâre. And she was a soul who needed to be reconciled with her Creator.

A door opened behind the dais, and sharp footsteps clapped on the polished floor. The Cypriot, Lucien Bouchard, marched around them and bowed low before Mâre. "*Vôtre Grâce*," he said in his foreign accent. "The woodcutters continue to ignore our commands and refuse to fell trees in the locations I demanded."

Andreas stood and crossed his arms, towering over Lucien Bouchard like a true prince of Savoy. "I heard you are careless with the trees."

"No, it is the woodcutters who are careless." Bouchard gave Andreas a sharp look, as if he didn't belong in the hall. "Those rebels must be put in their place. For too long they and the forest steward have managed things as they wished, but no longer." He approached the dais and offered his hand to Mâre, making sure Andreas saw it. "I am sure the woodcutters are in league with Philip, Vôtre Grâce. They seek to undermine the authority of the House of Savoy."

"Andreas wishes to speak about Philip." Mâre reached toward Bouchard and took his hand.

Andreas grimaced at their show of affection.

"I heard Philip the usurper entertained you at Château de Ripaille." Bouchard said, "and that you groveled before him."

"I don't know who told you that, but I did no such thing." Andreas lowered his brows but refused the temptation to insult the Cypriot. "Philip holds my family hostage, and he will release them only if he and my pâre come to some sort of agreement."

"Impossible. Philip only wants to use the duchy for his own hedonism."

"He is willing to negotiate." Andreas turned to Mâre. "When is the last time you spoke to Philip?"

As Mâre opened her mouth to speak, Bouchard answered for her. "He is the rebel, not your parents. The responsibility to reconcile lies in Philip's hands alone."

Andreas paid no heed to Bouchard. "Invite him here for a feast—ask him to bring my family too. He and Pâre can speak, and I believe they will reach an understanding." He positioned himself between Bouchard and Mâre, forcing Bouchard to release her hand. Andreas knelt before her and held her hands. "Please, Mâre. I yearn for my wife and children, and I fear for their safety."

She turned toward Bouchard. "Could we send an invitation to Philip? Surely a feast with the whole family would produce some cordiality in this beleaguered house."

Bouchard stood silent for a moment, his focus wandering from the construction project to Andreas and then back to Mâre. "I suppose it would be safer than going to Ripaille. Yes, we should dispatch an invitation to Philip." He nodded at Andreas. "It is an intriguing idea, Lord Andreas."

"Make sure Philip brings my family too. If he doesn't, the agreement is void."

"A shrewd negotiator, your son," Bouchard said to Mâre, a smile on his face. "I will be certain to include that in the message."

Mâre coughed harshly into the cloth and reached out for assistance. Andreas offered his support, and her coughing gradually abated. Before long, two servants arrived to escort her from the hall. Andreas tried to embrace her, but she was too weak to reciprocate. As Lucien followed her and the servants out, Andreas was left alone with the masons in the vast room.

Soon soldiers escorted him from the citadel and through the gates. He turned left and gazed over the expanse of Lac Léman, its tranquil waters muted beneath the pall of autumn's overcast sky. The usually vibrant hues of the lake now blended seamlessly with the somber tones of the surrounding landscape. Despite the gloom, there was a raw beauty to the vista, a reflection of the prayers Andreas now lifted from his heart.

Dear Lord, bend Philip's will toward reason. Encourage Constanza and the children—Elionor too. He turned from the lake and walked toward the village. *And be with these simple believers here. Protect them from those who want to harm them, and give them . . .*

What did they need? Certainly a Bible and its teachings. That morning, before Andreas left for the château, Antoine had invited him to teach the Scriptures at a gathering the next day, saying as many as thirty souls would meet in his home.

God, I feel so anxious about teaching them. I don't know why they asked me, but I suppose I'm the only one they know who owns a Bible . . . and can read it.

He had a day to prepare, but what could he, a noble son turned farmer, teach these peculiar yet genuine Christians of Thonon? At least the time in study would make the hours between him and his family pass faster. Soon Philip would receive the invitation to the feast, but only God could sway his heart to accept it. *Your will be done, Father.*

The streets of Thonon bustled as Andreas wound his way through them. Small crowds gathered and talked outside the inns. Food carts lined the streets, their vendors hawking their wares with enthusiasm. The scent of freshly baked bread mingled with the aroma of simmering stews, enticing patrons with promises of warmth and a full belly.

The Renaud home also brimmed with activity when Andreas arrived. Five of Antoine and Marie's grandchildren ran around the house, chasing Johan with wooden spoons and calling him their friendly giant.

Andreas sat at the hearth and warmed his hands over the fire. "When we're back in Piedmont, Johan, I should invite you to my house more often. My children would enjoy chasing the friendly giant too."

Weeks had passed since someone had last called Andreas papà. Memories lapped at his mind like waves on the shore of Lac Léman. Irene's laughter as she danced through the vegetable garden, her eyes sparkling with innocence. Ezio's eager questions about the stars and his wonder at the vastness of creation. Fosca's kindness toward the smallest creatures. Ave's unwavering determination to help others. Silvia's tender hugs and earnest prayers. Guido's adventurous spirit. Roberto's mischievous grin and quick wit. Bino's instinct to make others laugh. Umile's quiet wisdom. Alessia's boundless creativity. Zama's infectious laughter. Prospera's fierce determination to keep trying even when she failed.

Johan slumped onto the bench near the table and let out an exhausted breath. "How did your meeting fare?"

"My pâre was weak and unwilling to make a choice either way, but at least my mâre and Monsieur Bouchard are willing to talk to Philip."

"Bouchard?" Antoine entered the room from behind a curtain and eyed Andreas curiously. "You spoke to him?"

"I have many reasons to despise him, but at least someone in that château was strong and decisive."

"My daughter's husband might despise him more than you do. He works the woodcutters too hard, he pays them too little, and he mismanages the forests." Marie set a plate with three morsels of pale yellow cheese and a piece of bread in front of him. "This is from a family we know in Abondance, and it's our favorite." She grabbed a piece of cheese and laid it in Andreas's hand. "Go, taste it."

"I doubt I'll enjoy this as much as the hard cheese I tried in Parma once," Andreas said with a teasing grin.

"Parma?" Marie scoffed. "What do Italians know about cheese? On our side of the Alps, we craft true *fromâjo*."

"You might be right about Savoyard cheese, but don't forget your neighbors on the other side of the mountains. Their cuisine possesses a certain . . . class."

Marie chuckled and nudged Andreas. "A class indeed, but let's not speak too highly of their pasta."

"Only their pasta? Oh, Dama Marie, you wound me!" Andreas savored the first bite of cheese, its rich flavor capturing his senses with a taste of home and tradition. But he grimaced, feigning disgust.

Marie fixed him with a stern gaze. "Stop this foolishness at once, Monsieur Bonomo. You like it, and I see it in your smile."

"It's delicious, dama. Merci bôcô!" Andreas laughed and placed another piece of cheese in his mouth.

The remainder of the afternoon and into the evening, Andreas sat near the hearth and pored through the parchment pages of his Bible. Constanza's handwriting, neat yet welcoming, flowed over the pages of the epistle to the Hebrews. Antoine and Marie lit candles as darkness settled over the room, while Andreas kept the fire alive.

Elias arrived after sunset, and the children all ran to him, one jumping into his arms.

"Must we leave already, *Tonton* Elias?" asked the oldest boy.

"Your mâre is waiting at home for you." Elias caught sight of Andreas. "I have news about your family, but not much has changed since yesterday. I'll tell you when I return." After the children put on their shoes, he ushered them outside and shut the door.

"Elias is a good son." Marie sat opposite Andreas in the early stages of knitting a garment. "Because Antoine is no longer able to cut wood, Elias provides for us. He is also obedient to his Savior and yearns to know more about Him."

"And your daughter?"

"She is a gem among women and the best mother I have ever seen. When I was younger, I wished for more than two children, but now I know the Lord has blessed us with a son and daughter who honor us. I could never ask for more."

Andreas closed his Bible but used his finger to keep his place. The Renauds certainly held wisdom he could tap into during his fading time here. "In Thonon, you're surrounded by people who are less than godly Christians. How did you raise a son and daughter who honor both you and the Savior?"

"They were not without their struggles." Antoine stood behind his wife's chair and placed both hands on her shoulders. "When Elias chose to become a soldier instead of a woodcutter, we begged him to change his mind. Our relationship was strained for half a year."

"What brought you back together?"

"Forbearance, especially on my part," Antoine said.

"From what I gather, Elias is one of the most trusted and talented soldiers in all the realm." Marie lifted her chin and smiled. "I heard that the duke himself knows the name Elias Renaud."

As Marie spoke his name, Elias opened the door and walked inside. He closed the door and turned toward Andreas. "Your family is well, Andreas. Earlier today, Lord Philip allowed Constanza, Elionor, and the children to walk outside for fresh air." He unfastened his boots and set them against the wall. "Better yet, just before I left Ripaille this evening, I received a command from Lord Philip himself. I will escort both him and your family to Château de Thonon for a feast with the duke and duchess."

Andreas lifted his clenched fist in triumph and breathed a sigh of relief. "Philip accepted the invitation. Praise God, the one who hears my prayers."

"And ours too!" Marie said, rising to her feet with a wide grin.

"I needed your prayers far more than I thought a few days ago." Andreas bowed his head toward the Renauds. "When is the feast?"

"On the day after tomorrow," Elias said.

Andreas unclenched his fist and let his shoulders sag. "Why two days from now?"

"I was wondering the same thing. Something is deeply wrong in Thonon. The streets are filled with foreigners, some from as far away as the Dauphiné. Frâre Andreas, your family is being watched, every moment of the day."

"Are they safe without you there?"

"Yes, the veteran guards at Ripaille are loyal to Philip. It's the new recruits who worry me."

Andreas voiced the obvious question. "Do you think they're Ascendants?"

"No doubt. But what are they planning?"

*   *   *

The next afternoon, just as Antoine had predicted, about thirty people crammed into the central room of the Renauds' house and awaited Andreas's teaching with eager postures. With elderly men and women occupying the few chairs, most of the guests sat on the floor in silence. As soon as they finished singing, Andreas stood in front of the hearth, opened his Bible, and read from Hebrews.

" 'For the word of God is quick, and powerful, and sharper than any twoedged sword.' " Everyone's attention was on him, including the children's. He quickly looked down at the Bible again. " 'Piercing even to the dividing asunder of soul and spirit, and of the joints and marrow, and is a discerner of the thoughts and intents of the heart.' These are the very words of God, meant to guide our faith, and a gift to all who have believed in His Son as Savior. Since the time of the apostles, men have tried to usurp God by diminishing His Word."

The fire popped behind him, but no one heeded it except him. His hands shook as they held the Bible. "Some would demote the Holy Scriptures to the same level as the traditions of the Church of Rome. Others say the Bible is completely true and effective, yet they promote prophecies, dreams, and revelations as equally true."

Several men and women nodded as he spoke. Andreas's heart beat faster, and a drop of sweat trickled from his brow. *I feel like such a fool standing in front of these people.* Most were older than he was and probably more knowledgeable in the day-to-day life of a Christian. Yet here they sat, eyes wide, yearning for more.

Johan sat in the back with two of the Renauds' grandchildren beside him. He gave Andreas a reassuring smile.

"I stand before you, not by the authority of the pope, not because of my own wisdom or position, but because I read the words God gave to us, His disciples. These words are not for only learned scholars, pious priests, and devout monks, but for all who will hear and obey them."

The remainder of the message passed quicker than a ripple in a pond, vanishing almost as soon as it started. Before the meeting ended, they sang one last song and prayed together.

Soon after the prayer, however, the congregants pelted him with questions ranging from the nature of the Eucharist to the mode of baptism. He answered them to the best of his knowledge, and when he didn't know, he admitted it.

Their hunger for God's Word was undeniable, and their search for truth insatiable. If only they could read the Holy Scriptures themselves and follow in the same paths he had found only a few years earlier.

As the last guests departed, Andreas settled onto his pallet. The next day held the promise of a reunion with Constanza and the children. Tomorrow, Lord willing, they would pack for the journey back to Piedmont.

23

Philip was a youth of high spirit and valor, but restless, stubborn, ambitious. At a very early age he had learned to despise his father, and rose in rebellion against him: he put himself at the head of the discontented barons, in opposition to the Cypriot minions of the duchess.

—Antonio Carlo Napoleone Gallenga
History of Piedmont, 1855

LATE THE NEXT AFTERNOON , Andreas paced across the stone path inside the gates of Château de Thonon. Three Savoyard guards loyal to the duke stood behind the closed iron gate. With God's grace and perhaps a few concessions to Philip, his family would soon be reunited. He would see Constanza again, gaze into her deep brown eyes, and hold her delicate form. The children would run to him, hug him, jump into his arms, and laugh with him.

When Philip released Constanza and the children and Elionor, Andreas could introduce them to the Renauds and the rest of the Poor of Thonon. After that, they could go home—back to the alpine meadows of their valley and back to their humble Vallense church. Once Andreas told the barbes there about these believers, Estève, Bertran, or some other barbe would surely pay Thonon a visit and perhaps bring a Bible too.

The Lord had used him in more than one way here. Though Andreas would have never chosen to be in the middle of such a situation, God had allowed him to encourage the Poor and come to a mild reconciliation with his parents. Surely this would strengthen the bonds of his own family too.

The clap of footsteps fell on the street outside. Andreas stretched on his toes and peered through the bars of the gate, trying to glimpse Constanza or any of the children.

Philip walked at the center of the detachment, clad in elaborately embroidered royal garments. Directly behind him, six armed soldiers walked abreast in a tight formation, one of them Elias Renaud. At least forty men-at-arms marched behind Philip and his officers. Andreas caught Elias's eye, and Elias responded with a slight but encouraging nod.

Andreas pushed aside two of the guards, wrapped his hands around the bars of the gate, and shifted from side to side. Where was Constanza? *Lord, let her be here!*

His gaze locked onto the clean white cloth peeking out from behind Elias. His heart skipped a couple of beats. There she was, his beloved, her chestnut hair tucked beneath her kerchief and her eyes alight with life. How could she be more beautiful?

For a moment, Andreas stood rooted to his spot, unable to tear his gaze away from Constanza. She walked behind the soldiers, her graceful movements drawing his heart closer with each step. She seemed unaware of his presence, her attention absorbed by the sights and sounds of Thonon.

"Constanza!" The word tore from his lips.

At the sound of her name, she turned, her eyes meeting his with a blend of joy and tears. All the distance and separation vanished. Even the iron gate between them seemed to melt away. Time stood still, and nothing else mattered.

Breaking protocol, Elias quickened his pace and allowed a gap to form beside him. Constanza pushed through and ran to the gate.

Andreas shook the bars. "Open this!" he shouted to the guards.

Constanza wept as she reached for him. "Andreas! How I've longed for you, Andreas!"

With trembling hands, he reached through the cold metal, fingers extended desperately toward Constanza's outstretched hands. Her touch ignited a burning desire to hold her, to kiss her, to let her weep on his shoulder.

"Guards, is something wrong with the gate?" Andreas asked sharply.

"No, my lord. Monsieur Bouchard instructed us to wait for him before allowing anyone to enter."

Andreas spun toward the guards, though he still held Constanza's hands. "Who is Monsieur Bouchard to me? I am the son of the duke, and you must obey me first."

"I . . . I can't do that. I would be punished."

"Then find Monsieur Bouchard and tell him Lord Philip has arrived." Andreas tried to conceal his impatience but failed. "Now!"

"Yes, my lord!" The guard stumbled backward and ran toward the citadel.

Andreas turned back to Constanza. "All will be well soon." Behind her, Philip, Elias, and the other soldiers still marched steadily toward the gate. Andreas kissed her hands through the bars. "Where are our children?"

"They made me come alone, Andreas." Her shoulders slumped slightly as she took a slow breath.

He shook the iron gate. "Philip, you deceitful *canaille*, where are my children?"

"Safe in my château." Philip said with a haughty smirk.

"You read the terms and accepted the invitation. Both my wife and my children must be here."

"No one makes demands of me." Philip stood a few paces back from the gate, his men flanking him. "Only by my generosity did I bring along your woman."

The guard returned from the citadel, breathless. "Monsieur Bouchard said to open the gate."

If the gate opened and the feast commenced, when would Andreas see his children? Would there be more offers, counteroffers, invitations, feasts, and conversations that all ended in frustration? He couldn't let this insufferable dance of wills continue. It stopped here, now.

He lifted Constanza's hand through the bars and kissed it again. "Trust me." He released her and walked to the guard who held the key. "Don't open it."

"My lord?" The guard scratched his neck.

"Lord Philip failed to meet the terms of his invitation, and he cannot enter."

"But Monsieur Bouchard—"

Philip's voice rose from behind the gate. "Do not speak that man's name in my presence."

At least on one thing, Andreas agreed with Philip. "Monsieur Bouchard is not here, and his word does not usurp mine. The gate remains closed."

The door of the citadel opened far beyond the guard, and Mâre walked out with two attendants. Her lavish red dress swished as one of the escorts held her arm and guided her forward.

Andreas turned to Constanza. "That is my mâre, Duchess Anne of Cyprus."

"She's stunning, just as I imagined her."

"Sickness has taken her, though, and the physicians say her time on earth is fading."

"As it is for us all." Constanza reached for his hand through the gate.

Andreas took two steps toward her and held her hand again. "T'aimi, Constanza. I can't tell you how much I've longed for you."

"T'aimi tanben." She lifted his hand to her cheek and nestled up to it.

"Open the gate." Mâre's command brought the guards to attention.

Andreas kissed Constanza's hand but continued holding it as he shifted his focus to Mâre. "Philip hasn't met the conditions. My children aren't here."

Mâre ignored him and focused on Constanza instead. "Is this she?"

Andreas nodded. "Constanza"—he made certain Mâre heard the next words—"my wife."

"A peasant indeed but at least a pretty one." Mâre motioned to the guards. "Continue opening the gates."

"The feast hasn't yet started, and already Philip is conniving." Andreas walked to Mâre and touched her shoulder. "You can't allow him to act like this."

She cast a reprimanding glance at him. "The realm always comes before family, which is something you have never learned. Honor and prestige have nothing to do with whom we love."

The gate creaked open, each side pulled inward by a guard. Heart racing, Andreas rushed to Constanza. He took her in his arms, pulling her close as if to reassure himself she was there. For a moment, his vision blurred and warmth welled at the corner of his eye.

As he kissed her cheek, he whispered her favorite promise. "Forever." Never again would he leave her. No matter what happened during the feast, regardless of what Philip said, Andreas would be both her champion and defender.

He kissed Constanza again, this time on her lips, then held her arms. "All will be well soon."

Philip's retinue moved as one into Château de Thonon, with Andreas and Constanza following close behind. Oddly, many of Philip's men-at-arms were allowed to pass through the gate too, though they remained in the outer courtyard.

Andreas and Constanza entered the citadel, arms and hands entwined. The air was heavy with the fragrance of exotic spices, and the flicker of countless candles painted frolicking shadows on the tapestries lining the walls.

Constanza turned about in wonder. "I've never seen so many riches. You were raised here?"

"Partially. Other residences too—Chambéry, Allaman, Chillon—but here at Thonon most."

"I'm not prepared for this." Constanza pushed strands of hair under her kerchief, then brushed a hand across her skirts. "Look at all these elegant dresses. And the ladies' hair."

"You are far richer and more beautiful than anyone who has ever graced these halls, Lady Constanza."

Andreas tugged her forward to catch up with Mâre. Once they reached her, he beckoned Mâre to halt. "Please allow me to formally introduce Constanza."

Mâre stopped, coughed into a cloth, and eyed Constanza.

"I am happy to meet you at last, madòna." Constanza's sweet, considerate tone softened the swirling tension. "If you'd rather, I can call you mamà . . . but I suppose you don't say that here. May I call you mâre?"

"My son's crude mistress, who thinks I am her mother." Mâre jutted out her chin and rolled her shoulders back. "No, woman, I am no relation to you."

Andreas bristled and tried to maintain his poise. "By insulting her, Mâre, you also insult your son. Before God and man, Constanza is my wife, and I her husband. No power on earth can break our bond."

Constanza held his arm a little tighter. Mâre turned, coughed, and continued into the great hall, the same place Andreas had met her two days earlier. The stone foundation in the center of the room had been completed, and to the right, near the arched windows, was the long dining table.

"Your seat is there, Andreas," Mâre said, pointing to a chair near the corner.

A few of his younger brothers and sisters conversed at the table already, all grown in stature since he had last seen them. But only one empty seat was among them.

"We need another place set." Andreas squeezed Constanza's hand. "One for me, and one for my wife." He emphasized the last word.

Mâre laughed as if amused. "You mock us, my son. Nobles never eat with peasants."

"She eats with the rest of us, or I leave."

Philip positioned himself next to Andreas. "Then you will leave by yourself, because the woman remains with me until you relinquish your title."

"Take my title." Andreas threw his hands up. "Call me whatever name you wish. Squash me like the peasant I am. All I want is to live in peace."

Philip grinned and dipped his head. "Very well, I'll have a document for you to sign soon."

"Andreas is my son, and Louis is his father." Mâre shut her eyes for a moment and sighed. "I have no doubts about Andreas's legitimacy."

Philip ignored Mâre and motioned toward Constanza. "Until all is official, the woman will sit with the servants in the kitchens so as not to stain our dignity with her stench."

"Even my adviser, Lucien, was not invited," Mâre said.

Philip scowled. "That was a wise choice, for I would have left as soon as I laid eyes upon that Cypriot."

"Do not forget, I am a Cypriot too—along with all my children, which includes you." Mâre nodded toward Constanza. "I mean no offense, but this table is for those of our noble house alone."

Andreas despised treating Constanza as if she were an item to be bartered for. But he wouldn't leave her side. "At least allow her to sit nearby, perhaps in a privileged position. Command the servants to carry a bench into the hall and set it behind me. I'm not staying here while Constanza sits with the servants."

Philip raised a finger to object, but Mâre spoke first. "For this evening only, I suppose she may sit behind you."

"She's a peasant, Mâre." Philip sneered at Constanza. "Let her eat with the dogs."

Andreas opened his mouth and readied a lashing of words. Constanza grabbed his arm but addressed Mâre. "Mercé—I'm honored you would allow me to dine in the same room as you."

"I am grateful my seat is at the other end of the table," Philip said.

Constanza gave him an exaggerated curtsy. "And I am likewise grateful."

Philip scowled at Andreas and spun away.

Soon two servants carried a bench into the room and placed it behind Andreas's chair. With a gentle touch and a reassuring wink, he guided Constanza to the bench and seated her. "It's you who deserves the place of highest honor in this hall."

"You should've come with me and eaten with the servants." She motioned for Andreas to come closer and leaned toward his ear. "They would make more enjoyable dinner companions."

Andreas took his seat at the table. The grandeur of the hall and the poised expressions of his siblings evoked memories of a life of riches and prestige. Instinctively he lifted his head and straightened his posture. *Always command the highest respect in the room*, Pâre had taught him long ago.

Duke Louis of Savoy presided over the table, but to his right sat the man who demanded more attention than all others in the hall. Nose raised high and sleeves puffed up like clouds of vanity, Philip sat tall with a commanding air none other could match. Mâre sat at Andreas's right, his sister Agnes to his left. Farther down the table, beyond Pâre and Philip, sat various uncles, aunts, and cousins.

Andreas motioned to his siblings but addressed Constanza. "Allow me to introduce Agnes, Jean Louis, Marie, Bona, Giacomo, and little François."

"I'm not little!" François looked at Mâre with a pouting lip. "Is he my brother?"

"Yes, Andreas is your older brother."

Andreas sat upright. "Do you not remember me, François?"

"Five years have passed since you last saw us," Mâre said. "The boy was an infant when you left for the abbey."

Twelve-year-old Marie stared at Constanza. "Why does she not dress properly for the feast?"

"She's not actually his wife," Agnes said. "The peasant woman is his mistress."

Constanza stirred in her seat, obviously uncomfortable.

"I have never taken a mistress, nor will I ever," Andreas said. "Before both God and man, Constanza and I became one, just as the Holy Scriptures teach us."

"Yet you did so without a priest and without the consent of your parents." Mâre sat upright in her chair, her poise perfect but her breathing labored. "By all that is legal in this realm, you are unwed, therefore making her your mistress."

Philip lifted his goblet and cackled. "That's quite a jump, Andreas—from a devoted monk in holy orders to a typical member of our noble house. I have taken a few mistresses myself—"

"A few?" Mâre leaned forward and craned her neck to look at Philip. "I am more surprised at which women in Thonon you haven't claimed."

Philip took a long drink of wine and held the cup toward Mâre. "No worse than my own mâre."

Silence fell over the table. Servants filed into the hall, their arms laden with platters and bowls. Steaming dishes of roasted game birds, golden skin glistening in the candlelight, released a rich, savory fragrance. Beside them, bowls of hearty root vegetables, freshly harvested from the fields, offered a riot of colors and textures. An opulent display of ripe fruits adorned the center of the table, their vibrant hues of red, orange, and gold alluding to the bountiful harvest.

"Committing yourself to the Church must have been difficult," Pâre said to Andreas as he filled his plate. "But you cannot waste your life on one peasant woman. You are a son of a duke, not some petty lord." He gave Constanza a wry smile. "I can see why you enjoy her company, though. She is a charming young woman."

Andreas drew in a long breath and clenched his fists under the table. As he sat here, with Constanza demoted to a bench in the periphery, his pâre, his mâre, even his siblings insulted her. She deserved far better than how his family treated her. He gave each nearby family member a grave look. "I have chased cultists, traversed the Alps, braved a raging river, and scaled a château wall to save my family. I would give my life for any one of them, most of all my wife."

Philip gave a quick shrug and laughed. "This should all be settled soon, and you will no longer need to worry about what we think of your . . . relationship." He eyed Pâre. "First, we must come to a suitable settlement."

Pâre and Philip spoke with muted voices as they ate. Andreas stared at the dishes of game bird, turnips, and lentils. *Dear God, let this ordeal come to an end, even while I eat. I'm willing to forsake every birthright, every inheritance, and every title to have my family again.*

He heaped a plate with as much as it would hold and handed it to Constanza.

"Are there two of me?" she asked, giving him a playful smile.

Andreas offered a lighthearted chuckle. "One of you is more than enough for me."

Her gaze shifted subtly as she hid a smile. How could she remain so cheerful amid the insults?

He smiled inwardly and remembered the little item he had carried all the way from Piedmont. He pulled the worn white cloth from his pocket and showed it to Constanza. "This is yours, I believe."

"My kerchief!" She turned to the side and unfastened the one she wore. "One of Philip's officers bought Elionor and me each one of these out of kindness, but this one suits me better. Elionor, though—"

Mâre's elbow jabbed Andreas's side.

"I'll tell you later," Constanza said, placing the kerchief from Andreas on her head.

His wife was better company than anyone else in this room, but soon this would all be over, and he could talk to her for hours. He closed his eyes and sighed, then opened them and turned to Mâre.

"You should have been heir," she said, leaning toward Andreas. "Since you were a child, I have thought that."

"Yet God chose otherwise. Instead He has given me a life far more fulfilling than anything I could have imagined."

"Perhaps, but you know as well as I do that Amadeus is weak. It is a pity you were not born first, for then none of this would have occurred. You are patient, you are strong, you are wise—like your grandfather before you."

"Don't say such things, Mâre. Amadeus is the rightful heir."

"Yet as we sit here, your younger brother Philip will claim the duchy for himself." She turned her eyes toward the negotiations unfolding to her right. Philip's hands rose and fell in rhythm with his mouth. Pâre's gestures, however, were subdued and hesitant, as if he were yielding to Philip without question.

Mâre coughed into her cloth. "I fear for my life if Philip gains a hold on the realm."

Andreas pushed the food around on his plate, eating little. Constanza had finished her course with ease and now sat content behind him.

At the corner of his right eye, Pâre and Philip rose in unison. Andreas's chest tightened as he turned once more to Constanza and whispered, "Pray."

"My son and I have reached an agreement." The duke's chest seemed to cave, and his shoulders dropped. "Because of Amadeus's and Andreas's illegitimacy, I name Philip my rightful heir and grant him the customary title Prince of Piedmont instead of Amadeus."

Mâre rose in protest, her legs trembling as she stood. "I am . . . I was a faithful wife. Amadeus and Andreas both are your legitimate sons."

Pâre stared at his wife and mouthed, "Forgive me."

"You cannot allow Philip to be heir. You have already weakened Savoy to near insolvency."

Philip held his head high and smirked. "No, it is you, Mâre, who has weakened our realm and brought shame upon her. Savoy will once again be prestigious—no, glorious, when I reign."

Andreas rose, placing his hands on the table and leaning toward Philip. "Then you will release my family? I've done what you've asked. Now return them to me."

Philip gave Andreas a sidelong glance. "With all that has transpired, you interrupt me with your petty concerns?" He pushed a piece of parchment across the table toward Andreas. "But indeed, as soon as you provide your signature and thus renounce any claims as a son of Louis of Savoy, the women and children will be released."

Andreas pulled the document toward him and read from the top. By signing it, he would be declared illegitimate and renounce all claims to the duchy.

He looked up at Pâre. "You would allow Philip to usurp you and disgrace our house?"

"In time, he will become a fine leader." Pâre scowled at Constanza. "At least he remains faithful to the customs of this house."

"You are the one who has been begging for this," Philip said to Andreas. "It is you who desired that all your ties to the House of Savoy be severed. You may take your little family and leave as you please, so long as you never again claim to be a legitimate son of Duke Louis of Savoy."

Philip passed a quill to Pâre, who passed it to Mâre. Philip motioned for her to offer it to Andreas. "Sign your name at the bottom, brother. Be done with this ordeal and return to your hovel in Piedmont."

"Even if I sign this, Amadeus never will. He is the Prince of Piedmont, thus heir to the duchy."

Philip sighed and shook his head. "Amadeus has no desire to be duke. We both know this. It is Yolande who holds the power in that family, and if she were allowed to reign, she would deliver Savoy to her brother, who will soon become the king of France. By signing, you also secure the sovereignty of our house for generations to come."

"Then you will become the Duke of Savoy?" Andreas took the quill from Mâre's trembling hand, and a servant placed an inkwell in front of him.

"In time, but while Pâre lives, I will act as regent."

"Much as I was to my father before I reigned," Pâre said.

"Philip won't allow you to lead." Mâre clasped her hands. "He will push you to the side and bring the duchy to ruin before he even ascends to his position."

"Ruin?" Philip held his hands aloft and motioned to their surroundings. "You and your Cypriot courtiers have already accomplished that."

Mâre sank to her seat and breathed heavily.

Andreas pushed his chair back, stood, and moved toward Constanza, his hand finding hers for reassurance. Signing Philip's parchment could secure his family's freedom, but what other webs of problems might that weave? Would it quell the intrigues or merely birth new ones? Yet if he refused to sign, Constanza and the children would languish in captivity. Each moment, each day he delayed only deepened their separation.

"How can I sign this?" he whispered to Constanza. "It would be lying and bearing false witness against my own mâre."

"Then you must do what is right."

Andreas flashed a half smile at her. "And rash?"

She squeezed his hand tight and smiled back. "Yes, and rash."

Andreas released her hand, returned to the table, and placed a hand on the top edge of the document, feeling as if the whole table held its breath. He scanned the faces surrounding him: his younger siblings, Mâre, Philip, Pâre, distant relatives. In the shadows beyond the table, Elias stood along the wall. How would this arrangement affect the Poor? And Philip's ascension would affect far more than just Thonon. If Andreas signed, all of Savoy, including Piedmont and Val Angrogna, would be subject to the new duke.

He pushed the parchment away, then moved toward Constanza, who rose to stand beside him.

Philip's face turned red. He snatched the parchment and tore it in two. "Then you have chosen to never see your family again."

Andreas lifted his chest and positioned himself in front of Constanza. "Do what is just and right, Philip, I beg you. With your first act as heir, grant me and my family mercy."

Philip let out a short laugh, grabbed his cape, and pivoted away from Andreas. He nodded toward another piece of parchment in front of Pâre. "Allons, fâs-le, Pâre. Do not be a fool like Andreas. Sign it, and your legacy will be preserved."

"You would treat the Duke of Savoy as a common servant?" Mâre stretched out her hand to grab the parchment but kept her gaze on Philip.

Philip pushed her arm aside. Pâre signed his name and turned, the parchment in hand. With his chin held high, he declared, "May all of Savoy rejoice with us on this day."

"The pope will never accept this treachery," Mâre said under her breath.

Philip held up a finger. "Guards, constrain the duchess."

Two men rushed to Mâre and pulled her away from the table.

"These are my men," Pâre said. "Guards, release her. She is your duchess."

"She *was* their duchess." Philip pointed at the document again. "Savoy now belongs to me and my heirs."

"I still live."

"No, due to your failing health I am now regent."

"Guards!" Pâre shouted.

Twenty or more armed soldiers suddenly entered the hall, but none obeyed the duke's commands.

"They are all mine." Philip chuckled. "I assumed you would resist, so as we sat here, my men seized all of Château de Thonon. You have no power, Pâre."

Andreas clasped Constanza's hand and backed away with her. "I expected no less of Philip. Stay close. I won't let them take you from me."

Mâre screamed and thrashed as a man pulled her from her chair. Others took Pâre and Andreas's younger siblings.

Someone grabbed Andreas from behind. Andreas spun and threw a fist at the man but winced when it connected with Elias's jaw. "You . . . you're a traitor. I thought—"

"Something here is odd." Elias's eyes darted around the room as he rubbed his jawline. "Pretend I'm your captor—both of you. Step with me into the shadows . . . carefully." He grabbed Andreas's arms and held them. "Struggle a little."

"What's wrong?" Every muscle in Andreas yearned to fight, but Elias sounded like he was telling the truth.

"I don't know most of these soldiers."

Three burly soldiers grabbed Philip from behind and jerked him away from the table.

"Faster." Elias pulled Andreas backward, while Andreas kept a firm grip on Constanza's hand. "Melt into the darkness with me."

"Release me, you fools." Philip glanced around in confusion. "I am your lord."

The men held Philip in place, ignoring his command.

From the hall entrance, five new soldiers appeared, and behind them strode a bald man wearing a dull brown cloak.

Constanza gasped. "The Prophet."

"The Prophet?" Andreas eyed the cloaked man. "No, that's Monsieur Lucien Bouchard."

"I know the face of the man who murdered my papà. Whatever his true name is, he is the Prophet of the Divine Ascendancy."

Lucien Bouchard marched toward Philip, his cloak swaying behind him. Pâre shouted for help, and Philip did the same. Swords clashed near the table as two soldiers seemingly loyal to the duke fought other armed men. The duke's few men were quickly subdued.

"You so easily sign away the duchy with the stroke of a quill?" Bouchard stopped in front of Pâre and frowned. "The House of Savoy is weak indeed."

Constanza shuddered and reached for Andreas. "That voice . . . I know he's the Prophet."

"You Cypriot canaille." Philip sneered at Bouchard despite the soldiers holding his arms. "I will feed your carcass to my cats. My men far outnumber your rabble and have already taken the citadel."

"Your men? Command any in this hall and see if they obey you." Bouchard's words echoed off the stone floor. "As of now, the Duchy of Savoy is no more. A new power arises."

"Lucien, what is this?" Mâre stared at him. "I love you. Are you not a loyal servant of my household?"

"Decadence, corruption, hedonism—these are the marks of your house, dear Anne. Today this ends forever." He waved dismissively toward Mâre. "The faithful will rule in your stead, for the day of the Lord is at hand."

A slow, humming chant swelled from every corner of the great hall. "Ecce lux prophetæ ducet nos. Ecce lux prophetæ ducet nos . . ." *The light of the prophet shall guide us.*

"Now do you see?" Bouchard addressed his followers. "All has come to pass exactly as I prophesied. Follow me and spread the message for all the world to hear. In five days, the skies shall confirm it again. Étoilembra shall blot out the sun over Thonon, and the crown of twelve stars shall be cast down. Then the Ascendants shall reign in a new world."

Andreas shook his head as his pulse quickened. All these months, Lucien Bouchard had wormed his way into the House of Savoy's graces, twisting his presence into every aspect of the duchy, from day-to-day responsibilities like lumber quotas and château management to the power that came from his relationship with Mâre. He must have been the one who had pushed Philip into open rebellion. It was also he who had murdered Nicolaus Pavarin and stolen Constanza and the children.

Andreas had stepped into Bouchard's trap of his own free will. But he could not allow that trap to close around him and Constanza.

He eyed the small door to the right. One lone soldier stood there. Andreas turned to Elias. "I know the way out if you help us through that door."

"The Ascendants won't take kindly to that."

"Then we'll force our way out. I'm heading to Château de Ripaille for my children and Elionor."

"Not alone," Elias said.

"Constanza and I will keep our heads down. Treat us like we're your prisoners again."

Elias shoved Andreas in the back and grunted at him. "Like that?"

"Harder."

The slow, melancholy chant of the Ascendants continued, growing louder with each verse.

Elias marched Andreas and Constanza around the edge of the hall until they reached the door. As the lone guard approached, Elias swiftly interposed himself between Andreas and Constanza, his grip firm on Andreas's arm while his other hand grasped Constanza's elbow. "I'm escorting these faithless to the dungeon."

The guard stared them down, unmoving. "Who are they?"

"A minor noble couple. Now move, soldier."

"Soldier? Who are you to command me? In the Ascendant Kingdom, all will be equal."

As Elias pulled Andreas and Constanza toward the door, the guard took a position in front of it. "We stay here until the Prophet is finished. This is the moment we've all been waiting for. Soon all will submit to Christ and the Prophet."

Elias released his hold on Andreas and Constanza. In a flash, he drew his sword and held it to the guard's throat. "Drop your sword, soldier."

The guard fumbled for his sword and dropped it to the ground. Its clatter reverberated through the great hall, interrupting the Ascendants' chant.

Andreas tensed, feeling Bouchard's unseen glare as sharp as a blade at his back.

Elias kicked the guard in the stomach and opened the door. Andreas seized the fallen sword, then grabbed Constanza's hand and led her outside. A flurry of pounding feet and yells rose behind them.

Elias shut the door. "I hope you know the way out."

"Follow me." Andreas took the lead, gripping the sword as they navigated the dimly lit corridors of the citadel. Each step echoed the pounding of his heart as he sprinted forward.

The narrow passageways twisted and turned like a maze. As boys, he and Amadeus had often played in this same hall—crusaders against the cursed Mohammedans.

Constanza followed close behind him, and Elias held the rear. The sound of pursuit rolled down the corridors. Andreas drew in a labored breath and ran faster.

As he rounded each corner, he scanned for danger lurking in the darkness. Each shout from behind, every flicker of movement, sent a jolt through his veins.

At last they reached the heavy wooden servants' door. Andreas turned and pulled Constanza close. "The stable is across the courtyard from these doors. Are you ready to ride?"

"If there are horses," Elias said.

"Let's pray there are. If not, this will be a very short-lived flight."

Elias pushed the door open while Andreas held his sword ready for a fight. A wash of moonlight spilled across the courtyard and illuminated the cobblestone path toward the stable, beckoning them onward with the promise of escape. Andreas slowly ventured outside and gestured for the others to follow. After a short jog, they reached the stable.

"I definitely smell horses," Constanza said.

Andreas led her and Elias into the stable. Moonlight filtered through the wooden slats, casting shifting patterns of light and shadow on the straw-covered floor. The scent of hay and musky warmth surrounded him as he hurriedly scanned the rows of stalls, his hand still firmly clasped around Constanza's.

At the sight of a sleek black steed, Constanza loosened her grip. "This one is as good as any." She lifted a saddle from a peg on the wall, and Andreas helped her throw it onto the horse's back.

"I found one too," Elias said.

Another black steed stood amid the shadows across from Constanza. Andreas approached it with measured steps, assessing its temperament while it regarded him with dark, intelligent eyes. It would serve him well.

Shouts rose from the courtyard. Andreas's heart pounded against his breastbone as he saddled his horse and helped Constanza mount hers. "We'll ride through the courtyard, but not too fast." Lacking a sheath for his sword, he found a length of old rope, looped it around the hilt and blade, then tied it to the saddle. At least it wouldn't swing while he rode.

Elias sheathed his sword and mounted the horse he had chosen. "I'll lead the way."

Andreas turned to Constanza. "Are you certain you can manage her?"

She flashed a confident smile at him. "I ride better than you."

With a quick glance at Andreas, Elias burst from the stable into the courtyard. Andreas spurred his mount, Constanza close behind.

The horses pounded across the cobblestones, the pace brisk but controlled as they crossed the courtyard.

Andreas gripped the reins tightly and followed Elias. Constanza's form swayed rhythmically beside him.

Soldiers ran from the principal door of the citadel, swords drawn. Elias urged his horse onward, and soon Andreas and Constanza matched his pace. They veered left toward the gate. But it was shut.

Elias pulled back on his reins and turned toward Andreas. "Any other ways out?"

There was the old lakeside gate, but the path was narrow and winding. Could horses navigate it? They would have to.

In one abrupt motion, Andreas pivoted his horse on its hindquarters until it faced the right direction. He gave the horse a light kick and led the way toward the lakeside gate.

A crossbow bolt whizzed behind him. They had to gallop faster. He nudged his heels into the horse's flanks. Its hooves pounded harder against the earth.

Vines grew over the gate, but it stood unguarded. At least ten soldiers pursued them, but the men weren't yet halfway across the courtyard.

Andreas leaned back, pulling the reins taut, and dismounted in a fluid leap. He ran to the gate and pulled. Locked. He kicked the gate, but it refused to budge.

The metallic rasp of a sword leaving its sheath scraped through the air. Elias came up alongside him and found the rusty lock. He slammed his sword hilt into it twice, and it fell into the grass.

Andreas let out a little chuckle as he and Elias pulled the gate open. They swiftly remounted their horses and urged them forward, ducking through the gate with Constanza following.

The thud of boots grew louder behind them, punctuated by urgent shouts and the clatter of armor. Carefully but still with haste, the three spurred their horses into a single file—Andreas first, followed by Constanza, and Elias in the rear.

On the hillside nearby stood a dense thicket of trees. Andreas spurred his horse toward it, then halted under the branches and listened for any sign of close pursuit. A single command rang out. The thump of marching feet swelled, passed along the lakeshore, then turned south into the town.

When all was silent, Andreas brought his horse alongside Constanza's, reached for her hand, and kissed it. "Elias and I will go to Ripaille alone. I don't want to place you in more danger."

"Please let me go with you. I want to help Elionor and our children too."

Elias scanned the edge of the thicket. "We have no time."

"We need all the help we can muster. What if we fetch Johan at your parents' home and leave Constanza there?"

Elias nodded. "Follow me."

They wound their way up a steep hillside, staying behind the cover of the trees, until they reached the outskirts of the town.

"We'll draw too much attention with the horses." Elias swung out of his saddle. "Leave them here."

Andreas dismounted, untied his sword, and helped Constanza to the ground. Elias quietly led them down a narrow alley, then veered onto a shadowy lane. Townspeople milled about as if all were normal. Church bells tolled in the distance, their chimes mingling with the low hum of conversation from the nearby tavern.

At last they reached the Renaud home. Elias made certain no one was following, then opened the door.

Johan rose from the hearth as soon as they entered. "You found her!"

"The children are still at Ripaille." Andreas placed his hands on his knees and took deep breaths. "We need your help."

Elias unbuckled his sword belt and tossed Johan his sheathed sword. Johan caught it. "What's this—"

"Use it. I have another."

"Where are we going?"

"We have to fight our way into Ripaille and rescue Elionor and the children."

Johan strapped on the belt. "Just the three of us?"

Constanza grabbed Andreas's arm. "Don't leave me here . . . I beg you."

"Antoine and Marie are good people—believers too."

"What if you can't make it back here? What if the only path of escape is away from Thonon?" Constanza threw her arms around Andreas's chest. "I won't fight. I'll stay somewhere nearby until you find the children."

"She'll be a help with the children," Andreas said to Elias.

"Asse sie, she can follow." Elias strapped on his other sword. "How was Elionor when you last saw her?"

Constanza flashed a mischievous grin. "Why do you ask, Lugotenent?"

His lips twitched as he suppressed a smile. "We can't waste time."

Andreas wrapped his arm through Constanza's and held her close. "Then let's knock on the door of Château de Ripaille."

24

To have the Gospels on one's table, in one's own home, written not in Latin, but in a comprehensible language, made possible a direct, personal relationship.

—Marina Benedetti
A Companion to the Waldenses in the Middle Ages, 2022

A BREEZE CARRIED the earthy scents of autumn through the crisp night air. Andreas walked alongside Constanza, while Johan and Elias took up the vanguard of their meager force. The town of Thonon now lay behind them, and after a half hour's walk, they would arrive at Château de Ripaille.

Andreas gave Constanza a brief account of his and Johan's journey. Then she explained her tale, from her papà's murder to Philip's announcement that she would see Andreas at Thonon.

Elias slowed his pace until he walked beside Andreas. "Philip nearly emptied Ripaille of men this afternoon so he could overthrow the duke."

"Yet little did he know that most of his men were Ascendants," Andreas said.

"I knew some had infiltrated, but I didn't realize how many." Elias shook his head with deliberate motions. "I should have seen it. Too many recruits joined in the past month."

"Bouchard must have been planning this for months."

"Or years," Elias said. "Adviser to the House of Savoy and leader of an end-of-days sect."

"My mâre's companion."

"And Papà's murderer." Constanza spoke in a low monotone.

They soon walked into the dark forest surrounding Ripaille, where the thick carpet of fallen leaves muffled their steps.

Johan drew the sword Elias had lent him and held it out, examining it. "Three of us against how many?"

"Some men must still be loyal to Philip—most likely the officers. But Bouchard would have made sure some of his men stayed behind with the children."

"Why?" Constanza asked.

Elias gave Andreas a sidelong glance.

Andreas squeezed her hand. "I'll tell you later."

The forest thinned, and the low walls of Château de Ripaille rose in the clearing ahead. Andreas pointed to a fallen tree within sight of the gate. "Constanza, you stay there."

"Where will you be?"

He nodded toward the wall. "Johan will help Elias and me over that wall. After that, we'll unlock the gate."

"There's only one man guarding it now," Elias said.

Constanza touched Andreas's cheek. "Please don't do anything rash."

"The line between rash and right is blurred tonight, I'm afraid." Andreas gave her a long kiss, then released her. Johan and Elias were waiting. "Soon we'll be together and on our way home."

As he had three days earlier, Johan provided Andreas a foothold to scale the wall, and once he was atop it, Elias followed. Andreas clasped Elias's hand and pulled him over the top.

Elias pointed to a window on the far left side of the château. "Elionor and your children are there."

"If they could climb down from windows and scale walls like we can, this would be much simpler."

"Which is why we need that gate unlocked."

Andreas craned his neck to look under the gate's alcove. "I can't see the guard from here."

"He's there . . . probably sleeping as usual. If we surprise him, we might not need to kill him."

"I've never killed a man." Andreas rubbed his thumb across the hilt of his sword.

"Be thankful for that, Andreas. Be thankful."

They dropped into the courtyard and hugged the shadowed edges of the outer wall, their movements deliberate and quiet.

The guard slept against the gate's wooden frame, his snores blending with the sounds of the night. With silent urgency, Elias gestured for Andreas to stand watch while he crept closer. He closed the distance to the slumbering guard, and with deft hands, he clamped the guard's mouth shut and grabbed his shoulder.

Andreas ran to the gate. Elias's grip on the guard's mouth remained firm. "Sleeping on watch?"

The guard stiffened with startled recognition and mumbled.

"Who is your lord, soldier?"

Again the guard gave a muffled answer.

"Take your hand off his mouth a little, Elias."

He lifted his fingers.

The guard gasped. "I'm loyal to Lord Philip, Lugotenent. He hasn't yet returned from Thonon. I'm sorry about sleeping on watch. Please, my wife and children live in town. I have a sick daughter. My family needs my wages."

"Are there other soldiers inside?" Andreas asked.

"Yes, all housed in the north wing—new recruits."

Andreas peered up toward the window and sighed. "Ascendants. I wish we had more men."

"How did you get in here, Lugotenent? I saw you leave with Lord Philip earlier."

"Don't worry about us. Open the gate and go home to your family."

"The Cypriot, Lucien Bouchard, has overthrown the duke," Andreas said, "and those recruits inside are loyal to him."

The guard hesitated, and Andreas leaned closer. "Vâ! Open the gate."

"Yes . . . yes, I will." The guard's hand trembled as he reached for the gate controls. The metallic clang of the mechanism echoed softly as the gate began its slow ascent.

The guard gave them a parting wave and scampered off onto the pathway that led to Thonon.

Johan crept toward the gate and joined them inside. "You did it."

With a wry grin, Andreas turned to face him. "Did you doubt us?"

"Elias, no. Only you, my friend."

With Elias and Johan on either side, Andreas took swift but cautious strides across the courtyard until he reached the front door. Shouts erupted from inside.

"They know we're here." Elias pulled his sword from its scabbard. "Ready to fight?"

Andreas and Johan both held their swords in readiness. Andreas turned his ear to the imposing wooden door, the grainy texture cool against his cheek as he pressed closer, straining to capture every nuance of sound. Amid the hurried footsteps that reverberated through the aged timbers, men's voices rose and fell.

The voices and footsteps gradually receded, their cadence fading into the depths of the château. Andreas turned to Elias and Johan. "They're moving away."

"This might be our chance." Elias pushed against the door. "Locked."

Johan rammed his shoulder into the door and recoiled, wincing and grabbing his arm.

"You make a poor battering ram," Elias said, chuckling.

The door's lock suddenly clicked. Andreas lifted his sword and tensed. Elias and Johan did the same.

The door creaked open to reveal a brown-haired woman with a guarded face—and behind her, Elionor Janavel and twelve children.

"Papà!" Alessia bolted from the doorway and jumped into Andreas's arms.

Elias lowered his sword. "Madeleine, how did you—"

"Come," she said, waving the children forward. "Those guards will be angrier than a den of badgers when they discover there are no attackers scaling the north wall."

Fosca grabbed Andreas's hand, and together they all dashed to the gate. Constanza greeted them with open arms as soon as they passed through.

"Into the forest," Elias said, keeping an eye on the gate behind them. "You can enjoy your reunion there."

He led them under the canopy and into a glade. There, beneath the starry heavens, the children enveloped Andreas with hugs, kisses, and weeping. Tears glistened in Constanza's eyes as she gathered the children closer.

Andreas lifted his prayer to the heavens. "Thank You, Father. Thank You! You heard my cry, and You answered."

With each word of reassurance, the weeks of separation fled away. The children clung to him, their faces bright with happiness. At last, in the glow of the moonlight, his family stood in inseverable unity.

In the periphery, Elias and Elionor spoke, fleeting glances passing between them. Elias approached Madeleine, arms swinging as he walked. "Andreas, Johan, meet Madeleine, my sâre."

"Your sister?" Constanza wiped a tear from her eye.

"She's one of the Poor like Elias," Andreas said. "They call each other frâre and sâre."

Elias smiled. "Yes, Madeleine is my Christian sâre, but she's my older sâre by birth too."

"Only by five years," Madeleine said.

"The children whom you've seen at my parents' home—they're Madeleine's."

Johan slapped his knee and laughed. "Ah, they've kept me active for the last few days."

"I suppose they'll keep me active during the days again." Madeleine chuckled. "My work at Ripaille has come to an end, I'm afraid."

"Why didn't you tell us you were brother and sister?" Constanza asked, laughing.

Madeleine tucked a stray hair behind her ear. "It was safer this way. If no one knew, no one could use us against each other—or against our families."

"Madeleine's husband and children, our parents, our Christian frâres," Elias added. "They're better protected if no one knows who we are."

Madeline gestured toward Andreas and his family. "And it let us keep a closer watch on our new friends."

Constanza walked to Madeleine and hugged her. "You have been such a dear friend, like a bright star in the night. And now I know you're a fellow believer, though I've suspected it for a few days."

Andreas bowed his head toward Madeleine. "Merci bôcô for your care to my family, dama."

Silvia gazed up at Andreas. "When do we go home, Papà?"

"We should start tonight."

Elias shook his head. "As soon as Lucien Bouchard and his men know you've escaped, they'll hunt you down. If you leave tonight, they'll find you. Come to my home instead."

"Rest tonight," Madeleine said. "My pâre and mâre would love your family."

Andreas hesitated, then nodded. They did need to rest tonight, and the Renauds were a family they could trust.

As they reached the welcoming glow of the Renauds' home, Andreas breathed a sigh of relief. The warmth of the hearth beckoned them in, promising safety and solace. Andreas and his family crossed the threshold, leaving the darkness behind them. Surrounded by those he loved, he felt his burden dissolve, like a heavy fog vanishing under the morning sun. Whatever trials lay ahead, his family would face them together.

Antoine and Marie greeted them as soon as they entered. "We've been praying since you left," Marie said. "And now we rejoice again in answered prayer."

Andreas and Constanza's children joined Madeleine's, bringing the number of children in the small home to seventeen. With the eight adults, that made twenty-five in total. The children found a place wherever they could, most of them lying down near the fire. Marie and Madeleine covered them with anything they could find, whether wool, buckskin, or hemp. Before long, every child slept soundly close to the hearth.

Marie spread a thin layer of straw for the adults in the same room and handed Andreas and Constanza a large blanket made of down. "I'm sorry we couldn't provide better."

"It's only for one night," Andreas said, taking the blanket from her. He sat on the floor near the slumbering Roberto and Ezio and covered both himself and Constanza with the blanket. "Thank you again for opening your home to all of us."

Marie nodded once and smiled, then retired to her room for the night.

Andreas lay down, using his arm for a pillow, and let out a long breath. He reached for Constanza's hand. "I have so much to tell you."

"And I have much to tell you." She met his hand and held it to her cheek.

"It's so late."

"My heart is still racing. I have a feeling sleep will be hard to come by." She turned to her back and stared up at the rafters. "This is all like a dream, but still, I knew you would find us."

"You've endured so much, Constanza." Andreas caressed her cheek with his thumb.

"Every time I remember Papà, I weep. And to think of Mamà without him makes the tears fall faster." Chin trembling, Constanza rubbed the neckline of her bodice. "I miss them."

Andreas slid his arm under hers and drew her close. "Soon we'll see your mamà and everyone else."

"I'm thankful I can hold you again." She laid her head on his shoulder, wrapped her arm around his chest, and sniffled.

For a moment, they lay in silence, wrapped in each other's arms. A few of the children snored nearby. Near the door, Elias sat in a chair, keeping watch over both the door and the woman who lay on the floor a pace away.

Andreas propped his head up with his elbow. "Tell me, how did Elionor find herself here?"

"She came for help one day. But in truth, she's the one who's helped me."

For the next few moments, Constanza recounted Elionor's return to the valley, the invitation for her to stay, and her capture by the Ascendants.

Andreas drew closer to Constanza. "I noticed . . . she looks . . ."

"Yes, she is with child. Brando is the father, but he abandoned her."

"Yet here she is, dedicated to both you and our children."

"Elionor wants acceptance and forgiveness, but the guilt and shame weigh on her." Constanza pointed her nose toward Elias. "He cares for her. Wisely, she evaded his glances for weeks. Then two or three days ago, he said he believes as we do."

"Elias has a heart of true honor, just like his parents."

"And his sister." Constanza smiled and propped her head up, mimicking Andreas's posture. "Tell me more about these people you call the Poor."

"They don't have a Bible of their own, and I don't think they'd ever seen one before I showed them mine. They still attend the Mass—"

"Why? It's idolatry."

"I don't understand all their practices either, but I have seen their gatherings. They hunger for the Holy Scriptures like no one I've seen. And you should hear them sing, Connie. Their neighbors might conspire against them, the Church of Rome might persecute them, but these believers of Thonon remain steadfast."

"The barbes have always told us about these kinds of congregations—people who've never heard the name Vallense or met a barbe."

"Antoine told me a barbe preached to them generations ago. Now after all these years, even without a teacher or the written Scriptures, God has preserved them."

Constanza sighed. "They need a Bible . . . and a barbe."

The door creaked open, and a burst of chilled air entered the room. Elias leaned against the doorframe and peered outside, then shut the door.

"We need to leave in the morning," Andreas said. "I wish you could become more acquainted with Antoine, Marie, and all the others, but I feel Thonon is the worst place for us to be."

Constanza turned to her back again. "Why would the Prophet want us? I still don't understand."

"From what I gather, Lucien Bouchard has been doing everything he can to weaken the House of Savoy, all while positioning himself to topple it. He became my mâre's lover to control her and gain a powerful position. At the same time, he used Philip to sway the peasants against the duke. This afternoon at the feast, all of Bouchard's designs came to fruition. Philip thought the soldiers he had brought to capture the château and overthrow the duke were his, when in fact they were loyal to Bouchard."

"He's the leader of a fanatical sect. Why would he want to overthrow the duke?"

"The day of the Lord is at hand, according to him. Yet I don't think he actually believes what he preaches. I've known men like Lucien Bouchard—so hungry for power that they'll blaspheme God's name and twist the Scriptures to gain fame and followers. The Ascendants say all will be equal in his kingdom—no lords, no peasants, no merchants. They believe all flesh is sin, whether it be earthly possessions, procreation, or eating meat. But in truth, I think Bouchard only uses these things as a means of control."

"But what is our family to them? Why did the Prophet kill my papà?"

"I don't know fully, but I think he's using us to prove one of his twisted prophecies. You heard him tonight, and I mentioned it to you before your capture—the crown of twelve stars."

"What does that have to do with us?" Constanza paused and gasped. "Are you certain?"

"That's why we must leave tomorrow."

"Why would he come all the way to Piedmont for us? Surely there are other families with twelve children. Why our family . . . our children? How does he know about us?"

"Think about it. We fit his distorted Scriptures perfectly. The crown—that's me. Twelve stars, our children."

"And the woman clothed with the sun," Constanza said, grimacing, "is that supposed to be me? Elionor? What about the moon under her feet? I know that part of John's Apocalypse, and it's about Jesus and the twelve tribes of Israel, not any of us."

"Bouchard is a false prophet. He found an obscure portion of the Holy Scriptures and is using it to prove his power. However contrived it might be, if anything occurs that resembles what he teaches, then more men will bow to him."

"If we're so important, why would he surrender the children and me to Philip so easily at the lake?"

"Remember, most of Philip's troops were in fact loyal to the Prophet. Perhaps it was a ruse. I don't think a group of brown-cloaked Ascendants holding two women and twelve children against their will would have passed any of the sentry points between Piedmont and here. Yet a contingent of Savoyard soldiers could pass without question. Again, I think Bouchard used Philip."

"Do you think the Prophet will forget about us if we leave? Will he let us live in peace while he reigns over the whole duchy?"

"If he has no crown of twelve stars on the fourteenth of October, then the Divine Ascendancy will crumble in unbelief. Then the lords of Savoy and the Catholic Church will easily depose Bouchard and reinstate my pâre."

"Wonderful, papists with more prestige." Constanza lay down, closed her eyes, and nestled close to Andreas. "This is what I deserve for marrying a prince of Savoy."

"Soon we'll leave all of this behind us. Months from now, we'll hear news of the Prophet's demise." Andreas laid his head down and let out a long breath. "Then we'll all rejoice."

25

This adherence to the letter of evangelical commandments characterizes the Waldensian movement as a whole, and it was to cause them considerable hardship, for it imposed certain attitudes and procedures which appeared provocative in the society of the time.

—Gabriel Audisio
The Waldensian Dissent, 1999

E LIAS PULLED THE DOOR OPEN just enough to squeeze through. Outside, the first embers of dawn shone between the houses and cast long shadows across the streets of Thonon. He ventured onto the cobblestones, the cool morning air sending a shiver down his back.

Before he closed the door, Elias let his gaze linger on the huddled figures that lay scattered across the floor. God had guided these Vallenses into his path. From the moment he had first seen Elionor's smile and Constanza's unwavering resolve, he knew it was his duty to stand as their guardian until they could find their way home.

But he hadn't yet fulfilled that duty. As long as the Vallenses remained in Thonon, they were in danger. And today he must deliver them from that danger.

His gaze inevitably found Elionor's peaceful form resting on the floor. Lit by the dawn rays, her light brown locks cascaded around her pretty face, framing features that spoke of both fortitude and grace. Though he couldn't name his feelings, in her presence he found the peace that eluded him elsewhere.

But today she would leave him. If it weren't for his duty to care for *Paï* and *Maï*, he would follow the Vallenses to Piedmont. He ached for Elionor every moment. Would it be too bold to ask her to stay for a season? If he asked, would she accept?

Elias closed the door, stepping out into morning chill. He wrapped his gray cloak tighter around him and walked toward the well.

"Where's your uniform, Elias Renaud?" It was Marcel, an old man who lived in the next house. He stood with his hands wrapped around the handles of a resting wheelbarrow.

"I'm not on duty today, Marcel."

"That's more peculiar than a hare with feathers. I heard something happened at the château last night—something big and important. I figured you were there."

Elias sighed. He didn't have time for this, but he couldn't appear suspicious, even to an old neighbor like Marcel. "I was there. Duke Louis was overthrown by Lucien Bouchard."

"I knew something was about to happen. I've heard strange talk lately at the tavern—stars, crowns, eclipses, the end of the world. Meanwhile, I'm just trying to sell these." Marcel reached into the wheelbarrow and tossed a purple carrot to Elias. "Bonjorn, Lugotenent Renaud."

Elias flipped his hood over his head and wound through the cobblestone streets, chomping at the carrot. First he scouted the south road toward the mountains, but a company of men in the uniforms of Savoyard soldiers stood guard at the gate, inspecting every traveler who left the town. The same held true on the northern road toward Château de Ripaille and the west road to Genève. Ascendant soldiers even watched the docks along Lac Léman. Some men Elias recognized, while others were fresh faces. Not one of the three paths out of Thonon was safe.

He hurried back home, but as he rounded a corner, four men pounded on the door of Bernard and Catherine, a young couple who frequently attended gatherings of the frâres. Elias melted into the shadow of an empty market stall.

"Open the door!" shouted one of the men. "We hear you in there."

Catherine answered, two children clinging to her skirts.

"We're searching for Dama Madeleine Dupont. Where is she?"

"Ah, Madeleine. I think I've heard of her."

"Don't mistake us for fools, woman." An Ascendant grabbed Catherine's arm, pulled her away from her children, and threw her to the ground. "We know you're one of the Poor, and Dama Dupont is too."

Catherine shielded her face as the children ran to her. "Please, my husband is away working. We are loyal to the House of Savoy—"

"That's your problem." The soldier kicked a cloud of dust into her face.

Elias, fists clenched, scowled across the open area between him and the soldiers. *If I carried more than a knife . . .*

"The Duponts live near the lake." Catherine pointed in that direction with one hand and brushed the dust off her face with the other. "The house with a stone doorstep, a few doors down from the inn."

Elias turned his face away and smiled. Every house near that inn had a stone doorstep. *Perfect choice of words, Sâre Catherine.* But soon the Ascendants would discover the truth. They would question more frâres and sâres, and the trail would lead them to his parents' house. When the soldiers knocked on that door and saw everyone on the floor, they would know. The Vallenses couldn't remain there. Elias had to warn them.

He ran home through the alleys, and once he was certain no prying eyes watched him, he slipped inside. "You must leave now."

Andreas fastened his cloak and slung a sack over his shoulder. "We're almost ready."

"You can't go like that. Bouchard's men watch every road out of Thonon." Elias shifted toward Elionor. If he wanted her to stay, he needed to ask soon, or he would lose her forever.

"Surely there's a way out somewhere." Johan stuffed a linen doublet into his sack. "Maybe a place in the perimeter that's easier to scale?"

"I've lived within these walls for all my twenty-five years. Every gate is blocked."

Maï sat with Madeleine's youngest in her lap. "The Vallenses can stay here until the air clears."

Elias caught Madeleine's attention. "They're looking for you, probably because you helped the children escape from Ripaille. The Ascendants could knock on our door within the hour."

Johan stood and rocked on his heels, cracking his knuckles. "Where's that sword you lent me, Elias? I'm ready for a fight."

"We're outnumbered a hundred times over. Fighting would only lead to slaughter."

"Then we must find our way out secretly," Andreas said. "What do you suggest?"

Elias touched his temple and sighed. "I don't know yet. Let me sit and think for a moment."

Maï tilted her head to the side. "The meeting is tonight, son."

Elias eyed her curiously.

"At L'Ermitage, the same as every October."

"L'Ermitage is to the south, and that gate is blocked."

"What's L'Ermitage?" Constanza asked, holding the hand of one of her sons.

"Remember when I mentioned it at the château?" Madeleine's eyes brightened. "I'm meeting my husband Jean there as I do every year. It's no more than an hour's walk from here."

Andreas narrowed his eyes. "What good would going there accomplish?"

"It's on the edge of the forests that will lead you toward Piedmont," Elias said. "We gather there every year to sing and pray for protection during the woodcutting season."

"Are the soldiers letting anyone out of Thonon?" Paï asked.

"It seemed so, but a family the size of Andreas's can't pass unnoticed." A spark struck in Elias's mind. Andreas's family didn't need to remain together on the way out of Thonon. If they separated for a time and reunited at L'Ermitage, they might evade the Ascendants.

Maï struggled to hold the fussing baby in her arms. "What are you thinking, Elias?"

"How many families are heading to L'Ermitage tonight?"

Paï pursed his lips and gestured helplessly. "Twenty or so in town, probably thirty more from the surrounding hamlets."

Elias nodded thoughtfully. "We could bring the children to our frâres' and sâres' homes."

Andreas planted himself in front of Elias, shaking his head. "I'm not separating my children."

"Would you rather stay here until Lucien Bouchard himself knocks on our door? Our time is short, and this is the only way. I know where everyone lives. Between me, my parents, and Madeleine, we could bring everyone safely to a dozen houses. If Ascendants inspect one of those homes, they won't know the difference with one or two extra children."

"They're looking for me." Madeleine took Henri from Maï's arms and nuzzled his cheek. "I won't be much help."

"We'll need to disperse your oldest four, Madeleine. The Ascendants will be watching for a mother with five children."

"I think Elias's idea will work." Elionor flashed a shy smile at him. "And I'll help in whatever way I can."

Elias's heart fluttered as he tried to contain his churning feelings. He nodded at her, his gaze settling on her face a moment longer than intended. "This afternoon, when our frâres and sâres head to L'Ermitage, we need to take separate routes. The Ascendants will still ask questions, but I doubt one or two extra children will alert them."

"Yes, once everyone is at L'Ermitage, we'll be safe." Madeleine cradled baby Henri in her arms as she began to nurse him. "It's in a secluded glade, and no one has ever disturbed us there."

Paï eyed Andreas, smiling. "You will meet many of our people there. Maybe you can teach us tonight."

"Perhaps, but we must leave there tomorrow. The longer we remain near Thonon, the more likely it is that Bouchard will find us."

The corners of Paï's mouth drooped, and a glint of disappointment replaced the sparkle in his eyes.

Andreas waved his children toward him. "You all heard Lugotenent Renaud. Either he, Monsen Antoine, or Madòna Marie will take you to their friends' homes. You will do exactly as they say." He took a long breath, and his eyes seemed to moisten. "We'll all be together again this evening."

Elias gathered Andreas's son Ezio and Madeleine's son Florian, then set off toward the home of his friends Françoise and Aline. After Elias explained the situation, Aline accepted the boys with welcoming arms, and Elias hurried home to fetch more children.

His heart raced as he escorted each child through the narrow streets. Some men wearing dull Ascendant cloaks lurked about, but they didn't give him more than a passing glance. At each house, he knocked softly, ushering a child or two inside with hushed instructions. The children's faces reflected a mix of uncertainty and trust, their small hands gripping his tightly as they left the familiar faces of their parents and siblings.

Hours passed until Andreas and Constanza were the last Vallenses waiting to be led away. Elias opened a chest and took out a sheathed sword, then offered it to Andreas. "I saved it for you . . . after I bested you in the hall. It's a well-crafted blade, though it sits a little loose in the scabbard and needs to be sharpened."

Andreas accepted the sword and strapped it on a belt beneath his cloak.

Elias ushered Andreas and Constanza to the home of another friend. When he returned home, only Elionor, Madeleine, and Henri remained. Elias kicked off his boots and collapsed into a chair near the hearth. "We've done our part. Now it's in God's hands."

Madeleine smiled at him and slipped behind a curtain with baby Henri. Elias stole a glance at Elionor. She sat in a chair at the opposite end of the hearth, skillfully mending a woolen stocking.

There was no better time than now. Elias had kept the words locked away for too long. He sat forward in his chair and leaned toward her. "Elionor, there's something I must tell you before we leave."

She turned to him, her gaze curious but guarded. "Yes?"

"I've admired you from the moment we met." His hands shook as he spoke, but he couldn't stop now. "Your strength, your virtue—everything about you has captivated me."

A blush touched Elionor's cheeks. Her brow furrowed, and her lips parted, as if she wished to speak but couldn't.

"I know, Elionor. I see the child you carry," Elias said. "There's no need to explain right now. I understand."

She bit her bottom lip and absently rubbed the wool between her fingers. "No, Elias Renaud, I need to explain everything. Then you will understand."

Out of sight, in a quiet corner of the house, Madeleine hummed a soft melody to Henri. Uncomfortable silence filled the space between Elias and Elionor.

God, please don't let my clumsy words break this bond we share.

* * *

The walls closed in around Elionor the more Elias's words settled into her mind. The door seemed a welcome path of retreat from this man's kind but unknowing declaration. He didn't understand, and he never could. She was weak, not strong—immoral, not virtuous. But she couldn't run. Elias had to know the truth.

Slowly Elionor recounted the story of her life. "I grew up as an orphan in the village of Chivasso. No one wanted me until a barbe brought me to a new family who lived in the mountains—" Her hands grew clammy. She pressed her fingers together and forced herself to continue, all the way to Brando's abandonment just a few months earlier.

Elias's kind, understanding expression remained. "Thank you for telling me everything."

"Do you see now? I'm unworthy of your kindness, Elias, and I can't accept your sympathy."

"It's not sympathy, not even compassion." Elias gazed at her, and though she longed to look back, she couldn't. "I've seen who you are. You love our Savior. You are loyal, courageous—" he faltered slightly "—and the most beautiful woman I've ever looked upon."

Elionor shook her head again, this time faster. "Don't you understand? I'm an impure sinner—"

"As we all are. I'm no more worthy of God's love and forgiveness than you."

"Maybe that's true, but in man's eyes, I'm tarnished. No, it's more—I'm forever marred."

"To some, but not to me."

Elionor cautiously accepted his gaze. Still, the truth remained: Honorable men like Elias Renaud desired honorable wives, not women like her. Now this handsome, admirable man knew her dark past. Why didn't he run faster than a hare fleeing a hunter's arrow?

She touched her swelling abdomen. Maybe it was God who had brought Elias into her life. Could a man like him truly give himself to a wretch like her? Her pulse quickened, and the heat from the fire felt suffocating, bearing down on her like a woolen cloak on a hot summer day.

She shifted uncomfortably on the chair, and finding no relief, she rose to her feet and fanned herself. "Forgive me, Elias." A wave of lightheadedness washed over her. She placed her hands on an empty chair as she struggled to regain some composure. "A man and a woman shouldn't talk of such matters."

Elias drew closer, but she lifted her hand, palm facing outward. "I need a little space . . . and time to think. Please don't think ill of me."

"I mean no harm, Elionor." He bowed his head slightly and took a step backward. "I had imagined we held mutual feelings for one another."

"You're not mistaken." Her fingers trembled slightly as she clutched the back of the worn wooden chair, her knuckles turning white against the weathered surface. She glanced up, allowing her gaze to linger on Elias. Every line of his face and every sinew of his arms testified to his masculinity, while quiet strength and steadfastness burned in his deep, passionate eyes. How could she ever be worthy of him?

Elias nodded once at her and stood a little taller. "We'll leave for L'Ermitage when the evening bells toll. By now, everyone should have passed through the guard posts."

With a laden heart, Elionor silently left Elias and took refuge behind the curtain that separated the central room from Antoine and Marie's.

Madeleine lay on the pallet, admiring the cooing baby beside her. "Henri is anxious to see his pâre."

"I'm not ready to be a mother." Elionor walked to the pallet, sat across from Madeleine, and stared at the floor. "The baby is months away, and I'm already overwhelmed."

"Have you picked out a name yet?"

"I haven't even been able to think about that. Where I live, the first child is always named after the husband's father, but . . ."

Madeleine sat upright and touched Elionor's arm. "Don't worry about that. What are your parents' names?"

"Mamà's name is Magdalena." Elionor smiled slightly.

"A beautiful name for a filha petita. And your pâre?"

"His name was Lambert." Oh, how she longed for his embrace, to hear his wise counsel, to feel his presence. Yes, if God gave her a boy, she would name him Lambert.

The evening bells rang outside, and Elionor tensed. Dusk was approaching.

"It's time to head out," Elias said from behind the curtain.

Madeleine quickly swaddled Henri in a wool blanket, then held him in the crook of her arm. "You'll enjoy L'Ermitage, Elionor. The gathering of God's people always lifts my soul and encourages me onward."

Elionor and Madeleine entered the central room as Elias strapped a sword to his belt. He threw a worn gray cloak over his shoulders and fastened another belt around it.

Madeleine giggled at him. "Isn't that a little small on you, frâre?"

"It's Pâre's. I can't wear my other cloak now. Someone might recognize me from this morning." He tapped the concealed sword underneath the cloak. "And I need to hide this."

"That's not your usual weapon."

"I gave that to Johan before he left, and Andreas took the one he found at the château. This one needs a little sharpening, but I'll do that with the whetstone the woodcutters use at L'Ermitage." He checked outside, then opened the door, motioning for Elionor and Madeleine to follow.

At the outskirts of Thonon, a small group of soldiers manned the gate. Had Andreas and Constanza passed through their guard post? Were all the children safe? *Father in heaven, veil these men's vision. Allow us to pass unnoticed.* Elionor's heart pounded in her chest. *And please grant me wisdom about Elias.*

The soldiers gave her a quick glance, lingering longer on Madeleine. "Is that your only child?" one asked her.

Elias pushed forward and answered for her. "This is my sister, and she's going to see her husband in the forest. The baby's name is Henri."

"The forest . . ." The soldier eyed Madeleine. "He's a woodcutter?"

"Yes, for ten years or more." Madeleine bowed her head and tried to press past the soldier, but he blocked her path.

Lord, avert his eyes, Elionor silently prayed.

Another traveler walked up behind Elionor and peered over her shoulder. "What's taking so long?"

The soldier let out a soft huff, shook his head, and waved Madeleine through. *Thank You, God!*

When the gate was far behind them, the traveler ran up beside Elias. "That was risky," Elias said, "but thank you, Baptiste."

"My wife took one of the children with her earlier, and I've heard nothing but encouraging news since this afternoon." Baptiste walked closer. "All are safe, as far as I know."

"Praise God," Madeleine said, nodding. She soon slowed her pace, and Elionor did the same. Elias and Baptiste spoke ten or more paces ahead, well out of earshot.

Elionor and Madeleine walked in silence. Rolling vineyards flanked the stony path, and dark, forested hills loomed in the distance. At the edge of the forest, Madeleine broke the silence. "Elionor," she said softly. "I heard your conversation with Elias at the house."

Elionor clenched her hands near the folds of her skirt.

"Know that you're not alone." Madeleine repositioned the baby in her arms.

"God is with me," Elionor whispered, barely above a breath.

"Yes, but I also know what you're feeling right now. Probably guilt . . . and unworthiness." Madeleine stared at the path ahead. "I thought I could never be healed of it. I was a few years younger than you, and a moral woman, or so I imagined. Jean and I had known each other since we were children, but we both succumbed to our temptations. I became with child before we were wed."

"At least Jean is your husband now. The father of my child was already married and is gone forever. My sin is far worse than yours."

Madeleine sighed and slowly shook her head. "All the Poor in Thonon knew our sin, and I refused to show my face to anyone for months. I was defiant, though. A priest married me and Jean, and we lived apart from our families and God for the first year of our marriage."

"But all has been healed for you. You live happily with your husband, and you're a devout Christian woman."

"That wasn't a guarantee. My pâre and mâre prayed for us, and after a long struggle, I finally sought God's forgiveness and repented of that sin." Madeleine's countenance fell, and tears welled in her eyes. "For Jean, it was much longer—only in the past year has he returned to our Savior."

"I have returned to the Savior," Elionor said, though she heard the uncertainty in her own voice. "But His forgiveness feels so distant."

Madeleine's expression softened, a thoughtful look crossing her face. "Satan is the accuser. Anyone who reminds God-forgiven saints of their sins does the work of the devil."

"What do you mean?"

"I mean that dwelling on past sins, constantly reminding ourselves and others of them, only serves to hold us captive to guilt and shame. But Christ's sacrifice on the cross has already paid that price. His blood washed us clean, and we're forgiven."

"But how can I move past it?" Elionor pushed a loose lock of hair under her kerchief.

Madeleine reached out and touched Elionor's arm. "By accepting God's grace and forgiveness, by allowing yourself to see the good in others, and by believing in their ability to witness your redemption and transformation. That, Elionor, is the work of Christ."

Elionor touched her curved belly.

Madeleine lowered her chin and touched Elionor's arm. "I know Elias is my frâre, but I understand him more than anyone else does. He loves you, Elionor. I've never seen him give more than a glance at even the most beautiful women, but you—" Her lips curved into a soft smile. "You are everything to him."

"How? Is your brother blind? Or is he a desperate fool who doesn't know that he deserves far more than a woman like me?"

"I think you know the answer to that. For a moment, forget what you think of yourself and try to see Elias's devotion. He knows your story now, and he knows you sinned, but he also sees your repentance. That's what he adores in you."

As the vineyards stretched out before them, colored by evening twilight, Elionor's gaze drifted up to the man walking in front of her. Maybe, just maybe, despite her broken innocence, Elias Renaud sincerely loved her.

26

These nightly gatherings, by the fireside, were occasions of warmth and fraternity which fostered the sense of a shared but forbidden secret, and the communal awareness of peril.

—Gabriel Audisio
Preachers by Night, 2006

A YOUNG MOTHER WITH TWO CHILDREN guided Andreas and Constanza through the cordon around Thonon and into the hills. They arrived at L'Ermitage just before the sun settled below the horizon. As the path led them into the rustic encampment, Andreas took a deep breath of the pine and woodsmoke in the air.

Near the fringes of the encampment, Johan greeted them with a smile and a single slow nod.

"Are all the children here?" Constanza gripped Andreas's arm with both hands.

Johan held his hand to the side, palm upward. "See for yourself."

A small group of people gathered in a circle, talking and laughing. Andreas's breath hitched as he scanned the crowd, catching sight of Zama's wild curls bouncing in the last rays of sunlight. One by one, he counted the children—twelve, all safe. His chest tightened, and a sudden overwhelming rush of warmth flooded through him. Without a word, he and Constanza broke into a run.

Umile eyed Andreas's cloak. "You have a sword, Papà?" He touched the hilt hidden underneath the garment.

"I only kept it until we all met here safely." Andreas reached inside his cloak, unfastened the scabbard from his belt, and extended the sword toward Umile. "Take a look."

Umile grinned as he took the sword by the hilt, but he used both hands after he felt its weight.

"Heavier than you thought, isn't it?"

Grunting, Umile struggled to pull the blade from its scabbard. Bino, Roberto, Ezio, Guido, and two of Madeleine Dupont's boys gathered around, bouncing on their toes.

"Let me try next!" four-year-old Roberto demanded.

"No, it's too big for you." Ezio stepped around Roberto, crossed his arms, and tapped his foot as he waited for Umile to unsheathe the blade. "I'm the oldest, so I'm holding it next."

"You always go first!" Roberto shoved Ezio from behind and flashed a mean grimace at him.

"No more fighting, boys," Andreas said. "You'll all have your turn."

Constanza and the girls watched, along with several others whom Andreas had yet to meet. Umile pulled the blade halfway out, but his stature wouldn't allow him to pull it farther.

"Let me help." Andreas wrapped his hand around the scabbard. "Now use both hands, pull hard, and don't hesitate."

Umile's face lit up with anticipation as he held the hilt and pulled back from the scabbard.

"Don't let the blade touch the ground—" Andreas reached out and caught the edge of the sword as it escaped the sheath.

"Papà," Ezio gasped, "you told us to never touch a sharp blade."

Andreas gave him a half smile. "I did, and that instruction remains." He rubbed his thumb along the edge. "I already knew it was dull."

"I'll sharpen that." Johan's voice came from behind Andreas. "In the shed, there's a stone I used to sharpen mine."

"That's not necessary. We leave in the morning and don't need the extra weight."

Johan hesitated, shifting his weight and clasping his hands. "Did you hear about those people in Thonon?"

Andreas shook his head.

"A whole family—man, wife, and three children—were thrown from their house and beaten in the street. They refused to say where the Renauds lived." Johan gave him a grave look. "They sacrificed themselves for us."

They sacrificed themselves for us. The words echoed in Andreas's mind. A few days ago, he had thought he could rescue Constanza and the children by himself, but God continued to show him how much he needed others.

"I'll sharpen your blade. Better to be prepared than left with a useless hunk of metal." Johan grabbed the hilt from Umile and smiled at him. "I'll bring it back soon. It's better to practice with a real weapon anyway." His attention suddenly snapped to the forest's edge. "Someone's coming . . . two men."

"It's Elias and another man." Constanza squinted at the figures and smiled. "And Elionor and Madeleine too!"

After many greetings, embraces, and stories, Elias led everyone into L'Ermitage. Andreas and Constanza walked hand in hand through the maze of wooden cabins, buildings that must have weathered many storms and bitter winters.

The gathering hall, nestled farthest back in the encampment, stood against a steep, forested hill. The glow of lanterns spilled from its windows and cast flickering shadows across the mulched path. Tall pines kept watch around the perimeter, their branches swaying peacefully in the breeze.

The laughter of playing children echoed through the crisp air, while a few old men gathered around fires, their voices low and solemn. Here the sense of solidarity and fellowship was undeniable. These Christians who called each other frâre and sâre didn't cower in fear before those who meant them harm. No, they lived—lived out their faith as best they knew, and with all Andreas had observed in the past week, they exemplified the Savior's precept: *By this shall all men know that ye are my disciples, if ye have love one to another.*

Antoine Renaud met Andreas outside the gathering hall. "Come inside, come inside, my friends! There is food aplenty, and then more!"

Inside, the hall hummed with conversation. The air was thick with the rich, savory aroma of roasting meat mingled with the earthy fragrances of other inviting fare. The children's mouths opened in awe at the sight of the table in the middle of the room, and a few children licked their lips.

The glow of torches illuminated the multitude of faces in the hall. Some people sat cross-legged on the straw-covered floor. Others leaned against the rough-hewn walls. Andreas shook his head in amazement. "There must be two hundred people here."

"Still," Constanza said, "it's mostly women, children, and elders. Where are the men who were supposed to be here?"

"Deep in the forest still, and they won't return for a few days." Antoine crossed his arms and let out a labored breath. "Always, the House of Savoy demands more lumber."

"At least we can still gather and pray." Madeline revealed a sad but hopeful smile as she held her baby.

"But first we'll eat until we've had our fill." Antoine motioned toward the lone dining table at the center of the room. "We saved seats for you and your wife, Frâre Andreas."

"Merci, but I'll sit on the ground with everyone else."

"I insist. This is your last night in Thonon, and until you leave on the morrow, you'll hold a place of honor among us."

"I'll take your children with me." Madeleine waved her children toward her too, then gestured toward a group of women and children seated on the floor. "We're sitting there, and the Bonomo children will be our guests tonight."

Elionor glanced at Elias, a glint in her eye. "We should help her."

All twelve Bonomo children timidly followed the Duponts, Elias, and Elionor. Once the children were situated, Antoine led Andreas and Constanza toward the center of the hall.

A hand lightly tapped Andreas's shoulder. He turned to find Johan grinning. "That was an impressive sword you let me sharpen. How old is it?"

"At least two hundred years. One of my ancestors carried it in battle during King Richard of England's crusade to recover Jerusalem."

Johan caught sight of the steaming food over Andreas's shoulder. "Do you see all that fine fare? I'm getting some." He hurried past Andreas and Constanza, then pivoted back around, though still slowly stepping backward toward the food. "Your sword is in its scabbard. I propped it up near the door of my cabin—second one to the left after you leave this hall."

"Mercé, Johan. I'll pack it for our journey home. My sons couldn't keep their eyes off it, and perhaps it will be of some use."

As Andreas and Constanza passed the rough wooden table adorned with an array of food fit for a feast, Andreas's stomach rumbled. The skins of two roasted hogs glistened in the torchlight. "That's what I've been smelling."

"I could eat it all right now." A subtle excitement danced across Constanza's face. "But I suppose everyone else needs to eat too."

Andreas pulled out a chair for Constanza and beckoned her to sit, then found his place next to her. Others, mostly elders, surrounded the rest of the table.

"Where is Dama Marie?" Andreas asked Antoine, who sat across from him.

Antoine nodded toward a side door. "Finishing the meal preparations outside, I think."

"I'll go help her." Constanza rose to her feet. "It's the least I can offer."

Andreas continued to gaze in wonder at the packed room. "Are all of these people . . . like us? Believers, I mean."

"Yes, many are from Thonon, and others from outlying villages."

"Does the Thonon parish know about this?"

"Father Maurice might. Most probably think we just come up here to greet our men, but it's so much more. Here we can freely worship God in spirit and in truth."

"Where did you hear that phrase, 'in spirit and in truth'? Did you know that's from the Holy Scriptures?"

Antoine traced a knot in the wood of the table. "My pâre used to say it when I was a boy, but I didn't know it was from the Scriptures." He rolled his shoulders back. "Some of the men and I were wondering, Andreas. We receive the Mass from the priest, more out of tradition than worship. God doesn't want that. Christ's death is a solemn thing, and I don't think any of us have properly partaken of the bread and wine."

Andreas waited a moment to answer, remembering the Vallenses and how they practiced Communion. "In Piedmont, the Eucharist is a symbolic act where we commemorate Christ's sacrifice. It's also a time of fellowship, when we come together in unity and reaffirm our commitment to Christ and His church. All baptized believers in our congregation can participate."

"We would love to partake in this true memorial instead of the tainted one." Antoine loosely clasped his hands in front of him. "Would you show us before you leave?"

Andreas raised his brows. "Me? I've never administered it, and I'm not sure if this is the right setting. A church practices the Lord's Supper, and here . . . I don't think it would be right. I am sorry."

"There is so much we don't know." Antoine's gaze dropped to the table. He unclasped his hands and twisted the edge of his sleeve with his fingers. "Perhaps if we had a Bible and a preacher who could teach us from it . . ."

"As soon as we return to Piedmont, I'll be sure to tell the barbes. Perhaps as early as next year, one will visit you."

"Have you considered staying with us for a season?"

Andreas shook his head vigorously. "I can't. I have a field to plant, a family to provide for, a church I love."

But as he spoke, guilt pricked his conscience, whispering doubts about those obligations. Antoine's earnest plea ignited a spark of desire to stay with these people—to teach them the Holy Scriptures and unite his family with them. Yet he was also a husband and a father. To leave the security of Val Angrogna and settle in a place ruled by a millenarian sect would be reckless and irresponsible.

"I fully understand, Andreas, and I trust your judgment." Antoine placed both hands on the table and gave a sharp nod. "The meal is ready, I see. Follow me and enjoy the fare of Savoyard peasants. Afterward we'll pray and sing!"

While Andreas and Constanza ate, they talked with their frâres and sâres in Christ seated around the table. Marie joined her husband after thanks had been given for the abundance of food. Throughout the meal, various elder men and women approached the table to greet Andreas and Constanza and offer blessings on their upcoming journey across the mountains. Between the introductions, Antoine and Andreas spoke of the Holy Scriptures, doctrine, and the Vallenses.

The cleanup commenced soon after Andreas dipped his last morsel of crusty bread into the meat juices on his plate. Constanza rose to help with the chores, but Marie waved her back down.

"The children will gather the plates and wash them. You sit and enjoy the fellowship." Marie leaned over to Antoine and whispered something in his ear. Antoine nodded along with her; then the couple offered Andreas and Constanza a thoughtful smile.

They spoke for a few more moments at the table, but as the children cleared the last of the food scraps and dishes from the hall, people began to congregate at the far end of the room.

Antoine stood, pulled Marie's chair out, helped her up, and nodded once toward Andreas. "You've seen a few of us gather in a small home but never a meeting like this. Follow us."

Andreas and Constanza moved to the edge of the room and sat on the floor with the Renauds. Soon Madeleine, the children, Elionor, Elias, and Johan weaved through the crowd toward them. Elias offered Elionor a seat beside him, and after a slight hesitation, Elionor accepted the invitation. Roberto jumped into Andreas's lap, and Alessia nestled into Constanza's.

Madeleine spread her skirts and sat near Antoine and Marie on the other side of Elias and Elionor. "If only Jean were here," Antoine said to her.

"A few of the other wives are staying a day or two longer so they can see their husbands." Madeleine chuckled. "I suppose my work for Lord Philip is finished, so I could too."

"You should," Marie said. "Otherwise you might not see Jean for weeks."

"Who will be there for you?"

Marie took Elias's arm and hugged him. "I have a good son to watch over us."

Leaning to look around Roberto, Elias caught Andreas's eye. "We packed sacks of supplies for your journey. They're in the storage shed. I'll show you in the morning."

"What's the safest way to the mountains from here?" Andreas moved Roberto to the side so he could see Elias.

"The Dranse is a short walk away. Cross the river as soon as you can and follow the east bank." Elias leaned closer. "Two villages of Ascendants are on the west bank. Avoid them."

"Do you think the Great Saint Bernard Pass is best?"

"Yes, but by the time you reach it, the snow will make the passage hard." He motioned toward the children. "Especially with them."

Antoine elbowed Andreas. "See, you should stay with us until spring."

Andreas laughed with him. "We can probably be there before November, and hopefully the snow won't be too deep."

A hush fell over the room as a burly, white-haired man in the middle of the crowd stood and called for everyone's attention. A sense of anticipation rippled through the hall like a faint breeze.

The prayers began. After one person ended, another would rise and continue, offering thanksgiving for nourishment, for family, for fellow believers, and most of all, for the gift of salvation. They praised God for His love, His holiness, His mercy, and His forgiveness. When they offered their requests, they did so in faith and humility, asking for health, provision, and protection from their enemies.

But a theme that continually flowed from their lips was their guests; they asked for God's benevolence and providence on Andreas and his family for their journey over the Alps.

Andreas closed his eyes and prayed along with each speaker as the moments slipped away. Other sounds punctuated the stillness—a baby's cry, a muffled cough, the swishing of straw on the floor—but they only served as an accent to the calm.

Gradually the prayers subsided. Quiet settled over the hall, the echoes of fervent petitions lingering in the air like whispers of a holy melody.

Then, like a gust of wind stirring the leaves of a forest, Elias stood and addressed the congregation. "Let's begin with 'The Lamb Victorious.'"

"Lead us in it, Elias Renaud," a man said from behind.

The first notes of the song spilled into the air, carried by voices raised in reverent harmony.

> The martyrs' cry, the saints' refrain,
> Âmin, alélouyâ!
> God's vengeance falls, His foes arraign,
> Âmin, alélouyâ!

The song flowed through the room, weaving a pattern of sound through the spaces between the singers. A radiant smile spread across Madeleine Dupont's face, her joy flowing to her children, who eagerly mimicked her. Head held high, Elias led with a clear melody. Andreas listened and tried to join in the unfamiliar song.

> Babylon's fall, the mighty cry,
> Âmin, alélouyâ!
> Her pomp and pride shall swiftly die,
> Âmin, alélouyâ!
>
> From heaven's throne, the elders sing,
> Âmin, alélouyâ!
> His judgment comes, the victory ring,
> Âmin, alélouyâ!

These phrases—they were alluding to John's Apocalypse. The barbe Raimond Durand had once said persecuted Christians through all ages had taken comfort in the words of that book, words that pronounced the final triumph of Christ and His followers over the forces of evil.

The voices converged, rising and falling like the tide, as men, women, and children alike joined in sacred song. Andreas reached for Constanza's hand and held it tight as he tried to sing. At least he had taken to the "Âmin, alélouyâ" part.

Shout "Worthy is the Lamb" for joy,
Âmin, alélouyâ!
The nations yield, their schemes destroyed,
Âmin, alélouyâ!

The Lamb victorious, worthy, crowned,
Âmin, alélouyâ!
The faithful's praise forever sound,
Âmin, alélouyâ!

The walls reverberated with that last verse, as if each note declared the people's faith in the Lamb's glorious victory. In time, God would defeat Satan and all his minions, whether they be the Catholic Church, the rulers of the world, or the Divine Ascendancy.

Andreas met Constanza's eyes and found a reflection of the love that bound them together. Constanza beamed, squeezing Andreas's hand tighter. "This is the love of Christ if I've ever seen it. This song—I've never heard anything like it. It's so meaningful . . . and biblical."

Without a pause, Elias asked another man to lead and sat back down beside Elionor. Song after song, the praise continued into the evening, each song a glimpse into the true religion of these believers.

As the fifteenth song ended, Antoine gave Andreas a light slap on the back. "Marie and I were talking during the meal. The journey back to Piedmont will be a long and weary one. You and your wife haven't seen each other in over a month, and you won't have a comfortable time alone for many weeks more."

Everyone suddenly rose to their feet, and Marie said, "This is the last song—our song of parting."

Antoine continued where he had left off. "The foreman of the woodcutters has a comfortable cabin up the hillside, and there's only enough room for two. With this being your last night before the journey, you and your wife should have some time alone."

"But our children—" Andreas held up his hand in protest.

"I will care for them," Madeleine said.

Elionor gave Constanza a little push. "And I'll be here too."

"You are the kindest of friends." Constanza blinked rapidly, and a tear fell from one eye.

"You two go and enjoy the rest of the night." Madeleine held the baby in her arms and swayed with him. "The path up the hillside is outside to the left. We'll see you in the morning."

The last song began, and every person in the gathering hall walked about and offered a handshake or embrace.

> My Christian friends, in bonds of love,
> Whose hearts in sweetest union join,
> Your friendship's like a drawing band,
> Yet we must take the parting hand.
> Your company's sweet, your union dear,
> Your words delightful to my ear;
> Yet when I see that we must part
> You draw like cords around my heart.

Andreas held his hand out for Constanza's, and together they drifted toward the exit, surrounded by the melodies of parting. With each handshake and embrace, the bonds of fellowship tightened like an invisible cord, drawing him closer to these Christians.

> How sweet the hours have passed away
> Since we have met to sing and pray;
> How loath we are to leave the place
> Where Jézu shows His smiling face.
> Oh, could I stay with friends so kind,
> How would it cheer my drooping mind!
> But duty makes me understand
> That we must take the parting hand.

As Andreas guided Constanza out into the crisp night air, the songs echoed in his heart. With a silent prayer of gratitude, he turned his face toward the starry heavens.

Constanza turned to the left and pointed up as two streaks of light raced through the sky. "The night after the Prophet captured us, I saw a few shooting stars. They reminded me of Papà. When we return home, somehow I still feel as if we'll see him shearing sheep or pulling up a tree stump."

Andreas stopped Constanza, looked into her eyes, and embraced her. "I am thankful for your papà's memory. He raised my wife, and he's the kind of man I endeavor to imitate. I want our children always to remember the heritage they share with him."

She sniffled as she buried her face in his shoulder.

Andreas rubbed Constanza's back. "I saw a shooting star too, perhaps even on the same night. I was barely awake, but I remember praying for God to let you see the same."

Constanza lifted her head and wiped away a tear. "He answered your prayer just when I needed it." She faced the path, wrapped her arm in Andreas's, and nestled close to his shoulder. "Where's this cabin of ours?" Her voice eased into a whisper as they continued walking. "There's something I need to tell you when we're there."

Andreas scanned the edge of the forest by the light of the full moon. The forest parted directly ahead of him, revealing a narrow path up the hillside. Constanza's fingers intertwined with his, and the delicate strength of her touch propelled him onward.

The trail meandered its way through the towering pines and soon led them to the cabin's threshold. Andreas opened the door for Constanza and guided her inside. A stack of wool blankets sat on a sizable bed, and a small table with two chairs held a candle. With logs standing ready beside the clean hearth, flint on the mantel, and a tinderbox on the table, Andreas began lighting a fire.

Constanza sat near the hearth as Andreas stacked the logs. "Back home, I remember hearing about believers like the Poor, but it always felt like a myth. Now that I've spent some time with them, I can't help but wonder if there are more like them."

"I think we Vallenses tend to think of ourselves as the only bearers of truth." Andreas set the last log in place and opened the tinderbox. "But now you and I have seen that's false."

"To me, it's still odd that they practice papist traditions—at least some."

"They don't have the Holy Scriptures nor anyone to teach them. And few can read. If they could see the truth, I'm certain they would follow it." Andreas placed a handful of tinder in the center of the logs and broke off splinters of wood from a small log.

Constanza traced a finger along the folds of her skirts. "They need more than just a barbe who visits them every two or three years."

She was entirely right. What would an occasional weeklong visit do for Christians who thirsted for God's Word but had no access to it? "I've wondered a couple of times in the past week—what if this is where God wants us? Not now, of course, especially with Lucien Bouchard reigning over his little fiefdom."

"What will happen to people like the Renauds with the Prophet in control? He already hates them. Even if order is restored soon, what horrors will he commit before he's overthrown?"

"I fear for all of Savoy. My pâre, my mâre, and my siblings will likely all die, if they're not dead already. Something in me feels that I should do something for the Poor too, but what?" Andreas took the piece of iron from the tinderbox and struck it against the flint, casting sparks into the tinder. He gently blew on the embers. "I can do nothing about Bouchard other than trust that God will triumph in the end. If I had an army at my disposal, I would retake Thonon and cast Bouchard into Lac Léman." The tinder ignited, and he added small pieces of wood to build the fire. "Lacking an army, though, I believe we should return to where God planted us—to our farm, to our family, and to our church."

Constanza placed a hand on his back and rubbed it as he stoked the flame. "You're a wise man, Andreas de Bonomo."

After the logs caught fire, he stood, took the candle from the table, and carried it to the hearth.

"The fire will give us plenty of light," Constanza said, touching his upper arm. "Everything is perfect here."

Andreas set the unlit candle back on the table. "I wish I could pack this cabin in my sack and take it on the journey."

"I know you're strong." She squeezed his arm muscle, stood on her toes, and kissed his cheek. "But not that strong."

Andreas scooped her up from the floor with ease and gazed into her soulful eyes. She laughed for a moment but soon rested her head on his chest. The fire crackled behind them, quickly warming the room.

"I have genuinely longed for this moment," Andreas said.

"Me too, but for more than one reason." Constanza showed a gentle smile. "We aren't the only two here."

"Did one of the children sneak up here?"

Constanza bobbed her head back and forth. "No, but in a way, one did follow us."

"What are you saying?"

She burst into a smile. "I'm with child."

"You mean . . . you're going to . . ."

"Yes, our child. We're having a baby of our own."

Andreas froze, his gaze dropping briefly to her abdomen. He tried to speak, but the words caught in his throat. Instead he drew Constanza closer, closed his eyes, and spun her around once, laughing.

"It's still very early," Constanza said. "The baby will probably arrive in late spring or early summer."

"Praise God for His blessings." Andreas set Constanza on her feet and placed both hands on her hips. He opened his mouth suddenly. "Can you travel? I've heard some women get sick—"

Constanza placed a finger on his lips and whispered, "The baby and I will be fine."

"If we need to walk slower or stop for a time, we can. We're in no rush."

"I trusted you before all of this, but now I trust you all the more, Andreas." She touched his cheek. "I have full confidence in my husband."

Andreas leaned down and met her lips with a long, passionate kiss. There was no place he belonged more than in this sacred space, amid the pines and whispered promises, his arms wrapped around the woman who held his heart in her hands.

27

And these are they who, through great tribulation,
Have washed their garments white in the Lamb's blood;
Who offer at the throne the heart's oblation.
Made glad forever by the love of God.
Of these earth was not worthy; though they trod
The lowly paths of life, and wandered o'er
Their dreary rocks, 'neath persecution's rod,
Yet Thou, whose praise they were created for,
Hast made them priests and kings to God, forevermore.

—Robert Baird
Sketches of Protestantism in Italy, Past and Present, 1845

AT DAWN, streaks of golden sunlight broke through the dense canopy of spruces and pines. The evergreens softly swished in the breeze, and the melody of birdsong filled the air. Andreas sat beside Constanza on the doorstep of the cabin, bathed in the dim glow of the morning. Through a gap in the trees, the sun rose over the distant mountains, painting the sky in hues of pink and orange.

Andreas wrapped his arm around Constanza as she leaned against his shoulder. "A baby—a child with our blood and our appearances. I wasn't expecting it, not yet at least."

"We've been married for half a year now." Constanza curled up closer and sighed. "I hope he bears my papà's likeness."

"How do you know it will be a boy?"

"I'm dreaming. It feels like everything is a dream now."

Andreas drew in a long breath and patted Constanza's arm. "I suppose the children are wondering where we are."

"I hope they're still sleeping. They'll need it as we set out today." She sat upright and wrapped her arms around her knees. "They are resilient, far more than I. Yes, they complain incessantly, and they quarrel like a brood of chicks after the juiciest worm in the mud. But they are strong, Andreas."

"They've all lost their parents, and then they lost Luca and Vitòria. Our children have seen more loss than most old men."

"Their strength comes from more than just hardships, I think. They see their strong, godly papà too." Constanza placed her hand on top of Andreas's. "You give all of us the confidence to stand strong."

A sudden shriek carried up the hillside from the direction of the encampment. Then another. Andreas straightened and listened.

"That's a woman," Constanza said.

Andreas held a finger to his lips. A flurry of shouts erupted from down-hill—men, women, children. He stood, still holding Constanza's hand. "Stay here until I return. Bar the door and don't open it unless you know who it is."

"I'm not leaving you, Andreas."

The shouts continued. Then came a clash of metal.

He gave her a sharp look. "I beg you, Constanza, stay here. There's nothing you can do down there. I left my sword with Johan, and I need to find it."

He dashed back into the cabin, his heart racing. Without another word, he slipped on his boots, fumbling with the straps. Constanza's worried gaze followed him as he jumped off the doorstep and launched into a run. The chill of the morning air bit his skin.

Down the path he sprinted. The shouts grew louder and more distinct, echoing through the still forest. One sounded like Silvia, and another like Ave. What was happening? Bandits? Inquisitors? But only one answer made sense.

As he reached the edge of L'Ermitage, women and children darted frantically between the cabins. Their panicked cries mingled with the intermittent clash of metal in the distance. Andreas stopped, catching his breath and scanning the commotion. Where were the children? And he still needed his sword. He darted toward Johan's cabin and burst inside.

Propped against the wall near the door was his sword in its scabbard. He unsheathed it, and the blade gleamed in the light seeping through the cracks of the window shutters. His fingers closed around the hilt.

He dashed out of the cabin, his boots pounding the earth as he raced toward the clanging metal. The clashes grew louder with each passing moment, raising his pulse and driving him like winds whipping through the trees just before a storm.

Through the maze of cabins he pushed himself. Images of Silvia, Ezio, Bino, Fosca, and all the rest flashed through his mind and spurred him onward.

Emerging into a clearing, he skidded to a halt. Johan and Elias stood like stalwart guardians, fending off four Ascendants. Elionor and eleven of the children cowered behind Johan and Elias. Where was Ezio?

Andreas surged forward to join Johan and Elias. His sword arced through the air, meeting the steel of an Ascendant with a resounding clash.

Beside him, Johan kicked an Ascendant and grunted. "Looks like we've stumbled into quite the brawl." The clang of metal against metal punctuated his words.

Andreas spared a fleeting grin. "We just need to be the ones standing when it's over."

Elias, his movements precise and calculated, fought with a silent intensity. He slew an Ascendant and pivoted to fight another.

From the corner of a cabin, three more Ascendants pressed toward the battle, one of them encased in chain mail and wielding a mace. Elias and Johan were strong, and Andreas would never surrender, but even together, how could they defeat this new foe, let alone the four other remaining Ascendants? Andreas gritted his teeth and steeled himself for the coming assault.

Johan grabbed Andreas's shoulder, pulled him back, and positioned himself in front of Andreas. "Go help Elias." He bent his knees slightly and took a deep breath, sword held ready. "I'll face this one."

Andreas grabbed Johan's elbow. "He's too heavily armored. And he'll crush you with that mace."

"Let me help you, Andreas." Johan ripped his arm away from Andreas. "Take your family and leave this place."

Andreas turned to Elionor and his children. A few paces from them, Elias fought three Ascendants by himself.

"Go, Andreas!" Johan waved him off and charged toward the armored Ascendant.

Andreas almost charged with him, but Johan's words echoed in his mind: *Let me help you, Andreas.*

Elias called for help from behind. Andreas spun back around and sprinted toward him.

Every movement became sharp and distinct. Elias felled another Ascendant. Though Andreas held his ground, weariness crept up his limbs.

An Ascendant singled him out, and with each blow they exchanged, Andreas stumbled backward. His muscles protested the strain, aching for rest. The man snarled at Andreas and rammed his whole body into him. Andreas fell to the grass.

No, I can't stop. He forced himself to his knees and thrust his sword forward, meeting the Ascendant's chest. With a final shuddering exhale, the man collapsed.

Elias grunted as he took a cut to the cheek.

Andreas whirled back toward Johan. The armored soldier swung his mace and slammed it against Johan's shoulder. Johan cried out in agony and fell backward.

Andreas dashed toward him. An Ascendant charged Andreas from the side. Until a few moments ago, Andreas had never slain a man, but now, with the lives of Johan and his children hanging in the balance, he fortified himself again for the grim necessity.

The man stabbed toward Andreas's neck. He sidestepped and kicked the man's leather-armored side. Leg aching from the impact, Andreas turned to face the man again.

The Ascendant's stance was too narrow. Andreas swung at the man's bare forearm and connected with flesh. The assailant grabbed his wounded arm, leaving Andreas with an opening. He launched himself at the man, rammed into his body, and shoved him to the ground.

Andreas held his bloodstained sword, panting, eyes darting to the trees. Elias slashed the last nearby Ascendant and threw him to the ground. They could still win this battle—no, they must.

Near a cabin, Johan lay on the ground, holding up his sword in desperation.

Andreas shouted and charged forward. Elias followed.

The armored Ascendant slammed his spiked club down. Johan grunted. The Ascendant swung again, glimpsed Andreas and Elias, then fled around the corner of a cabin.

Andreas pressed ahead, sweat making his sword grip shift. He should have stayed with Johan. He could have helped. *Dear Lord, don't let Johan die.*

Two slain Ascendants lay nearby, a testament to Johan's heroism. Andreas slid to his knees next to Johan and tossed his sword aside. "Johan, are you hurt badly?"

Johan gasped for air. "Are the children safe?"

"Thanks to you."

"I'm sorry." Johan's hand shook as it lay on his chest. "I couldn't pierce his armor."

"You saved us. We're all alive because of you." Andreas touched Johan's shoulder. "Can you stand?"

But he already knew the answer.

*　　*　　*

The eerie silence pressed against Constanza's chest as she leaned against the wooden door and shifted anxiously. Andreas had told her to stay in the cabin, but she couldn't stay here while her husband and her children and her friends were likely fighting for their lives. What if someone was wounded? Who else could tend to the injured in the encampment?

No, she would not stay cooped up here like a frightened *marmòta* in its burrow while others fought and bled. If something horrible had happened to Andreas, then staying in the cabin only delayed the inevitable. And if he had triumphed, then all was safe. She lifted the bar and pulled the door open.

Cold air filled her lungs as she descended the worn path, each footfall seeming to echo through the calm forest. Her hands clenched and unclenched at her sides. *Please, God, let them be unharmed.*

Voices resonated from inside the cabins as she approached the encampment. Ahead, a woman and two children walked to a well. Constanza let out a little sigh of relief and fixed her gaze on the cabin where the children had been staying with Madeleine.

She hurried through L'Ermitage, scanning the encampment for any familiar faces. Some she had seen last night praying and singing.

From the corner of her eye, she spotted Andreas and Elias kneeling next to a man who lay on the ground. Constanza's breathing quickened.

Elionor stood nearby with the children, their faces drawn and concerned as they shifted their focus between Andreas and the man.

Johan. Constanza's heart jolted, seizing her breath. She ran to Andreas, putting herself between the children and Johan's bloodied body. "What happened?"

Andreas gazed up at her, his expression empty and uncertain. She had never seen that look on his face. Was he angry at her for leaving the cabin?

"All are here except Ezio." Elias stood and sighed deeply. "He's in the gathering hall with Madeleine."

Andreas nodded toward Johan. "I don't know how bad it is. An Ascendant struck him with a mace . . . multiple times. Can you help him?"

She knelt beside Johan and prepared herself to see the injuries. A sword lay in the grass beside him. His sturdy frame lay broken and vulnerable, his breathing shallow. His blinks came at slow, sporadic intervals, each one heavier than the last.

She touched his shoulder and worked to capture his focus. "Johan, it's Connie."

"My old rival." A raspy breath escaped his mouth. "And my friend."

"I'm going to look at your wounds now. I'll try to be gentle." Constanza moved his blood-soaked cloak aside and winced inwardly. Crushed ribs, bluish skin, a sucking sound from his chest as he tried to breath—she couldn't do anything for him. These wounds were mortal.

But she had to try. "Andreas, help me prop him up. He can't breathe."

"You were right, Connie . . . about me." Johan shook and wheezed as she held the back of his head. "A dawdling man, you called me. I was. Forgive me."

Andreas supported Johan's back, but Johan's breathing only grew weaker. "That's in the past, Johan. There's no man in the world I would rather call my friend."

"I'm still selfish." His chest heaved, but he couldn't take more than a shallow breath. "I wish I would've washed more feet . . . like Jesus. Been a servant instead of a burden."

Andreas clasped Johan's hand as Constanza motioned to lay him back down. "You are a servant, and I want my boys to be as strong as you someday."

"I wish . . . I wish I could've taught them to hunt." Johan closed his eyes for a moment, and the corner of his lips turned upward. "Teach them to loose an arrow better than you do."

An elderly man approached them, panting. "We saw an Ascendant . . . behind the gathering hall."

"I'll follow you." Elias pulled his sword from its scabbard and glanced at Elionor. "And return soon."

Constanza kept her hand behind Johan's neck, but nothing was helping. She prayed for a miracle.

"I'm not leaving you here," Andreas said to Johan.

"Our paths are parting." Johan strained to speak as he flung a feeble glance at Constanza. His gaze settled back on Andreas. "Your family needs you. Fight for them."

As Johan's chest stilled, his breath escaping in a final whisper, Constanza's own breath faltered. An emptiness settled over her, as if the very air had been sucked from her own lungs. For all her life, Johan had lived just down the hill. They had competed, and they had quarreled, and they had shared many memories together. Now he had departed for the eternal realm of heaven.

Andreas crumpled to the ground, his body racked with silent sobs that matched the stillness of their surroundings. She had never seen him like this. With a tender touch, she reached out, offering a little solace. Tears flowed down her cheeks, mirroring his sorrow.

Elionor knelt beside Constanza and placed a hand on her back. Silvia ran to Andreas and latched on to him, sobbing, while the other children gathered around Constanza. How had it come to this? Johan Lauras, dead. He would never again pick up a hunting bow or blurt out some foolish jest and wait for everyone to laugh at him.

"I shouldn't have let him come to Thonon with me." Andreas fought to stifle his sobs, but they broke free and only grew louder. "But he insisted. I should have stood with him at the end, Constanza. Instead he laid down his life for me, for our family." He swallowed, then sniffled. "We were so close—almost rid of dukes, lords, prophets, cultists."

"We did what we thought was best," Constanza said.

"But it wasn't the best." Andreas let out a forceful breath. "I should have stood up to Lucien Bouchard."

"You were only trying to protect us. This isn't our fight."

Andreas slowly shook his head. "No, it's been my fight all along. Bouchard and his fiends hate us. They hate our faith, they hate our family"—his gaze shifted toward the gathering hall—"they hate our brethren in Thonon."

Constanza laid Johan's cloak over his lifeless face. "How can we fight the Prophet? He's the master of the whole realm now."

"Which is why fleeing to Piedmont won't help us. He needs our family so he can prove his power. He's already proven his willingness to pull us from our homes, and he'll do it again. Besides, we can't leave our new friends to fend for themselves. If the Divine Ascendancy isn't dealt with here in Thonon, the evil the Poor have faced will soon seep into Piedmont."

"We have no army. One more attack here might be the end of us . . . and our friends."

"Then we can't let that happen." Andreas set his jaw, raised his head, and stood. "Those woodcutters despise Bouchard and his followers even more than I do. They're returning here later this week, and with their numbers, we might be able to push back against this kingdom Bouchard imagines he has established."

Andreas gazed at his ancestor's sword, its metal reflecting the determination chiseled across his face. He reached down and grasped its hilt. "We may not have an army, but we have courage." He gave Elionor a slow nod. "And we have Elias Renaud. Until those woodcutters arrive, we'll stand against whatever the Ascendants throw at us."

With each word, his strength seemed to grow, as if he could dispel all Constanza's fears and doubts with a single glance. *He is the embodiment of a man.* She leaned close and embraced him. With Andreas leading their family, they could confront any trials that dared challenge their unity.

A distant clash of metal, like the dark tolling of a bell, jolted them from their embrace.

Andreas spun to scan the surrounding cabins. "We must move!"

*   *   *

The clanging of weapons ignited a fire in Andreas's veins. He motioned for everyone to follow him. "The gathering hall is the safest place here. Ezio is waiting for us."

Constanza hesitated as she looked at the slain body before her.

"The battle isn't finished yet." Andreas gave Johan's body a quick glance, but he couldn't afford to mourn now. "We'll bury him when we're able."

Swiftly Andreas rallied his family and Elionor and led them farther into the encampment. Women and children, their faces lined with fear, hurried toward the relative safety of the cabins. A small group of older men armed with axes and bows hurried toward the sounds of battle, ready to confront the threat.

As Andreas pressed forward, the clamor of battle grew closer. The hall was in sight, and once everyone was safe there, he would join Elias and the other men.

Behind them, two armed Ascendants rushed toward Elionor, who held the rear. The pursuers were too close and would soon overtake her and the children.

Andreas skidded to a halt and ran back to face the attackers. "Elias!" he shouted. "I need you, Elias!"

Andreas gripped the hilt of his sword, bracing himself to fight alone if he must. He could not fail. Constanza, the children, the Poor—they needed him alive.

"Stay behind me." He planted his feet and faced the attackers. "If there's a clear path, head toward the hall."

Constanza shouted from behind, and Andreas turned toward her. The warrior clad in chain mail ran at Constanza.

A blow struck Andreas on the back of his head, sending him stumbling forward. His grip on his sword faltered as hands seized him and wrenched the weapon from his grasp.

"Andreas!" Constanza's voice pierced the air.

He peered through the legs of the men surrounding him. Just ahead, Constanza knelt on the ground, weeping and pleading with the armored Ascendant.

Andreas tried to stand, but a boot pressed him to the ground. He reached for his sword but couldn't free himself. Twisting his head, he glared up at his captors. "What do you want?"

No answer came, only whispers between them. An Ascendant reached for him, rope in hand. Andreas kicked and threw wild punches, but soon his hands were tied behind his back. Tensing and struggling, he freed one hand from the rope and catapulted himself toward Constanza. But the arms that held him were too strong.

A sudden blow landed squarely in his stomach, driving the air from his lungs in a sharp, gut-wrenching gasp. He doubled over but couldn't find his breath.

Shouts rang out in the distance, and Andreas turned his head. Against the backdrop of a cabin stood Elias and at least fifteen older men, including Antoine. With that many men, they outnumbered the Ascendants. Elias called out a command and charged.

More Ascendants appeared from the woods. Instead of staying to fight, they constrained Andreas, Constanza, Elionor, and the children, then quickly retreated into the forest. With the little strength that remained in him, Andreas fought against his bonds and his captors, trying to slow them enough for Elias and the others to arrive. Yet despite all the exertion, he barely impeded the retreat.

The Ascendants dragged them into the depths of the woods. Andreas glanced at Constanza and gathered the will to speak. "All will be well. I won't let anything happen to us."

"Papà!" Zama reached for him, shaking with sobs, but an Ascendant yanked her back. "Where are we going, Papà?"

"Stay close to Mamà and Elionor. And don't fear, Zama. I will protect you." He gazed at Constanza and the rest of the children. "All of you."

Holding back his own tears, Andreas breathed in deeply and winced, his stomach still aching from the punch. Each step carried his family farther from the safety of L'Ermitage and deeper into the unknown. Was there an escape from this that didn't include pain or death? *Dear God, protect us. I don't know what to do.*

But as he finished those few desperate words of prayer, a line from last night's singing reverberated through his memory like a rallying cry: *God's vengeance falls, His foes arraign, Âmin, alélouyâ!*

28

A prophet possessed a further qualification: a personal magnetism which enabled him to claim, with some show of plausibility, a special role in bringing history to its appointed consummation. And this claim on the part of the prophet deeply influenced the group that formed around him. For what the prophet offered his followers was not simply a chance to improve their lot and to escape from pressing anxieties—it was also, and above all, the prospect of carrying out a divinely ordained mission of stupendous, unique importance.

—Norman Cohn
The Pursuit of Millennium, 1970

BELLS RANG through the streets of Thonon, seeming to further chill the already cool air. Ascendants clad in brown cloaks, both men and women, lined the foremost street that sloped toward Château de Thonon. Though it was close to midday, gray skies cast a gloomy pall over the procession of prisoners.

Andreas tried to push his way through the Ascendants toward Constanza, but each time they shoved him back. Elionor walked to his left, while the children, most with their heads hung low, marched in front.

The Ascendants along the street watched with tense expressions as the captives were paraded past them. Some incessantly chanted "Ecce lux prophetæ ducet nos," while others remained silent. Shadows danced along the cobblestones, mirroring the simmering whispers that seemed to permeate every corner.

As they entered the city square, Andreas stared in amazement. The once-bustling marketplace now lay desolate, its stalls overturned and goods strewn across the cobblestones like refuse. The cathedral, its bells still tolling, stood defaced and vandalized, its symbols marred by crude graffiti and its broken statues littering the entranceway.

Farther down the road, the houses of merchants and magistrates, once representations of the prosperity and stability of the duchy, now bore the scars of pillaging. Windows were smashed, doors torn from their hinges, and thresholds littered with belongings. The air itself seemed to smell of anarchy and rebellion.

In just two days of the Ascendants' supposed heaven on earth, Thonon had devolved into miserable decay. This was certainly not the Thonon of Andreas's childhood but rather a twisted image of its former self, consumed by the flames of fanaticism and tyranny. The duchy that generations of his noble family had built now lay squandered and wasted—almost overnight.

An opening appeared toward Constanza, and this time, their captors didn't notice as Andreas slipped through. He yearned to hug her, but his hands were bound. Instead, he brushed against her arm.

Constanza nudged him in return, but her chin trembled. "Ezio . . . where is he?"

"If he's still in L'Ermitage, he's in capable hands. Madeleine is there, and so are Marie and Antoine and of course Elias."

"What will happen to us? Why can't the Prophet just let us all be?" Her questions came in a desperate staccato.

Andreas had no answers, but even if he did, he wouldn't blurt them out. If the Prophet truly wanted to use them to instill fear and gain power, Andreas didn't have the stomach to say it.

As he walked beside Constanza, something over her shoulder caught his eye. The warmth drained from his body, and all that remained was cold numbness.

Four bodies swayed from a gallows, their limbs bent at unnatural angles. Two men, a woman, and a boy of no more than fifteen. Their faces were twisted masks of pain, eyes staring at nothing, the injustice etched into their lifeless forms.

Constanza's grip tightened on his arm, her breath hitching. She turned away and shook her head. "Andreas, please. I can't—"

"I won't let it come to that." But how could he promise that when he had no power to fulfill it?

Though the children up ahead were obviously frightened by the men surrounding them, thankfully they were too short to glimpse the gallows. He needed to protect them, but at the same time, Ezio was beyond his control. Would Andreas see him again? Though Elias seemed to have formed a small force of older men to defend L'Ermitage, there were still far more Ascendants in these lands.

Andreas rubbed at the rope around his hands and peered up at the ominous gray château. Though dark waters lay ahead, he could not despair.

The gate clanged open in front of them. Under its stone arch stood the crimson-cloaked Lucien Bouchard. Even in the dim light, his posture displayed his pride in his rise to power. He took a long breath and caught Andreas's eye. "Lord Andreas . . . and your wife." He walked through the midst of the Ascendants, stopped a pace from Constanza, and pushed Andreas aside.

Andreas resisted, but two arms pulled him backward.

"I've been saving something for you." Bouchard pulled a handful of deep red petals from his pocket and held them toward Constanza. "Our destinies have again intertwined, Dama Bonomo." He glanced at the hands tied behind her back and reached out to her.

"Don't touch her!" Andreas lunged at Bouchard but couldn't escape his captor's arms.

Bouchard disregarded Andreas, circling Constanza to untie the knot with ease. As the rope slithered to the cobblestones, he gently deposited the petals into her hands. "Do not reject them this time." He moved to Andreas and loosed his bonds, then addressed the Ascendants. "I count only eleven here. Where is the twelfth?"

"All twelve are here," one answered.

Bouchard's gaze swung from one child to the next and finally settled on Elionor. "She is not one of them. The oldest boy is missing. Where is he?"

"Probably still in the woodcutters' camp with the Poor," one man answered.

"Again I ask—why is he not here?"

"Armed men attacked us. Several faithful were lost, but we slew one of the Poor."

"And you retreated?"

"If there were more of us, we could find the boy to complete the crown."

"Then gather more men. There are scores of ègals here who would be enthralled to have a part in the fulfillment of the prophecies."

Andreas jerked one shoulder away from his captor. "What do you want with us, Bouchard? I'll give you whatever you want in exchange for our freedom."

"A negotiation?" Bouchard chuckled. "I am not some haughty noble who takes interest in your titles, lands, or birthrights." His mouth twisted into a smile. "We have brought an end to the old systems, and soon Christ and His faithful will reign. Have you not seen Thonon? We have vanquished the oppressors, laid waste their wealth, and cast down their pride. In their place, we have established a new kingdom, one of fraternity, equality, and humility."

Constanza's countenance hardened as Bouchard spoke. Her shoulder twitched slightly, and red dust fell from her fingertips as she crumbled the petals.

Bouchard caught sight of the petal fragments on the ground and exhaled sharply. "I hear you have chosen to cast your lot with the Poor. Did you not see what became of them, that unfortunate family hanging by their necks? The boy proved useful, though. While he screamed like an infant, he revealed where you and the Poor had fled. Soon you will see what becomes of the rest of them."

He turned and addressed the soldiers gathered in the courtyard. "Gather all fighters and any soldiers willing to join us, then secure the twelfth star. Tomorrow, as the heavens align with the great wonder of the sun and moon, the crown of twelve stars shall be cast down. Let it be known that those who dare oppose the

Divine Ascendancy and its prophet shall meet their end. The offering shall seal our power and bring all doubters to their knees."

"You can't do this. We're innocent. You don't have to—"

Bouchard shook his head. "I understand your feelings, Lord Andreas, but the end of days is here, and this is what heaven ordained long before either of us was born. Innocence is irrelevant. Power demands sacrifice." He turned and whispered something to an Ascendant, then gave Andreas and Constanza a parting nod.

A hand grasped Andreas's shoulder, pulling him away from Constanza and the others. He turned, panic rising, only to meet the steely gaze of an Ascendant.

Andreas dug his heels into the ground, muscles tensed and jaw clenched in defiance as he struggled against the man dragging him away. He shouted, but a calloused hand silenced him. With each step, he grew weaker, but still he twisted and pulled. A blow struck his ribcage, and he staggered back, crashing onto the steps in front of the citadel's wooden door.

Constanza screamed his name.

Andreas sprang up to run, but the iron grips of three Ascendants latched on to him, unyielding as they wrenched him farther from his family. The heavy oak doors shut behind them, and inside the citadel, the stillness amplified his grunts and heavy breathing.

Even if his body would no longer resist, he could not surrender. To the right, cracking and pounding echoed from the great hall. The roof had been torn away in whole sections, exposing the gray skies above. Laborers had even begun to dismantle the heavy beams that had once supported the roof. Beneath it all stood the strange platform that had been under construction during the feast three days ago. It was as if Lucien Bouchard and his followers had stripped away all that had once been awe-inspiring and majestic, leaving only bones and memories.

The Ascendants dragged Andreas up the stairs and pushed him down the long corridor that led to the duke's quarters. Each footstep echoed off the stone walls, calling up long-buried memories he had tried so hard to forget—the scent of polished mahogany, the rustle of tapestries, the ever-present trickle of water from the courtyard fountain. The past rose to meet him, pulling him deeper into the citadel he had once called home.

They passed the little chapel where Pâre had spent many of his waking hours. Then they marched past Mâre's quarters and finally the duke's. Pairs of Ascendants stood guard at the four doors at the end of the hall, one of which led to the room Andreas had shared with his brothers in their youth. The men holding Andreas whispered to the guards, then opened the door and pushed Andreas inside.

The same heavy drapes still hung from the windows, casting oddly familiar shadows on the worn floorboards. The scent of hearth smoke wrapped around him as it had during the countless hours he had spent here as a child. The chamber remained frozen in time, like a relic of the past that now felt like a dream. The tapestries on the walls depicted scenes of knights and battles. Their colors had faded with the years, but their stories were still woven into the fabric of his memory.

Philip sat in the shadows beside the window. Andreas tensed.

Philip gazed at Andreas, shoulders sagging and lips downturned. "Brother."

Andreas bit his bottom lip but otherwise remained still. Memories of childhood games and shared laughter clashed with the events that had driven them to this place. "Philip," he said at last.

"I never wanted this." Philip stood and peered out the leaded windows.

"But you caused it." Andreas approached him, his stomach and side still aching from the struggles of the past few hours. The words of the Hebrew prophet Isaiah came to mind: *It is he that bringeth the princes to nothing; he maketh the judges of the earth as vanity.*

"It wasn't supposed to happen the way it did. How could Mâre entwine herself with such a snake as Lucien Bouchard?"

"That's not what I'm talking about. I was enjoying the life God had blessed me with until you shattered all of it."

"I didn't abduct your family. That was Bouchard and his rabble."

"You used my family for your own gain, Philip."

"I rescued them from the cultists."

"And dragged them over the Alps, away from their home, all so you could attain more power."

"You knew this day would come, brother. Pâre, Mâre, Amadeus, Bishop de Romagnano—they all knew where you've been hiding. For months Pâre has summoned you, but you refused to answer. Perhaps you thought it possible to abandon your noble lineage and fall into heresy without anyone noticing, but now you see how mistaken you were."

Andreas clenched his fists and almost lunged at Philip, but he didn't have the strength. Instead he turned his back to his brother, found a chair, and dropped into it, sighing as he laid his hands on the armrests. "Remember how we would quarrel as boys?"

"Do I remember?" Philip chuckled as he dragged his chair across the floor. "I still wonder how both of us survived without maiming each other for life." He sat, crossed his legs, and lounged against the cushion. "How did you end up here? I thought you would be on your way back to Piedmont by now."

"We were to leave this morning, but the Ascendants found us first."

The bells rang their midday chorus by the time Andreas finished telling Philip about the flight from the feast, the rescue of the children from Ripaille, the secret escape from the town, and the skirmish at L'Ermitage.

Philip leaned on one armrest and rubbed his cheek as Andreas came to the end of his story. "You truly love Constanza, don't you?"

"Love might be the first word that comes to mind, but it's only the beginning." Andreas coughed, his throat dry with thirst.

"At least those Cypriots left some water for us." Philip stood and walked to a table with a clay pitcher sitting atop it. He filled two earthenware cups to the brim and offered one to Andreas.

Taking the cup, Andreas nodded once. "Thank you."

Philip raised his cup. "To Andreas, my elder brother, who has found the secret to happiness and long life."

"And to my brother Philip," Andreas said, mimicking the gesture and smiling, "who has done everything in his power to bring it to an end."

They both sighed, then downed the stale water.

"What will become of us, Andreas? Will the Cypriot hang us or fillet us? Or perhaps he'll drown us in Lac Léman."

"I can't let it come to that."

"What can you possibly do to stop it? Our fate is entirely in the hands of Lucien Bouchard."

"I'll do everything I can, but most of all, I have faith that God will triumph over His enemies, either now or at His coming."

Philip placed his cup on the floor. "Now *you* sound like a maniacal heretic."

"No, the opposite. God is sovereign over the affairs of the world, and the timing of His kingdom is known only to Him." He paused, his gaze steady on Philip. "The world is so steeped in sin that it can't be redeemed by human hands, and Bouchard's promises to create a perfect world are just like all tyrants who came before him or will come after—bound to fall into the cesspit of antiquity."

Philip's gaze wandered the room. "I must admit, your commitment to this . . . alternative path has puzzled me. Forgive me if I fail to comprehend how you could forsake your rich, comfortable life to become a common peasant."

"Being poor isn't what matters. If I wanted that, I would've remained a monk, for at least then my life wouldn't be in peril."

Philip crossed his arms. "You choose to risk your life, Andreas, but for what?"

Andreas pondered that for a moment. This path had begun in his mind, even as a novice in the abbey. His pressing questions, the depravity of his own soul, the need for everlasting redemption—then, at his lowest point, the Lord had sent a preacher who had showed him the truth in both word and deed. Through Jesus Christ alone, God had forgiven his sin, redeemed his soul, and sanctified his spirit. After all the Lord had given him, how could Andreas offer anything less than his whole life?

"I forfeit my life for the truth," he said. "For the truth that can set any man free, the truth that transforms the heart, the truth that leads to eternal life. I can't turn from what I know to be true, regardless of what happens to me."

"You make everything sound so easy. You're married to a woman you love, you took little orphan children in as your own, you don't back down from your beliefs." Laughter rumbled in Philip's chest. "If you weren't a heretic, Pope Pius himself would canonize you. Your name would be remembered through the ages, like Saint Maurice or even Saint Francis."

Andreas's voice softened as he met Philip's eyes. "If my name were forgotten but the love and truth I've tried to live endured, then I would count this a life well lived."

"Even if the Cypriot kills you and leaves your wife a widow?"

Andreas shuddered at the thought, not for fear of death but for those he would leave behind. To imagine Constanza and the children without him, to never see the child Constanza carried—no, he couldn't imagine. "I won't allow Bouchard to harm Constanza or our children."

"If anyone in this room deserves to live, it's you, brother. As for me . . ." Philip slouched in his chair and sighed. "My life is over. Even if the Cypriot keeps me alive, Pâre will take everything from me—titles, land, inheritance. History might remember me as Philip the Landless."

"All of that pales in comparison to your position before God." Andreas leaned forward. "I want you to know the Savior too."

Philip threw his head back and laughed. "I'm the most debauched noble in all of Savoy. Why would I surrender my happiness so I can become a dull peasant like you?"

"Because that debauchery requires a punishment, as mine did before my conversion."

"While I'm paying my debts in purgatory, perhaps you could help pray my soul out of it."

"Purgatory is an invention of the Catholic Church. It only serves as a tool for the clergy to control and exploit the masses."

Philip waved that away. "Now you sound like that man Hus from a few decades ago in Bohemia. You know what the pope's council did to him, no?"

"They burned him at the stake after they lied to him and promised safe passage."

"And I don't wish to share his fate. Perhaps that's your life's calling, but not mine."

"Life on this earth is short, but it's here we must either believe the gospel of Jesus Christ or reject it."

Philip clasped his hands behind his head. "I choose to live as I wish until I feel the need to change."

"And I will pray the Holy Spirit shows you that need before it's too late."

Philip did not answer. Andreas rose and strode to the window, leaving his brother to ponder.

Across the vast expanse of Lac Léman, the Vaudois shore lay cloaked in gray hues, and distant mountains rose on the horizon. In the stillness, Andreas's thoughts turned to Johan, who had given his life for his friends. Andreas's chest tightened at the memories they had shared, both bad and good. In the end, Johan had chosen to follow Christ instead of worldly pleasure, and his testimony, especially in the last month, was one to be admired.

Thoughts of Constanza and the children came next. Were they somewhere in the château, or had the Ascendants taken them elsewhere?

Andreas closed his eyes and offered a prayer for their protection. There was nothing else he could do.

29

Kings shall serve us, and any nation that will not serve us shall be destroyed. The Sons of God shall tread on the necks of kings, and all realms under heaven shall be given unto them.

—Taborite manifesto, c. 1430

THE DAY PASSED INTO EVENING , and the evening into night. Andreas lay on one of the three curtained beds in the room and stared at the rafters. Thuds, slams, and creaks sounded throughout the château, making sleep impossible to find, though Philip had already been sleeping for hours.

Sometime in the night, the noise ceased, and Andreas fell into a deep slumber.

An abrupt shake startled him awake. His eyelids flew open. Above him stood the actor who had played Jacques at Château de Ripaille a week ago, now wearing the cloak of an Ascendant. "The Prophet will see you now. Come with me."

Andreas rubbed his eyes and yawned. "May I wash my face and drink a cup of water first?"

Jacques raked his hand through his hair. "Make haste. He waits for us."

"And a sharp blade would be helpful," Andreas said, rubbing his stubbly neck.

Jacques ignored the comment and motioned to the washbasin on the other side of the room. After a swish of water in his mouth and a quick cleanse of his face, Andreas met Jacques at the door. "What about Philip?"

"The Prophet requested only your attendance."

Two more Ascendants met them outside. Not a single candle guided their path as they walked through the nearly pitch-black halls. At each closed door, Andreas wondered if Constanza waited behind it. Were the children frightened and alone in one of these dark rooms, or were they with Constanza and Elionor? If only he could know for certain.

Instead of descending the stairs, Jacques led him into what had once been the duke's quarters. The heavy door creaked open before Andreas and revealed the dim chamber within.

Lucien Bouchard sat upon a carved wooden chair, still wearing his crimson cloak. His figure was cast in stark relief against the glow of torchlight.

"Andreas de Bonomo. I hear that is what you call yourself now."

Jacques and another Ascendant prodded Andreas forward until he stood a few paces from the chair. After a nod from Bouchard, the Ascendants walked back to the door and stood watch.

"Did you sleep well?" Bouchard asked, sounding concerned.

"I slept." Voice still raspy, Andreas cleared his throat. "Where is my family, Monsieur Bouchard?"

"Your family, Monsieur Bonomo, is exactly where they need to be. But let us not waste time with trivialities. There are far more pressing matters for men like us to deliberate, would you not agree?"

Murderer of Constanza's father, abductor of Andreas's family, persecutor of the saints—there was nothing to say to Lucien Bouchard. Andreas planted his feet and set his jaw.

"No answer? So be it. I have some questions for you." Bouchard rose and strode to Andreas. "Your dedication is admirable. Few men have the strength to walk the path you have chosen. You also understand the worth of every man. People need someone to follow, to believe in. If it were not for men like you and me, they would follow someone else, likely someone far less kind."

Andreas curled the corner of his lip. "We are nothing alike. The Holy Scriptures speak of men like you, and not so gently."

"That is where you falter. You are tied to one reading of the letter instead of using God's words to advance what you deem is right."

"That's called twisting the Scriptures. Have you deemed it right to imprison me and my family?"

"I know it's hard for you Vallenses to understand the world outside your insignificant sect. Once you experience the power that comes from harnessing religion instead of allowing it to control you, then you, too, can have all your soul desires." Bouchard raised his fist. "The Catholics hold to their traditions, the Vallenses to their scriptures, both of which I also hold in high regard. But do you not see that there is more? You cannot confine the revelations of God to the pages of ancient scriptures. Let them live and breathe in the present, allowing you to ascend to greater heights and attain true fame and prestige."

Andreas lowered his brows. "Fame and prestige are not the chief ends of man."

Lucien shook his head. "Do you not see the limits of your faith? You are an intelligent leader, far wiser than those you surround yourself with. Take what is yours, cast aside the rigid rules, assert your position. God created men like you and me to control those who are easily swayed, never to serve them."

"Scripture alone stands as the bedrock of my faith." Andreas straightened his back. "The Bible isn't something to be used for worldly gain. It's the unchanging

Word of God. To gain power and prestige by distorting the Scriptures is to stray from the path of truth into the treacherous realm of deception."

"But see how much you are surrendering. You have sacrificed so much for your beliefs, but have you ever wondered if there is an alternative path—one where you can hold on to your faith without losing everything you love?"

Bouchard reached out and grasped Andreas's hand, the grip as firm as iron shackles. Andreas tried to pull back, but Bouchard's hold was uncannily strong.

"Imagine your life in Piedmont—Constanza at your side, children of your own playing in the fields, the burden of nobility gone. The Vallenses could live in peace, with you at the helm of a movement that transcends petty divisions. It is not impossible."

Andreas peered beyond Bouchard toward the window. His family at peace back in Val Angrogna. Could that truly be his? A pang of guilt coursed through him. No, he could never abandon his loved ones, forsake his new friends, or destroy his character. He shook his head and flashed a cold smile at Bouchard. "I would never cooperate with a man like you, not if I were promised the world itself."

"Be rational. You and the Vallenses, I and the Divine Ascendancy—we hold so much in common. We both despise the Church of Rome. The clergy hunt us and try to stomp us out, yet still our followers flourish because of men like you and me."

"As I said, we are nothing alike." Andreas pulled his hand from Bouchard's grip. "True believers don't persecute those who disagree with them. They don't seek glory and power. They don't walk about bending the Scriptures to control the masses and inventing crooked doctrines like declaring marriage a sin. Bouchard, we are as different as light and darkness."

"I am offering to release you, along with your wife and the woman with child. You could be back in Piedmont with Constanza before the winter sets in."

"You never mentioned my children." Andreas rubbed his biceps.

"That is another matter entirely. If I do not show my followers and the rest of the populace that I have both the will and power to fulfill my promises, then I will lose all credibility. Leadership is not about kindness. It is about making choices others are too weak to make."

"I'm not leaving the château without my wife, my children, and Elionor."

"That is not an option. So what will you do? None but I can give you the freedom and peaceful life you desire."

"I already have friends in Thonon, and they have no association with you."

"The Poor?" Bouchard licked the corner of his mouth. "Do you imagine them as your friends? Men like us don't need the help of friends. We trust in ourselves and take advantage of those willing to stand by us. The Poor will soon be nothing but a memory, remembered only by how hot their flesh burns."

"At least they seek the truth of the Scriptures instead of listening to your manipulative teachings."

"There are always those who resist change and cling to the past." Bouchard clasped his hands together. "History is a harsh teacher. Those who resist the tide of change are often swept away. I would hate to see someone of your potential be cast aside." He motioned for the guards. "You have until tomorrow, October the fourteenth, the day of the eclipse, to decide. No matter your choice, the crown of twelve stars will be cast down, exactly as I have said. All Savoy, and very soon all the world, will bow to me."

Andreas planted his feet firmly and squared his shoulders. "There is only one whom all men will bow before. And He is no mere mortal."

Bouchard signaled his men to escort Andreas away. "When the sun disappears tomorrow, so too could all that you hold dear. Think carefully. The dawn may bring you peace, or it may bring anguish. Either way, the world will know the power of my words."

30

The Christian man, it seems to me, is the noblest style of man; the freest, bravest, most heroic, and most fearless of men. If he is what he should be, he is, in the best sense of the word, a man all over, from the crown of his head to the sole of his foot.

—Charles Haddon Spurgeon
A Good Start, 1898

How HAD HE LET ELIONOR GO? Elias repeated the question over and over in his mind. When the Ascendants had attacked yesterday morning, he had gathered what men he could. But with fanatical strength, four Ascendants had stood as a rear guard, fighting like rabid hounds while their cowardly friends retreated with Elionor and the others.

Sweat beaded on Elias's brow as he dug the second of two graves for the brave men who had perished yesterday. The first one had been Gaspard, who should have lived out his years doting on his grandchildren, not lost his life to a battle wound. And the grave Elias prepared now was for the brave Vallense, Johan Lauras.

With the hole deep enough, Elias threw the shovel up over the side, heaved himself out, and dusted himself off. Johan's body lay under a tattered old cloak near the newly dug grave. Too young, this Vallense farmer. Though a bit boisterous, Johan had been a valiant man, a strong man. He would've made a good soldier.

Perrin, one of the old men at L'Ermitage, helped Elias lift Johan's body and lower it into the hole. "I never thought it would come to this, Elias. We've never sought conflict, and we've only ever wanted to live in peace. Now here we are, surrounded."

"The Ascendants will destroy us all if we don't hold them back."

"With a few old men and some rusty axes not worth carrying into the forests? The Ascendants probably don't care about us. We know they wanted the Vallenses most."

"Lucien Bouchard wants all of us dead, and we still have one of the Vallense children with us. And do you know what day it is?"

Perrin looked at Elias inquisitively. "The thirteenth of October."

"Tomorrow is Bouchard's day. You've heard his prophecies. They need all twelve children to complete their crown, and right now one is missing. If we hold back the Ascendants, their prophet loses. His followers will falter, and his kingdom will collapse."

But as Elias spoke, his thoughts drifted to the beautiful woman who had captured his heart. He and the other men at L'Ermitage needed to do more than hold back the Ascendants. Elionor was Bouchard's captive, and Elias had to help her. If he didn't, he couldn't bear the thought of living.

Perrin picked up his shovel and threw dirt into the grave, and Elias grabbed the other shovel and did the same. They buried the dead in silence.

"I need to check the perimeter." Elias leaned his shovel against an old fencepost. "Come with me if you wish."

Perrin walked beside Elias as they made their way to the edge of the clearing. "The Ascendants will attack again."

"Then we'll fight back." Elias scanned a thick patch of briars for signs of Ascendants. "We can't stand back and sacrifice our Vallense frâres to the Prophet."

"It's the young woman, Elionor, isn't it?" Perrin kicked a stone from the path. "I understand your love for her. She sang behind me the other evening in the gathering hall. But I did want to warn you—"

"Thank you for your concern, but others have already warned me." Elias stopped and faced Perrin. "I know what I need to know about Elionor."

"What do your pâre and mâre think of her?"

"They know only what Madeleine and I have told them." Elias tightened his belt and began walking again. "But none of that matters if we don't help her and her friends."

Perrin swung his hand toward the trees. "We're surrounded, and soon the Ascendants will know how few men we have here."

"Then I pray God blinds them."

After the thorough appraisal of the perimeter, Elias hurried to the hall. Madeleine's children ran about the open areas with other young ones, but otherwise the feeling inside was quiet, somber.

Madeleine sat against the wall feeding the baby as Elias approached. "The children are hungry," she whispered. "We had planned to stay here only one night, and we have no more food. We can't stay here much longer, frâre."

"We can't surrender either." Elias leaned his sword against the wall and sat facing Madeleine.

"We're mostly woodcutters' wives and children, not soldiers."

"I'll lead the defense, but I need you to stay with the other women here. Pray for deliverance, pray for the Vallenses, pray for Elionor." Elias tensed his hands at his sides.

"Indeed you love her." Madeleine gave Elias a warm smile. "I completely approve of Elionor. She is as compassionate and selfless as any woman I've met."

"Some think differently."

"The naysayers will always abound, frâre, but I think you understand what it means to marry a woman with a child. Yes, there is risk in any relationship, especially marriage. I hold many regrets from my youth, but Jean is a good husband and father, and he's becoming a good Christian man instead of watching from afar." Madeleine placed her hand on Elias's. "But you and Elionor are both devoted disciples of Jézu. I've seen her remorse, and I believe she has confessed and forsaken her sin."

"I know she has. And do you know how I know?" Elias pointed toward Madeleine. "Elionor doesn't desperately pursue me."

"Yet she adores you. When you're near, her eyes blaze with almost as much intensity as yours. She can barely contain her smiles with you in the room."

"I'm so used to being aggressive, firm, strong. But with Elionor, I forget how to speak. I want to give her everything, but I don't know how to start."

"All she wants is you, Elias." Madeleine pushed a lock of hair under her headscarf and grinned. "Give her that, and she has everything."

"I still don't know if she's alive." Elias sighed, his mind aching from all the possibilities. "What if Bouchard has already executed her?"

Madeleine pushed his shoulder. "Always imagining the worst, exactly like when you were a boy."

"Maybe if my elder sister hadn't told me bears lurked outside, ready to devour little boys—"

"Did I say that?"

Elias shot a sideways glance at Madeleine.

"Maybe I did make you a little more gloomy than you already were." She giggled, laid the baby over her shoulder, and patted his back. "But it's been good for you. You're much wiser and more discerning than I was at your age."

After a few moments of silence, Elias reclined against the wall and breathed deeply.

"When was the last time you slept?" Madeleine asked.

"Two nights ago." Elias peeked from under an eyelid as Madeleine stood.

"Then I'll try to keep the children quiet for you."

Weariness washed over Elias like a wave. His eyelids grew heavy, and soon he drifted into a light slumber.

A shout from the door snapped him back into the present. How long had he been dozing? It felt like all day, but everything was exactly as it had been before he had fallen asleep.

Perrin ran to Elias, panting. "The Ascendants are back, and in greater numbers."

"Bring all the women and children inside." Elias bolted up and grabbed his sword. "Barricade the entrance. Where are they coming from?"

"All from the north—at least sixty of them. Baptiste saw them in the forest, ready to attack."

Sixty Ascendants, many of them soldiers who had once served under Elias, stood against him and fifteen old men. He hurried to the door, sword in hand, and instructed Ezio de Bonomo on how to barricade the entrance.

Elias surveyed the rugged terrain surrounding L'Ermitage. With odds as they were, he and the old men couldn't defeat the Prophet's men. But he would never surrender. Maybe he could outwit them instead.

The elderly men gathered around him, rusty axes and weathered spears in hand.

"They need to think we have more men than we do," Elias said. "Spread out along the edge, hide in the shadows, make as much noise as you can. We'll use every trick we have to confuse them."

The men met his words with nods of understanding. This was the moment to turn the enemy back, to show the Ascendants that the Poor would not be easily overrun.

"Spread out, but stay in sight of each other. A couple of you walk quickly from one spot to another. Make them think we patrol every foot of our perimeter."

As the men dispersed, uncertainty gnawed at Elias, but he pushed aside the doubts and focused on the task at hand. Moving swiftly from one position to another, he directed the placement of the men. "Shout to each other. Call out the names of men who aren't here—your pâres, your gran-pâres, the pope, whoever. Make them think we're many."

In the distance, the sound of crunching leaves and snapping twigs carried across the terrain. His heart pounded against his breastbone as the Ascendants crept through the brush.

With bated breath, Elias waited. Only two Ascendants were in front of his position. He sprang up and moved to where he had stationed Perrin. Two more attackers approached there.

And then, as if by some miracle, the first signs of confusion clouded the Ascendants' faces.

"They're hesitating," Perrin whispered in disbelief.

A burst of triumph coursed through Elias's veins as the Ascendants stopped and fell back. The ruse was working.

But even though the Ascendants had paused, this surely wouldn't be the end. The enemy would return, but with greater numbers. And when they did, the Poor would be ready to meet them.

"We have to keep this up," Elias said to Perrin. "All day, all evening, all night. When the sun sets, light the torches and keep them moving."

"For how long? They'll discover our deceit soon enough."

"Until the woodcutters return."

"They're woodcutters, not soldiers. Besides, that could be days, if ever."

"Then I'll make sure it doesn't take that long." Elias glanced back toward the hall and the forested hills beyond. "Where are they cutting right now?"

"I don't know. Somewhere up the Dranse." Perrin shrugged. "One of the wives is bound to know."

Yes, Madeleine. She would know where Jean was. After some parting instructions for Perrin, Elias jogged to the gathering hall and pushed on the door. Locked. He knocked in a furor. "It's Elias. Open the door."

The door cracked open, and the boy Ezio peeked out.

"We're safe for now." Elias opened the door and scanned the room. "Where's my sister?"

Ezio pointed at the back corner. "All the mothers and children are over there. A few of us boys are standing guard at the doors."

"Good." Elias offered him a smile and a single nod. But if the defenses failed, the boys' efforts, though valiant, would do little. The Ascendants would cut them down without mercy.

Madeleine's voice came soft and melodic as Elias approached her. Hélène, her daughter, sat nearby rocking the baby as Madeleine taught seven or eight children a song. Long ago, when he was a boy, she had taught him the same.

> A little faith does mighty deeds,
> Quite past all my recounting;
> Faith like a little mustard seed
> Can move a lofty mountain.
> A little charity and zeal,
> A little tribulation,
> A little patience makes us feel
> Great peace and consolation.

Elias joined in on the last two lines, and all the children listened, some smiling, others curious.

"You can still sing it, frâre!" Madeleine clapped and smiled.

Elias motioned for her to follow him. In a private corner a few paces away, he asked, "Where are Jean and the rest of the woodcutters?"

"In the forests . . . cutting wood."

"I know that. But where exactly?"

"Elias, you know I don't think about these things. I have four children and a baby to care for. For the past week or more, I've been trying to keep Constanza and her children safe . . . Elionor too. Now we're in danger, so please forgive me if I don't know the name of the place where my husband cuts down trees."

"I'm sorry, Madeleine. We're holding back the Ascendants for now. They think we have more men here than we do. But the ruse won't last long. It could be tomorrow or even tonight when they attack. We need help, and Jean and the other men are our one hope."

"Aline will know where Françoise is." Madeleine led Elias to the other side of the room and asked Françoise's young wife where her husband was working.

"In the hills above Bellevaux." Aline pursed her lips and gave Elias a curious look. "Why?"

"I need to find the men and hurry them along. With their strength, we might fray the Ascendants' noose."

Madeleine blinked rapidly. "Do you know where this Bellevaux is?"

"To the south. If I leave now, I'll be there by nightfall."

"We need you here, Elias. The old men can't defend the whole encampment by themselves. They need your expertise, your leadership."

"Wouldn't it be better to have a hundred men like me here, some stronger?"

Madeleine shook her head. "What if the Ascendants capture you in the forests? Then we'll be without our one strong defender, and still our husbands won't know our plight. Let me go instead."

"Never. Besides, you don't know the way to Bellevaux. It's I or no one." Elias's gaze swept over the women and children huddled about the room. What if the Ascendants who lurked beyond the trees attacked? Could he live with himself if he didn't return before then?

No, everyone here relied on him, and he wouldn't fail them. "I'm going," he said to Madeleine.

"When?"

"Now, as soon as I pass through those doors. I trust the men here, and they'll keep up the ruse through the night. But you need Jean." He nodded toward Aline. "And you need Françoise. Every wife here needs her husband, and every child his pâre. Lord willing, I'll return by noon tomorrow with a hundred strong, fearless woodsmen."

Madeleine threw her arms around Elias's neck. "I trust you, frâre, and we'll all be praying for you."

Elias made his way outside and scanned the perimeter one last time. The elder men stood guard with a fierce determination carved into their faces. Though the sun hadn't yet set, they had already lit torches. Light flared from twenty or more points along the northern perimeter—exactly what they needed. But in the distant shadows, the Ascendants had also lit torches.

As Elias slipped into the forested slope to the south, he whispered a prayer. *Lord, please let this ruse hold until I return. Help me find the men. And give Andreas strength. I imagine he needs it right now.*

With each step, the weight of his choice pressed down on him. Madeleine, the children, Mâre, Pâre, Elionor . . . all those he loved were in danger, but he wouldn't rest until he had won their safety and put an end to Lucien Bouchard and his tyranny.

31

I had a vision—and I saw white spirits and black spirits engaged in battle, and the sun was darkened—the thunder rolled in the heavens, and blood flowed in streams.

—Nat Turner
Testimony of his insurrection, 1831

THE SUN DIPPED BELOW THE HORIZON and cast its final rays across the room where Elionor and the children were confined. Elionor traced the patterns etched into the walls, marveling at the opulence that surrounded her. She had never set foot in a place so grand, so exquisite, with its towering ceilings, its walls adorned with elaborate tapestries, and its polished wooden floors that gleamed in the light.

The hearth fire, their lone source of warmth for the past day, had dwindled to glowing embers, and the air held a chill that seeped into Elionor's bones. Despite her attempts to coax more heat from the dying flames, she and the children had run out of fuel while the guards outside remained indifferent to their plight.

Silvia briskly rubbed her hands together and blew into them. "I wish Papà and Mamà were here."

"Me too." Ave huddled close to Silvia and smiled up at Elionor. "But I'm happy you're here with us, madomaisèla."

"I think it's time to sleep now."

"But it's so early." Guido covered a yawn and hid a sheepish smile.

"Come now, to the bed. There's not much else to do here anyway."

"I haven't heard the coughing much today," Silvia said. "I hope it's not like last night. I could barely sleep."

As the children settled in for the night, the baby fluttered within Elionor, bringing warmth to her cheeks and a smile to her face. The day when she could hold this little life couldn't come soon enough. But how long would she and the children be confined in this room? Days? Weeks? She shuddered at the thought of months.

Despite everything that had happened since the day she had come to Constanza in desperation, Elionor thanked God that He had led her down this path. With Constanza and the children, she had found belonging again. And Elias—

The thought of him made her heart thump, and the baby moved a little more too. Elias's strength, his loyalty, his love—they anchored her. In his presence, she felt a courage and resilience she had never known before. He was her hope, her guide through the stormy waters ahead. No clouds of doubt about his devotion passed over her. He would fight for her without flinching.

As Elionor drifted toward sleep, the coughing started from the neighboring room. She rolled to her back, and the baby stirred in response. The cough echoed through the silence, punctuated by rasping breaths.

Silvia sat up beside Elionor and sighed. "Again?"

"I know it's hard to sleep, but someone is suffering in there. We should pray for her."

Silvia bowed her head as Elionor interceded on behalf of the unknown woman. By the time Elionor finished, Silvia's breaths were long and heavy, and her eyes remained closed.

The door creaked open, and a man's voice rang out. "Woman!"

Elionor sat up in the bed and covered herself with a blanket.

"Come here, we need you." The man stared at her. "Make haste!"

"The children are coming with me."

"No, only you. They stay here."

Elionor shook her head as she slid farther back on the bed. "They're my charge, and I can't leave them here alone."

Another man entered the room and strode to the bed. "We won't harm you, woman. We just need your help."

Prospera clung to Elionor's arm. "What's wrong, madomaisèla?"

"Stay with me and all will be well."

A man clasped Elionor's arm and tore her from the bed. A few children jumped out and pulled her back, crying. Elionor flailed her arms and kicked, but the man dragged her to the door while the other man restrained the children.

"Madomaisèla!"

"Don't fret!" Elionor shouted back as she was thrown to the floor. The door shut behind her, and the two Ascendants loomed over her.

The other pointed to the next door down the corridor. "You've heard all that coughing. Make it stop."

"I'm not a healer." Elionor slid backward and leaned against the wall, shaking her head. "I beg you, let me return to my room."

"Either hush that invalid woman or stand guard with us in this cold hallway." The taller Ascendant offered Elionor a hand, but she recoiled. He grabbed her hand anyway, wrenched her up, and pushed her toward the neighboring room. "That's your choice."

Elionor took slow steps to the door and looked back. The men stared at her and motioned for her to continue.

The coughing greeted her as soon as she opened the door. A single flickering candle on the bedside table illuminated the faces of three young girls clustered around a bed. Their eyes were red rimmed, their faces marked with worry and fear.

A woman lay propped up on a mound of pillows, her features gaunt and hallowed, each labored breath rattling in her chest. Despair hung in the air like a suffocating fog, and the room was heavy with the stench of sickness.

"Can you help her?" one girl asked in a flat, hopeless tone.

Though Constanza had taught Elionor a little about caring for the sick, this was far more than a sniffle or childhood cough. Her heart ached at the sight of the woman's pain, but what could she do? The girls, none of whom was more than fifteen years old, hovered around the woman's bedside, their hands clutching hers in a desperate bid for comfort.

But Elionor couldn't turn away from someone in need. With tentative steps, she approached the bedside. "Is this your mother?" she asked the girls.

The one who seemed to be the oldest nodded. "She has been sick for many months, but it's worse now. We don't know what to do. Can you heal her?"

Elionor examined the three girls' finely embroidered garments. The intricate designs spoke of the wealth and status that surrounded them. The lilt of the girls' speech, tinged with the refined accent of nobles, further confirmed their position.

Gently, Elionor reached out to the woman, her touch light against the clammy skin. She adjusted the pillows beneath the woman's head and eased her into a more comfortable position. "My name is Elionor Janavel."

"Who?" The woman's voice came in a lifeless sigh. Her breathing seemed to ease at Elionor's touch, and her features relaxed.

"Elionor. The men outside wanted me to help you."

"Her name is Anne," said the oldest girl. "I am Agnes, and these are my sisters, Marie and Bona."

Elionor offered them a warm smile. *"Planer de vos véser."*

"Where are you from?" Agnes asked. "Your accent is quite different from the other servants."

"Oh, I'm not a servant here. I'm from the mountains of Piedmont."

Marie raised her brows. "Two of my brothers live there."

"One of them is a heretic," Agnes said. "He even married a peasant girl."

Elionor's jaw nearly dropped. These were Andreas's sisters, and the woman—this was the Duchess of Savoy herself. Elionor Janavel—orphan, outcast, peasant, Vallense—was touching the most highborn woman in all the land. She pulled her hand away, held it to her cheek, and retreated from the bed.

She shouldn't be here. To them, she was lower than a lame mule. *Dear God, why did You put me here? I am nothing, and I have nothing to offer them.*

A whisper of divine guidance stirred the stillness. God hadn't placed her here by accident. This was her call to extend compassion, just as so many others had done for her. When Elionor was a child, Monsen Raimond had pulled her from the mire of Chivasso and brought her to the Vallenses. Soon afterward, Papà and Mamà had taken her in as their own daughter. And even after she had forsaken so much of what she had been given, Constanza, her dearest friend, had shown her compassion. Then there was Elias, who loved her with pure, selfless, unwavering devotion. No matter the duchess's status, Elionor would do what she could.

"Come, girls," she said to Agnes, Marie, and Bona. "There's much we can do to ease your mamà's discomfort."

She guided Agnes toward a nearby basin filled with water. "Dampen this cloth and gently press it against your mamà's forehead. It will help to soothe her fever."

Turning her attention to Marie, who stood wringing her hands anxiously, Elionor offered a tender smile. "You can help too. Knock on the door and ask the guards for more water. Your mamà needs to keep drinking."

"They'll say no."

"Give them a big smile and lighten your voice a bit. They brought me here to help, so I think they might oblige us." Elionor led the youngest girl to the bedside. "You sit with your mother, Bona. Hold her hand and speak to her softly. Your being near will bring her comfort."

As the girls hurried to their tasks, Elionor turned to the Duchess of Savoy. "Vôtre Grâce." Was that the right way to address her? She sighed and carefully adjusted the pillows beneath the duchess's head. "You are not alone, Vôtre Grâce. I'll be here as long as you need me."

Duchess Anne stirred, her eyelids fluttering open. A weak smile graced her lips as she gazed up at Elionor. "Thank you." She reached out a trembling hand, her fingers twitching as they brushed against Elionor's own.

Elionor met the duchess's hand with a light squeeze. "The Lord is gracious and merciful to us all, Vôtre Grâce."

Anne's eyes reflected unshed tears as Elionor spoke softly about everything she could think of—the mountains, Elias, the coming winter. Agnes periodically dabbed her mother's brow, Marie offered the duchess drinks of water, and Bona rubbed her hand. But all three listened as Elionor recounted her stories.

"You know our brother?" Agnes asked. "Do you know his wife too?"

"Ah, my friend Constanza. She is the brightest gem in all the world."

"But she's a peasant, a shepherdess. She is pretty, but—"

"Not all beauty shines with polish, dear Agnes. Your brother Andreas is as honorable a man as any, but if you knew Constanza, you would see that she's as rare a jewel as he is."

Elionor told stories about her home and childhood well into the night, but in time, the three noble daughters fell asleep on the bed. The duchess still coughed and stirred, but the pain seemed to have lessened. Elionor laid her head near the foot of the bed. The Bonomo children needed her, but God had placed her here with the duchess for now. Her prayers put her mind at ease despite the darkness around her.

*　*　*

Three filthy, brown-cloaked Ascendants stood at the threshold of Constanza's windowless cell. A short tallow candle, the sole light in the room, illuminated their ugly countenances.

"Come with us," one of them said. "And don't delay."

Constanza waved them away. "Close the door so I can ready myself."

"No need for that, dama. The Prophet is waiting."

The mention of him sent a biting chill down her spine. She couldn't face that man, especially not alone. After what he had done to Papà—

No, she couldn't dwell on those images. She pressed a trembling hand to her abdomen, where the promise of new life lay nestled within her womb. But where were the children? Was Ezio still safe, or had the Ascendants captured him too? What had happened to Elionor? And Andreas . . . *Please, Lord, protect him.*

Two of the three Ascendants stomped into the cell and yanked her up from her mat without a word.

Constanza pulled away from their grasp, stood on her own feet, and lifted her chin high, refusing to be a puppet in the hands of these wicked men. "I can walk myself." She followed them through the door and into the hallway.

The air clung to her skin like the chill mist of early morning, seeping into her bones and leaving her shivering. Each shadow seemed to leer and taunt her.

The men forced her up a flight of rough stairs and into an expansive hall. Constanza's breath hitched. A few days before, the splendor of this hall had impressed her, but now it lay bare under the open sky. At the center of the room stood a wide stone platform.

The hall teemed with Ascendants. Men and women alike made up the throng, but most of their features were obscured by their hoods. The air seemed to crackle with tension.

Constanza's heart seized as her gaze settled on the thirteen familiar faces amid the Ascendants. Andreas stood before the children, his steadfast countenance a torch of pure strength as they huddled around him. Holding her ground at their side, Elionor lifted her head in quiet defiance despite all she had endured.

Constanza bolted toward her loved ones, her heart pounding louder with each step. The world narrowed to just the space between her and Andreas. Without hesitation, she flew into his arms. Andreas's embrace swallowed her up. She buried her face in his chest, feeling the steady rhythm of this heartbeat. The noise and chaos faded away, leaving only Andreas and the children.

A hush fell over the crowd, and Constanza lifted her head. Lucien Bouchard emerged from the crowd of Ascendants. Instead of the crimson cloak Constanza had seen before, he now wore the same brown cloak as all the others. If not for his bald head and sharp features, he would have been no different from the rest in the hall.

His piercing gaze bored into her. An icy grip tightened around her heart. She couldn't bear to look at him.

Andreas tightened his hold on Constanza for a moment before moving her gently aside, his scrutiny fixed on the Prophet. "Where is my son?"

"Delayed, I'm afraid," Bouchard said. "But don't fret, he will arrive soon. Your family will be completely reunited . . . for a time."

"Why are you obsessed with us?" Andreas stepped in front of Constanza, shielding her.

"It is not obsession when God has chosen me to be the interpreter of His prophecies." Bouchard reached into his pocket and removed an old, stained parchment. "Have you not read what God has given us? All the faithful who are gathered here know it by heart, but allow me to read it for you. Perhaps then you will understand."

Andreas shook his head. "God has given you no revelations beyond creation and His Holy Scriptures. All you claim as prophecy is a farce. You told me yourself."

"A farce?" Bouchard turned to the Ascendants. "He sees all we have accomplished in Thonon and doubts it is the will of God. What do you say?"

A clamor of boos and hoots cascaded through the great hall.

Bouchard turned back to Andreas with a crooked smile. "We have already seen so much come to pass. Let me read." He held the parchment at arm's length, squinting to focus. "'And there appeared a great wonder in heaven; a woman clothed with the sun, and the moon under her feet, and upon her head—'"

"My children are not your crown of twelve stars!" Andreas shouted.

Bouchard laughed. "You are blind. We have overthrown the House of Savoy, we have in our possession the crown of twelve stars—indeed, you and your twelve orphans." He pointed up toward the hole in the roof. "And soon, if anyone is still so ignorant as to doubt me, we shall all witness the convergence of the sun and moon. Watch and see."

Constanza frowned. Did he believe his own delusions, or was he simply preying on the minds of peasants who had never been taught to discern truth from fables?

Andreas's gaze on Bouchard sharpened. "That portion of John's Apocalypse says nothing about a prince, nor children, nor an eclipse. It's all a concoction from your distorted mind."

"No, you are the one who is confused. Allow me to read the very next words. 'And she being with child cried, travailing in birth, and pained to be delivered.'" The Prophet extended his hand toward Elionor, who turned her head away. "Yet another fulfillment."

Constanza had studied John's Apocalypse, and whatever interpretation the Prophet had imagined was far beyond a stretch. How had he so easily manipulated all these Ascendants?

Bouchard turned and slowly advanced toward the children. "Next these prophecies speak of casting down the twelve stars."

"What?" Constanza gasped, holding back a scream.

The Prophet folded the parchment and stuffed it underneath his cloak. "In this sacred hour, the veil between the earthly realm and the heavens shall be drawn thin. The faithful have gathered in Thonon as I have commanded. Today, during the eclipse of redemption, the kingdom of heaven shall be established upon earth."

Andreas suddenly released Constanza's hand and gestured to the whole gathering. "Do any of you truly believe this?"

"Despite what a faithless man like you declares, today is the day of the Lord," Bouchard said. "Soon after midday, Étoilembra will blot out the sun, and all that was destined to come to pass will be fulfilled. As we speak, the final star of the crown is heading toward us. It will be cast down and the world will be set right."

Andreas shook his head slowly. "You blaspheme the name of God, Lucien Bouchard."

"We shall all know the truth soon. When the crown of twelve stars is presented, when darkness falls upon this holy place, we will know that the light of the prophecies is indeed true."

"Or God will simply strike you down as He has all other antichrists before you."

"Listen to yourself." Bouchard leaned toward Andreas just enough to dominate the space. "Don't fret, though—your time among us will be short. It appears you have chosen the path of weakness, and your presence will no longer be necessary."

Each word seemed to echo within Constanza, sending a tremor of fear up her spine. She pulled the children closer, shielding them from the Prophet. How could such madness, such manipulation, exist in this world?

Andreas turned to look at her, his expression mirroring her thoughts. She nodded as if making a silent vow, a pledge to stand united against Lucien Bouchard and his Ascendants. No matter what.

32

By signs in the heavens it would be made known to me when I should commence the great work. And on the appearance of the eclipse, I should arise and prepare myself, and slay my enemies with their own weapons. And immediately on the sign appearing in the heavens, the seal was removed from my lips, and I communicated the great work laid out before me to do.

—Nat Turner
Testimony of his insurrection, 1831

THE MORNING DRAGGED ON as the throng of Ascendants patiently waited for the spectacle their prophet had promised them. Andreas stood like a fortress wall in front of Constanza, the children, and Elionor, praying that God would protect them.

At this very moment, the Ascendants might be launching their attack on L'Ermitage. Elias and the few men there had shown their bravery, but they couldn't hold out against so many. What then? Just as with the other children yesterday, Lucien Bouchard would parade Ezio through Thonon on his way to the citadel.

Andreas drew in a deep breath and gazed over the crowd. He tried to imagine a miraculous salvation, but this time, no Savoyard army would march in and save the day, and the host of fanatics wouldn't suddenly experience a change of heart.

Constanza placed a hand on his shoulder, and Andreas lifted his hand to meet it. "Stay strong," he whispered. "Don't let them see fear in us. No matter what happens, God will defeat His enemies."

As the sun rose higher in the clear sky, Bouchard paced below the platform, from one end to the other, stopping at intervals to whisper to various followers.

Just before midday, a man in armor ran inside, disheveled and panting, and spoke to Bouchard. The Prophet sighed and gazed up at the sky. He mouthed something to himself, then marched toward Andreas, anger radiating with every step.

Andreas curled the corner of his lips and shook his head. "It seems you won't have your twelve, Monsieur Bouchard." He raised his voice. "Now you all see. Lucien Bouchard has robbed you of your consciences. Men, he has forced you to leave your wives. Women, he has taken your husbands from you to serve his own purposes. Lucien Bouchard isn't a prophet of God but a manipulating liar. Today his fiefdom comes to an end. Turn from your error while you're able."

Bouchard crossed his arms and chuckled. "Clever, your pleas, but we all know they are nothing except your last desperate gasps of life." He walked to Elionor but glanced at the sky again instead of at her. "The woman in travail. I knew it all along, of course. God meant her to be the twelfth star, not the boy."

"Because all you say is false," Constanza said under her breath.

"She will take her place on the altar with the others to fulfill the prophecy." Bouchard grabbed Elionor's wrist and pulled her toward the platform.

Andreas sprang forward to defend Elionor, but as he did, Bouchard's men took hold of first Roberto and Umile, then the rest of the children. Andreas pivoted toward them, steeling himself for a fight.

Someone shoved Andreas to the ground and kicked him in the side. He groaned in pain. An Ascendant threw Constanza down beside him and held one foot over her, ready to stomp.

Andreas lunged at the man, seized his ankle in midair, and wrenched it backward. With a burst of strength, Andreas pushed himself up and toppled the man, pinning him by his throat. "I'll kill you before you touch her."

Powerful arms from behind threw him backward and slammed his head into the stone floor.

Andreas lay stunned. The world swirled around him as a dull ache spread from the point of impact. His thoughts were foggy, disjointed. Every movement sent torrents of pain through his skull.

He staggered up, but two men quickly clasped his wrists and ankles in iron shackles. Constanza screamed for him as the same happened to her. Behind her, the Ascendants bound Elionor and the children with heavy ropes, then dragged them to the platform.

Bouchard loomed over Andreas and Constanza. "Take them away. They will not be permitted to spoil the occasion."

Two Ascendants clad in plate armor broke from the crowd in answer to Bouchard's signal. Those faces—where had Andreas seen them?

Château de Ripaille. These were the two actors from *The Misadventures of Pierre and Jacques.* The way they walked in their Savoyard armor was awkward, as if it hadn't been properly fitted for them.

"You will find a boat docked on the shore." Bouchard nodded at Andreas and Constanza. "Let the lake devour them."

"What crime have we committed?" Andreas yanked his shoulder away from the man who held him. "You can't execute innocent subjects of the Duke of Savoy."

"Savoy is no more, and soon the rest of the world will either bow to the Divine Ascendancy or perish." Bouchard lifted a hand toward the open sky. "The great wonder of heaven is coming."

His temples still throbbing and his side aching, Andreas lifted his head and stared directly at the Prophet. "You condemn yourself, Monsieur Bouchard. God's wrath will fall on false prophets like you, not upon the innocent. If you murder me, my wife, my children, or my friends, you will bring nothing but damnation to your soul."

"You cling to your feeble faith and are blinded by your weakness." Bouchard waved dismissively. "Take them away. They will see the truth soon enough."

Andreas's heart pounded as Pierre, Jacques, and a few other Ascendants dragged him and Constanza through the dimly lit corridors of the citadel. The clank of their iron shackles echoed in the empty spaces. Andreas stole a glance at Constanza. "I'm right here," he whispered. "I will never leave you."

"I know." Constanza's eyes shimmered with tears. "T'aimi, Andreas."

"God hasn't forgotten us. We don't fight this battle alone."

An Ascendant shoved Andreas away from Constanza and positioned himself between them. They descended a narrow staircase, each step leading them farther into the abyss.

At the gate, the blinding light of the midday sun blurred Andreas's vision. Ascendants crowded the streets of Thonon, their fervent chants rising like a deformed hymn.

A small skiff waited at the dock on the waters of Lac Léman. The Ascendants threw Andreas into the boat's confines. A long sculling oar rattled as his knees slammed against the slimy hull. Constanza fell next to him, groaning as her elbow hit one of the thwarts. Pierre and Jacques—or whatever their real names were—stood at the helm, their callous gazes betraying no remorse.

"What will happen to the children?" Constanza's tears dampened Andreas's tunic as she buried her face in his chest. "I don't want to drown."

If he were able to loose himself from these shackles, he would defy the Prophet's followers and wrap his arms around Constanza, showing these fanatics the unwavering love of a husband and wife. But instead he guided his feelings into prayer. "Dear God, You are all powerful and all knowing upon Your throne. Defend us. Cast down Your enemies and show Your might to the world."

Pierre and Jacques each took an oar and pushed off from the dock. As the boat glided across the surface of the lake, Andreas intertwined his fingers with Constanza's despite the shackles. High above, the bright sun and full moon drew closer to each other.

On the shore, a crowd of onlookers watched the spectacle, some gazing up at the converging sun and moon while others pointed at the boat. Behind them loomed Château de Thonon and its roofless, desecrated great hall.

What horrors were Elionor and the children experiencing? Had the Ascendants found Ezio and the Poor? Andreas pushed the gruesome possibilities aside and turned his mind toward the Lord instead. *Yea, though I walk through the valley of the shadow of death, I will fear no evil: for thou art with me; thy rod and thy staff they comfort me.*

*   *   *

A soft tapping stirred in Elionor's womb as she sat bound with the children under the shadow of Lucien Bouchard's altar. Sometimes the Ascendants' voices swelled into a chant, and other times the hall fell into an eerie silence. Where was God amid this sea of evil? Andreas was right—God would have vengeance upon His enemies—but would their blood be spilled before then?

"What are they doing?" Silvia asked.

Elionor recalled distant memories of her childhood before Papà and Mamà had adopted her. "When I was a girl, I thought no one cared for me. Except for my cat, I was alone . . . or so I thought."

Irene's face lit up with hope. "God was with you."

"Yes, and though I felt alone, He still protected me from evil."

"Like now, madomaisèla?"

"Even now, Irene." The Ascendants transitioned into yet another chant while, high above, the sun and the hazy moon drew closer together. "Even now."

Though her hands were tied, Irene managed to wiggle herself onto Elionor's lap. "Where are Mamà and Papà?"

"Just as God is with us, He's also with them."

But as Elionor spoke, Bouchard moved toward them. With each step, he seemed to grow more imposing. Elionor prepared to resist, but he walked past her to the altar itself. He lit a series of candles encircling the platform as he chanted with his followers in an unfamiliar language.

Beside the altar, a richly adorned knife lay in the sunlight, its blade reflecting the glow. Bouchard lifted the blade toward the sky, and the chants of the Ascendants ceased, bringing a searing silence broken only by Bouchard's murmured refrains.

A shiver crept down Elionor's back like icy fingers, chilling her to the bone. Her heart raced, each beat seeming to echo in the stillness of this desecrated place.

Irene's chin trembled. "What's he doing?"

"Don't look. Close your eyes, pray, and don't fear." But how could she say that when fear had already struck her? She had to protect these children from the Prophet. How, she didn't know, but she couldn't sit and cower in helplessness.

Bouchard lowered the knife, glancing over his shoulder as if to make sure his audience was captivated. With deliberate care, he touched Roberto's head, then Irene's. "'And upon her head a crown of twelve stars.'"

Elionor turned away from him when he reached for her. She closed her eyes but still felt his ominous presence as she pulled Irene and Roberto closer. If only she could hold all the children and shield them from this.

A flicker of resolve ignited within her, and she nurtured it as if it were the last ember of a dying fire. *Lord, give us Your grace. Grant us Your courage and deliver us from evil.*

She had to do something, at least for the children's sake. With trembling hands, she moved Irene gently to one side and pushed herself to her feet.

Ignoring the tremors that threatened to overtake her, she fixed her gaze defiantly on Bouchard and his followers. The Prophet was the enemy of God, and she would not allow him the pleasure of his supposed prophecy coming to pass so easily.

"God's mercy will prevail over your profanity." Her hands clenched into fists at her sides as the children gazed up at her. "And God's justice will be swift."

Bouchard paid her no heed and lifted his hand toward the sky. "It is all coming to pass, exactly as I have foretold."

Chants exploded across the room. "Ecce lux prophetæ ducet nos. Ecce lux prophetæ ducet nos."

Not a single Ascendant showed signs of wavering. Bouchard held his hand out toward Elionor and the children. "See, all except you know the truth."

In the bright sky high above the château, the sun and moon seemed locked in a dance as they neared their convergence.

"Behold the heralds of the kingdom." Bouchard's declaration rose above the chants of the Ascendants.

Elionor gathered the children together. "Even if it gets dark, the Lord is still with us."

The words were as much for herself as for them.

33

I have a firm conviction that I am immortal till my work is done.

—Lottie Moon, 1895

THE BOAT'S ANCHOR splashed into the shimmering waters of Lac Léman, dragging the creaking boat to a halt. The scent of minerals and fish mingled with the crisp air. Waves splashed against the side of the boat, rocking Andreas to and fro. The sun shed brilliant rays across the lake.

Pierre's plate armor clanked as he removed his oar from the oarlock, laid it across the thwarts, and stepped over the ropes coiled in the hull. He reached down and gripped Andreas's shoulders. "I'll make this more painful if you resist."

"We're innocent, and you know it." Andreas refused to budge from his seat in the hull. "Or are you too ignorant to discern that for yourself? You simply obey whatever Bouchard tells you, like a little puppy."

"You won't sway us, oppressor." Jacques forced Andreas up to sit on a thwart.

Pierre grabbed a long pole from the side of the vessel. "Look above, look around you. The Prophet has already chosen your fate." He gripped the pole with both hands and rammed it into Andreas's stomach.

Andreas heaved and gasped for breath but stayed atop the thwart, shielding Constanza below. He would die before a man ever rammed a pole into her like that.

"Your end is nigh, Lord Andreas, Prince of Savoy." Pierre pulled up Andreas by one arm and pushed his foot into the back of Andreas's knees, forcing them to buckle.

Andreas twisted and jerked. The pole struck him across the back. He reared back and shouted as Pierre jammed the pole behind his knees and forced his arms behind it.

Just out of arm's reach, Constanza stretched out a hand, weeping. But Andreas could do nothing constrained like this.

Pierre wrapped ropes around Andreas's elbows, his legs, and the pole, then unfastened the iron shackles and tossed them aside. With a little more room for movement, Andreas strained against the new, oily bonds but couldn't free himself.

All his hopes would be drowned in these deep waters. His life with Constanza would end less than a year after it had begun, and he would never see the child who grew within her. In a matter of minutes, he would stand before the gates of heaven, ready to meet his Creator.

He drew in a long breath and set his jaw. He had to remain strong for Constanza, had to show these Ascendants that he did not fear death.

"I am here with you until the end," Andreas said.

Tears streamed down Constanza's cheeks. She mouthed, "I know."

"But you're going first, my lord." Pierre chuckled as he grabbed the pole and heaved Andreas up to a kneeling position on the thwart.

Far in the distance, snow brightened the tops of the gray Alps. Somewhere beyond those mountains was a place that seemed more distant than ever—home. Forests rolled gently down toward the lake, their patchwork of hues interrupted by pastures and green pines. Andreas prayed that Elias, Antoine, Marie, Madeleine, and the rest of the Poor would find refuge somewhere in those deep forests. Someday, perhaps they would find a man to teach them the Holy Scriptures.

On the cliffs along the shore stood Château de Thonon and its desecrated great hall. Lucien Bouchard and his machinations had humiliated Pâre, Mâre, Philip, and even Andreas. And somewhere in that mighty citadel, the children and Elionor faced the Prophet alone.

Pierre nodded toward the shoreline. "Look over there."

Ascendant onlookers—as many as fifty or sixty—stood on the docks and the stony beach, shielding their eyes from the sun.

"They're here to watch your demise." Pierre clamped his hands on Andreas's shoulders and turned him toward the crowd. "Listen to those cheers. We're entertaining them, giving the audience what they desire." He shoved Andreas toward the gunwale.

The skiff rocked from side to side, and Jacques shifted to the other side to maintain his balance.

Andreas pressed backward against Pierre's pushes. Pierre moved in front of Andreas, grabbed the pole, and yanked him toward the edge of the boat.

Andreas grunted, hooking one foot around the bottom of the thwart.

"Throw him overboard." Jacques picked up another pole and tapped Constanza's shoulder with it. "We still have her, and we have an offering to witness when the sun is blotted out."

Pierre twisted the ropes and jerked Andreas off balance. The edge of the thwart scraped against Andreas's shins as Pierre forced him forward. Andreas tried to dig his heels into the narrow space between the thwart and the hull, his bound arms straining against the pole. Pierre leaned over him, sweat dripping from his brow, his hands gripping the pole tightly as he heaved again. The gunwale pressed against Andreas's ribs.

Along the shore, the murmurs of the crowd swelled into the now-familiar, devilish chant.

"Please, mercy!" Constanza's shout rose over the chants. "Have mercy on us!"

Jacques hauled her upright, unlatched her shackles, and forced her knees to buckle. "At least you'll die with your husband, dama."

Andreas clenched his fists. If he could save Constanza, his own death would be vindicated.

He gazed down at the surface of the lake, then at Pierre's Savoyard armor. If Pierre fell overboard, it would be impossible for him to swim.

Andreas tilted his body sideways, wheeling to topple back into the boat. Pierre held the pole tight. The ropes bit into Andreas's flesh as he pressed against the weight of Pierre's foot.

With a fierce twist of his body, Andreas ripped one side of the pole free. Its end slammed into Pierre.

"Push him over, Pierre!" Jacques shouted over Pierre's grunt.

Pierre grabbed both ends of the pole and heaved Andreas back to the edge. "Try that again, and I'll make your wife suffer."

Andreas tensed the muscles in his arms, back, and legs. As much as he could, he shifted his weight to his feet. Leaning forward, he tested Pierre's hold on the pole. Tight.

Dear God, if it wasn't before, my life is Yours alone.

With a swift lunge forward, he propelled himself and Pierre into the watery abyss below.

*   *   *

Constanza landed on the bottom of the boat as Jacques pushed her aside and rushed to the boat's edge. Ripples radiated from the point where Andreas and Pierre had sunk.

"Pierre! I'm coming!" Jacques bent and hastily loosened the armor around his legs.

If heavy armor had sunk Pierre, it would sink Jacques too. Constanza scanned the boat for something, anything that might help her.

A wooden oar caught her eye two arm's lengths away. As Jacques focused on the water and removed his armor, Constanza crawled to the oar, grabbed it, and stood. The boat rocked, almost sending her back onto the deck.

She fixed her gaze on Jacques and gripped the oar tightly, her knuckles whitening. With a swift, fluid motion, she raised the oar to her side. Her heart pounded. *Just like casting a shepherd's crook at a stubborn goat.*

With a resounding cry, she swung the oar with all her might.

The blow thudded against Jacques's side. He gave a shout and faltered at the edge of the boat.

Constanza swung again, this time at the back of his head. The oar connected with a smack. Jacques's arms flailed and he plunged into the water.

Constanza shuffled toward the edge as the splash subsided and the murky depths consumed him. She searched the waters frantically, her breath coming in gasps. Where was Andreas? This lake was nothing like the shallow creeks near home. If she dived in, she would die. She clenched her fists and dug her nails into her palms, as if the pain could ground her.

Tears welled in her eyes and blurred her vision as she searched for any sign of Andreas—a ripple, a bubble . . . a body. *Dear God, let Andreas live. I can't bear to live without him.*

*   *   *

Andreas strained and jerked against the pole, but he continued to plummet into the cold unknown. *I can't die like this.* He forced his eyes open but found only a blur. The water pressed against him from all sides. The deeper he sank, the more his eardrums hammered.

His lungs burned as if set on fire. He swallowed, but that only further tightened his chest. If he could find one breath of air . . .

He fumbled desperately for any weakness in his bonds, any opportunity to escape. But the ropes were too thick and too tight.

He strained and pulled against the pole and the rope. Every sinew screamed in protest as he fought the embrace of the depths. *I need to live—for Constanza, for my sons, for my daughters, for everyone who needs me.*

He twisted and slammed the end of the pole into the rocky lake bed. Again. The rope beneath his fingers started to fray.

The pole shifted behind his knees. The ropes slackened. He flung his legs outward and pushed the pole into the bottom again. With a final wrenching twist, he tore free from the ropes and pole. He launched himself from the lake bed and broke free from his watery prison with a gasp of sweet, life-giving air.

Andreas moved his arms in slow circles and worked his legs beneath him, pulling in every breath with gratitude. A rush of triumph flowed over him. He opened his eyes, but nothing except the lake and the distant shore lay before him. No, that was the Vaudois shore. He spun the other way and braced himself to fight Pierre and Jacques despite his exhaustion.

A lone figure stood in the boat.

Constanza.

"Andreas!" She reached toward him. "Oh, Andreas."

He swam toward the boat, every movement fueled by the fierce desire to reach her. As he drew closer, she reached out a trembling hand. Her fingers entwined with his as he pulled himself from the water's grasp.

He crawled over the side and collapsed on a thwart, his breaths uneven. "Constanza," he whispered as waves lapped against the boat. "I don't know how—"

"Pierre and Jacques are gone. They won't trouble us again."

Andreas opened his mouth slightly. Pierre had fallen in with him and must have sunk immediately. "But how is Jacques gone too?"

"I showed him the strength that runs in Pavarin blood." Constanza sat beside Andreas, the rugged determination of her alpine upbringing evident in her firm gaze.

After a long sigh, Andreas sat upright, wrapped his arms around Constanza, and held her close. Their hearts seemed to beat in time with the rocking of the boat. "I thought I was going to die."

"I knew you wouldn't. Remember, you've already whispered your promises of forever."

A breeze swept across Andreas's soaked clothes and sent a shiver from his skin to his spine. Ascendants thronged at the edge of the water, while Château de Thonon towered on the cliff above. Surrounded by drifting gray clouds, the sun and the blurry shape of the moon drew closer together.

Lucien Bouchard would begin his offering soon. Andreas and Constanza had no time to linger here, floating on the lake, while the Prophet proceeded to murder their children.

Andreas reached into the hull and found the long shaft of the sculling oar. With a grunt, he hefted it out, the wood worn smooth from use. "I'm rowing back to shore."

"Those Ascendants will capture us as soon as we reach the dock, Andreas. Isn't there something else we can do?"

"Find a shore without a hundred cultists standing on it?" He angled the oar's blade toward the water, fitted the shaft into the open notch of the stern's oarlock, and pushed the oar downward to seat it. "Bouchard could begin the killing at any moment."

"We have no weapons, no armor, nothing." Constanza's lips quivered and her shoulders sank.

"I'm going alone." Andreas sat on the sternmost thwart and dipped the oar into the lake, then swept it back and forth. "Watch as I row and steer. When I'm close enough to swim, I'll slip overboard. Row as fast as you can to the Vaudois shore. It will take you the rest of the day, but you'll be safe there. Find your way back to Piedmont—"

"And raise our child alone, a helpless widow who turned her back on her husband, her children, and her closest friend?" Constanza sniffled and wiped her nose. "No, I'm going with you, and I'll face whatever you face."

Andreas shifted the oar and steered toward the nearest dock. "There's nothing you can do."

"And what can you do? They'll kill you the moment we land." Constanza sat beside Andreas, placed her hands on the shaft beside his, and began rowing with him. "You are my husband, and they are my children too. God alone can save our family and Savoy from the Prophet."

Andreas shook inside as he rowed, his muscles begging for respite. The standard of the House of Savoy still fluttered atop the château. Apparently the Divine Ascendancy hadn't bothered to replace it yet.

The faces of the men and women on the docks grew more distinct the closer Andreas rowed. Hatred, devotion, ferocity—the Ascendants would tear his skin from his limbs the moment he climbed onto the dock. But he would never retreat.

"The whole world lies in darkness." Andreas gritted his teeth in defiance against the forces arrayed against them. Soon the boat would touch the dock, and the battle would begin. He gave Constanza one last smile. "It's you and I against the world."

"We are not alone." Constanza gazed at the shore over his shoulder, beaming.

"I know, God is always with us." Andreas closed his eyes and drew in a deep breath.

"No, Andreas, look. Truly, we're not alone."

He flung his eyes open. No more than three boat lengths away, the Ascendants on the dock hurried to the shore. A shocked murmur rippled through them, growing louder as they peered up the slope.

Elias Renaud stood atop the cliff, his sword gleaming like a flaming torch under the failing sun. Behind him were at least a hundred men, axes in hand.

"The woodcutters," Andreas mumbled to himself and rowed the boat against the side of the dock. He threw a loop of rope around the post and leaped from the boat, then lifted Constanza to the dock and gave her a brief but passionate kiss. "Remain here until it's safe. It appears we have some help."

"Our friends." Constanza smiled wide with recognition.

Bouchard's words from yesterday echoed in Andreas's mind: *We trust in ourselves and take advantage of those willing to stand by us.* But that wasn't the way.

Some of the Ascendants scattered toward the flat beach to the left and the forests beyond, while others started up the slope to resist Elias. The axmen swept down the slope to meet the challenge, their charge accompanied by a roar. The Ascendants faltered, unable to match the strength of men accustomed to felling trees. One by one, Elias and his men dispersed the Ascendants until none remained.

With one sword in his hand and another dangling from his side, Elias ran toward the shore, another man on his heels.

Andreas met them at the trail leading up the slope. "My son Ezio—"

"He's safe with my sister," Elias said.

Andreas grasped Elias's arm. "You mustered the cavalry just in time, mon frâre."

"The Poor of Thonon don't stand by while our friends are in danger." Elias unfastened the scabbard from his belt and handed it to Andreas. "For you."

Andreas pulled the sword partly out of the scabbard and felt the newly sharpened blade. It was the sword that had been displayed at Ripaille, the one his ancestor had wielded.

Elias motioned to the man beside him. "Jean Dupont, Madeleine's husband and the strongest man in this corner of Savoy."

"Your family honors you well," Andreas said.

"Where is Elionor?" Elias asked, his countenance grave.

"In the château with my children. Lucien Bouchard and his followers intend to murder them at the eclipse."

Elias peered upward, shielding his eyes from the dim sunlight. "There's not enough time. The citadel gates are locked, and Ascendants hold the gate with pikes and crossbowmen."

"We'll break the gate before sunset," Jean said. "Our men are already cutting trees to use as battering rams." Without waiting for a reply, he turned on his heel and hurried off.

"We need to find another way in." Elias scanned the walls.

A spark ignited within Andreas. "The lakeside gate."

"The Ascendants must have discovered it by now."

"It's our best chance." Sword in his right hand, Andreas turned back to the shore. Elias followed close behind.

They raced up the winding path, their footsteps crunching the dead foliage and clapping on the ancient stones. Vines draped the gate like a shroud, partially obscuring its rusty surface. Andreas slammed his shoulder into the gate, and it creaked open.

"Well done." Elias advanced into the courtyard and peered up at the destroyed roof of the château. "What happened?"

"It's the chamber for Bouchard's altar. That's where we'll find Elionor and my children."

A loud crash echoed through the courtyard, then another.

"It's Jean and the other woodcutters," Elias said.

"But that gate won't budge easily." Andreas motioned him forward. Together they swiftly crept through the grass, avoiding the open areas and trying to stay clear of the sentries along the wall.

A shout resonated off the citadel stones. "Intruders in the courtyard!"

Andreas ducked into a doorway and tried the door. Locked. He slammed his sword hilt into the latch once, twice. On the third time the lock gave way.

The air inside the door hung heavy with the scent of age and decay as Andreas led Elias through the familiar passages. A glimmer of light caught Andreas's eye and beckoned him through the darkness. He followed the glow to a narrow staircase, its steps worn smooth by centuries of footsteps.

With each step, the air grew colder, sending shivers up Andreas's arms. At the top of the staircase, he and Elias entered an empty, dimly lit chamber.

Andreas motioned toward the set of ornate double doors at the far end of the room, their ancient wood warped and weathered by time. Veins protruded from his forearms as he held his sword. "Ready?"

Elias nodded once. "No retreat."

34

And the light shineth in darkness; and the darkness comprehended it not.

—The Holy Bible
John 1:5

ANDREAS AND ELIAS each grabbed a door handle and pulled. The hinges creaked, and a burst of fresh air flowed through the gap. Before them stood the mass of Ascendants, probably two hundred in all. Their movements and chants were synchronized with morbid anticipation.

The sky hung dark and ominous through the gaping hole in the roof. The crescent of the sun hovered in the heavens, almost completely covered by the black circle of the moon.

At the edge of the stone altar stood Lucien Bouchard, holding a knife as he and the crowd stared at the celestial event above them. On the altar lay seven girls, four boys, and Elionor, most weeping and all bound in ropes.

Little Alessia caught Andreas's eye. "Papà!"

The other children cried out for him.

Andreas's pulse quickened. The closest Ascendants looked away from the heavens and dropped their jaws. "Oppressors!"

A loud crash resounded from the other end of the hall. Bouchard slowly drew his gaze across the room and stared at Andreas. In the unnatural light of the eclipse, the Prophet's eyes shimmered with pride and expectancy.

The light suddenly vanished. All that remained of the sun was a simmering flare at its fringes. A hush fell over the dim room.

Bouchard raised the knife high above his head.

Andreas launched himself toward the altar. Elias matched his pace as their footsteps echoed through the chamber. The Ascendants formed a wall of resistance, their faces twisted with fanatical devotion. But they would not deter Andreas.

His muscles strained against the tide of bodies as he pushed through the throng. Elias fought beside him, his sword flashing in the faint light, cutting through the air with lethal precision.

Bouchard's figure loomed. Elionor and the children, bound and helpless, trembled as the blade hovered above them. The tip was aimed at Silvia's throat. *No, God, please no!*

With a primal roar, Andreas bounded up to the platform, his free hand outstretched toward Bouchard's dagger. Time crawled. The dagger started its descent, an arc of death poised to shatter his family.

Andreas closed his hand around Bouchard's, defying the darkness. A sliver of sun emerged from behind the moon.

The chamber erupted into chaos. Andreas fixed his attention on Bouchard. "Your kingdom ends here."

"The desperate words of a helpless man." Bouchard pulled away from Andreas's grasp. Scores of Ascendants clamored around the altar.

Another thud boomed through the hall, followed by a loud crash. The main door splintered and fell, debris scattering across the floor. Axmen poured through the opening.

Bouchard took a step back, and the color left his cheeks. "This is our hour!" he cried. "Fight for the kingdom!"

Three Ascendants, swords drawn, rushed toward Andreas. He gripped his own sword, muscles tensing with determination.

Before he could act, Elias blocked the Ascendants' path. "I'll fight them. You protect the innocents."

Andreas hesitated. The old urge to face every threat alone, to shoulder the burden himself, boiled within him. But he had tried to fight alone, and it had nearly broken him.

"Merci," he said, and turned back to the altar.

Bouchard eyed Elionor and the children. Andreas skirted the altar toward the Prophet, his sword reflecting the growing sunlight.

Bouchard's knife whizzed through the air like a hornet, cutting and stabbing with practiced accuracy. Andreas clenched his jaw as he dodged slice after slice. A flash of searing pain traced his ear and cheek, but he could not falter.

Behind him, the sounds of battle gave way to a discord of chaos and despair. Bouchard shifted his stance ever so slightly—a momentary lapse in his guard, a fraction of hesitation before a counterattack.

As Bouchard adjusted his grip on the knife, Andreas shifted his weight and positioned himself to seize the opportunity.

Bouchard struck. Andreas parried the blow and sliced through the gap. The edge of his blade cut through Bouchard's neck with ease.

The Prophet stood for a dazed moment, then collapsed to the stone floor in a pool of red.

The chaos of combat faded, the clash of steel replaced by utter stillness. The full light of day cleansed the chamber with golden radiance. Andreas turned from Bouchard's body and allowed his gaze to linger on the children. Tears still streaked their cheeks, yet their eyes no longer darted in panic. Mouths that had trembled with mumbled prayers or stifled cries now softened, the first flickers of relief breaking through. These were the lives Bouchard had tried to destroy but failed.

Andreas moved among the children, severing their bonds with a steady hand, his sword now a symbol of liberation rather than violence. Irene, eyes brimming with tears, reached out to touch him. "We knew you'd come, Papà."

"Where's Mamà?" Alessia asked.

"Safe." Andreas breathed a sigh of relief and gratitude. "Thanks be to God, she is safe."

Umile couldn't tear his gaze away from Andreas's sword. "You're our hero, Papà."

Andreas came to Elionor last, but as he reached to cut the ropes around her wrists, a firm hand touched his arm.

"I can handle this one." Elias stepped around Andreas, his hair tousled and his forehead glistening with sweat. He wiped the blade of his sword on his breeches, then gently grasped Elionor's hands and sliced through her bonds.

The glance he exchanged with her carried the hope of a bright future. There was a tenderness in Elias's face—devotion with a hint of vulnerability—and Elionor's warm gaze mirrored it.

As Elias helped Elionor off the altar, the children regarded them in wonder. Irene, Fosca, Ave, Silvia, Guido, Roberto, Bino, Umile, Alessia, Zama, and Prospera stood together, their expressions reflecting the tumultuous journey they had endured. Some smiled through tears, while others stood in quiet contemplation.

Andreas laid his bloodstained sword on the altar. All the remaining Ascendants stood along the wall, their weapons strewn across the floor before them, their defiance replaced with humiliation and utter defeat. The woodcutters formed a line in front of them, axes still in hand.

Jean Dupont approached Andreas. His chest heaved, and his sleeves were torn, revealing sinewy muscles rippling beneath weathered skin. He wiped the sweat from his brow with the back of his hand and grabbed Andreas's shoulder. "Monsieur Bouchard's fiefdom lasted about as long as that midday darkness." He nodded toward Elias. "And thanks to my wife's brother here, it seems we arrived just in time."

"What did you do?" Andreas asked Elias.

"Yesterday I slipped through the perimeter around L'Ermitage. I found the woodcutters late in the evening, and we traveled through the night until we reached L'Ermitage. After we scattered the Ascendants there, we headed straight to Thonon."

"And that's when you appeared on the cliffs." Andreas bowed his head in thanksgiving, then raised it as a question struck him. "How many men died?"

"Ascendants?" Jean bowed his head and his voice softened. "They fell on our axes as if they had no will to live."

"No, how many good men?"

Elias sighed. "A few."

All for me and my family. Andreas's throat tightened.

"You did nothing wrong," Elias said. "This was all Bouchard's fault. Every sorrow, every tear today was his doing."

"My family was in danger too." Jean shifted his weight to the other foot and scanned the great hall. "We fought for justice and against tyranny."

Elias peered at the shattered throne on the opposite side of the room. "Is Duke Louis still alive?"

Andreas nodded. "As far as I know, he, my mâre, and my siblings are locked in their chambers upstairs."

"Do we have to let them out?" Jean asked, half smiling.

Elias gave Andreas a pointed look. "There's no one stopping you from becoming duke now."

"No, that's not what God wants for my life. I'll go upstairs and free them." He smiled at Elias and Jean. "Enjoy your few moments without a duke while they last."

Elias chuckled. "I suppose old Louis is much better than Lucien Bouchard."

Andreas addressed Elionor next. "Will you find Constanza and bring the children to her? She should be near the lakeshore. Please tell her I'll be there soon."

As Elias, Elionor, and Jean escorted the children outside, Andreas climbed the stairs to the living chambers. He freed Philip first, then moved to his younger brothers, Pâre, and finally Mâre and his sisters.

Andreas knelt at Mâre's bedside, and the rest of his family gathered around him. Mâre's breaths were shallow and her cheeks pale. Agnes, ever the nurturing soul, attempted to rouse her, but Mâre remained still.

Hand trembling slightly, Andreas reached out and clasped her frail fingers in his own. They felt so much different than they had years ago. He leaned down and pressed a soft kiss to her hand. "I love you, Mâre," he whispered.

He breathed the same air she did, each shallow breath mirroring hers, his mâre—the woman who had given birth to him and raised him as a prince of Savoy—now so frail and vulnerable.

If only he could rewrite their history, mend the fractures between them. But the past was immutable. All he could offer now was his love and forgiveness, praying that somehow she would find solace and peace in Jesus Christ.

A hand touched Andreas's shoulder. Startled, he turned to see Pâre standing beside him.

"Andreas," he said, "your mâre needs rest."

Andreas released Mâre's hand and rose to his feet, meeting Pâre's gaze with a sense of resignation. "Savoy is yours again."

Philip approached Pâre, his head bowed. "I want to apologize—"

"Don't speak to me. You have forfeited your appanages and inheritance, and you will forever be known as Philip the Landless. Go to France and see if they will take you in."

"But . . ."

Pâre turned his face away from Philip and gave him a dismissive wave. "Leave now while I still feel merciful."

Philip stomped away and hurried down the stairs.

"And as for you." Pâre let out a long sigh as he stared at Andreas. "I am grateful for your loyalty."

"All would have fallen into ruin if it weren't for some of your loyal subjects. You might know them as the Poor—"

"Heretics nonetheless, and soon they will be no more. Lucien Bouchard expelled all the priests in Thonon, and by now, the Diocese of Genève has heard what has happened. They will bring their inquisitors here, and all who oppose the Holy Roman Catholic Church will be tried and sentenced."

"But the Poor opposed Bouchard. They had nothing to do with the rebellion, and without them, you wouldn't have a duchy."

"Ecclesiastical intrigues, inquisitions, crusades—I have no say over what the Church does, especially not after I allowed a mad sect to fester around me. If you want to save your friends, tell them to leave—and soon."

Andreas tightened his lips, thinking. "What if they return to Piedmont with me?"

"I cannot permit them anywhere in my realm. Forget about them. Take your wife and your children and enjoy your peasant life. If you manage to conceal your heresy, you will find peace. But do not waste your life by casting your lot with the Poor."

After a few parting words and embraces, Andreas left the chamber, walked out of the citadel, and passed under the gate into the streets of Thonon. Pâre's words echoed in his mind. Forget about his frâres and find peace—how could something seem both so right and so wrong? Was comfort, even peace, the aim of life?

As he walked toward the lakefront, the cool breeze brushed against his skin, carrying the promise of new beginnings. Constanza stood beside the tranquil waters, her beauty radiant and her grace as captivating as ever. The children buzzed around her, full of joy and life.

With a swift stride, Andreas closed the distance. His heart swelled as he gathered Constanza and the children into his embrace.

"Never forget how God preserved us," Andreas said. "Tell it to your children and your grandchildren, tell it to your friends and the merchants in the street—may the faithful's praise forever sound."

"Âmin, alélouyâ!" Constanza added, finishing the Poor's song from two nights ago.

The moments dissolved as Andreas listened to his family share tales of courage, sorrow, and hope. Many of the Poor gathered along the shore with them, including Jean and Madeleine Dupont and the Renauds.

Elias stood with Elionor, moving the sand around with his boot. He suddenly lowered himself to both knees, his gaze on Elionor unwavering. "T'aimi, Elionor Janavel, and I will forever. I will love you unconditionally. I will care for your needs with unending loyalty. I will be this child's pâre." His tension seemed to unwind in her presence. "And I will never forsake you."

Elionor gasped and held a hand to her mouth. She didn't speak.

"Marry me, Elionor."

"You know what I've done, Elias. If we had known each other a year ago—"

"We know each other now, and that's what matters." Elias took both of her hands. "Will you be my wife, Elionor?"

"I don't deserve this." A single tear traced a path down Elionor's cheek.

"Say yes, madomaisèla!" Prospera's wide grin added a touch of innocence to the moment.

Andreas lifted Prospera into his arms and held a finger to her lips.

Elionor nodded, her smile tinged with wonder and gratitude. "Yes, Elias Renaud," she whispered, "I will be your wife, and I will devote myself to you alone . . . forever."

Elias caught Andreas's arm. "Will you marry Elionor and me?"

Andreas laughed as he held Prospera. "What's wrong with a Catholic priest?"

"The Ascendants drove them all from Thonon. Besides, I want to separate from Rome entirely. I didn't know the reasons before, but after hearing what you've preached from the Holy Scriptures—"

"I've never married anyone. I'm barely an ordained barbe."

"You're the closest we have." Elias folded his arms. "Marry us, Andreas. It's a simple matter—we require witnesses and your assurance of our consent, and then the blessing of marriage is ours."

"Here? Now?"

Elias laughed heartily. "No, I think we can find a more pleasant setting. Perhaps in a few days."

Elionor's eyes sparkled as she turned toward Elias, a playful smile sneaking onto her lips. "Do we need to wait so long?"

"Not a moment longer than required." Elias's laughter softened into a warm chuckle as his eyes met Elionor's.

Andreas nodded as he shifted his focus between the pair. "A few days it is, then."

"Elionor will be the next Renaud!" Elias announced to the those nearby.

Amid the shouts of congratulations, Constanza embraced Elionor first, then stepped back as Madeleine and Marie followed.

While the women spoke with Elionor, Andreas set Prospera down and motioned for Elias to follow him. He approached the other men and spoke in hushed tones, warning them of their fate if they remained in Thonon.

"For years, we've known this day would come." Antoine sighed and nodded. "I suppose we'll need to find a place more welcoming."

"When are you setting out for Piedmont?" Elias asked Andreas.

Andreas looked out over the waters of Lac Léman. Without a doubt, the relative safety and familiarity of Val Angrogna beckoned. There the Vallenses had flourished for generations, centuries. Yet there were also new places and a people who yearned for God's Word.

He hesitated, his gaze drifting between the lake, the children, and Constanza. Something sparkled in her, as if she could sense his thoughts and held the same feelings he did.

"My frâres and I are all in agreement," Antoine said. "We want you to be our teacher, and whatever we hear from the Scriptures, we will follow and obey. The choice is yours, but know that you, Constanza, and your children would be welcome among us."

That evening in the tiny Renaud home, after all the children had fallen asleep, Andreas and Constanza sat alone at the crackling hearth.

"This path—it's not without its challenges," Andreas said. "Are you prepared to leave everything you've known and journey to a new land with people you've known only for a few days?"

"I've already done that, Andreas. God led us to Thonon, to true believers who need His Word and someone to preach it."

Andreas leaned back in his chair and chuckled. "This reminds me of when we chose to adopt the children, except now there's no one to seek counsel from. Antoine is a wise man, and so are several of the other men I've met. But we would have to leave everything—our way of life, our home, our church—and venture out into the unknown." He stared into the roaring fire and sighed. "Are you certain?"

"Yes." Constanza gave one firm nod. "I only wish we could tell everyone back home, so they won't fear for us."

Andreas held Constanza's hand and kissed it. "We'll send word to them as soon as we can."

35

But where you hear of a poor, simple, cast-off little flock, which is despised and rejected by the world, join them.

—Anna of Rotterdam
Her last testament presented to her son, 1539

THE LIGHT OF TWOSCORE FLICKERING TORCHES marched down the slope toward Andreas and his family. The dawn's glow painted the distant mountains in hues of pink and gold. To the west, over the deep blue waters of Lac Léman, lay a new life.

At the head of the line of torches walked Elias Renaud, accompanied by his new bride, Elionor. Antoine and Marie Renaud followed them closely, trailed by Jean and Madeleine Dupont, their five children in tow.

A knot formed in the pit of Andreas's stomach, twisting tighter with every man, woman, and child who gathered around him. These believers had chosen a path fraught with uncertainty, yet their steadfastness and eagerness showed their faith in Christ and commitment to the truth of the Holy Scriptures.

Elias's nod signaled that all was prepared.

Andreas turned to Constanza. "Are you ready?"

She looked down the line of children, then met his gaze with a reassuring smile. "We are."

Over the past five days, the Poor of Thonon had packed their belongings into the boats the duke had lent them. They would set out for the shores of Vaud and from there into Swiss lands. Rumor said the bishops there were less zealous, and perhaps the Poor would find a place to serve and worship God freely.

Andreas reached into his pocket and removed the Bible that Raimond had given him two years ago. The brown leather might be tattered and the ink smudged in places, but the words inside had never been newer. He flipped to the Apostle Paul's second epistle to the Corinthians and read.

" 'Therefore if any man be in Christ, he is a new creature: old things are passed away; behold, all things are become new. And all things are of God, who hath reconciled us to himself by Jesus Christ, and hath given to us the ministry of reconciliation; to wit, that God was in Christ, reconciling the world unto himself, not imputing their trespasses unto them; and hath committed unto us the word of reconciliation. Now then we are ambassadors for Christ, as though God did beseech you by us: we pray you in Christ's stead, be ye reconciled to God.'"

As he finished, a hush fell over the congregation. Then, like a breeze stirring in the leaves, a few of the Poor began to sing, their words filled with emotion. The sound strengthened and rose above the lapping waves and the rustling trees. One by one, more joined in the song, their voices blending in harmony and flowing across the lake waters.

> And since it is God's holy will,
> We must be parted for a while,
> In sweet submission, all as one,
> We'll say, our Father's will be done.
> My youthful friends, in Christian ties,
> Who seek for mansions in the skies,
> Fight on, we'll gain that happy shore,
> Where parting will be known no more.

The final notes faded into the wind, and a calm settled over the shore. Andreas led his family to one of the waiting boats, Constanza's hand clasped in his. Elias and Elionor joined them at the water's edge, and together, they guided the children into the boats.

With a final glance back at the shoreline, Andreas took a deep breath and stepped onto the deck. The sails of the twelve boats unfurled and fluttered in the morning breeze. Andreas cast off from the dock, and with each gust of wind in the sails, the boats glided farther from the familiar shores and deeper into the unknown.

Andreas wrapped his arm around Constanza, surveying his family and new-found friends. To some, they might be the Poor. To others, Vallenses. But in truth they were neither. They were believers united in the unbreakable love of their Savior, Jesus Christ.

Epilogue

Twelve years later, May 1472

"**D**O YOU SEE THE BOULDER HERE? This is where I first met your mamà." Andreas smiled at his children, then wrapped an arm around Constanza's shoulders and drew her close. "Though I would say she was less than friendly then."

"A strange man with a shaved head appeared in my goat pasture. Wouldn't you want our daughters to do the same as I did?"

Andreas glanced at sixteen-year-old Alessia and seventeen-year-old Zama and Prospera. "I'm certain I would never want them to entertain the company of a Catholic monk. So yes, flashing a knife was perhaps the right choice, Connie."

Prospera held a hand over her mouth and laughed. "I still can't believe you used to be a papist, Papà—and with a shaved head too."

"He was still handsome, though." Constanza stood on the tips of her toes and kissed Andreas's cheek. "You look so much better now with a beard and a full head of hair . . . but I do see a few specks of gray in your beard these days."

As the morning sun covered Val Angrogna in a golden hue, Andreas led his family along the narrow path that wound its way down through the terraced pastures and orchards. For this visit to Piedmont, Silvia, Ezio, Guido, and Umile had chosen to remain in Zurich. Both Silvia and Ezio had children of their own now, and their families were pillars of the church there.

Constanza walked beside Andreas, her expression alight with reminiscence. "These terraces were my papà's pride, and they brought him much joy and fulfillment. He spent years carving them from this slope and transforming them into the beauty you see now. When I was a girl, I heard men say this was his greatest accomplishment."

Andreas shook his head. "No, Nicolaus Pavarin's greatest accomplishment walks alongside me now." After twelve years and five children, Constanza had never been more beautiful.

The firstborn of their own, eleven-year-old Nicolaus, picked a ripe apple from a tree that hung over a nearby pond. "I wish I could have met him."

"There are many I wish you could have met," Andreas said. "Your papeta; my old friend Johan Lauras; Victor, the courageous man who helped us find the Greek manuscript; and Raimond, the barbe who showed me the way to Christ."

"He's the one I'm named after!" said seven-year-old Raimond de Bonomo.

"Indeed." Andreas swung the youngest of the children, three-year-old Johan de Bonomo, into his arms. "And you're named after my good friend." He sighed and peered out toward the green slopes of Mount Vandalino. Though the scars of those men's loss lingered, each of their lives had molded Andreas, and their testimony encouraged him onward in his service for Christ.

Eighteen-year-old Ave knelt, picked a small pink flower, and smelled it. "Fosca, do you remember when we gathered a bouquet of these to bring to Mamà?"

"But they never made it to her, thanks to Bino." Fosca nudged Bino playfully on the shoulder.

He flashed a teasing smile. "The goats were hungry."

Ave gathered a few more flowers and handed them to Constanza. "What are these called, Mamà?"

"*Flor dau barbe*—flower of the barbe." Constanza removed a stem from the bouquet and tenderly tucked it into the front lacing of Andreas's doublet, her fingers lingering a moment as she smiled. "Quite fitting for our barbe."

Prospera rested her hands on her hips and faced the farmhouse far down the slope. "I still remember the morning we first came here. We were all exhausted and filthy after traveling all night from Turin."

Zama nodded along. "Mamà's brothers and sisters brought us all blankets and clean chemises."

Bino held a finger up. "Fresh goat's milk and bread too!"

Ave took a deep breath and let it out slowly. "I still can't believe we lived in this valley for only a year."

"I always heard everyone talk about this place," Nicolaus said, his eyes full of wonder, "but it's even more amazing than I thought."

Constanza took a long breath and smiled. "My papà always believed in both strength and wisdom, and he had both. But he never thought of this land as his own. He was only a steward of God's blessings." Her gaze drifted down the slope toward the house. "He taught me everything, but most importantly, he taught me and your *tantas* and *oncles* the Holy Scriptures. Far more than being strong or smart, Papà was wise and godly."

As they continued their walk, Andreas recalled his talks with Nicolaus Pavarin while Constanza told stories about her childhood as a Vallense girl. The terraces cascaded down the hillside in a patchwork of vibrant colors, each one well tended and overflowing with life. Thousands of flowers bloomed, and the lush greenery of the fields stretched to distant heights. This was where Andreas had been drawn to the Savior, where he had learned to love the lost, and where he had surrendered to God's will.

So much had changed since those fateful autumn days twelve years ago when God drew them away from this beautiful land and placed them in a new one. What should have ended in disaster, God had transformed into a glorious victory.

Power-obsessed Lucien Bouchard and his fanatics were but a wrinkle in Andreas's memory, and what God had wrought in those tumultuous weeks stood as a landmark to His providence.

The family descended from the terraces and made their way toward the Pavarin home nestled at the bottom of the hill. The air was filled with a quiet reverence as they approached the two gravestones that marked the resting places of Constanza's papà and mamà.

The Bonomo family gathered around the graves, their heads bowed in silence. Constanza's mamà, Armanda, had died a year ago but had left behind a legacy of love and strength in her children and grandchildren.

Andreas eased into a more comfortable stance and crossed his arms loosely as he addressed the children. "What do we believers receive from Christ at our death?"

All answered in unison. "We are made perfect in holiness and immediately pass into glory. Our bodies, still in Christ, rest in their graves until the resurrection."

"And what do we receive from Christ at the resurrection?"

"The Savior will openly acknowledge and acquit us in the day of judgment, and we will be made perfectly blessed both in soul and body in the full enjoying of God to all eternity."

"And where in the Holy Scriptures does it show us that?"

"In Matthew's gospel," Raimond said. " 'Whosoever therefore shall confess me before men, him will I confess also before my Father which is in heaven.' "

"And in the epistle to the Thessalonian church," Anne said, always ready to outdo her younger brother. " 'Then we which are alive and remain shall be caught up together with them in the clouds, to meet the Lord in the air: and so shall we ever be with the Lord.' "

Andreas placed his arm around Constanza and led the family in a brief prayer, thanking God for the blessings of their heritage. When he finished, he rubbed Constanza's shoulder. "It's time."

Constanza nodded and lingered near the gravestones for a moment longer before she turned to the children. "Come, let's say our adieus."

They left the Pavarin farm and descended farther into the valley. Young children eyed them curiously as the family passed by the crossroads. Did the Vallense boys and girls of Val Angrogna know who these foreign visitors were? Surely they had heard the stories—the defeat of Friar Marco Spada at the old fort, the rise and fall of the Lord of Luserna. Perhaps they had even heard rumors from Thonon about the downfall of Lucien Bouchard and his Divine Ascendancy. But to these children, the names of Andreas, Constanza, Elionor, and Johan were nothing more than that—names.

To the right was the farm Andreas and Constanza had called home for the first few months of their marriage. Though they had imagined they would spend their whole lives here, God had chosen otherwise.

Andreas and his family walked side by side, their footsteps scraping against the dirt path. The air was filled with the sweet scent of wildflowers and the sound of sheep bells ringing in the distance.

They soon reached the lush, sweeping pasture outside the hamlet of San Lorenzo, where the gathered Vallenses offered longing embraces and warm handshakes. The field overflowed with well-wishes as old friends and neighbors bid the Bonomo family adieu.

"I heard Elionor Janavel lives near you," one woman said to Constanza. "Is it true?"

"Yes, but she hasn't been Elionor Janavel in years. She married Elias Renaud, and they have seven children, perhaps eight by now. Both are part of the church in Zurich."

Bertran, now barbe to the Vallense church in this valley, gave Andreas a firm embrace. "I wish we could have talked more about the foreign believers you've joined."

"We practice our faith as you do here—we follow the Holy Scriptures, we reject Roman dogma, we live in humility." For a moment, Andreas peered off into the distance. "But few of them realize there are like-minded believers here in Piedmont, just as you know almost nothing about us."

"Would you still call yourself a Vallense?"

Andreas scratched his beard. "Vallense—wasn't that a name your enemies gave you?"

"Maybe, but what do you call yourselves in Zurich?"

Andreas smiled slightly. "A church."

"So be it," Bertran said, chuckling. "I'll pray the Roman Church and the magistrates keep their distance from you, the same as I pray for the flock here."

"The fires of oppression temper us and sharpen our resolve. God has given us His Word, and it's within churches like yours and mine that the truth lives." Andreas nodded toward his family, who stood in the shade of a chestnut tree, ready to depart for home. "I want to pass the same truth down to my children and for them to carry it on as long as Christ tarries."

After the last embrace Andreas and his family walked the ancient path out of the valley toward their home across the mountains. Andreas held Constanza's hand as they gazed out over the land that had shaped their lives. Memories flooded his mind—the trials, the joys, the moments of doubt, and the unshakable faith in a mighty God who had carried them through it all.

"We've come so far," Constanza said, reaching for Andreas's hand.

Andreas curled his fingers around hers. He drew in a deep breath and relished the warmth of the sun on his face. It was a stark contrast to the icy pail of water that had greeted him years ago, just before God had rescued him from the mire of sin and guided him onto the path of redemption. "We have indeed, and every step was worth it."

Acknowledgments

This series has been one of the greatest journeys of my life. From the moment I first imagined writing a tale about medieval Waldensians (Vallenses) to this conclusion of the series, I have been blessed with love, support, criticism, advice, feedback, and encouragement. I could never show all my gratitude here, but I would like to mention a few highlights.

Above all, I am thankful to my Lord and Savior, Jesus Christ. Through the ages, many have lived and died for Him. Many names have been forgotten, but they share one trait in common: service to their Savior. And it's all because He alone is worthy of praise and honor. I write for His glory first. Where readers are inspired or entertained, it's only because of God's enablement.

My wife, Andrea, has been a patient listener through each step of writing, from inspiration to the finale. Some of the most valuable criticism and insights have come from her. My four children, Allen, Eric, Aliza, and Emma, have also been patient and understanding. Whether I'm brainstorming, drafting, or editing, my family's smiling faces encourage me, and their lives help breathe life into the characters of my stories. Also, I believe that in order to write well, one has to first read well; beginning in my childhood, my parents have helped develop me as a reader.

I could never thank Mt. Zion Baptist Church of Brogue, Pennsylvania, enough. I am so grateful I can raise my family among such God-honoring believers, and I can't imagine writing a book like *Prince of Savoy* without their support and encouragement. Some have read my stories, but far more important are the testimonies of the Christians I serve with and worship alongside every week.

Before this story reached the form you just read, it met the eyes of several devoted beta readers: Andrea Speckhals, Vonda Murdock, Diana Wilbur, and Jenna Starr. All of them have helped me since the beginning, and their thoughts truly made this story better. Jayna Baas was the perfect copyeditor; her corrections, questions, and suggestions save me from embarrassing mistakes, help me as a writer, and bring a level of professionalism that wouldn't be possible without her talents and proficiency.

The research process for *Prince of Savoy* introduced me to dozens of works I hadn't yet seen. I finished Will Durant's *The Renaissance* and *The Reforma-*

tion—part of the larger series History of Civilization—a few months before planning this book. Though I didn't originally read his books for research purposes, Will Durant gave me a rich overview of early modern Europe that helped fill gaps in my own knowledge.

To all my readers who have journeyed with me through each book in this series, I offer my deepest gratitude. Your dedication and enthusiasm have been a source of constant encouragement. Whether you've been with me from the first page or joined along the way, your support has meant more than you realize. Thank you for embracing these stories and allowing the characters and their journeys to become a part of your lives. It's been an honor to share this adventure with you, and I hope Andreas, Constanza, Elionor, Elias, Johan, and others have inspired, challenged, and moved you as much as they have me.

Historical Notes

Of all the stories of the Witnesses of the Light trilogy, Prince of Savoy has the most ties to verifiable, documented historical events and people. It was thrilling to discover the threads, intrigues, and personalities that would inspire the characters and plot of this story. Though this series focuses on Waldensian characters who lived in fifteenth-century Piedmont, Prince of Savoy forced me to branch out into new cultures, traditions, and languages.

The House of Savoy

With the exception of Andreas, all characters from the House of Savoy are historical figures: Duke Louis of Savoy, Anne of Cyprus, their son Philip, Amadeus and Yolande, and even Andreas's younger siblings. Andreas was substituted for the duke's son Louis, Count of Geneva, who was of a similar age and familial position; this approach allowed for the exploration of a Savoyard prince who forsakes his noble status to live among the Waldensians.

Philip was a rebellious usurper whose goal was to overthrow his father and mother. Just as it's represented in this book, he thought his mother, Anne, and her Cypriot courtiers had brought the Duchy of Savoy to decadence. In October 1462, Philip and men loyal to him sacked Thonon and imprisoned both Louis and Anne. (I took the liberty of moving these events exactly two years forward to coincide with the previous books in the series.) Two months after Philip's rebellion, Anne died from what is now thought to have been tuberculosis. However, the lords of Savoy soon overthrew Philip, who was then exiled to France. Ironically enough, after Amadeus, Yolande, and their offspring all died young, Philip became the Duke of Savoy at fifty-nine years old, and it was through him that the dynasty continued.

Both Duke Louis and Anne are represented as they are described in historical documents. Louis was known as a weak, incompetent leader, especially in his later years. At his ascension to duke in 1440, Savoy was in its prime, but by his death, it was in steep decline, only to be further dragged down by his son Amadeus IX and daughter-in-law Yolande of Valois.

The Divine Ascendancy

Short-lived religious sects flared up frequently throughout western Europe in the late medieval and early modern periods. These groups were often millenarian, believing they would bring about the end of the world and establish a divine kingdom on earth through apocalyptic change. The Divine Ascendancy, though fictional, is a synthesis of these real sects. Each belief represented in Prince of Savoy can be attributed to real movements: end-time doctrine to the Zwickau Prophets; communism to radical Taborites; condemnation of marriage and children to Cathar Perfecti.

Seldom did cults achieve supremacy in a region as the Divine Ascendancy did fictionally in this story. However, the Münster Rebellion of 1535–1536, one of the most infamous instances of a radical religious sect taking control of a city, is a key example of the extreme fervor millenarian movements inspired.

The Prophet, though also born of my own imagination, is a combination of various cult leaders. His political connections to Savoy and relationship to Anne of Cyprus are based on Giacomo Valperga, who was executed by Philip during Philip's sack of Thonon. Religiously, Lucien Bouchard's beliefs and personality were inspired by Thomas Müntzer, John of Leiden, and the much later leader of a slave uprising, Nat Turner. Did these real figures believe what they preached? It would be hard to determine that with any degree of certainty, but in Prince of Savoy, I gave the Prophet motivations I felt were believable for the historical era while not delving into areas I felt were too dark or occultic for my readers.

In crafting the Divine Ascendancy and its leader, I aimed to capture the volatile mix of political ambition and religious fervor that characterized similar movements of the time. Just as historical figures like Thomas Müntzer and John of Leiden blurred the lines between religious conviction and personal ambition, the Prophet in *Prince of Savoy* embodies the dangerous allure of unchecked power cloaked in spiritual authority.

The Poor of Thonon

Medieval Waldensians were far from monolithic. Though Piedmont is probably the most well-known region they dwelled in, there were many similar groups throughout Europe, most of which never referred to themselves as Waldensians in any form. A self-description that occurs more than once, however, is *poor*. In fact, some of the first people ever named Waldensians were also called the Poor of Lyon.

What unified these groups, and why do modern historians typically refer to all of them as Waldensians? Many have attempted to answer this question, but one conclusion seems to predominate: the barbes.

These itinerant preachers, many of whom came from the Alpine valleys of Piedmont, would visit small congregations throughout Europe as infrequently as once every three years. The teachings of the barbes and their Holy Scriptures reached east to Poland, south to Calabria, west to Portugal, and north to the English Channel. Some held orthodox beliefs, while others held beliefs I would consider heretical. The Poor of Thonon, though fictional, are meant to represent what one of these disparate groups could have been like. Though they would not come to any prominence in the historical record until the sixteenth century, the Swiss Brethren also played a small but important role in my portrayal of the believers of Thonon.

LANGUAGES

Old Occitan (called Romaunt in this story), fifteenth-century French, Piedmontese, and Latin were all used in previous books in this series. As I mentioned in those books, these languages are at least five hundred years old, so representing them exactly as they were in 1460 is impossible. When I could not find an accurate word in a lexicon or dictionary, I consulted modern versions of words and phrases.

Franco-Provençal (Savoyard) is the primary new-to-me language I researched for this book. It is still spoken in parts of southwestern France and Switzerland, but like Occitan, its use has dwindled, especially in the past century. Though in the same family as Occitan, it required new dictionaries, lexicons, and phrase-books. I tried to localize the dialect as closely as possible to the actual region of Thonon, but when that was not possible, I leaned on the vocabulary of Chambéry, the cultural center of Savoy.

SONGS

Four songs are featured in *Prince of Savoy*, each depicted as part of the traditions of the Poor. Unfortunately, very few songs from groups like the Poor or the fifteenth-century Waldensians have survived to the present day. This left me with the challenge of either creating original hymns or selecting songs that could plausibly reflect Waldensian beliefs as conveyed in writings such as *The Noble Lesson* and *On Antichrist*. To maintain a sense of historical authenticity, I drew from eighteenth- and nineteenth-century American church hymnals, finding hymns that, though more modern, captured the spirit and themes that might have resonated with the Poor.

The first song, "The Lord into His Garden Comes," is attributed to an anony-mous author and is sung in chapter 20 when Andreas first meets the Poor at the

Renaud home. While I made some modifications, the majority of the text comes from hymnals dating as early as 1801.

In chapter 26, during the Poor's gathering at L'Ermitage, two songs are sung. "Âmin, Alélouyâ!" is an original composition I created, drawing on themes from Revelation—particularly how persecuted Christians might have found solace in passages like Revelation 5:12, 11:17–18, 14:7, 15:3–4, 16:7, 17:14, and 19:1. The second song, "The Parting Hand," was written by John Blain in 1818, though I made adjustments to the lyrics to suit the setting. Another verse of the song is sung in chapter 35 as the Poor set sail across Lac Léman.

In chapter 30, Elias hears Madeleine singing "Come, Little Children, Now We May." The origin of this hymn is unknown, but it first appeared in hymnals in 1835.

Historical Accuracy

As Dan Carlin of the *Hardcore History* podcast has said, I do not consider myself a historian but a history enthusiast. I benefit immensely from academic historians and their countless hours of research, writing, and fact-checking. Though I have labored to make *Prince of Savoy* fact based, I am not above error. Anything here that might be misrepresented or ahistorical is entirely on me, the author.

In writing *Prince of Savoy*, my goal was to create a story that, while rooted in historical reality, also allowed for the creative freedom necessary to explore the lives and struggles of Andreas, Constanza, Elionor, and Elias. By weaving together documented events and fictional elements, I aimed to provide readers with both an engaging narrative and a glimpse into the complexities of fifteenth-century Europe. Though some liberties were taken to enhance the story, I have endeavored to remain true to the spirit of the era and the people who lived through it. My hope is that *Prince of Savoy* not only entertains but also sparks curiosity about the rich and tumultuous history that inspired its creation.

Selected Bibliography

Audisio, Gabriel. *Preachers by Night: The Waldensian Barbes*, 15th–16th centuries. Boston: Brill, 2007.

Baird, Robert. *Sketches of Protestantism in Italy. Past and Present.* Including a Notice of the Origin, History, and Present State of the Waldenses. Boston: Benjamin Perkins & Co., 1847.

Braght, Thieleman. *Martyrs Mirror.* Translated by Joseph F. Sohm. United States: Mennonite Publishing Company, 1886.

Bruchet, Max. *Le Château de Ripaille.* France: Librairie Charles Delagrave, 1907.

Cohn, Norman. *The Pursuit of the Millennium: Revolutionary Millenarians and Mystical Anarchists of the Middle Ages.* United States: Oxford University Press, 1970.

A Companion to the Waldenses in the Middle Ages. Netherlands: Brill, 2022.

Cameron, Euan. *Waldenses: Rejections of Holy Church in Medieval Europe.* United Kingdom: Wiley, 2000.

Comba, Emilio., Comba, Teofilo Ernest. *History of the Waldenses of Italy: From Their Origin to the Reformation.* United Kingdom: Truslove & Shirley, 1889.

Flour de Saint Genis, Victor Benigne. *Histoire de Savoie.* France: Conte-Grand et Company, 1868.

Gallenga, Antonio Carlo Napoleone. *History of Piedmont.* United Kingdom: Chapman and Hall, 1855.

Gray, Thomas. *The Confessions of Nat Turner.* United States: T. R. Gray, 1832.

Morland, Samuel. *The History of the Evangelical Churches of the Valleys of Piemont.* United Kingdom: Henry Hills, one of His Highness's printers, 1658.

Müntzer, Thomas. *The Collected Works of Thomas Müntzer.* United Kingdom: T & T Clark, 1994.

Key to Foreign Words and Phrases

Fr.-Prov.: Franco-Provençal, the regional Romance language spoken in parts of Savoy and surrounding areas.
Fr.: French, spoken more formally and among nobility or clergy.
Gr.: Greek, the language of scholarship and the original New Testament.
Lat.: Latin, commonly used in religious texts, services, and academic writing.
Occ.: Occitan, the vernacular language spoken by Waldensians and others in southern France and northern Italy.
Pied.: Piedmontese, a Romance language native to the Piedmont region.

adieu (Occ.; ah-DYUH): farewell.

allons, fâs-le (Fr.-Prov.; ah-LOHN, fahs-luh): let's go, do it.

amb plaser (Occ.; ahm plah-ZAYR): my pleasure.

âmin, alélouyâ (Fr.-Prov.; AH-meen, ah-lay-loo-YAH): amen, hallelujah.

apparemment (Fr.; ah-pahr-ah-MAHN): apparently.

asindinsa divina (Occ.; ah-SEEN-deen-sah dee-VEE-nah): divine ascendancy.

asse sie (Fr.-Prov.; ahs see): so be it.

babbo (Pied.; BAH-boh): dad.

bela petiòta (Fr.-Prov.; BEH-lah peh-tee-OH-tah): pretty little one.

belle épouse (Fr.; bel ay-POOZ): beautiful wife.

bensur (Fr.-Prov.; behn-SOOR): of course.

bienveunue (Fr.-Prov.; byan-vuh-NYOO): welcome.

bon après-midi (Fr.-Prov.; bohn ah-PRAY-mee-DEE, meh-SYUH): good after-noon.

bon homme (Fr.-Prov.; bohn om): good man.

bon vêpre (Fr.-Prov.; bohn VEH-pruh): good evening.

bon vespre (Occ.; bohn VEH-spray): good evening.

bon-a sèira (Pied.; bon-ah SAY-rah): good evening.

bones femes (Fr.-Prov.; bohn fehm): good women.

bonjorn (Fr.-Prov.; bohn-ZHORN): good morning.

bonjorn (Occ.; bohn-ZHORN): good morning.

bonjour à nouveau (Fr.; bohn-ZHOOR ah noo-VOH): hello again.

canaille (Fr.-Prov.; kah-NYEH): scoundrel.

casa (Occ.; KAH-sah): home.

chasteu (Occ.; SHAHS-toh): castle.

ché pa bon (Fr.-Prov.; shay pah bohn): It's not good.

chòtas (Occ.; SHOH-tahs): tawny owl.

compreni pas (Occ.; kohm-PREH-nee pah): I don't understand.

dama (Fr.-Prov.; DAH-mah): missus.

demoisèla (Fr.-Prov.; deh-mwah-ZAY-lah): miss.

Deus vult (Lat.; DAY-oos voolt): God wills it.

diable (Occ.; DYAH-bluh): devil.

dianthos (Gr.; dee-AHN-thohs): carnation.

Dies Natalis Domini (Lat.; DEE-ess nah-TAH-lis DOH-mee-nee): Day of the Lord's Birth.

dominus (Lat.; DOH-mee-noos): lord.

effectivement étrange (Fr.; eh-fek-TEEV-mohn ay-TRAHNZH): odd indeed.

ègal (Lat.; EH-gahl): equal.

era una blaga, tranqui (Occ.; EH-rah OO-nah BLAH-gah, trahn-KEE): it was a joke, take it easy.

èroe (Occ.; EH-roh): hero.

espècia-te (Occ.; es-PEH-see-ah-teh): hurry (literally, spice it up).

étrange (Fr.; ay-TRAHNZH): strange, peculiar.

excellente, excellenta (Occ.; exs-seh-LEHN-teh, exs-seh-LEHN-tah): excellent (masc., fem.).

filha (Occ.; FEE-yah): daughter.

filha petita (Fr.-Prov.; FEE-yah peh-TEE-tah): little girl.

fraire (Occ.; frayr): brother.

frâre (Fr.-Prov.; frahr): brother.

fromâjo (Fr.-Prov.; froh-MAH-zhoh): cheese.

gàrgola (Lat.; GAR-goh-lah): gargoyle.

gran-pâre (Fr.-Prov.; grahn-pahr): grandfather.

grossi (Pied.; GROSS-ee): silver coins.

honrea loteo paire elatoa maire (Occ.; oh-NRAY-uh LOH-teh-oh PAH-ree eh-lah-TOH-ah MAH-ree): honour thy father and mother.

je suis désolé, les djanas (Fr.-Prov.; zhuh swee day-zoh-LAY, lay zha-NAH): I'm sorry, ladies.

jeune seigneur (Fr.-Prov.; zhuhn say-NYUHR): young sir.

Jézu (Fr.-Prov.; ZAY-zoo): Jesus.

jòga amb ieu (Occ.; ZHOH-gah ahm yoo): play along with me.

la mia ca 'l'é toa (Pied.; lah MEE-ah kah l-ay TOH-ah): my house is yours.

lugotenent (Fr.-Prov.; loo-go-TEH-nahnt): lieutenant.

ma maîtresse (Fr.; mah meh-TRESS): my mistress.

machinacions (Occ.; mah-shee-nah-SEE-ohns): machinations.

madama (Pied.; mah-DAH-mah): missus.

madomaisèla (Occ.; mah-doh-mah-AY-lah): miss.

madòna (Occ.; mah-DOH-nah): missus.

maï (Fr.-Prov.; mie): mom.

mamà (Occ.; mah-MAH): mommy.

mameta (Occ.; mah-MAY-tah): grandma.

mamie (Fr.-Prov.; mah-MEE): grandma.

mâre (Fr.-Prov.; mahr): mother.

mare nostrum (Lat.; MAH-ray NOH-strum): Mediterranean Sea.

marmòta (Occ.; mahr-MOH-tah): marmot.

mercé (Occ.; mehr-SAY): thank you.

merci bôcô (Fr.-Prov.; mehr-SEE boh-KOH): thank you very much.

mes jeunes amis, savez-vous parler la langue française? (Fr.; may zhuhn ah-MEE, sah-VAY voo pah-LAY lah LAHNG frahn-SAYZ): my young friends, do you speak French?.

mirabell (Occ.; mee-rah-BEL): impressive.

mon ami (Fr.; mohn ah-MEE): my friend.

mon amic (Occ.; mohn ah-MEEK): my friend.

monsen (Occ.; mohn-SAYN): mister.

monsieur (Fr.-Prov.; muhn-SYUH): mister.

nò (Pied.; noh): no.

nou (Fr.-Prov.; noo): no.

oncle (Occ.; ONK-luh): uncle.

paï (Fr.-Prov.; pie): dad.

papà (Occ.; pah-PAH): daddy.

papeta (Occ.; pah-PEH-tah): grandpa.

papi (Fr.-Prov.; pah-PEE): grandpa.

pâre (Fr.-Prov.; pahr): father.

parfète, parfèta (Fr.-Prov.; pahr-FAYT, pahr-FAY-tah): perfect (masc., fem.).

per los cèus (Occ.; pehr lohz SAY-oos): by the heavens.

perdon (Occ.; pehr-DOHN): sorry.

perfècte, perfècta (Occ.; per-FAYKT, per-FAYK-tah): perfect (masc., fem.).

pi dispias (Pied.; pee dee-SPYAS): I'm sorry.

pietat (Occ.; pee-eh-TAH): oh, pitty.

pinson (Fr.-Prov.; pan-SOHN): chaffinch.

planer de vos véser (Occ.; PLAH-ner deh vohs VEH-zehr): pleasure to see you.

poleta (Occ.; poh-LEH-tah): chicken.

poulet (Fr.; poo-LEH): chicken.

qual pretié (Occ.; kahl preh-TYAY): what a dainty one.

quattrini (Pied.; kwah-TREE-nee): copper coins.

que ridicle (Fr.-Prov.; kuh ree-DEE-kluh): how ridiculous.

quinzèna (Occ.; KEEN-zay-nah): period of fifteen days.

raison d'être (Fr.; ray-ZOHN day-truh): purpose for living.

ridicule (Occ.; ree-dee-KOOL): ridiculous, ludicrous.

sâre (Fr.-Prov.; sahr): sister.

sèi desolat (Occ.; say day-zoh-LAHT): I'm sorry.

seror (Occ.; seh-ROHR): sister.

sì (Pied.; see): yes.

solide (Occ.; soh-LEED): strong, firm, solid.

t'aimi (Occ.; tay-mee): I love you.

tanben (Occ.; tahn-BEN): too, as well.

tanta (Occ.; TAHN-tah): aunt.

tonton (Fr.-Prov.; tohn-TOHN): uncle.

ulit (Occ.; OO-leet): carnation.

usurpateur (Fr.; oo-zoor-pah-TEUR): usurper.

vâ (Fr.-Prov.; vah): go.

viandanti (Pied.; vee-ahn-DAHN-tee): travelers.

vôtre grâce (Fr.-Prov.; VOH-truh grahss): your grace.

Name Pronunciation Guide

Agnes of Savoy (AG-nis)

Alessia de Bonomo (ah-LAY-see-ah day bo-NO-mo)

Amadeus IX, Prince of Piedmont (ah-mah-DAY-ooss)

Andreas de Bonomo (ahn-DRAY-ahs)

Anna-Maria Maridan (AHN-nah mah-REE-ah mah-ree-DAHN)

Anne of Cyprus (AH-nuh)

Antoine Renaud (ahn-TWAHN reh-NOH)

Armanda Pavarin (ahr-MAHN-dah pah-vah-REEN)

Ave de Bonomo (AH-vay)

Aymon Dupont (eh-MAWN doo-PAWN)

Bertran Arnaldi (BAIR-trahn ar-NOL-dee)

Bino de Bonomo (BEE-noh)

Bona of Savoy (BOH-nah)

Charlotte of Savoy (shar-LOT)

Clarisse Dupont (klah-REES)

Claude Montagnard (klawd mon-tahn-YARD)

Colletto Corsone (kohl-LEHT-toh kohr-SOH-neh)

Constanza de Bonomo (kohn-STAHN-sah)

Dominica Maridan (doh-mee-NEE-kah)

Elias Renaud (eh-LIE-uhs)

Elionor Janavel (eh-lee-oh-NOR zhah-nah-VEHL)

Estève Malan (eh-STAY-ve mah-LAHN)

Ezio de Bonomo (ETZ-ee-oh)

Florian Dupont (FLOH-ree-uhn)

Fosca de Bonomo (FOS-kah)

François of Savoy (frahn-SWAHZ)

Giacomo of Savoy (JAH-koh-mo)

Giuseppe Maridan (dzhoo-SEHP-peh)

Guido de Bonomo (GWEE-doh)

Hélène Dupont (ay-LEHN)

Henri Dupont (AHN-ree)

Irene de Bonomo (ee-RE-nay)

Jean Louis of Savoy (zhahn loo-EE)

Johan Lauras (yo-HAHN loh-RAHS)

Lorenzo Maridan (lohr-EHN-zoh)

Louis I, Duke of Savoy (LOO-ee)

Lucien Bouchard (loo-SYEN boo-SHAR)

Ludovicus Romagnano (loo-do-VEE-kuss ro-mahn-YAH-no)

Madeleine Dupont (MAD-uh-len)

Marie of Savoy (mah-REE)

Marie Renaud (mah-REE)

Matteo Ghos (mah-TEH-oh GOH)

Nicolaus Pavarin (nee-koh-LOWSS)

Philip of Savoy (FIH-lip)

Prospera de Bonomo (PROS-per-ah)

Roberto de Bonomo (roh-BAIR-toh)

Silvia de Bonomo (SEEL-vee-ah)

Umile de Bonomo (OO-mee-le)

Yolande of Valois (YEW-lahn de VAH-lew-ah)

Zama de Bonomo (TZAH-mah)

Andreas and His Noble Lineage

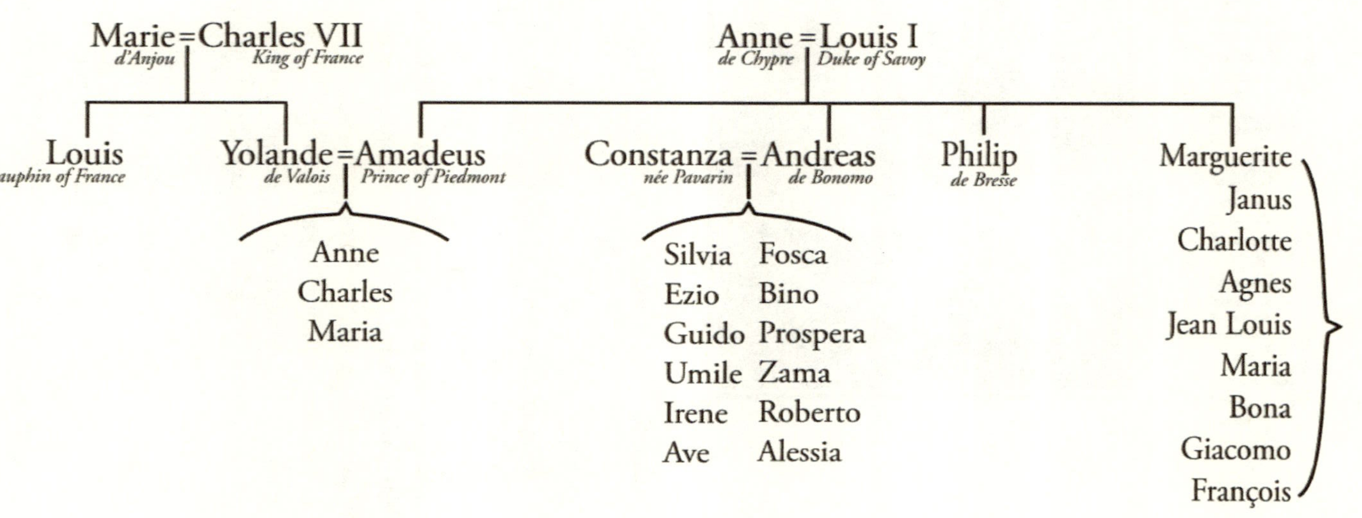

About the Author

D. J. Speckhals is the author of the Witnesses of the Light historical fiction trilogy, which transports readers to fifteenth-century Europe to explore the resilient faith of the Waldensians.

From a young age, Dustin has held a deep, lifelong passion for history and geography. He spent many school nights studying *National Geographic* and *Rand McNally* atlases, striving to capture a glimpse of the world beyond his home in Michigan. After receiving his B.A. in Pastoral Theology in 2009, he married Andrea and relocated to southeast Pennsylvania, where he has established a successful career as a software developer.

When not immersed in writing and research, Dustin enjoys serving in various ministries at his church, running, pursuing the perfect slice of pizza, and embarking on adventures with his wife and their four children.

www.djspeckhals.com
Facebook: @DJSpeckhals
Instagram: @d.j.speckhals
Twitter: @DSpeckhals

If you loved this book, please give it a review online. Positive reviews help so much. Thank you.

If you loved *Prince of Savoy*, There's more!

Heretics of Piedmont: A Novel of the Waldensians
Witnesses of the Light #1

A monk banished for sins he didn't commit. A secret mission that could redeem him—or condemn him utterly.

The Lord of Luserna: A Novel of the Waldensians
Witnesses of the Light #2

One book could change the world—
Or cost them everything.

The Outcast of Chivasso: A Novella of the Waldensians
Witnesses of the Light #0.5

His enemies want him to flee.
One little girl needs him to stay.